ALSO BY MELISSA GOOD

Dar and Kerry Series
Tropical Storm
Hurricane Watch
Eye of the Storm
Red Sky At Morning
Thicker Than Water
Terrors of the High Seas
Tropical Convergence
Storm Surge: Book One
Storm Surge: Book Two

Stormy Waters

Melissa Good

Yellow Rose Books

Texas

ISBN 978-1-61929-082-2

First Printing 2012

9 8 7 6 5 4 3 2 1

Cover design by Donna Palowski

Published by:

Regal Crest Enterprises, LLC
229 Sheridan Loop
Belton, TX 76513

Find us on the World Wide Web at
http://www.regalcrest.biz

Printed in the United States of America

Sometimes my real life and my stories accidentally converge and so I would like to in this case acknowledge both my previous employer, EDS, and my current one, Norwegian Cruise Line for bits and pieces found inside these pages and note that it would have been a very different story had certain events not taken place.

~ Melissa Good

Chapter One

DAR POURED HERSELF a glass of juice, then returned to her desk and settled back into her leather chair. A thick, white printout was already in her inbox. She lifted it out and plopped it down in front of her as her computer hummed in the background, collecting her email.

Security reports. Dar winced slightly as she started reading. "Damn, what a mucking little troublemaker I am." She shook her head ruefully. "Aye, yi yi yi yah...Mark I owe you dinner, at least for this one." Her fingertip traced one intrusion attempt that had come perilously close to finding a crack, being turned aside at the very last second by the random roaming parser that dipped continually into the data stream and examined the traffic it found there. "Wow."

The parser had been around since a twenty something year old bored Operations Manager had put it in place years ago and recently had to defend keeping it. Dar hadn't really expected to have her stubborn insistence in leaving her code in place vindicated so explicitly, but she was never one to look a gift goat in the ass either.

She opened a new mail window and typed rapidly. Next time someone tells me we don't need any of my old programs, they're fired. She reviewed it, then sent it on its way to Mark's inbox. Satisfied she went back to reviewing the report.

A soft knock interrupted her a few minutes later. Dar put the page down and leaned on her elbows. "C'mon in."

The door opened and Maria poked her head in. "Good morning, Dar."

Dar leaned back in her chair and studied her assistant. "Morning." She lifted a hand and curled a finger, beckoning Maria inside the office. "Siddown."

Looking slightly apprehensive, Maria did so, taking a seat across from Dar in one of her comfortable visitors chairs. "Si?"

Dar steepled her fingers. "I have a meeting with Mariana in about an hour over your little incident at that restaurant last week."

Maria sighed. "Dar, I am so sorry."

"Shh." Dar waved her off. "Don't apologize. I only wish you'd gotten some pictures. The two of them were up to no good, and I'm happy Kerry didn't end up there with them."

"They were very nasty women, Jefa."

"I know." Dar said. "The problem is, they're also a huge honking pain in the ass, and it's to their advantage to make us look as bad as possible."

Maria sighed. "We should not have gone to that place. It was a wrong thing to do, Dar. Even if you do not say so."

Dar shrugged. "And at that tech conference, I shouldn't have challenged every hacker on the planet to break into our systems. But I did, and here we are." She nudged the stack of papers. "So, what I want you to do is just let me handle it okay?"

"Jefa?" Maria looked confused.

Dar got up and walked around to the front of the desk, perching on the corner of it. "I'll meet with Mariana and take care of whatever bullshit she got handed. Kerry's up to her ears in this damn bid, and I don't want her bothered with it."

"Okay, Dar, if you say so." Maria still looked unsure. "But the policeman came to us on Friday, and I spoke with him. I think it is fine. He said to me that what they were was some nuisance?"

Nuisance. Dar chuckled inwardly. "All right. Listen, I'm going to need to schedule a security meeting after lunch. Book the big conference room, and get all the operations department heads in there."

"One o'clock?"

"That's fine." Dar nodded.

Maria started to get up, but paused. "Dar, I did not get to ask you—did this thing you were in New York for go all right?"

"It did."

"Was Kerrisita a good help for you?"

Dar's blue eyes twinkled warmly. "Couldn't have done it without her."

Satisfied, Maria stood up and headed for the door. "Is good. Mayte will be very glad as well. She was very concerned that everything would go nicely."

Dar went back to her seat and dropped into it, pulling her report back over. A motion on her screen caught her attention, and she looked over studying the security alert flashing.

Damn. "I think I'm going to end up embarrassing the hell out of myself with that damn challenge." She exhaled, resting her head on her fist. "What an idiot I am."

KERRY CAME AROUND the corner of her office entrance and plowed into her administrative assistant. "Whoa!" She hauled up short and put a hand out to steady Mayte, who had bounced off her. "Hey, Mayte."

Mayte's eyes widened. "Oh, Ms...Kerry. Hello. Good morning." Her expression was a cross between apprehension and concern. "You are here so early."

"C'mon inside. I want to hear all about our rock 'em sock 'em admins." Kerry grinned indicating her office door. "I've got a staff briefing at ten, but we've got some time to talk."

Mayte followed her inside and closed the door, and stood a little awkwardly beside Kerry's desk. "Kerry, my mother is very upset with us. She said for me to come to you and to apologize."

Kerry put her tea mug down on her desk and came over to face her assistant. "Why?"

"Because we should not have confronted those ladies."

"Ah." Kerry folded her arms. "Well...I'd agree with you, except that...remember the story Dar said for you to ask me about, when you told us what happened?"

"Yes." Mayte fastened her eyes on Kerry's face.

"Once upon a time, back when Dar and I first started seeing each other..." Kerry turned and wandered over to the window, peering out. "And we were still keeping it secret from everyone..."

"Except my mama."

Kerry chuckled. "Uh...er...yeah, except for her. From everyone else, though," she amended. "Mariana and Duks asked us out to dinner. We knew Mariana suspected what was going on, so we were trying really hard to pretend we were just friends while at the restaurant."

Mayte merely watched her, fascinated.

"Now that I look back, I doubt we were fooling anyone, but we were trying hard, and we thought we were doing pretty good." Kerry turned and leaned against the glass. "Until one of Dar's old girlfriends showed up and started needling her in front of all of us."

"Oh, that is terrible!"

"Uh huh. It was," Kerry agreed dryly. "Until I got up and pushed her in front of a tray full of Thai food and she ended up with eel guts up her nose while she swam on the floor in a puddle of peanut sauce."

"Oh." Mayte covered her mouth with one hand and tried not to laugh.

Kerry came back over to her. "So, they're probably pretty lucky," she admitted. "Because if I'd have been there, and they'd have started talking trash about Dar, I would have done a lot worse than dump chili down their shirts."

"Really?"

Kerry's face turned suddenly serious. "Yes." She drew in a breath. "Dar means everything to me. If I wasn't there to watch her back, I'm glad you two were."

Mayte looked a touch overwhelmed at that. "Then, no matter what my mama says, I am glad too," she replied softly. "It did not feel like a bad thing to me." She paused. "Until the policemen arrived."

"It wasn't." Kerry stepped closer, then impulsively held her arms out. "C'mere." She enfolded Mayte in a hug, giving her a gentle pat on the back. "Don't worry about anything. If they make more trouble, Dar will take care of them." She released the girl, but clasped her shoulders. "You guys have nothing to worry about."

Mayte was blushing. "T...thank you."

"Okay." Kerry gave her a pat on the arm, then let her go and perched on the edge of her desk. "Now, we've got a lot of work to do to get ready for this ship bid. I'm going to need some rush orders on equipment, and I'll need you to get hold of Elaine and see what we can do to pressure the vendors."

"I will call her right away," Mayte replied softly. "Did...did Jefa's thing in New York come out...did you fix the problem there?"

Kerry smiled inwardly at the half nervous stutter. "Oh yeah," she reassured Mayte. "Dar had it pretty much resolved before I even got there. I just added some moral support for a couple hours and then we spent some time out in the city."

Mayte's brow puckered a little. "You left so quickly I thought?"

"That I was going to save the day?" Kerry went to her chair and sat down, giving her trackball a roll. "Nah. I just went to be with Dar. Sappily romantic, but true." She propped her chin on her fist and gazed at her assistant. "Occupational hazard with us."

Mayte recovered her composure and smiled. "I hope to be finding that out someday also," she said, as she escaped toward the door. "I will set up the meeting with accounting for this afternoon."

"Thanks." Kerry watched as her assistant disappeared, then she shook her head and took a sip of her tea. She turned to her computer and checked her email. "Ah."

She clicked on the one from the Port of Miami's agent and leaned on her elbow, studying the schematics that had been provided. There were four possible places for the four ships to dock, and she had no idea which spot would be filled with the ship they'd be assigned.

And yet, waiting for that information before she ordered a working circuit was just idiotic. Kerry gazed at the scattered buildings, and pondered her choices. Four docks, four dock buildings, four choices of places to drop a line. The agent did not know which dock would be assigned to which ship.

Well, poo. Kerry sent a note off to Quest, asking him which ship they'd be working on. If she had that maybe she could gently nudge the port agent into assigning it a pier, and if that worked, then she could call Bellsouth and drop the circuit.

And they'd need a satellite. Kerry sent a note off to Mark. They had a regular provider, but she didn't think they knew anything about marine satellites. However, they might know someone who did.

At least it was a start. They had their work cut out for them, though.

Something chittered at her elbow, making her jerk and look up to see Gopher Dar peeking out from behind her mail window. "Hey!" She chased it with her pointer, and caught it by the tail. "Aha! Gotcha!"

"Ooooooo." The Gopher Dar flopped on its back and squiggled causing her to release the mouse button as she started laughing. Immediately, the creature bounced to its feet and scurried away, wagging its finger at her. "Oh, you are so damn twisted." She leaned closer, peering at the thing. "Hey! What t-shirt is that?"

Gopher Dar sashayed across the screen now that he wasn't being molested. He had a tiny white t-shirt on that bore the words "Hackerz suck!" Kerry sighed, and watched as he pulled out a magnifying glass from his non-existent shorts and started peering around her desktop.

Apparently Dar had her work cut out for her, too.

KERRY REMOVED HER sunglasses as she came to stand near the pier wall, gazing thoughtfully at the concrete structures around her. It was so hot the pavement was giving off heat waves, and the place was pretty much deserted here in the noon time sun.

She walked to the edge of the fence and peered through it spotting a couple of maintenance men walking slowly down the empty docks. One was kneeling beside an iron tie cleat painting something on the concrete surface, and another drove a forklift toward a stack of pallets.

"Hmm." Kerry turned and walked to the front of the pier building that consisted of a few glass doors, and a series of garage type roll entrances. She checked her watch, then blew her already sweaty bangs off her head with a long breath and leaned against the wall to wait.

The humidity was almost overpowering. Kerry debated waiting in the Lexus, then spotted a Miami Dade truck trundling slowly her way and decided to give it a chance that her port agent was inside.

The truck creaked to a halt and the door opened, and a tall, gray haired woman with a clipboard exited. She came around the end of the truck and approached Kerry. "Ms. Stuart?"

"That's me," Kerry agreed. "Are you Agnes?"

"Yes. Thanks for coming over." The woman gestured toward the glass doors. "Let's go inside." They went from the muggy heat to a frigid interior as she closed the doors behind them, locking the locks again before she went on. "Sorry. We get so many vagrants out here I've got to keep the doors closed or we'd find them under the floorboards."

"Ah." Kerry murmured, as they crossed a large open space, and went through two sliding glass doors into a larger room in the back.

"Okay, this is pretty typical of all four piers," Agnes said. "These are four older buildings we've decided to renovate for the next cruise season, so no one's using them. It'll be better than using the cargo piers anyway. There's no space back there and we'd be moving you every other day."

"Okay." Kerry nodded agreeably. "So this is where they normally put the cruise liners? Where the passengers get on? Because one of the things we're supposed to do is make it so they can check the passengers onboard while they're in the waiting area."

Agnes brightened. "Well, that'll work great then. Yeah." She led the way over to one side of the room. "Over here is where we usually put the boarding agents, and in here is a small office I guess you guys could use. Otherwise, it's pretty open."

Kerry peered into the tiny room, which bore the scars of many years of administrative use. It was grungy, but it had a lockable door, and—she peered under an overturned table—wall jacks. "Okay." She sighed. "Is there a telecommunication closet?"

"Around the back here." Agnes led her through two sliding doors, and they entered a stifling hot interior garage. "This is where they put the luggage," she explained, "so customs can get to it."

"Ah." Kerry grunted.

Agnes opened a closet at the back of the garage and they peered in. On the back wall was a punch down block, and the rest of the room was ringed with power panels. There was one black case on the wall near the door, however, that looked a little familiar. Kerry unlatched it and folded the door open, spotting the mounting hardware inside for a network switch. "Ah."

"That's for the wiring in the building, but you'd have to put your own equipment in there," Agnes said. "Now, the problem is, as I told you, we won't know which ship is going into which pier until they get here."

Kerry closed the switch case. "Why? I mean, you know they're coming, why not just assign them?"

"Wish we could." Agnes waited for Kerry to leave the closet, and then she closed the door. They walked back toward the main building. "But the port won't, since they've never seen these, and they don't trust the specs we were given. The draft or how deep the hulls are below the waterline is really important because the piers vary."

"Uh huh." Kerry could understand that since she knew what a draft was, and knew there were places in some of the smaller islands she and Dar visited that the Dixieland Yankee had trouble getting into because of the draft. "So that'll be..."

"The day they get here. First one that shows up will be assigned, and so on."

Drat, drat, drat. Kerry sighed as she edged through the non-working doors and back into the air conditioning. "Okay." She put her hands on her hips and studied the space again. "I can't wait until then to drop circuits."

"Yeah." Agnes seemed sympathetic. "I know, the other people that are doing this thing called, and they said the same thing."

"Really? So what are they going to do?" Kerry asked casually.

"Use cellular. Some kind of new process."

Some kind of untested, barely adequate process. Hmm. "Well, I'd use that for one computer, but not for an office." Kerry decided. "Okay, I know what I need to do. Thanks for meeting me down here, Agnes. It's greatly appreciated."

The woman smiled at her. "Absolutely. No problem. Having four ships in here in the summer is a big windfall for the port. We'd be glad to do anything we can to make it good for you."

"Except pre-assign the piers," Kerry said wryly.

"Well..."

"It's okay." Kerry started for the front doors. "We'll manage it somehow."

She bid Agnes goodbye and crossed behind the Agnes' truck toward the small parking lot in front of the pier. Her Lexus sat there in the heat looking very blue and lonely. She slid behind the wheel with a grimace as the hot leather hit the back of her legs. "Ugh."

She started the engine and got the air going, then leaned back and pulled out her PDA. She opened a new message and tapped out a directive, then paused, tapping the stylus on the edge of the device as she thought about what she was doing.

It wasn't really a risk, per se. It was an expense. The question was, should she incur the expense, and accept the cost in order to ensure she had the environment she needed to do the job? Kerry nibbled her lip, counting the days they had left.

Well, she had leverage with Bellsouth. With a slight nod, she sent the message. She put down the PDA then shifting the car into reverse, backed out and drove carefully out of the parking lot

She checked her watch again, then opened her cell phone and hit the speed dial. "Hey, sweetie."

"Hey." Dar's voice sounded relaxed. "Just got out of my meeting with Mariana."

"Aha. How'd it go?" Kerry asked, making the turn onto Biscayne.

"I don't think Telegenics' lawyer likes me."

Kerry chuckled low in her throat. "There's a shocker. Listen, before you tell me more, I'm heading to the Bread Factory. You want a sandwich?"

"Mm, chicken curry," Dar responded instantly. "And that spicy soup if they've got it."

"Okay. Now, what did the lawyer say?? Kerry navigated carefully through the traffic. ?Are they really serious about pressing charges??

"Not anymore."

"Ah, that's good."

"I basically told them since it was off company property, and off company hours, it wasn't a company problem."

Kerry blinked. "Um..."

"And if they wanted to pursue it on a personal basis, I'd welcome a suit that explained why his clients were trying to entice my partner out to convince her what a scumbag I was."

"Ugh." Kerry winced. "Hon, I don't think that's exactly what they were up to."

"Doesn't matter. It was enough to scare him off. Besides, that was the subject matter that made our battling burritos dump the chili bowl, so..." Dar chuckled a little. "Anyway, one less thing to worry about, but listen..."

Uh oh. "Yeah?"

"Maria just told me that Mayte told her that you got an invitation from Quest to a kick off reception at the port this Saturday."

"Just me?" Kerry pulled into the small strip mall that held one of their favorite sandwich shops.

"You and a guest."

"You and me, then." Kerry sat back. "Okay, so here we go again. Can I hope, maybe, that Telegenics will send someone else to do the bid now that it's on?" She got out of the car and headed for the restaurant. "I've just scoped out the port, Dar. It's going to be a pain in the ass working here."

"Uh huh. I figured."

"I'm dropping lines into all four possible spots we could be. I'll just cancel the ones we don't need," Kerry said, holding her breath a little as she waited for her boss's reaction. Dar hated wasting provisioning and she knew it.

"Hmm."

"Two chicken curry on croissants, provolone, nothing else, two spicy soups, one coffee." Kerry told the attendant, still listening to the pensive silence on the other end of the cell. "Hon, I had to. I couldn't risk not having it, and they won't tell us where they're putting the damn things until the last minute."

Dar sighed into the phone. "Yeah. I know. I just—"

"Hate wasting the money." Kerry handed over some cash. "I know."

Dar clucked her tongue a few times. "But you know what? This is your project," she finally said. "So go for it. I've got hacker bees flying around my head like gnats, so that's what I'm going to concentrate on."

Kerry felt uncertain all of a sudden. "Okay," she said slowly. "Are you sure you don't want to..."

"I'm sure." Dar sounded confident. "Kerry, my being involved is only going to make it tough on you, we both know it. In fact, why not take Mark to the reception?"

"Mark?"

"I'm the problem," Dar said.

Kerry frowned. "Can we talk about this later? I need to think about it."

A bit of silence. "Okay," Dar said. "Sure."

"It's not that I don't think you're right..." Kerry said in a rush. "I just...I want to talk to you about it."

"You don't want to take Mark?" Dar hazarded a guess. "If you want, I'll go with you, Ker. I was just trying to make things a little smoother."

"I know." Kerry relaxed a little. "It surprised me, that's all."

"Okay. See you in a bit?"

"Be right there," Kerry nodded, "just getting the sandwiches. See you in a few minutes." She folded the phone and tucked it into her belt, and tried to reassemble her thoughts while waiting for her order.

Dar was right. She knew that. The core of their problem with Telegenics was the personal issue Shari had with Dar. But now, it might even be more than that given what had happened last week. Would Dar's stepping out really solve anything? Or just make it worse? Kerry gazed off into the distance, facing her own insecurity with a grimace. The truth was she didn?t want to face Shari and Michelle alone, and the reasons had nothing to do with business. She wanted Dar there, antagonist or not. Despite her big ideas before she?d gone to New York about how she was protecting Dar from having to be involved, despite her confidence.

Damn.

"Here's your order, ma'am." The boy behind the counter handed her the bag courteously. "Have a nice day."

"Thanks." Kerry took the bag and headed out the door. "For the thought, anyway."

Damn, damn damn.

DAR EDGED PAST the rows of switches, ignoring the apprehensive looks of the on duty techs in the Ops center. She dropped into a seat in the back row at the master console that wasn't generally manned and keyed up some views. She wrapped her hands together and rested her chin against them as she studied the results.

"Ma'am?" One of the techs got up and faced her. "Can we do something for you?"

"No." Dar gave him a baleful look. "Just siddown and leave me alone."

He did so quickly, burying his nose in the console without a backward glance.

As though she could feel Kerry's wry look on her, Dar sighed. "Listen up, all of you."

Four heads turned timidly toward her.

"I'm not trying to be rude, okay? I'm just working on something, and I know this place better than any of you. So don't worry about it."

The techs relaxed. "Yes, ma'am," the one who'd approached her said. "We know that...we just wanted to help you if we could."

"Thanks. Now siddown, and leave me alone."

This time the man grinned a little. "Yes ma'am." He went back to his reports, and the rest of the techs did as well, but the atmosphere was definitely a little lighter.

Dar shook her head and went back to her own display. She called up the network topology, and studied it intently. The main part of the attack had hit them in specific places. Not their external websites, those were bypassed entirely. This had hit them in their tier one interfaces, where the big circuits connected them both to the Internet and their global network.

That meant, Dar reasoned, someone had some pretty solid information on their infrastructure. She didn't like the idea, but knew it was almost impossible to prevent some information from leaking out. After all, the Telcos were big companies with lots of people making generic wages who could be paid to punch up their provider account and read off circuits and patch points.

So...

If she was going to design a global threat solution, where would she put it? At the network core? Dar's finger traced a few lines. No, because if the threat got that far, she was screwed. Her fingertip stopped over the exterior access ports. No, it would have to go between their infrastructure, and the outside circuits, and that meant a secure appliance.

However, she couldn't put a bottleneck in the network. That would negate all the hard work she'd done over the last few years to remove the damn things. That meant that anything she put in place had to be able to analyze all the data traffic, and yet, not impede its performance.

It was a huge puzzle. Dar gave the diagram a fond grin. She loved puzzles. If she could solve this one, not only would she be in a position to solidify their network offering, she'd also be off the hook for being the idiot who'd made them a target the size of Antarctica.

She pulled out her PDA and tapped a new message addressing it to their hardware provider. She scribbled a note and sent it off, her mind running over the possible approaches she could take on the thing's programming.

It was exciting thinking about something brand new. Designing the network had been fun too, but she really hadn't created anything that hadn't already been there. She just designed the best possible one she could. This was something quite different.

"Ms. Roberts?"

The voice brought her out of her musing with a start. "Yes?" She glanced up sharply at the console tech.

"Sorry ma'am." The man gave her an apologetic grin. "But you're being looked for." He pointed at the door.

Dar looked up to find Kerry in the doorway, holding a bag and grinning impishly. With a slightly sheepish look, she got up and circled the consoles heading for her partner. "Ah...thanks." She joined Kerry at the door. "I'll be back."

As she left, she sent one last look back at the master console grinned and let the door close.

Yeah. She'd be back.

KERRY PEERED AT her reflection in the mirror as she inserted a jade earring in one ear. The color not only matched her eyes it complimented the sea green dress she was wearing. She stepped back to assess the combination with a satisfied grunt.

"Something wrong?" Dar appeared at her shoulder, glancing curiously at her.

"No...except that this is the second time this week we had to get gussied up, and it's not nearly as much fun as the first time."

"Eh." Dar shrugged one shoulder. "The way I figure it, we'll go for a little while, and then bow out. Nothing says we have to spend all night there."

Kerry inserted her other earring nodding a little in agreement. Her stomach had a few butterflies anyway, since it was going to be the first time she'd seen Michelle and Shari since she'd...well, since she'd blown them off.

No other way to say it, really.

Blown them off and triggered a food attack on them by her staff. Kerry almost chuckled. "Okay. Then we can come back here. How about a swim in the pool when we get back? I bet we'll be all sweaty just from the drive up and back."

"Good for me." Dar finished putting her necklace on. "Do I need to bring my boxing gloves? Or you think they'll be civilized?"

Kerry indulged herself in a moment's fantasy of Dar in her black silk sheath, clobbering their Telegenics competitors with the cute red boxing gloves she used for class. "Heh."

"Was that yes, or no?"

"That was me wishing they'd be uncivilized," Kerry admitted. "Ah well. Let's get going. Want me to drive?"

"Sure."

Kerry walked into the living room, shadowboxing as she walked. "Boom...boom...boom..." She paused as they reached the front door and cocked her head to one side. "Wouldn't it be cool if we had the motorcycle up here? I'd love to pull up on that."

Dar stopped. She leaned on the door and looked Kerry up and down. "Hon, think about that a minute and how you have to ride a bike," she said. "If you think I'm giving all of downtown Miami a view like that, you're nuts."

Kerry looked puzzled, then glanced down at herself. A snort emerged. "Oh," she muttered. "Yeah. I see your point."

Dar opened the door and gestured toward the outside. "Exhibitionists first."

"Nyahh."

PIER 12 APPEARED somberly festive as they walked up the flight of stairs into the port facility. Dar handed the white gloved receptionist their invitations and waited to be checked off whatever list the woman had, then gave her a brief nod as they were allowed past.

A glance at the banners told her that Quest wasn't quite the expansive host he'd presented himself to be. It was clear that the cost of the party was being borne by the Port which tied in with what Kerry had told her about them being glad of the business in an off time.

They rode the escalator up to the second level where there were tables filled with various edible items. A bar anchored each end of the room and both were busy with well-dressed schmoozers taking advantage of the free alcohol.

Dar spotted Michelle and Shari at the far table and steered Kerry toward the closest table, reasoning there was no sense in getting into a fistfight before even getting a beer out of it.

Quest approached them just as they reached the bar looking quite pleased with himself. "Good evening, ladies." He greeted them cordially. "Glad you could make it."

"Thanks. It was a nice thing for you to do." Kerry replied. "I realize we're all competing, but the goal of the project is to give you a solution you can use and that we can implement," she said. "And besides, we're all adults, right?"

Dar handed her a cold beer.

"Exactly." Quest agreed. "I'm very glad you have decided to take that view." He turned slightly and ordered a drink from the bar, then leaned on it and looked back at them. "Especially since one of our applicants has chosen to capture this process on film." He indicated behind them.

Kerry turned her head to see a cameraman and an assistant over in the far corner. "Why did you let them?" She turned back to Quest. "I thought you wanted this to be low key."

The man shrugged. "Once it was out, it was out. No point in hiding it anymore. This way, we get some good press for free. What can I tell you?"

Practical. Dar silently agreed. "Look at it this way, Ker. One day you'll end up watching yourself on the Discovery channel."

"Travel Channel." Quest corrected her succinctly. "They've already signed the deal. My people weren't that thrilled, but they never put a restriction in the contract so we're stuck with it."

Dar studied him. "Be a lot of pressure for Telegenics to win the bid then," she remarked casually. "Otherwise, makes for bad TV, doesn't it? No happy ending for the little guy."

"Doesn't it?" Quest tipped his drink toward her then walked off in the direction of the camera crew.

Kerry strolled away from the bar with Dar at her heels. They both stopped in a relatively empty spot reviewing the room together. "Hmm," Kerry said. "Why does this whole thing just get slimier and slimier every time we turn around?"

"The smell of mildew is in the air. Let's go see what they've got over there." She nudged Kerry toward the canapé table. Halfway there, she realized they'd been spotted by Michelle and Shari, but she just kept walking one hand coming to rest on Kerry's back as they reached the line. "Ker?"

"I see them." Kerry observed the choices. "Oh, look, hon...lots of little potential weapons. I bet those stuffed potato puffs would sting."

"Contain yourself, Jesse James." Dar handed her a plate. "Maybe it'll be civil."

"Maybe our dog will learn to fly."

Dar offered her plate up to the uniformed attendant and watched as he placed several canapés on it. Her peripheral vision picked up their adversaries approaching and she took a moment to sort out her possible responses before she turned and made eye contact with them. "Evening." She decided on a gracious nod.

Kerry's shoulders squared visibly before she looked up. She merely returned the stares evenly, allowing Dar to do the communicating for the both of them.

"Evening." Michelle responded, taking a breath to continue. But after a second, her jaw closed and she merely picked up a plate and continued down the line.

Shari glared at both of them. Dar lowered her head slightly and subtly altered her posture as an icy edge came into her eyes.

The camera man from the filming crew closed in focusing on them tightly, and with a twitch of her lip, Shari also turned and went down the line, cutting in front of them and grabbing a plate of her own.

Kerry smiled pleasantly at the cameraman. "Hi."

"Hi," the man returned her greeting cheerfully. "So, what do you think about the party?"

"It's been just charming so far." Kerry said. "Hope it stays that way." She added just loud enough for her voice to carry.

Neither of their adversaries turned, but both backs stiffened.

The man moved off to follow Shari and Michelle followed by another man who was talking into a recorder.

Kerry removed a generic puffy something from Dar's plate and popped it into her mouth chewing with thoughtful vehemence. After a second, she stopped chewing, and, with a weird expression on her face, hastily washed her food down with a swallow of her beer. "What was that?"

"The establishment of primate dominance as a vestige of our ·biological lineage," Dar replied succinctly. "Or did you mean the spicy mushrooms and anchovies? Thanks for trying it for me, by the way."

Kerry digested both pieces of information. She took another swallow of beer to get the last of the taste from her mouth. "Ook, ook."

"Me Jane, you Jane, you know how it is." Dar sounded more than amused. "Let's go talk to those guys from Cangen. I think that second one in the corduroy trousers used to work for us."

"Cords in summer?" Kerry muttered, as she followed her partner across the tile floor. "Bet he didn't work for us long."

JUST HER LUCK, it would be the bathroom again. Kerry found herself face-to-face with Michelle as she stepped up to the sink and leaned forward to wash her hands. The red haired woman was dressed in a caramel colored cocktail dress that did not flatter her at all. "Hi."

"Hi." Michelle responded. "I've got to hand it to you, Kerry. You surprised me."

Kerry concentrated on washing her hands. "Did I?

"Yes." Michelle leaned against the sink and waited for the other woman washing her hands to finish up and leave before she continued. "I thought you were civilized."

"Ah." Kerry straightened up and reached for a towel. "Well, you know, most of the time I am." She faced Michelle squarely. "But you stomped all over my last nerve to such an extent that I just lost the ability to deal civilly with you. Isn't that a shame?" She tossed the balled up paper towel into the basket and walked past. "Good night."

"Kerry."

Michelle was, if nothing else, persistent to the core. Kerry debated a moment, then paused and waited. "Yes?"

"I know you think we hate you..."

"No," Kerry interrupted firmly. "I don't think that at all. I think your partner hates Dar, and you both will do anything to beat us. I don't mind competition, just don't put a friendly face on it. Be square."

Michelle folded her arms over her chest. "We can compete and not be enemies." She suggested. "I know there's an issue between Shari and Dar, no question. But you and I always got along."

"Until you starting playing dirty tricks."

Michelle's eyebrows arched. "Says the woman who sent thugs from her office to attack me?"

The characterization of their staff just struck Kerry as sadly funny. "They didn't go there for that," she told Michelle. "They just wanted to let you know I wasn't coming." She paused. "I had to leave town on unexpected business."

"Your way of sending a message?" The other woman countered with a touch of sarcasm. "Nice."

"No." Kerry turned and opened the door. "I didn't send them. I would have just let you sit there and rot." She gave Michelle a last smile, and walked out.

Michelle stood for a moment in quiet thought, her eyebrows lifting. "Now that is a damn surprise." She murmured to herself. "I guess the old divide and conquer isn't flying anymore." With a shake of her head, she walked out of the bathroom and headed across the floor. "I knew I should have stayed at the hotel tonight."

Kerry was ahead of her angling toward the other side of the room where she suddenly spotted Dar and Shari facing off, Dar's body language aggressive and exuding energy.

Michelle sighed gustily. "Oh, crap." She hastened her pace, then, just as suddenly, she slowed again. "You know what?" She said to the air. "To hell with it. If she's opened up her mouth again, let her take the consequences this time. I'm over it." With a nod, she turned on her mid height heels and headed back for the bar.

KERRY REACHED DAR'S side just as she heard her partner say something she hoped wasn't related to Shari's biological origins. "Hey." She put a hand on Dar's side.

"Sorry, that's just bilge wash," Dar replied crisply, then glanced to one side. "Not you."

"Why is giving a customer a low cost solution bilge wash? Because it can be done cheaper than you can do it?" Shari countered.

"Because it doesn't work," Dar said. "Not long term. There isn't a piece of software out there that can't be hacked or modified without firmware backing it up."

"Oh, that's bull."

Dar refused to lose her temper. "No, it's not bull. It's just how technology is. Engineers know that." She exchanged a slight nod with her counterpart at another of the companies. "If you want to have real control of the process, you have to control it at a machine level."

"But hardware costs more." Shari argued.

"Failing costs more than whatever you pay to succeed," Dar said. "If you ignore that, you set up your clients for failure." She continued, "Here's an example. A client puts in production a new application, whose over WAN link bandwidth had never been quantified."

"That's not my problem as the network provider," Shari said. "I sell a service and a pipe."

Dar's blue eyes glinted with sharp glee. "That's the difference between being a business partner and a vendor. I don't just sell pipes."

"No." Shari didn't miss a beat, very aware of the cameraman focusing on them. "You sell insurance, at a premium."

The man Dar had been talking with, interjected a hand wave. "Yeah, but it's like clean underwear. You don't have a pair, boy, you end up needing 'em," he said. "I don't go for all the high priced goodies you do, Dar, but there has to be some ass covering. I don't ever trust just one piece of anything to be the only solution."

"Pithy way of putting it Don." Dar produced a grin.

"In my time, I've seen more software than hardware take a dump, ma'am." He shrugged unrepentantly. "I, for one, do not intend on pushing a low ball I can't sleep at night over just to get a contract."

The cameraman's assistant winced a little at the language, but indicated to his partner to keep filming.

"It's got nothing to do with low balling!" Shari broke in. "It has to do with not waving the latest and greatest and most expensive at people who don't need it!"

"But why shouldn't we offer the latest technology?" Kerry asked. "Isn't that the whole point?" She frowned. "You all talk like using the best and the newest stuff available is a handicap. Hello? We're in the technology business, folks. It changes every ten minutes. If all customers want is a canned, old solution let them go to BestBuy."

"Are you nuts?" Shari now addressed her directly. "People want the cheapest solution the fastest way possible. They don't want to be cutting edge."

"No, but we do." Dar smoothly took back over. "You've got it all wrong, Shari, just like always. People don't want the cheapest solution. They want the one that is most economical for them."

Shari rolled her eyes. "Ah yes, Professor Roberts, who probably barely passed freshman English. I see the difference."

"ILS doesn't pay me to write essays." Dar still maintained her composure. "But if you don't know the difference between economical and cheap, that'll explain things when those companies you sold bargain basement solutions to all fall apart and come crying to a real IT company for a solution."

"You wish."

"No, ILS does pay me for in depth analysis and trending. I don't wish. I know." Dar replied coolly.

The cameraman seemed totally engrossed in the exchange sliding the lens back and forth between the talkers. He lingered on Dar. She noticed, and turned her head slightly to look right into the blank, black eye. She winked at it, and unexpectedly grinned. "Now remember. I'm the bad guy."

The assistant grinned back at her, making an okay sign with his fingers.

Shari glanced around, but apparently did not find what she was looking for. "Well, we'll find out which one of us has the right approach soon enough. Excuse me."

Dar watched her go, feeling a sense of vague personal triumph that she hadn't let Shari's jibes rattle her. Outwardly, anyway. She took a deep breath feeling Kerry move just a little closer to her, her partner's body heat gently toasting her left side.

Did Kerry sense how she felt? Dar let out her held breath slowly, only marginally paying attention to Don's subject change. The cameraman was still standing there fussing with his gear, and the assistant took the opportunity to approach them.

"Well, that was a great piece of film," the man said. "I think that was one of the best we have so far. Ms. Roberts, mind of I ask you a few questions?"

"Well..."

"Just a few?" The man coaxed. "Let's go over there where it's a little quieter."

"Go on, boss." Kerry poked her a bit. "I'll go get you a refill." She captured Dar's glass and plate.

Dar gave her a brief, uncertain look, then shrugged and indicated to the cameraman to lead on. "Can't guarantee I'll answer, but you can ask."

Kerry waited for them to move off, before she headed back toward the tables, running her mind over what had just happened. Dar had won the exchange, she realized, and without getting mad in the process. She'd also impressed the television people, and used her charm on them to very good effect.

Wow. Kerry handed the bartender her empty glass. "Can I have a...um..." Beer? Scotch? Something cocktailish to match Dar's newly burnished image? She leaned forward and put her hands on the edge of the bar. "Do you have any milk?"

The bartender paused in the act of pouring a glass of wine and looked at her. "Milk?"

"Milk."

He finished and handed the glass to a woman standing by waiting. "Uh...yeah..."

"I got some ginger ale?" The man offered with polite persistence.

"Milk." Kerry repeated again. "Don't make me go find a Farm Stores."

"Okay." The man gave up gracefully and produced the milk. "Here you go." He handed it over. "I never argue with a woman wearing a snake on her chest."

Kerry almost gave her snake a milk bath, but managed to regain control over her grip on the glass and retreated toward the food table intent on finding something appropriate to go with it.

DAR SAT DOWN at one of the small tables on the far side of the room and fiddled with a table tent as the camera assistant joined her.

He started off by extending his hand across to her. "First of all, I don't think we actually met. I'm Derren Eschew."

Dar warily took his hand and shook it. "People say 'bless you' a lot to you don't they?"

Derren chuckled good naturedly. "Oh yeah." He agreed. "Bless you, gesundheit, want a tissue, have a cough drop...you name it I've heard it six million times since first grade." He leaned back in his seat once they'd released their grasps. "You have a pretty unusual name too, don't you?"

"Roberts?" Dar lifted a brow slightly. "In Miami, sure."

"Hehheh. I meant your first name." Derren clarified. "Is it short for something?"

"I've never been short for anything. No. It's just Dar."

The man opened a small notepad and studied its contents. "You characterized yourself as the bad guy." He looked up at her. "Why?"

Dar paused a bit before she answered, considering her words. "You're framing Telegenics as the good guys," she said. "So that makes me the bad guy."

"Because, they're a little, struggling company and you're the IT giants? David and Goliath kinda thing? They have worked incredibly hard to get an inroad into a very tough business that you seem to own. Isn't that right?"

Dar propped her chin up against her fist. "No." She replied. "That's not right. We only own the contracts we've won, and despite Telegenics opinion to the contrary, we won those contracts by being the best choice for the companies who signed them."

"But they're going out and changing that." Derren flipped a page and made a note.

"Are they?"

The man stopped writing and looked up. "You don't think they are?"

Watchful blue eyes focused on him. "I think it's a tight economy, and they're taking advantage of companies looking to cut expenses to tempt people with short term savings." She stated quietly. "Whether it was the best choice for them remains to be seen."

The man scribbled another note. "Naturally, you don't think so." he said.

"Naturally." Dar agreed, with a flash of neat white teeth. She let her eyes drop to the table, then turned her head sideways as she sensed Kerry approaching. Her partner was carrying a glass and a plate, and as their eyes met, Kerry broke into a warm smile.

"Your company does a lot of work for the government. Isn't that right? Military work?"

Dar nodded.

"Bet you're glad the 'don't ask, don't tell' policy doesn't extend to contractors, huh?"

The question caught Dar by surprise, and she let potential answers percolate for a second or two while Kerry set the plate and glass down, and took a seat next to her. "Why?" She cocked her head. "Despite what you've been told, corporations, even big ones like mine, are sexless."

Kerry came in right on the sexless. Her head jerked a little in as she gave her partner a bemused look. "I leave to get you a drink, and I come back and you're talking sex? I thought this was for the Travel Channel?"

Derren leaned on his elbow. "So working with a bunch of GI's who would be glad to give you the boot doesn't bother you?"

Kerry leaned toward him. "Does it bother you?" She asked. "Did you tell when asked or something?"

A guarded look crossed the man's face, and he straightened up and moved back from the table. "Nah, I just wondered. Politics and contracts make strange bedfellows, I guess." He got up and closed his notepad. "Nice talking to you, Ms. Roberts. Hope we get to do it again." He held out a hand, and clasped Dar's briefly. "Night."

He walked off trailing the cameraman behind him.

Dar studied her glass. "You got me milk." She commented.

"And cookies." Kerry nudged the plate closer. "Have some."

"Wonder what that last part was about." Dar commented, breaking a cookie in half and nibbling it. "Looking for a racy angle?"

Kerry shook her head. "After all, they're gay too." She pointed at Michelle, who had rejoined Shari near the dessert table. "Or maybe that's the angle?"

Dar grunted, focusing on her treat.

Kerry sighed. "Are we having a good night here?"

"Damned if I know." Dar took a sip of the milk. "Damned if I know, Kerry. There's something just not clicking in this whole thing. I'm missing something."

She drummed her fingers on the table. "Something."

Chapter Two

KERRY TURNED THE page of the book she was reading, enjoying the cool breeze off the water as she swung idly back and forth in the swing chair. It was just past six and they'd left work early after a long, long week.

Fortunately after the party Quest had left them all alone, and neither she nor Dar had heard anything more about the project all week long which had turned out to be a damn good thing.

Disasters tended to come in spurts. This week she'd had to deal with six of them, one for each day and two on Monday that had almost resulted in her being on an airplane to someplace boring and unpleasant.

But she'd worked it out in the end, and now she was blissfully enjoying the quiet decompression of sitting on the deck watching the sun's light slowly fade.

Behind her, the glass door slid open releasing a puff of chilled, garlic scented air along with Dar's tanned and mostly bare body. "Hey." Kerry lazily rolled her head to one side as Dar joined her on the swing chair, dressed in only a pair of soft cotton shorts and a colorful scarlet sports bra. "What are you up to?"

"About six and a quarter." Dar put her feet up on the stone porch balustrade, flexing her toes against the warm surface. "Busy week."

"Uh huh." Kerry laid her book down and let her head rest against Dar's shoulder. "I'm glad it's over. Between my fubars and your hackers, I wanted to call Florida Power and Light and have them take the power out again." She leaned closer and sniffed Dar's skin curiously. "Why do you smell like bubble gum?"

"I was playing ball with Chino and her new toy." Dar displayed a clump of cream colored hair dusting her shorts. "It's a giggle ball, and it smells weird."

"A giggle ball?"

"Uh huh." Dar said. "Like you." She reached over and tickled her partner who obliged her by giggling and smacking her hand.

"Dar!" Kerry tried to tickle her back, but found her hands caught and gently held. "You punk."

Dar released her, as she chuckled. "Yeah, I've been a punk all week. I'm driving the Ops crew nuts. I think they wish I'd go back to yelling at people in meetings."

"That's not true. They love it," Kerry said. "I heard them in the break room. You were the entire subject of conversation the last six times I went through there." She added, "At least until they spotted me. Then it switched to soccer."

"Soccer?" Dar sounded pleased nonetheless. "Yeah, I've been giving them some pointers as long as I'm taking over the console." She wiggled her toes contentedly. "Been sort of fun."

"They're in awe of you, you know that, right?" Kerry smiled, rocking them both a little. "Hey, I've got an idea—you up for a night dive tonight?"

"Oo." Dar's eyes lit up. "Yeah!"

Ah. Kerry felt the stress of the week slip away from her. Warm air, warm water, and the stars. "You'll protect me from cuttlefish, right?"

"With my life." Dar promised.

"I'll grab dinner, you grab the towels. Let's go get deep."

"C'MON, CHINO." Kerry herded their pet onto the back of the boat watching her frisk about, and busy herself smelling every square inch of it. After watching the dog for an indulgent minute, Kerry continued on into the boat's cabin and put down her armful of supplies.

She set the full pot of spaghetti and meatballs on the small stove, putting the locking arm in place to keep the contents from becoming interior decoration when Dar started the boat moving. The wine she put in the small fridge to chill, along with the dessert, a six pack of yogurt, and some baby chocolate milk chugs.

The boat rocked lightly, announcing Dar's presence and a second later she joined her in the cabin. She dropped a mesh bag containing Kerry's gear on the deck and tossed her own nearby. "We're outta here."

"Go go Gadget." Kerry went to stow the diving gear. "I'll get us loose."

Dar ducked outside and headed up to the controls while Kerry dodged the curious Chino and hopped onto the dock to untie the lines. The sun had just gone down, and the breeze had picked up, tossing her hair back as she jumped back on board. "Okay!"

The low rumble of the diesels starting up vibrated the deck beneath her feet. Chino barked in surprise, and backed up as the water churned behind them. Normally, Kerry would go up and join her partner as they motored out, but she knew if she did their pet would stand at the bottom of the ladder and bark, so she parked herself in one of the wood and fabric deck chairs instead. She was barefoot and wearing a sleeveless muscle t-shirt. She completed her outfit by snagging one of Dar's baseball caps and putting it on backwards to keep her hair out of her eyes once the wind came up.

Chino went over to stand near the edge of the deck as they backed into the quiet marina waterway, her tail wagging idly as she watched the other boats go past.

Kerry stretched her legs out and leaned back as the island slowly receded, the lingering bands of sunset still painting the sky to the west.

It was warm, but with the breeze, very comfortable. Kerry allowed herself a few more lazy moments until they reached the buoy and Dar kicked the engines into higher gear. Then she pushed herself to her feet and got to work preparing their gear for the dive.

"Hey, Dar?"

"Yeap?"

"Did you wash these wetsuits?"

"Yeap." Dar answered promptly. "Found some new stuff in the dive shop last time I went. You like the smell?"

Kerry sniffed cautiously. "Smells like tangerines!" She yelled up. "I like it!" She set the neoprene suits down with a grunt of satisfaction. Then she went to the built in lockers and removed their BC's and regulators, laying them out on the counter and going over them with a careful eye.

They were only doing a reef, and a somewhat shallow one at that, but Kerry had never bought into taking chances with their favorite sport.

Satisfied, she opened the bottom cabinet and removed two tanks, lifting them with some effort onto the low bench on the side and bungee tying them in place as the boat shifted in the waves.

Tanks falling on your toes sucked. Kerry had two formerly broken ones to attest to that. She picked up Dar's BC first and untied one tank, slipping the rig over the top and sliding it down by wiggling the straps against the snug fit. She re-looped the bungee while she positioned the rig, tightening the tank clasp with a firm hand.

The boat shifted and rocked, making Chino bark in surprise. The dog scrambled back next to Kerry and pressed against her legs, eyeing the spray coming over the bow with dubious eyes.

"It's okay, Cheebles." Kerry patted her on the head. "Mommy Dar just wants to get us where we're going fast." She reached over and picked up Dar's regulator, then went back to her task.

So far, so good. Kerry secured Dar's instrument console to the D-clip on the right hand side and prepared to repeat the entire process with her own gear.

Once finished, she took their masks and sat down with a tube of no fog, applying it as Chino curled up at her feet on the deck. It was a comforting and familiar task, and the smell of the sweet, salt air and the feel of the spray against her put her heart at ease as they headed into their own private world.

DAR POPPED UP out of the water, reaching for the steps with one hand as she cleared the surface. She removed her regulator and gave Kerry a nod. "Okay, we're tied off," she said, licking her lips. "Nice down there, no current."

Kerry was standing by in her gear, or more to the point, sitting by, since she was on the back deck with her flippers resting on the wooden diving platform next to the ladder. Chino was standing up on the inside of the wall, peering over at Dar as she wagged her tail.

"Cool." Kerry prepared to stand up, readying her balance as she lifted herself plus forty pounds of assorted gear onto her fins. She put her regulator in her mouth and took a breath, then put her hand over her mask and stepped out into the sea.

The water was pleasantly cool, and it quickly penetrated her short wetsuit and reduced some of the heat built up inside it. Kerry got her equilibrium and looked around spotting Dar immediately nearby.

This was her favorite kind of night dive when they descended while it was still a little light out. She could see shadows under her, and the outline of the reef more comforting than going down in total darkness.

Dar pointed downward. Kerry nodded and let the air out of her vest, feeling her body settle deeper in the water as she changed from vertical to horizontal and headed down to the bottom.

Dar had picked one of their favorite reefs with lots of undercuts and coral for critters to hide in. Kerry settled on her knees in the sand just clear of the coral and got her camera gear arranged watching as ghostly schools of fish whisked around her and started to dissipate.

A big sea bass appeared swimming idly through the reef pretending not to notice all the potential dinner candidates heading away from him. He swam closer to Kerry and she simply kept still and waited, her camera raised so she could look through the offset crosshair.

The bass seemed as curious about her as she was about him. He finned closer, tiny bits of iridescence reflecting the last of the light from the surface as he came within her easy reach.

Kerry cautiously closed the shutter button, wincing right along with the fish as the strobe went off and sent a brief silver flash of light everywhere. The bass gave her an insulted look and swam off, flicking his tail at her as he disappeared into the gloom.

Kerry felt pleased with the shot however, and she turned to find something else to take a picture of. As though in total cooperation with her effort, Dar swam into view a little above Kerry's head outlined against the pale surface of the water.

Another flash of silver secured the portrait.

Kerry pushed up off the bottom and finned toward the reef. It was getting darker, and now if she peeked under the coral ledges she could see the beginnings of the eerie phosphorescence the night brings.

It was like a magic world that hid itself from the night. Kerry decided to just experience the change. So she settled carefully down on the bottom again, folding her fins under her and getting herself cross legged somehow.

She focused the lens on the darkness of the overhang aware, from the corners of her eyes, of Dar's nearby floating presence.

In the shadows, several little bioluminescent fish suddenly appeared nibbling at the pale scarlet polyps. Kerry captured it, then nearly lost her mind as the occupant of the dark hole, a green moray eel, came rushing out to confront her with open jaws.

Seated as she was, there was no way for her to get out of the way in time. However, just as she had started to unwind her body, she felt herself lifted up and away by a powerful yank on her gear. The next thing she knew she was twenty feet away over another part of the reef.

In the gloom, she saw the eel retreat, but not without giving her a vicious glare.

She let out her breath in a stream of bubbles and looked over her shoulder into Dar's watching eyes. Kerry wiped the back of her hand over her mask, and nodded as her partner gave her a pat on the butt.

Dar held up two fingers, then indicated her own eyes, then indicated Kerry's. She shook one of the fingers at her in semi-mock remonstrance.

Yeah, she was right. Kerry nodded at her, accepting the scold. *I'm in the ocean, not in an aquarium. These are wild animals.* She got her composure back, and floated for a moment. She spotted more glowing coral and started toward it, more cautiously this time.

"OOOHGH." Dar finished putting their gear up and dropped down into a deck chair. "Nice dive."

A perfect canopy of stars now covered the sky over them, obscured only in spots by drifting clouds. Kerry continued out from the cabin and put two plates down, taking her seat across from Dar with an equally contented grunt. "Killer."

Dar leaned over and got hold of a strand of spaghetti between her teeth, slurping it in until it broke and left her with a smattering of sauce across her nose. "Whoops."

Kerry lifted a glass of chilled wine and took a sip of it, swirling its tangy sweetness around in her mouth to cleanse it of the last of the saltiness. "Thanks again for saving me from Captain Eel, Dardar. Man, that scared the poop out of me."

Dar chuckled, picking up her plate and propping it against her knees. "Me too." She attacked the pasta with a fork, swirling a big mouthful and consuming it, her body demanding something to replenish the energy she'd just expended.

Kerry took another sip of wine instead, gazing out over the dark waves she'd recently been beneath. Looking at it from above, like this, it seemed almost insane to think about diving into it. It represented, in a way, the totality of the unknown. She now felt a connection to the sea she'd never had before she'd met Dar.

Far off, near the horizon, she spotted a darker shadow against the clouds. She watched it idly, then squinted a little as it seemed to elongate. "Hey, sweetie? What is that?" She pointed.

Dar looked up from biting a meatball in half. "Uh?" Her eyes focused on where her partner was pointing. "Um..." She swallowed hastily and put her plate down, getting up and walking to the back of the boat. "Hah."

"What's funny?"

"What do you suppose the odds are of you and I being out on our boat the very same time as Quest's ships are making the turn for the cut?" Dar asked.

"Is that what they are?" Kerry joined her at the back of the boat, peering out into the darkness. "Really?"

"Four big ships being pulled by eight little ones." Dar confirmed. "I don't think it can be anything else."

Kerry turned and regarded the opening to the cut, which was just to their south. "We're going to get a good look at them, that's for sure."

Dar returned to the table, only just barely saving her spaghetti from a Labrador tongue. "Yep, we sure are." She settled back down and put her feet up. "Front row seats."

The line of ships crept slowly closer, their superstructures only sparsely lit, rolling slightly in the almost calm seas.

DAR KEPT THE Dixie idling just past the turnoff into the port's pier area, getting as close to the last ship as she could without incurring the wrath of the circling pilot boats. There was a customs fast boat cruising around too, but Dar figured she'd be pegged as a bored rich boater with nothing better to do than sightsee, rather than a potential threat or smuggler. "Which one, Ker?"

"I think it's that one." Kerry pointed at the ship aligned on the northeast side of the port. "Yeesh, they're big."

"That they are." Dar studied the vessels. They were all roughly the same size, but all four had different configurations. Two seemed to be tall and squat; the other two were long and lower. Even in the dark, they all bore signs of having better times behind them. She could see patches upon patches of metal on the sides if the light from the streetlamps lining the harbor hit them at a certain angle.

The one on the northeast that Kerry had pegged as "theirs" was one of the longer, lower ones. Dar steered a little closer, keeping a wary eye out for the authorities, her eyes measuring the length and breadth with automatic accuracy. "Damn thing must be a thousand feet long!?"

"Lot of portholes." Kerry noted.

"Oh yeah." Dar agreed softly. The Dixieland Yankee slid a little sideways in the tide, and a strip of moonlight splashed between her and the boat. It hit the water, and Dar leaned forward her eyes catching a ripple on the surface that didn't look quite right. "Hey, Ker?"

"Yeah?"

"Check the bilge real quick, huh? Are we leaking something?"

Kerry scrambled across the deck and hopped over the back wall leaning over and peering at the back of the boat. She held on with one hand and fished her mini flashlight off her belt with the other, keying it on and studying the spot where the engines were churning the water. "Can't tell." She yelled up at Dar. "You're breaking up the water too much."

Dar cut the engines after looking around to make sure they weren't going to drift into anything. "Look quick."

Kerry studied the water, then leaned way over and stuck her hand in, bringing it up and sniffing. Her nose wrinkled. "This stinks, but not of diesel."

"Okay, get up." Dar started the engines again and backed the boat away from the pier, getting to an angle against the moonlight again. She spotted what had worried her — a silvery film on the water they?d just passed through that extended across the surface of the water behind them.

Carefully, Dar turned the boat and followed the oily stripe with her eyes. It went right past them and headed across the cut, fading out from her view as it reached the ship in the northeast dock. "Figures."

"What is it?" Kerry was at the bottom of the ladder peering up.

"Should have thought of that first. It's one of them leaking something." Dar pointed.

Kerry turned and looked, shading her eyes against the streetlamps. Now that Dar had pointed it out to her, she saw the line on the water, and in fact if she went to the side— "I can smell it." She called up. "Smells like kerosene."

Dar moved their boat sideways out of the stain. One of the customs' boats was now heading their way, apparently noting the odd maneuvers she'd been executing. "Shoulda just stayed out on the reef. Better go grab the registration just in case, Ker."

The other boat pulled alongside and Dar set the Dixie into idle keeping her hands on the controls as the customs officer grabbed hold of the railing. "Hi." She called down.

"You having a problem?" The man called up to her, apparently more concerned for her safety than suspicious.

"No. I saw a slick, and thought I was causing it." Dar pointed. "But it's that tub over there."

The officer shaded his eyes then crouched. "Ah! Yeah." He nodded. "You just out for a ride?"

Kerry emerged, carefully locking Chino inside the cabin. "No, we were diving." She indicated their gear. "We live over there. We saw these big ships coming in, so we were curious."

The customs officer gave her a once over. "Well, don't be too curious. That's our job." He pushed off from the railing. "You folks have a good night."

"Night." Kerry replied politely. "You too."

The customs boat backed away, but placed itself conspicuously between the ship and the Dixieland Yankee. The officers on the rear of the boat watched them as Dar idled for a moment more, then swung the bow around and headed off toward the marina on the far side of the island.

Kerry climbed up onto the flying bridge and joined her partner. "That was weird."

"Of course it was. Do normal things happen to you and me?" Dar asked, as she glanced behind her. "But in fairness, I don't think oil leaks are their department." She took the right fork around the island instead of the left, coming even with another of the ships as she moved slowly through the no wake area.

This was the first ship that had come in, and it was already tied up. There were several figures standing on the deck leaning on the rails, looking at the sights. One waved at them.

Kerry waved back.

The figure stepped forward and exposed himself laughing loudly.

Dar picked up the mic clipped to the console and switched on the Dixie's PA system. "Throw it back, buddy. It's too short."

Kerry snickered, leaning against Dar and hiding her face in her shirt sleeve.

The man's companions laughed as well, slapping the miscreant on the back and shoving him back against the wall. One of them then advanced to the rail, but backed up again as the Dixieland Yankee turned into the marina channel and started to disappear from view. "Hey girlies! C'mon back, yeah? I got me a big one!"

"You know what?" Kerry sniffed reflectively. "I sure hope Shari and Michelle get that one."

Dar chuckled. "I'm sure ours won't be much better. Old salts are old salts."

"Hmm. We could bring our own old salt with us." Kerry mused. "He's still on the payroll, and I bet he'd probably keep those guys off our backs."

"Hmm."

They came around the south side of the island and entered the marina basin, slowing their already slow speed to just above idle. Most of the marina was empty–the owners moving their boats to a more comfortable climate during the summer along with themselves.

Dar angled toward their slip putting the Dixie neatly into place as Kerry scooted down the ladder to jump ashore and tie them off. Her thoughts, however, were on Kerry's last suggestion. Not that she really thought they needed Dad around on their ship.

But wouldn't it be interesting if he were hanging around the others?

Dar shut down the diesels and leaned against the console, weighing the conflict of aiding their business goals at the expense of asking her father to be a part of something not quite...

Would he consider it dishonorable? Or just good strategy?

"Dar? You coming down from there or should I bring coffee up?"

Dar shut down the console and pocketed the keys, then started for the ladder still pondering the question.

KERRY SETTLED INTO her seat glad of the very early morning quiet of the office on a rainy Monday morning. She had a meeting scheduled in an hour with Mark and the technical team for the bid, and she intended on using the time before then to square away the project and tie up a few loose ends.

"Hey, Mayte?" She pressed her intercom. "You there?"

"Yes! I am."

"Did we get the circuit completion on the pier?" Kerry asked. "I don't have anything here on it."

"I will check." Mayte promised. "They were saying on Friday that it would be done."

"Okay, thanks." Kerry set that problem aside. She pulled over a folder with requisitions for the project, and reviewed them. "Yikes! Is this just for the setup team?" She sighed, leafing through the pages. Money to establish an office at the pier and get that up and running, and provisioning for the gear to equip the office. "Damn, IT is expensive." She shook her head and signed the pages, closed the folder and tossed it into her out bin.

"Kerry?" Mayte's voice crackled in.

"Yeesss?" Kerry answered.

Her assistant laughed softly. "You sound so funny when you do that."

"Do I sound like Dar?" Kerry's eyes twinkled.

"A little." Mayte admitted. "Only not so big."

Kerry's eyebrow lifted.

"The circuits have come complete." Mayte went on. "The Bellsouth man says it is terminated in the local office on Brickell. He needs to know from you which to patch here."

"Tell him the Pier 10 one." Kerry replied. "But hold on to the other ones. I might be able to rent them." She hummed softly in satisfaction. "Okay, we're good to go." She typed a message to Mark then took a sip of her morning tea.

The door opened and Mayte slipped inside coming over to her desk with a folder in her hands. "Good morning."

"Morning!" Kerry pointed at her outbox. "Can you make sure that gets down to purchasing? We're gonna need it." She glanced at her assistant. "That's a pretty shirt. I like it."

Mayte blushed visibly. "Mama got it for me this weekend." She fingered the silk shyly. "I think she was trying to make it up to me for getting me in so much trouble when you went to New York." She hesitated. "Kerry, you were talking last week about going diving. Do you like that a lot?"

Kerry leaned back in her chair. "Absolutely," she said. "In fact, Dar and I went on a night dive on Friday night. It was wonderful. I saw a moray eel."

Mayte nodded seriously. "I think I would like to try that. Do you know where I could find out about it?"

"Sure. Matter of fact, you can borrow my study materials to see if you like it. Remind me and I'll bring them in tomorrow." Kerry promised. "It's a great sport...ah, did you tell your parents you wanted to do this?"

"No." Mayte grinned a little. "I did not think they would like it. Mama is always worried the sharks will eat you and La Jefa when you go." She confided. "Have you seen a shark?"

"Sure." Kerry said. "But it was in a tank at Disney World. Does that count?" She grinned at her assistant's look of bewilderment. "Anyway, I'll bring the stuff in and you can read it. Really, it's a lot of fun."

"Thank you. I will tell Mama afterwards. Yes?"

"You learn fast." Kerry winked. "Hey, maybe you can come out diving with us if you decide you like it. I think your mama trusts us to take care of you."

Mayte's eyes lit up. "I think so too!" She blurted. "Thank you!" Her gaze dropped to the folder in her hands. "This came for you." She held it out. "I am sorry I am taking up your time."

Kerry took the folder, and watched in some bemusement as Mayte trotted for the door and escaped into the outer office. "Huh." She put the folder down and opened it. "What got into her, I wonder?"

"You."

Kerry nearly jumped out of her seat before she recognized the voice. "Jesus, Dar." She looked over at the inner door. "You scared the poo out of me." Her brow creased. "What do you mean me?"

Her partner strolled over and took a seat on the edge of Kerry's desk. "You haven't noticed yet she has a crush on you?"

"Oh, she does not." Kerry scoffed. "Get out of here. She's a nice kid, and she loves working here. What, because she's interested in diving, you think she's got a crush on me?"

The corners of Dar's eyes creased as a little grin appeared. "Okay, don't say I didn't warn you. Did those lines come in?"

"Yes." Kerry nodded. "I was going to send Mark and a team there to get the office set up and facilities working. Did you want to go look at the ship?"

Dar got up and went to the window looking out as she pressed her fingertips against the glass. "No." She did a few vertical pushups. "I've got something I'm working on in ops. Maybe I'll go over tonight, after the crowds take off."

"Okay."

"I just talked to Alastair."

Kerry half turned to face her partner. "And?"

"The contracts this contract is tied into will either make or break the quarter, he thinks."

Nothing like a little pressure. "Okay, but the quarter just started."

"New business is down forty percent on the month." Dar kept doing her pushups. "Alastair said people are waiting to see what happens with this one. It's too public."

"What do you mean, too public? Kerry lifted a hand. "You mean the filming people? They aren't done yet!"

"People know," Dar said, "about us and Telegenics. It's all over the tech press."

"So we have to win it." Kerry exhaled. "No options."

"Something like that." Dar nodded. "I've got to go to ops." She pushed away from the window. "Tell Mark I'm sure Telegenics and everyone else is going to be crawling over our people at the pier. Pick the right people to go down there. I don't want a leak inside."

"All right." Kerry watched the door close behind her. "I'll do that." She added softly.

Things were getting serious. She figured it was only going to get uglier as they went along, and at the end? What if they just couldn't put in a competitive bid? Would Dar agree to a money losing contract to secure the more lucrative one behind it?

Kerry picked up her pen and chewed the end of it, thoughtfully.

"OKAY." Kerry removed her sunglasses as she entered the port building, looking around and spotting one of their security people near the back door. "Hey, John."

"Ms. Stuart." The man hurried over. "Glad you're here. There are some people over in the office causing a problem. The pier folks brought them over."

Kerry sighed and stuck her glasses into the pocket of the red camp shirt she'd put on for her visit to the port. "Lead on." She gestured toward the back. The building was a lot noisier than it had been on her previous visit, and she could hear the sounds of various power tools going as the infrastructure staff put together their temporary office.

They walked through the entryway and into the back hall. Kerry spotted Michelle Graver's distinctive figure in the doorway to their office along with her camera people, and she only just prevented herself from audibly growling. "What's going on here?" She asked instead, putting a sharp note into her voice.

Michelle turned, along with the cameraman, and the port agent.

The port agent had the grace to look apologetic, but Michelle certainly didn't.

"We're just documenting the first of many instances of ILS's attempt to sabotage everyone else's efforts." Michelle said bluntly. "In this case, by taking all the spare pairs into the port and preventing us from putting a circuit in." She advanced aggressively on Kerry, pointing her finger at her. "Didn't think we'd find out?"

Kerry waited for Michelle to stop walking then she made the most of her few inch height advantage. "If you can the Joe Friday routine, I'll rent you one of the lines. Otherwise, take yourself out of my administrative space, please. I have work to do." She was very aware of the camera focused on her, and the wide eyed stares coming from her people inside the office, but she kept her even gaze on Michelle's face. "And for the record, my forethought does not equal your sabotage. Now take off."

"Forethought? No one knew what building we'd be in." Michelle shot back.

"That's right. So I had lines dropped in all of them." Kerry replied. "Now, if you're interested in that rental, we'll talk price. If not, goodbye."

"And help you recoup the cost you'll have to charge the client? Over my dead body." Michelle moved around her and motioned for the cameraman to follow her. "We'll find another way." She brushed by Kerry, coming very close to making physical contact before she got past and headed for the door. The port agent hurried after her, but not without giving Kerry a frazzled look.

"Nice way to start the day." Kerry exhaled, turning back to the office. "Brenda, give the other two piers a call. Offer them use of those lines for a pass through cost, with a two percent administrative charge for our carrying them and paying the bills."

"Yes, ma'am." Brenda went to a phone immediately and dialed after consulting a small directory.

"Smooth, boss." Mark commented. "Slick idea to trip them all up."

Kerry sat down on the edge of one of the folding tables. "Wasn't really the plan. I just needed to be sure we'd have a line on startup. I had no idea they were short on pairs." She admitted wryly. "Ah well. How are we doing here?"

Mark came over and sat next to her. "Pretty good. The line's up to the office, and I just got the router in place. This room is crap for security, though."

Kerry looked around and had to agree. The office had light plasterboard walls and a single door with a simple bolt lock. No alarms, no reinforced panels, nothing. They were putting in six computers and the requisite network gear to support them, and aside from the need to protect corporate data, there was also the question of protecting the hardware itself from being taken. "Can we put a monitoring rig in here?"

"Sure," Mark said. "But when it goes off, it'll take us about twenty minutes to get down here before it all walks off. Not to mention, the line comes in to a public Telco punch down."

Ugh. Worse and worse. "Okay, put a full encryption suite on the data." Kerry sighed. "I'll see what we can work up to put security out here. Otherwise we'll have to make these boxes boot to the network, and keep everything at the office."

Mark nodded. "See what I can do." He got up and went back to work. Kerry remained where she was for a few minutes watching the activity, then she got up and left the office to head over to the ship.

The port agent entered from the front just as she was heading up the escalator. She paused at the top waiting for the woman to catch up with her. "Hi."

"Listen, I'm really sorry about that." Agnes apologized. "I had no idea Ms. Graver was going to do that or that she'd bring those men! What's this all about?" The woman seemed very agitated. "The port didn't bargain for anything like this!"

Where to start? Kerry decided no amount of explanation would really be adequate. "It's business." She explained shortly. "Just try to steer clear of it."

The woman eyed her. "Was she right? Did you do that to stop those people from working?"

Kerry blinked. "That's really none of your business," she replied. "I'm telling you — don't get caught up in this. It's just going to be messy for the port if they try to get involved."

The woman's radio spluttered and she listened intently. A man's voice came through sounding rather desperate, asking for her to come mediate another dispute on the next pier. "That might be easier said than done." She told Kerry. "So far it seems like all you people want to bring here is trouble." She turned and headed down the steps two at a time, talking into her radio.

"Yeesh." With a shake of her head, Kerry went to the outside door and pushed it open, emerging into a blast of shimmering sunlight.

She had plenty of time to look at the ship in the daylight as she walked along the endless outdoor passage that eventually led her to the gangway. The bottom was painted a dark blue and the upper part was once apparently white, but now rust covered a good portion of the exterior and it was more a mottled yellowish gold color.

It looked sad and worn, and she wondered again if all the work obviously needed to make it functional would be worth it. She ran a hand along the railing, the chipped paint spots feeling harsh and almost sharp against her fingers. The port showed its many years resting here on the waterfront. Its concrete was pitted from wind and rain, and the walkway she was on had cracks both near the railing, and more ominously, near the wall.

Kerry eyed a large split as she walked past, and reasoned that if it had held legions of cruise ship passengers en mass, it probably was fit to hold her hundred and thirty five pounds, but she scooted past it anyway just to be sure.

There was a guard hanging around the end of the gangway, but he just nodded as Kerry showed him her corporate badge and went on gazing listlessly down the pier, watching men with forklifts move boxes around.

Kerry walked up the gangway and across the metal bridge leading onto the ship. The railing had been folded back, and she found herself on the outside deck about mid way up the vessel.

She looked down and found worn, salt scoured teak that in some places was so discolored it was almost impossible to see a grain. But it was teak nonetheless. She recognized it from her experience with the Dixie, and as she walked toward the inside doors, it oddly comforted her.

Inside the doors her first impression was one of overwhelming mildew. She stopped short and stifled a sneeze, staring around her in disbelief. The interior of the ship was, to put it mildly, a wreck. She was standing in what was apparently the main reception area, and all she could see was broken, dusty furniture, a ceiling in pieces, some of it hanging down almost to the ground, and dozens of rotting wooden boxes.

The stench was disgusting. It got inside her throat and she could taste it on the back of her tongue, leaving a tinge of bad sewage lingering on its edges. "Ugh." Kerry swallowed hard, glad she hadn't stopped for lunch before coming over. After a moment, she got control of her stomach, and proceeded on picking her way carefully through the debris. The interior of the ship seemed to be a total disaster, and it appeared to her that everything would have to be rebuilt to be usable.

This would work for her purposes since she'd have to put cabling in ceilings and walls and that was always easier when they were being constructed. But she had to wonder, yet again, at Quest's purpose in refitting these old vessels. Surely it would take more money than the darn things were capable of recouping.

A man appeared dressed in white overalls. He spotted Kerry and stopped, looking her up and down with frank appraisal. "You want something?" he asked, in an odd accent not quite German.

"IT contractor." Kerry responded briefly, holding up her identification.

The man grunted and turned his back on her, continuing on his way without a further word.

Kerry edged down a partially blocked hallway and almost collided with another white jump-suited body. "Oh, sorry. Hi there. Can I help you?" A slim, good looking man with curly blond hair turned around. "Are you looking for something??"

Kerry stepped back a little. "Not really," she said. "I'm from the IT contracting company. Just looking around to see what we're going to have to do."

The man scratched his nose. "Oh, okay," he said. "It really looks worse than it is." He turned and peered back the way she had come. "The old girl's really got solid bones. It's all cosmetic stuff out there."

Kerry recalled the holes in the hull she'd seen, and reserved judgment. "Are you part of the ship's staff?" She asked politely.

"I am. I'm Tally Johnson, and I'm the captain's personal assistant. And you are...?"

"Kerry Stuart. From ILS. Do you have a few minutes to show me those bones you mentioned?"

The man positively beamed. "I sure do. You're the computer people, right? We heard we were going to get computers." He started leading Kerry further inside the ship. "The captain's not so sure about that, but I heard we're even going to be able to get email. Is that true?"

Well, having a few friends in middling places was a good thing. Kerry decided she liked perky Mr. Johnson. "That's a very good possibility, yes. We're planning on a satellite, and a new charging system, maybe even VOIP telephones."

Tally laughed. "Okay, you just went past me, Ms. Stuart."

"Kerry, please." Kerry gave him a charming smile. "Nah, it's not that bad, just phones that run over the computer network. You don't have anything like that now, right?"

"No way. We've got manual cash registers, and one old PC the purser used to use to make up the pax folios."

Kerry chuckled. "Now you just went past me," she said. "What's a purser, and what's a pax?"

Tally led her into another, smaller hallway with stairs going up and down. The destruction did seem to be less. Tally headed for the stairs holding his hand out to her. "The purser is the fellow who handles all the money, and the pax are the passengers. C'mon, let me show you the old lady from the bottom up."

Kerry followed him, avoiding the railing and its thick coating of dust, and glad of her jeans and sturdy boots in negotiating the torn up carpet and broken steps. As they went down, the sounds of work, hammering, and banging increased and she had the sudden sensation of descending abruptly into another world.

THE FOREMAN CHECKED off names at the gangway, glancing briefly at each worker as they came up to his desk. He eyed the next to last of them, a big guy wearing a sleeveless sweatshirt and very worn jeans. "Next?"

The man ambled up and presented a set of papers.

The foreman scanned them. "General work." He read. "You got a seaman's card?" He looked at the one presented and nodded. "Service?"

"Navy."

"What'd you do?"

"Little a' every damn thing."

The foreman looked closely at the putative worker noting the scars and the air of definitive but understated competence. "All right, Roberts. Just give this to the guy at the ramp, and have at it. Contract's as long as the tubs are here. Understand?"

"Yeap."

The foreman scribbled a note on a card and handed it over. "Here." He fiddled with his pencil as the newcomer walked away and turned to the man sitting next to him. "Can't believe some of the guys they're passing through the security check, can you?"

The other man shook his head. "Want me to double check that one? I can have Alberto rerun him."

"Nah." The foreman made a rude hand gesture. "As long as he works, I don't give a crap. We've had worse on the docks, and at least this guy showers."

"And speaks English." The second man pointed out.

The foreman snorted as he waved forward the last applicant. "Yeah. Probably make him a supervisor just for that."

DAR PROPPED HER laptop up a little more comfortably against her knee, and typed in another command. She was flat on her back underneath one of the racks, a pale blue cable extending from the jungle of equipment to the back of her machine.

The floor was cold against her skin, but she'd found a relatively all right piece of metal to rest her head against and at least for now, the odd position wasn't interfering with her ability to concentrate.

"Ms. Roberts?"

The techs, on the other hand... "Yeees?" Dar rumbled.

"Um, can I run a cable out here for you? That looks really awkward."

Dar wiggled one foot. "What does, my typing style?"

"Well, the floor, ma'am. Can't really be comfortable, huh?"

Dar typed in another command and reviewed its effect. She scowled and reversed it, tapping the enter key with unnecessary force. "Have you ever tried it?" She glanced quickly at him, before returning her attention to her task. "Lying on the floor?"

There was a moment's silence then a squeak as the tech moved in his leather chair. "Uh...well, sure...we have to do that all the time under there. That's why I said we'd...um..." He cleared his throat. "Ma'am, it's uncomfortable."

"Well, I like it." Dar informed him. "It's good for your back."

"It is?"

"Sure." Dar tried to ignore the annoying object between her

shoulder blades that she suspected was a screw removed from the rack
and never replaced — a pet peeve of hers. "Better than my waterbed as a
matter of fact."

The two techs moved around causing more squeaks. The younger
of the two, blond crew cut Dave, leaned his elbows on his knees and
gazed over at Dar. "You like waterbeds? I tried one once, but it moved
too much for me. I got sick."

"I have a semi-waveless." Dar answered, distracted as a readout
gave her an answer she hadn?t expected. She switched to another
screen and checked a monitor she had running, then frowned again and
tried something else. "Damn it."

"Is that one that don't move, ma'am?" Dave said. "At all?"

"Not really." Dar muttered, biting off a grimace as she mistyped a
command and had to redo it. "Depends on what you're doing in it."

It took a few seconds for the utter silence to penetrate her
concentration. Then Dar turned her head to see two shocked faces
looking back at her, jaws hanging. She took a moment to review her
words, grinned. "Too much information, huh?"

Both techs nodded. "No offense, Ms. Roberts." Dave managed to
get out.

"None taken." Dar replied graciously. "Didn't mean to freak you
out."

They left her in peace for a while, shuffling and squeaking just out
of her vision behind the racks, and she took advantage of it to continue
the slow process she'd started two hours prior.

She set the monitor running again and tried a new command
setting a complicated algorithm on one of their outside interfaces. The
device accepted it, and then began processing traffic with the
instruction, causing her other screen to start spiking wildly. "Hmm."

"Ma'am?"

"Not you." Dar typed a note to herself on yet another screen she
had open, and then she went back to the device and removed the
command. "Just something I'm doing."

"Uh. It's not like you freaked us out or anything."

Dar stopped typing in mid motion, and turned her head again.
"No?"

Dave had scooted his chair over a little toward her. "No, I mean —
you're really cool and all. We figured that out the last week or so."

"Thanks." A low beep interrupted this enlightening conversation.
"Excuse me." Dar pulled out her PDA and glanced at the screen. "Ah,
heh."

Hey sweetie. Bet you'll never guess where I am!

Dar pulled out her stylus and scribbled a reply. Can you top
lying under a router rack being grilled about our waterbed
activities by the ops staff? She hit send, and then waited
patiently until she saw the light stutter on.

Uh...no. Not by a long shot. How did that happen?

Dar tapped. Eh, good question. Got myself into it somehow.
Anyway, where are you? Thought you were going to the ship?
I'm in the morgue.

Dar stopped, blinked, and put her PDA down, pulling out her cell
phone instead. She speed dialed Kerry's number and kicked impatiently
at the corner of the rack until the line was answered. "WHAT?"

Her partner delicately cleared her throat before answering. "Hi,
honey."

"Where are you?" Dar dispensed with the niceties.

"Not nearly in as much trouble as you are, apparently." Kerry
answered with a wry chuckle. "I'm in the ship's morgue. Did you know
they had morgues? As well as a whole lot of other places?"

"Uh..." Dar collected her composure. "Well, I guess I did. I mean,
they have to. What else are you gonna do if someone croaks on a cruise?
Put 'em in the freezer? That'd be gross."

"Sure would," Kerry said. "Now, tell me about our waterbed?" Her
voice took on a slight echo, as though she'd cupped her hand around
the phone. "You're not really talking to them about um...you know."

Dar glanced at the techs that were pointedly not looking at her.
"About what we do in bed? No." She admitted. "They wanted to do me
a favor and I'm giving them a hard time. So, how's it look?"

Kerry sighed. "It's a mess." She replied. "Dar, it's going to be such
a pain in my butt getting cabling in here. They're going to have to
puncture solid steel firewalls."

"Ig."

"And it all has to be shielded twisted pair."

A sigh. "Yeah, I figured that. It is on the Navy ships," Dar said.
"Though I think there's less interference running around a cruise ship
than on one of those."

"You'd think." Kerry said. "I'm going to have the tech team come in
here and start estimating for cable, but Jesus, Dar, they barely have
telephones here! They still use handsets they plug into a live line!"

Dar winced. "It's going to be like cabling Grant's tomb," she said.
"Okay, tell the guys to do it right. Find out every place they're gonna
need anything, and let's just get out the bad news first."

"Will do." Kerry said. "Hey, Dar?"

"Mm?" Dar shifted, crossing her ankles and gazing up at the
bottom of the routers. "Did you know you could see the fiber optic
LEDs from underneath these things? They look like Christmas trees."'

Silence. "Uh, sweetheart, why didn't you have the guys run a serial
line for you?" Kerry asked. "Instead of you lying under the racks?"

"That'd be too easy." Dar muttered, peeking at the techs. They
peeked back at her with nervous little grins. "So, what did you want?"

"Eh?"

"You said, 'hey Dar.'"

"Oh." Kerry pondered a minute. "You distracted me, and I realized
I wanted the waterbed with you in it. But that wasn't what I was

thinking about. Give me a second here."

Dar watched the LEDs flicker over her head, idly daydreaming about the scent of clean linen while she listened to Kerry's faint breaths on the other end of the line. "Glad I wore jeans today, or this could have been really scandalous."

Kerry muffled a snorted giggle. "You're so bad. Okay, I remember now. I've been hearing music from the Hard Rock every time I go out on deck. You want to have dinner over there when you come out later?"

"Sure." Dar replied, watching her monitor now. "But do you really need me to come out there? Sounds like you've got it all worked out. I could just pick you up." She juggled the phone against her ear and typed a command. "How about it?"

Kerry didn't answer for a bit, and when she did, her voice had changed, a touch of uncertainty entering it. "Yeah, I guess," she said. "But don't you want to see the place for yourself?"

"Not really. I trust you."

"Dar, you said this was really important."

Dar released her laptop and took hold of the phone again. "It is, and you're really good at what you do, and I'm perfectly happy to leave it in your hands. Is there a problem with that?" She queried, unsure of what was going on with her partner. "Ker?"

"No, it's not a problem at all. Thank you for the vote of confidence. I know how critical this is, and I'm glad you trust me to take care of it."

Dar waited. Nothing else was forthcoming. "But?" She prompted.

A sigh.

"But you want me to look at it anyway?"

"You have much more maritime experience than I do." Kerry explained, not bothering to confirm her guess directly. "This is a new world for me, and I want to make absolutely sure I size it right the first time. I would appreciate your insights, yes."

Well, that was true enough Dar admitted to herself. Kerry knew enough about boats to get the Dixie out of dock, but there was no way around the fact that Dar had spent her childhood around big ships, and she just knew a lot more about their peculiarities. "Point made." She gave in gracefully. "Meet you there at six?"

"You're on." Kerry sounded much happier now. "I'll meet you out by the front. Oh." She cleared her throat. "By the way, I'm the Demon of the Dock, I'll have you know."

"You are?"

"I deliberately took all the pairs into the pier to keep everyone else out, and am now making a scandalous profit renting them."

"Bwaahahhahaaha..." Dar started laughing, almost banging her head on the bottom of the rack. "If I stop and get you a pair of devil's horns, will you wear them to dinner?"

"Pffft. Just for that, I'm going to stick you with my pitchfork."

"Just for that, I'm going to grab your —"

"Dar, aren't you in the ops center?" Kerry interrupted innocently.

"Ahem."

"See you later. I have to go on the rest of my tour with my new friend Tally." Kerry chuckled. "I get to see the crew mess next. They want to put internet in there."

Dar chuckled as well. "Have fun. See you later." A moment after folding the phone closed, she glanced at the console. Both techs had their faces buried so far into their screens she feared they were absorbing the electromagnetic interference right through their skins.

Ah well. Dar went back to her router. So what were a few more scandalous stories, anyway?

IT WAS TWILIGHT before Dar was walking across the concrete toward the pier building Kerry had specified. The heat had lessened a little, and there was a nice breeze coming in off the water.

Dar sucked in a lungful of it, and paused to look at what she could see of the ship. "Hmm." She rocked on her heels once or twice. "Now ain't that a bucket of coasters being held together by paint chips."

The flag clips on the bare nearby poles clanked in agreement as she continued on across the grass and up onto the building's steps. As she got to the glass doors, one was opened, and a uniformed guard studied her suspiciously.

"Hi." Dar produced her identification dutifully. "Can I come in?"

The man studied her badge, then looked at her carefully before he stepped back and opened the door, allowing her to enter. Dar walked past him into the pier building, her nose wrinkling at the scent of incipient mildew overpowering the air conditioning.

The pier building had seen better days, she decided. The walls were covered in a layer of moderately fresh paint, but it was obvious this layer had been put down over many, many others, and the carpet underfoot did not have the luxury of any padding, the better to resist the persistent moisture.

It had a government feel to it. Dar rubbed her nose, stifling a sneeze. She quickly crossed the back room and stuck her head into the alcove where the office was, noting approvingly the locked door and, even more so, the security guard sitting stolidly outside. "Hi, Don."

The guard looked up from his book, surprised. "Oh. Ms. Roberts." He greeted her with a smile. "I didn't think I'd see anyone else here tonight. They closed up the office about an hour ago."

Dar walked over and inspected the door. "Open it?"

The guard got up quickly and did as she asked, unlocking the door and pushing it open. "There you go."

Dar entered and flipped the lights on with a negligent motion of her hand. She prowled around the small space, examining the newly installed gear, and then gave it her grunt of approval before she backed out and waved a hand at the guard. "Feel sorry for whoever has to work in there."

Don wrinkled his nose. "Smells like three week old bread." He agreed. "You just come here to check that out, ma'am? I could'a just told you over the phone." He lifted his cell.

"Wasn't why I came." Dar headed toward the escalator that led up to the ship's boarding gangway. The moving stairs were turned off this late, but she made light work of trotting up them, pushing her way out the back door and getting her first good look at the bulk of the ship. "Jesus."

She stopped in her tracks and leaned against the metal rail. The ragged, paint chipped surface was rough under her fingertips. Growing up on a naval base meant she'd seen her share and far more of old rusting hulks, ranging from fishing boats to destroyers. But the last vessel she'd seen in this condition was heading out to be sunk for an artificial reef.

Dar turned and hurried down the long walkway. Tied up or not, shallow water or not, having Kerry on board the damn thing gave her a hive and the faster she got her partner off the dangerous and, to her eyes, listing vessel the happier she'd be.

As she reached the entrance to the ship, she spotted Kerry heading her way. "What?" She turned as a man blocked her path, glowering at him until she realized he was just looking to see her ID. She held it up, and then brushed past him as Kerry cleared the inner door and came out onto the deck to greet her. "Hey."

"Hey." Kerry gave her a more than cordial grin. "I was just coming out to find you. You're early."

Dar took her arm and backed up until they were both safely on the metal gangway. Then she stopped. "Anyone else of ours on that thing? Hope not."

Kerry turned and looked, then swiveled back to face her partner. "Huh?"

"It's gonna sink."

"Oh, c'mon Dar, no it isn't." Kerry chuckled. "It's not really that bad inside. C'mon, let me show you around." She hooked a finger through Dar's belt loop and tugged.

"I'm not boarding that damn thing." Dar resisted the pull. "Did you see those holes? Look!" She pointed at the side of the ship, which did, indeed, sport several healthy sized gaps in its metal sheathing. "I've seen bathtubs more seaworthy."

Kerry leaned back against the iron rail. "Hon, it made it across the ocean." She reminded her. "I'm sure it's okay sitting here in the Port of Miami and besides, it's only forty feet deep here. Even if it did sink, I could sit on the pool deck up there and get a suntan while it was going down."

"Mmph."

"C'mon." Kerry gave her another tug. "It's really not that bad, Dar. Once you get used to all the chaos inside. I got a really nice tour of the ship, and honestly, it's better than I thought it would be."

"Uh huh." Dar allowed herself to be drawn toward the deck again. "And you have how many ships to judge this against?" She queried, with a wry grin. "How about letting me judge how scary this crate really is?"

"Okay, sailor girl." Kerry tolerantly led the way across the deck to the inner door. "How's the office?"

"Annoying as usual." Dar paused inside to look around. The air of tattered, tired elegance reminded her of some of the old beach hotels she'd occasionally wander into in her youth, with much of the same scent of age and disappointment.

They were in the center of the ship, a large, somewhat open area that extended up several decks now obscured in scaffolding and torn old wallpaper. There were water stains on the walls under the wallpaper, and the exposed girders were thick with rust. "Point one." Dar said. "Rain inside? Bad thing." She indicated the girders.

Kerry peered at them. "Can't that be from the humidity or the sea air?"

"No." Dar patted her on the back. "But that's all right, cause it means they need to rip all that drywall and plaster out, and that means we can get wiring in at a lower cost than if we have to pull it all."

"Hmm, yeah, I talked to the construction chief about that. He said they'd be ready in about a week to strip everything." Kerry agreed as they walked past worktables and through a propped open glass door at the back of the open area.

Dar found another half destructed space that had a few old desks and walls covered in the typical grunge you often found in office buildings. "Back office?"

"Uh huh. Want to see where they suggested we put the computer systems?" Kerry took her hand and led her forward, shoving open a half stuck panel just wide enough to admit Kerry's slim form and then stepping back. "Here."

Dar gave her a suspicious look, and then slowly poked her head in. After a moment, she drew it back out. "And the joke is?" Her voice rose. "Kerry, you couldn't fit our dog in here, much less what we're going to have to run this thing on, and there's no air conditioning."

"Right. It's a linen closet." Kerry agreed. She peered inside at the room, a scant three feet by six feet not including the hot water pipes running along one wall. "I told them we could use this to store spare parts, but only if they stuck a wall mount AC unit with a drip drain on that long part."

"Good answer." Dar shook her head as she watched Kerry shove the door shut again. "They have no clue, do they?"

"Nope." Kerry leaned against the door. "I told them we're going to need this room instead." She pointed at the larger space. "They freaked."

Kerry walked across the floor, looking up as someone called her name from the outside entrance. "Oh, hi Tally." She turned. "This is my boss, Dar Roberts. Dar, this is Tally. He's been showing me around." She gave her new buddy a grin. "And watching me shock the pooters out of the construction guys."

"Hi." Tally gave Dar a brief smile. "Um, Kerry...listen, you really, really, really got the stripes mad about this room here." He indicated the space. "It's the Purser's office."

Kerry perched on the corner of one sad old desk. "And?"

"Ah." Dar scratched her jaw. "Pursers kind of run everything, Ker."

Tally turned on Dar with a grateful look. "You've been on ships?"

"Not this kind." Dar managed a half grin. "But yeah, enough to know the politics." She got up and put her hands on her hips. "But the problem is Kerry's right. We'll need about this much space for the system your owner wants."

Tally looked just aghast. "But the old system just fit under Drucilla's desk there." He pointed. "Honest!"

"Okay, let me give you some idea here." Kerry stood up. "First, we're going to put in two big switches about like this." She spread her arms out to either side, then raised one and lowered the other. "And like this."

Obviously lost, Tally merely nodded.

"And then, two racks of computer equipment about twice the width of a refrigerator and about that tall." Kerry added. "And that doesn't even include all the space for cables."

Tally sighed and sat on the desk. "I don't know what we're going to do. They won't give up this space; I'll tell you that right now. They've been talking for a month about how it's going to be redone." He looked around in a worried sort of way. "It's the biggest office on the ship."

Kerry paused in mid-step and peered around her. Then she looked at Dar.

"Okay." Dar said. "Then we'll give you the space this stuff's going to need, and your people can tell us where they want us to put it. We can't shrink any of it. It's just the size it is." She walked to the wall, glancing back to see another figure in the doorway. She took a marker from her pocket and drew an X. "The racks are from here." She made another mark. "To here. That's for the servers. Then the network core is here." She drew a large box on the wall. "To here."

"Why do we need all that?" The newcomer asked.

"Oh, hi Drucilla." Tally said.

"Your boss wants it." Dar told her. "Add this for consoles and monitoring stations. And you get this much space." With a flourish, she drew on the rest of the back wall, and then took six big steps into the center of the room. "Out to here."

"That's ridiculous." Drucilla came into the room. "We don't need all that! We work just fine with what we have, that NCR register system and my machine." She pointed at the drawing. "We don't have room for all that! What's it for, anyway?"

"Point of sale. Email. Computers for everyone. Interactive television, IP phones, and internet." Kerry ticked off things on her fingers.

"On here? You surely are joking."

"Nope." Dar went over to Kerry and leaned her arm on the smaller woman's shoulder. "I'm not. We've been asked by your company to put that," she indicated the wall, "in here. Now, if you don't want to give up this space, you need to get together and decide where you want to put our stuff."

"Oh, my god." The woman put her hand on her head. "This is insanity. I have to go." She turned and left.

Kerry and Dar exchanged glances, and then they both looked at Tally.

"Internet?" Tally's eyebrows quirked up. "Really?"

"Now, here's a guy with the right priorities." Kerry chuckled. "C'mon, Dar. Let me show you the rest of it."

Dar stepped carefully over a piece of rotted, rolled up carpet as she followed them out, suspecting the rest of the tour was only going to roll rapidly downhill.

"SO THAT'S IT." Kerry stood on the very back deck of the boat alone with Dar after their tour. It was dark now, and the less than soothing cantaloupe colored lights of the pier lit everything around them and washed the stars almost clean out of the sky. "What do you think?"

Dar cautiously tested the railing before she leaned against it. "I think it's going to be a Mongolian cluster fuck." She replied, crossing her arms. "No matter how we do it there isn't enough space." She ticked off a finger. "Enough cableways..." She ticked another finger. "Or enough patience in my body to deal with all these frustrated sea dogs who make my father look liberal."

"Hmm? Kerry joined her at the rail and looked over. The salt water lapped gently at the rusting metal, making little swirling sucking noises as it curled around a jagged edge. "So. What are you saying that we don't do it?"

Dar exhaled heavily.

"Dar, nothing says everything we do has to be easy." Kerry poked her gently. "It's a challenge. Isn't that what you told me sometime forever ago?"

"Yeah, I know." Dar grimaced wryly. "C'mon. Let's go home."

Kerry followed her as Dar led the way around the back of the ship toward the gangway. It was dark on the exterior with only a few of the windows lit from within here on the upper decks.

A cruise ship moved past in the channel and the ship rocked slightly in its wake. The creaks and groans from the old structure were not in any way comforting, and Kerry wondered in her heart if Dar wasn't really right after all.

Was there a point to all this? Could Quest really be meaning to take these old hulks and put them back in service with modern customers that are used to every sophistication?

Kerry turned her head and regarded the passing modern cruise liner. It was all glass and shiny metal, as far from their poor, rusting hull as could be. Four or five decks taller, and half again the width of the ship she was on, the differences were so striking she had to wonder in truth what the hell they were thinking.

She shook her head a little as they walked off the ship giving the guard a nod as they traded the gentle motion of the ship for the stillness of the concrete walkway. "I don't know." Kerry pointed at the cracks she'd noticed on the way in. "I think that ship's in better shape than this pier."

Dar inspected the cracks, then walked to the railing and jumped up and down several times experimentally.

"Dar!" Kerry squawked.

Dar chuckled, and moved on. "Relax," she said. "There's rebar all in there. It's not going..." Dar paused, and went to the rail again, leaning against it as she watched the pier below. "Ah."

Kerry went to her side and peered past her shoulder. "Oh ho." She recognized Shari's form pacing on the concrete outside their ship. "Should we say something?"

"Nu uh." Dar drew back into the shadows of the walkway and pulled Kerry with her. They stood in silence as their nemesis strolled along the side of the ship examining it.

"Dar?" Kerry whispered.

"Mm?" Dar put an arm around her, resting her cheek against Kerry's head.

"Does the fact I want to shove her in front of Majesty of the Seas over there mean I'm going to hell?" Kerry wondered. "What's she up to, just checking the boat out?"

"Ship," Dar said. "Yeah, not much else she can do from down there. Hatch is closed." She pointed at the hull. "Maybe she's seeing what we got versus what they got?"

As if to confirm it, Shari reached the end of the pier, then she turned and wandered back, apparently losing interest in the vessel. Dar and Kerry turned and walked along even with her unseen in the shadows until Shari passed the end of the ship and they were at the end of the walkway.

Shari stopped and looked back, putting her hands on her hips before shaking her head and continuing on down the pier toward the ship Telegenics had been assigned. By freak chance, it was in the slip right behind theirs, and Dar wondered suddenly if they hadn't been spotted on the aft deck while they were talking.

But why would Shari bother to come out on the docks for that? Dar dismissed the idea, and steered Kerry back through the doors toward the escalator. It still wasn't working so they plodded down it in amiable silence, their footsteps alerting the guard stationed at the office below.

"Hello?" The guard came out into the area at the end of the escalator, one hand on his hip.

"Just us." Dar waved a hand at him. "Roberts and Stuart causing trouble as usual."

The man's hand dropped and he smiled, returning the wave. "Oh, hi ma'am's," he said, obviously relieved. "Sorry, forgot you were up there." He waited for them to get down to his level. "I've had some of the crew out there try to get in, trying to get free phone calls, I guess."

Kerry patted the guard on the shoulder as she walked past. "Hang in there," she said. "We'll get something a little better set up for you guys soon. This is pretty Antarctic."

The man went back to his metal folding chair and sat down picking up his book and opening it. "No problem, ma'am. We'll survive."

Dar and Kerry walked through the outer room toward the front doors the silence of the big building broken only by their footsteps and the air conditioning units cycling on. "This is a pretty grungy place to have people go on a luxurious cruise ship, huh?" Kerry commented.

"Eh. No worse than most of the airport." Dar shrugged, pushing open the outer door and holding it for Kerry to pass through.

It was very dark outside and they both paused as several shadowy figures near the edge of the building stirred and looked their way as they came out. There were trees next to the pier doors, and the area apparently appealed to the homeless who were camped beneath them.

Kerry's heartbeat picked up slightly, but the men merely turned back around and continued their conversation not interested in them at all. She felt a little irritated at herself for the assumption of bad intent and acknowledged she had a way to go to erase her upbringing.

It was odd, those little unconscious biases that poked up from time to time. She liked to think of herself as a fair minded person, but she'd found that sometimes she just hadn't had the right experiences to be able to take away things picked up from so many years of living in the family environment she had.

It bothered her. She'd realized when she'd worked with the girls at the church that their lives were, to a large extent, alien to hers and she wondered just how much in touch with them she'd really been.

"Ker?"

Dar's voice startled her. Kerry looked quickly up to find the scattered moonlight reflecting off Dar's pale eyes. "Yeees?"

"You got quiet."

"Just thinking." Kerry sighed. "Long day."

Dar stuck her hands in her pockets. "Well, I offered not to come down here," she said. "Only made it longer, and I doubt I helped your plan any."

All thoughts of equality and WASP sensibilities flew out of Kerry's head. She took hold of her partner's arm and stopped pulling Dar to a halt as well. "Why do you keep saying stuff like that? Don't you want to be a part of this?"

They were only a few feet from their cars, Dar having parked right next to her in the now empty lot. It didn't seem to be a good place for a discussion, but going anywhere meant they'd have to separate, and Kerry really wanted to hear the answer to her question before they parted. "Dar?"

Dar twitched a half shrug that ended in her lifting her free hand and letting it fall. "Honestly? No."

Kerry exhaled, caught a bit by surprise. She thought a moment on the answer, and then decided maybe she wasn't surprised after all. "Because of how tough the job on the ship is going to be?'

"No." Dar turned and went over to Kerry's car, leaning against it and crossing her legs at the ankles. "I just don't want any part of Telegenics." She studied the tarmac, most of it cracked and weed ridden.

Kerry joined her, leaning on the car right next to her, their shoulders brushing. "Oh." She murmured. "I thought you were kinda past that."

Dar shrugged.

Kerry really couldn't think of much to say after that. She kicked herself a little for not spotting Dar's reluctance before and realized maybe she'd been deliberately ignoring those not so subtle hints.

Finally, she sighed again. "Guess we'd better go home." She pulled her keys out and chirped the door to her car open. "Anyway, thanks for coming out and giving me your insights. They really did help."

Dar remained leaning against Kerry's car, watching under half lowered eyelids as Kerry eased past.

Since the cars were parked next to each other it meant Kerry had to pick her way carefully, placing her feet down between Dar's extended ones. She brushed her lightly and put a hand on her stomach for balance as she scooted by.

Dar reached out and captured the hand holding it. She waited for Kerry to turn and face her, then blinked in surprise when she simply leaned against her, patting her side in silence. "I'm becoming a chickenshit," she murmured. "Sorry, Ker."

"It's all right." Kerry said, listening to the stuttering heartbeat under her ear. "Let's go home, and we can talk about it. I'm tired of the sauna, and my piggies hurt." She gave Dar a quick hug, and pushed back, glad to see a faint grin in all the shadows crossing her partner's face. "Race you?"

"You're on." Dar unlocked her car, and they parted to head out toward home.

Chapter Three

THERE WERE DISTINCT advantages to working from home. Kerry leaned back in her chair and put her feet on her desk, propping her keyboard on her lap at a comfortable angle. Wasn't something she could do at work, at least not during business hours and she appreciated the difference as she peered at her screen and continued typing.

"How's the line working?" Dar entered with her laptop. She took a seat on the small couch across from Kerry's desk and opened it. "I messed with it this morning." Chino ambled in after her and curled up on the carpet near Kerry's desk.

Kerry looked up. "Great. It's a heck of a lot faster since you put DSL in. I thought you had squirmies over the security with it though."

"Eh." Dar had focused on her own machine. "I tested it. It's all right, as much as any remote connection is." She replied. "And the surfing's a hell of a lot faster."

"That's for sure." Kerry watched Dar work for a moment, and then spared another thought wondering why she'd given up her comfortable sprawl on the couch downstairs for the smaller confines of Kerry's office. She really didn't think the need to ask about the circuit prompted it, since Dar seemed content now to sit quietly pecking at her keyboard.

Just wanted to be close? Kerry found herself smiling at the thought, since she'd been regretting the fact that her own laptop hadn't contained her needed files so she could move down into the living room.

They'd had a light dinner, and then gone to the gym together but the subject of Dar's working on her project hadn't come up even once since they'd gotten home. There was something left to be said about it, though and Kerry suspected that those words were behind this instinctive drive they both seemed to have to be in the same place at the same time so when the words came out, they'd be there to hear them.

Until then, though, she was happy just to continue working; typing out an initial assessment of the ship project for the team meeting she'd scheduled the next day while Dar persisted in her programming project. They worked together in a comfortable silence, broken only by the rattle of keystrokes and Chino's dreaming whines.

"Know what I wish?" Kerry asked idly, as she waited for the deck plans of the ship to insert into her document.

"Uh?" Dar grunted in question.

"Wish we were at the cabin. I feel like a midnight salt water swim." Dar paused and looked up. "Hmm." She shifted the laptop a little.

"We could go in the pool." She offered. "Not as romantic, but there's no seaweed and sand either."

Kerry tapped the enter key and continued typing. "Eeeeehhh...it's not really private enough for what I had in mind." She heard Dar's keystrokes stop, and she waited a second before she looked over at her to find sharply raised eyebrows and a slight grin facing her. "Don't you give me that look. It's your fault. You turned me into a hedonist."

Dar pointed a thumb at her own chest, and widened her eyes.

Kerry stuck her tongue out.

They both went back to working, but the faint grin remained on Dar's lips as she typed. After a few minutes, she paused again. "Know what I wish?"

"Does it involve hot fudge?" Kerry murmured, erasing a sentence and drumming her fingers on her keyboard as she pondered a replacement.

"Heheh." Dar snickered softly. "Save that thought for later. No. What I was wishing for was that we could go back about three weeks and start over again."

Ah. Kerry wiggled her big toe. "Before Orlando?"

"Yeah."

Kerry added a paragraph, and then paused again. "What do you think you would have done different?" She asked. "I mean, about the show or dealing with them or..." She kept her voice casual and her eyes on the screen, not wanting to stifle any revelations.

Dar was a little funny that way. If she said something, and you came back with 'what did you mean by that?', she often stopped her train of thought and switched to something completely different. It was almost like on a personal level, she didn't deal with being challenged while she was trying to communicate something

Dar shifted her position, wiggling her shoulders into a more comfortable spot on the couch. "Keep my mouth shut a lot more, for starters." She scrolled her touchpad with one finger and put her other hand behind her neck, stretching the muscles out with a grimace. "Handled the two of them better, maybe."

"Ah." Kerry ran the spell checker on her document. "I don't know, honey. I don't think most of that was us. They came into this whole thing gunning dirty."

"Mm. Well, I don't think it's going to get any better," she replied. "One of the reasons I don't want to be involved."

Kerry thought about it as she watched the spell check end. She scrolled up for another view of the report, scanning it lightly with her eyes. "Maybe you're right," she finally said. "Why don't we just table it for a while, let me get the whole process started, then you can see what you think."

They both continued in silence for a little while. Dar reached down and scratched Chino's belly, then at last tipped her head back and raised her eyes from the screen. "What I think is...that sounds a hell of a lot like what I said to you when you didn't want to be the Vice President of Operations."

Kerry looked over her shoulder and batted her eyelashes.

Dar smiled and shook her head.

"Dar, don't worry about it." Kerry said. "We'll just work it out."

Chino woke up and flipped over, sneezing. She got up and went to Kerry's side, standing up on her hind legs and giving Kerry a sloppy kiss on the cheek.

"Thank you, sweetie." Kerry took hold of her muzzle and kissed her on the head. "I love getting kissies from you almost as much as I love getting kissies from your mommy Dar."

A moment later, she found herself encircled by Dar's arms. Teeth closed gently on her earlobe. She could feel the intensity of the emotion behind the squeeze that nearly stopped her breathing.

"Damn, I love you." Dar whispered.

Kerry reached up and cupped her partner's face, pulling her forward a little and kissing her on the lips. She then pressed her cheek against Dar's and exhaled, a low sound of contentment sounding deep in her throat. "Damn, I love you."

"Know what I think?" Dar reached over and pulled the wireless keyboard out of Kerry's hands, setting it on the desk. "I think work's over. Want to join me and a glass of champagne in the hot tub?"

Kerry abandoned her machine without a second's thought. She swung her legs off the desk and stood up, hooking her fingers inside the waistband of Dar's shorts and following her as she walked out of the office and started down the steps. Chino bustled past them reaching the bottom landing and whirling around in a circle as she waited for them to catch up.

As they reached the dog, however, the phone rang. Dar glanced at the clock on the entertainment center, and her brows lifted. "Who the hell's calling here now?"

"Only one way to find out." Kerry went over to the side table and picked up the cordless phone, keying the answer button and putting it to her ear. "Hello?"

"Hey, sis." Angela, Kerry's sister, replied. "Busy?"

Dar had cocked her head to listen. Now she gave Kerry a pat on the butt and pointed toward her own bedroom, mimicking stripping out of her clothing as she walked past.

"A little. What's up?" Kerry gave her partner thumbs up, and then dropped into the couch. "How are you? How's the munchkin?"

Angie cleared her throat. "Munchkin and I are fine," she said, and then hesitated. "But we're kinda looking for a new place to live."

Kerry blinked. "Huh?"

"Richard found out about Brian." Angie said. "He filed for divorce."

"He's divorcing you?" Kerry sat straight up, her voice rising. "No shit. Really?"

Dar kept one ear on the conversation in the living room as she changed out of her t-shirt and shorts. She was halfway glad Kerry's family had conveniently provided a distraction, to chase the subject they'd both been dancing around, out of the way for a while.

It would be easier, she thought, if she knew what the hell her problem really was. As Kerry had hinted, she'd thought she was past the bullshit. Kerry thought she was past the bullshit. So why was she doing everything in her power to avoid having to deal with the ship project?

Dar glowered at her reflection in the mirror. Stormy blue eyes were reflected back at her, and she scowled, feeling a mixture of frustration and impatience with herself. Could she really just toss the project off on Kerry's shoulders, knowing how important it was, and how much Alastair was counting on her?

On the other hand, could she really justify not trusting Kerry to handle it? Dar sighed. "Fuck." She addressed herself. "I think you need a head enema."

"Yeesh." Kerry interrupted her self-chastisement. "Poor Angie!" She entered the bedroom and halted as Dar turned, her expression altering to one of sultry interest. "Hmm. Maybe I should convince her to try something other than guys for a little while."

Dar put one hand on her hip. "Oh, I'm sure that'd be a popular suggestion. Especially for Brian," she said. "What happened?"

Kerry pulled her t-shirt off. "Angie thought she'd blown him off about Andy's blood tests, but I guess he got suspicious. He had DNA tests done without her knowing."

Dar snorted. "Nice!" She slipped behind Kerry and undid her bra, giving her a scratch between her tanned shoulder blades. "So she's going back home?"

"No." Kerry folded her bra and set it on the counter next to her already folded t-shirt. "Oh, my mother offered, sure, but Angie, she wants to get out on her own."

"With Brian?"

Kerry didn't answer for a moment, and then she turned and faced Dar. "She's not sure."

Dar cocked her head in question.

A shrug. "She said she doesn't want it to be a case of he needs to take care of her now. She wants to do it on her own." Kerry put her hands on Dar's waist, rubbing her thumbs on the soft skin there. "Maybe I started a family trend. In any case, she was asking what the housing prices were like down here."

"Ah."

Kerry eased forward and brushed her lips over the curve of Dar's breast. She felt Dar's fingertips run up and down her back and it encouraged her to move closer, fitting her bare body to Dar's and reveling in the sensual jolt it gave her. "Y'know, water sounded good..."

"There's water in that bed." Dar suggested, kissing her neck.

"Just what I was thinking." Kerry gladly gave up the idea of the hot tub, and started exploring Dar's skin instead. "Mm...maybe I should tell Angie..."

"Shh." Dar bumped her toward the bed. "If we start telling the heteros, they'll all want to be gay." She tumbled with Kerry into the center of the bed, as they both chuckled.

"HEY, COL." Kerry carried her teacup into the break room and set it down. "What's up?" She asked, waiting her turn at the hot water spigot.

"Same old, same old." Her friend replied, with a grin. "Hey, any chance of you making it out to the beach this coming weekend? We've got a 'cue planned."

Kerry dunked her teabag up and down a few times. "Hmm. Let me get back to you on that. Maybe. Hey listen, are there any units open in the complex?"

"Mine?" Colleen asked. "Two, I think. Why?"

Kerry poured a little milk into her tea and put the bottle back in the refrigerator. "Might need one on short notice." She explained. "You going back to your office? I'll fill you in."

Colleen picked up her coffee mug and followed Kerry out into the hallway. She caught up with her friend a few steps down. "So, what's up?"

"My sister," Kerry said. "Following my very bad example. C'mon inside and I'll tell you all about it." She entered her office, toasting the newly arrived Mayte with her cup. "Morning!"

"Morning, Kerry." Mayte smiled at her, as she went to her desk and slid behind it.

Colleen trailed after Kerry as they both entered the inner office, and Kerry shut the door before going to her own desk and taking a seat. "I get this call last night." She said. "My family's hit the Enquirer again."

"Oh no." Colleen sat down across from her. "Now what? Is your nephew an alien?"

"Worse." Kerry sipped her tea. "A bastard and his father found out about it." She watched Colleen's eyes widen in amazement. "Did I forget to tell you my sister had an affair with my ex-boyfriend?"

"Jesu." Colleen covered her face with one hand.

"Hmm. Thought for sure I told you that one. Anyway, Richard found out and he's suing Angie for divorce. She was hinting about places down here so I figured..."

"I get the picture." Colleen held her hand up, palm out. "Let me talk to the landlord and see what he's got open. I know there's a one bedroom, but I'm thinking for her a two would be better, right? How's she going to survive? I thought you told me she's a housewife."

Kerry sighed, leaning back in her chair. "She is. She can do some light office work, though, and she's not stupid. She knows how to use a PC, do some bookkeeping, that sort of thing."

Colleen made a face.

"I know." Kerry acknowledged the grimace. "Honestly, Col, she'd be better off going back to Mom's house, but I'm not really the one to tell her that, you know?"

"Mm." She nodded. "I know. Is she cut out for Miami?"

"Was I?"

"You didn't have a kid, and no skills." Colleen said with blunt honesty. "Not that I'm knocking her looking for something new, eh? It's just that I think she doesn't realize you got where you are because you earned it."

Kerry looked around at her office, hand-picked and hand-decorated by Dar, filled with knick-knacks and cute, yet mute, symbols of their partnership. A brief grin crossed her face as she sipped again at her tea. "True." She acknowledged. "But I think what she wants is to make it on her own before she lets Brian come back into her life and it reverts to stodgy traditionalism."

A soft knock came at the door. "Yes?" Kerry raised her voice.

The door opened and Mayte stuck her head in. "Kerry, the conference room is booked for your meeting at nine, but Mr. Mark says to tell you he is running a little late. Something about a wipe-up."

"Uh, oh." Kerry winced. "I think he means wipe out. That doesn't sound good. Okay. Thanks Mayte. I'll start the meeting without him. Hope he's all right." She shook her head, and reviewed her page of mails, most of which were marked with red urgent flags. "Yeesh. What a way to start the day."

Colleen stood, and chuckled wryly. "Well, my friend, I'll be on my way to start my day, and hope it's not nearly as raucous as yours. I'll let you know what the landlord says." She waggled her fingers at Kerry and headed for the door.

"Bye Col." Kerry turned her attention to her inbox, clicking on the first red flag. It was a plea from marketing—on a new account. She leaned forward and studied it thoughtfully, then shifted her window over and clicked on their network diagram. When it came up, she typed in a circuit identifier and scanned the results.

Her fingers drummed lightly on the keyboard. "Marginal." She nibbled the inside of her lip. The new account wanted a guaranteed amount of bandwidth, and the minor pipe they were running on, an offshoot of the main network in a far out part of Oregon, was approaching their self-imposed saturation limit.

Should she agree and hope for the best? Should she ask for a bandwidth increase? They wouldn't get any more money if she had to make a bigger pipe there, unless they could bag more business in the area.

After a moment's more drumming of her fingertips, Kerry went back to the mail program. She hit reply, and typed a response. "Okay, John. I'll go for the guarantee, but you guys better understand that's a very tight area. Nothing else goes in there for any existing customers and that pipe stays that size unless you book me more business."

She hit send and then sat back. After a second, she went into her sent mail file and selected the note she'd just delivered, forwarding a copy of it over to Dar. "Juuuuust in case."

Then she went on to the next note, another plea, another account, another decision to justify. Kerry found herself wondering how long it was before Dar had gotten tired of handling stuff like this? She'd developed a technique of scaring the hell out of everyone so much no one asked her for favors, and so she had a lot less of the kinds of emails to deal with than Kerry currently did.

Kerry was perceived as 'nice'–she knew it, and she knew that often played in her favor, but in cases like this, it often caused her to have to make calls she really shouldn't have to, just because people knew they could approach and ask her for it.

So, was Dar's way of operating really more efficient?

Hmm. Kerry exhaled, then jumped as Gopher Dar appeared, chittering at her from behind her mail window. "Yow. You little stinker." She laughed, clicking at Gopher Dar with her mouse. Today her little pal had on a t-shirt and overalls, and was wearing a baseball cap with the letter K on it.

Gopher Dar shook his finger at her and then pulled out a placard, sashaying across Kerry's screen so she could read it. "Nerds Rule, huh?" She chuckled. "Dar, Dar, Dar."

"Yes?"

Kerry jumped again, despite herself. She turned and gave her boss a mock glare. "Wench."

Dar sauntered over. She was dressed in jeans again, and carrying a shoulder pouch full of various nerdy things. "I'm going to the main patch closet. If anyone's looking for me, tell 'em I've got my head up a router somewhere."

Kerry gazed affectionately at her. "You going to be lying on the floor all day again? Here." She pulled a small sheepskin pillow from her large desk drawer and handed it to Dar. "Park your buns on that."

Dar accepted the fluffy thing and held it up. "You want me to walk through the hallways carrying this?" She laughed. "Kerry, I don't need a duff muff."

"Well, tell them it's my muff." Kerry replied, with a twinkle. "Actually, it's for your head. It's not good for you to have your head on the cold concrete, honey. I don't want you getting sick."

Dar tucked the pillow under her arm and sketched a salute at Kerry as she headed for the door. "Oh." She paused with the door half open. "Good decision on Oregon." Then she scooted through and shut the door after her, leaving Kerry in momentary silence.

"Thanks." Kerry said to the closed door. "Nice hat on the gopher." She added with a grin as she spotted Gopher Dar now sleeping in the corner of her screen, the hat tilted over his eyes.

With a shake of her head she went back to work, checking her watch for the time. It was nearly eight, and she had to get through the rest of her red flags before she left for her meeting at nine, and for a minute she wished she were working with Dar on her project instead.

"Bad Kerry." She resolutely clicked on the next mail.

IT HAD BEEN a very long time since Dar had wandered down to the first floor of their building and into the big central core telecom room. She propped the door open from long habit, looping a piece of old Ethernet cable tied around a conduit, just for that purpose, over the door handle and proceeding inside.

It was far from a glamorous place, concrete block walls lined with rack upon rack of circuit cards, cables, and routers. It also held two big UPS units to power the room if they lost outside electricity, its own air conditioning unit, and a, thankfully, raised floor so she didn't actually have to lie on concrete.

The walls were covered in steel conduit that lead to every other floor of the building, and there was a set of bright red pipes that indicated the lines coming in from outside. Those had tiny camera attachments to one side that allowed a fiber optic thread to penetrate the pipe at the top and give the security department visibility through the conduit to its terminus outside.

There were also cameras pointed toward them inside the patch room, a bit of extra insurance Dar had installed a year or so back. It never paid to take chances, and admittance to this particular room was restricted to four people inside the company, she being one of them.

Kerry and Mark were another two, and the fourth key resided in Plano in the hands of the corporate security officer, in case of disaster.

Dar set her bag down and ran her eyes over the racks to re-familiarize herself with the configuration. She'd supervised the original installation in this room, but it had been a while since she'd seen the hardware. She ran her fingers over the patch panels, peeking behind them to inspect the jacks.

Everything looked in order. Dar circled the room one more time, and then she selected a spot on the floor and knelt, pulling out her laptop and a set of cables. She plugged the end of the cable into one of the two master routers and sat down, leaning against the rack and putting Kerry's pillow behind her head to cushion it.

It added a bit of unexpected comfort that was welcome, considering the number of hours she suspected she'd be sitting here on the floor working. Dar smiled, taking an Ethernet cable from her bag and attaching the back of her laptop into the network with it. Kerry was so cool sometimes.

Okay, most of the time. In fact, there were times Dar did wonder what exactly she'd done in a past life to deserve meeting Kerry in this one.

Ah, well. She booted up her laptop and pulled a can of Yoohoo from her bag, opening it and setting it at her side in direct violation of the strict no beverage rule she'd put in place for this room.

The screen came up and she started up her analysis program, and then booted the network monitor. She cracked her knuckles and started typing, calling up the router configuration on one screen while she set the monitor running on another.

An alert flashed. Dar paused and looked at it, surprised. "What the?" She pulled up the monitor and made it full screen, her eyes flicking over the readouts. Her attention zeroed in on one escalating counter, and with a curse, she switched to the router screen and started typing like a demon.

"Son of a bleeping pissant hacker. Wait till I get you—"

"YOU OKAY TO walk from here, sailor boy?" Ceci put the truck in park and peered across the bridge leading to the port. "Or you want me to drop you down inside?"

"Naw." Andy gathered up his hard hat and a small sack lying next to him on the seat. "This here's fine. Don't want them beagle brains wondering nothing." He paused to regard the line of old ships stretching out down the cut while plucking a seam on his jeans.

Ceci watched him with a faint grin. "Well, go have fun then." She nudged his shoulder. "My husband the corporate spy."

Andy chuckled turning his head and giving her a light kiss on the lips. "Just doing Dardar a favor." He opened the door and hopped out giving the side of the truck a slap before he moved off down the sidewalk toward the bridge.

"Hmm." Ceci leaned on the truck steering wheel resting her chin on top of it. "I'm not sure who did who a favor." She made a mental note. Her beloved husband had settled into retirement, but Ceci knew him well enough to know having something to do was coming as a definite relief.

The fact that it was a truly interesting, actually important task, only made it all the better. Had Dar known that before she asked?

Well. Ceci mused. The apple didn't fall far from the tree, to quote a hoary old saying, and very probably her daughter had an inside insight into mentally hyper-driven, restlessly active behavior that she, thankfully, didn't.

In any case, Andy was excited as a kid with a new slingshot, and she found herself surprisingly grateful to Dar for making him that way. She looked around, spotting Bayside just to her right. Hmm.

Maybe she could get Dar a present to say thank you. With a brisk nod, she put the truck in gear and made a swift U-turn, crossing six lanes of traffic with placid non-concern.

Andrew walked slowly down the pier, nodding briefly at the few men wandering in to start work along with him. "Lo." He greeted the foreman who was standing near the gangway drinking a cup of coffee.

"Hey there, ugly." The foreman responded with an easy grin that stripped the insult of most of its sting. "Listen, buddy. The folks inside gave me a good write up on you."

Andrew stopped at the edge of the gangway and leaned on the chain rope. "Yeap? That so?"

The man nodded. "That Norskie said it was nice to have someone who spoke English but kept their mouth shut for a change."

Andy chuckled. "Them fellers inside done chatter a bit, that's true." He allowed. "Didn't seem any too organized, though." He added offhandedly. "Lots of them boxes went all over the place."

The foreman sighed and shook his head. "Yeah, I know. I heard that." He frowned. "Problem is the people who ordered all the stuff for the fixing up didn't palletize it."

"Yeap." Andy nodded.

"So we've got dishes mixed with plumbing fixtures. What a mess." He showed Andrew his clipboard that held reams of receiving invoices. "Look at this. You're going to have an even bigger mess coming in today."

Since he so nicely offered, Andrew took the board and examined the papers. "Wall." He leaned on the chains again and pointed at one of the lines with a scarred finger. "See that there?"

"Yeah?" The man looked at the line warily. "What about it?"

"Way back when, in the Navy, that there used to be called a source tick." Andy told him. "I ain't got a half clue what them boys back in the office do with it, but all them with the same number done belonged together."

The foreman looked around quickly. "Yeah?" He studied the number, then flipped a few pages, and looked at another invoice. "Son of a bitch! Look! Cups, saucers, and silverware, all the same one!" His voice rose excitedly. "If we can get a couple of big magic markers we might make sense of this damn crap. Hang on...I'll be right back. Ugly, you're a genius!"

Andrew watched him hurry off. "Lord." He moved on in search of a roach coach, spotting one outside the walkway. "What the hell these people being paid for I do wonder. Mah kid come in here and this whole basket'd been tossed head over keester by now."

There was a small crowd around the wagon and he joined it,

standing in line to wait his turn, then pointing mutely at the coffee and holding up an apple he'd taken from the back of the coach when he got to the front. The vendor handed him a steaming cup and took his proffered money, then moved on to the next guy in line as Andrew set the cup down and put as much of everything he could to get it to stop tasting like watery coffee.

It was already warm, and he was sweating under his t-shirt, but as he walked over to stand near the gangway again and sipped his coffee, he felt good to be there anyway. He leaned against the huge cleat the ship was moored to and crossed his ankles, his military issue boots showing dark against the white concrete.

Two figures approached from down the pier, attracting his attention. He remained in place, however, idly munching on his apple as the two women approached. They were talking as they walked, looking around, but not really paying much attention to the men standing around on the pier.

As they came even with him, though, Andrew dropped his eyes to his cup, cocking his ears to listen instead.

"I'm telling you, Shari. It's going to take three weeks to get the damn wireless gear in here, and even then the best I can hope for is maybe a two megabit pipe to that rented office over there."

"We are not giving those bitches one flat dime, Michelle," the taller, older of the two women retorted. "I don't care if we have to move the office here. Rent space in that damn Catholic trailer. I don't give a shit. I've got other people working on screwing ILS, so I'm not going to sit here being screwed by them in the meantime."

"Well, hell," the shorter woman replied. "I say let's bury the hatchet long enough to get a connection, for Pete's sake. I need the access to the system, Shari! I can't run the hardware part of this with a fucking tin can and a roll of string!"

"Fine." The taller woman stormed onto the gangway, brushing right by Andrew as she did so. "Do whatever the fuck you want. Go screw the little blond rat you're lusting for. Maybe that'll get you what you want."

The smaller woman stopped at the edge of the gangway. She glared at the other woman's retreating back, then glanced at Andrew.

"Mornin'." Andrew tipped his coffee cup to her.

With a disgusted look, the woman turned and stalked off, her heels clattering loudly on the concrete.

"C'MERE...C'MERE..." Dar was focused intently on the screen, her body arced forward and hunched over the laptop. She had three windows open, and she was running traces in all of them, using a fourth to scramble rapidly after the would be hacker as they probed the gateways into her network.

It was a tough balance, trying to follow the hacker around while at the same time not revealing her presence and at the same time running traces on him to find out where he was from.

Instinctively, she'd thrown up a zone around the router he was attacking, locking off the security to her login alone, and restricting all inbound traffic to reroute through her analyzer. So there was no danger in letting him poke around because there was literally no place for him to go.

And maybe she could learn something about what he was looking for if she let him keep looking. But the probes did not seem to have any particular intent. The hacker was looking for something, anything, as though he was just opportunistically searching for any crevice.

Which, if she thought about it, made a peculiar kind of sense given the jerk wad challenge she'd tossed out there.

Without looking, Dar picked up the can of Yoohoo and took a swallow, then set it down quickly as her nemesis apparently decided to give up and backed out of the gateway. "Ah, ah, ah..." Dar glanced at the trace and then chuckled wickedly. "Ah, gotcha."

She followed him back out, away from their hardened entry point, back through the backbone he'd come in on, back to his own front door.

He vanished, his IP disappearing behind a firewall, but before he did Dar got one last bit of information from him she hadn't expected, an unusual port that she took a chance on and went in after him.

She never expected it to work, but the next thing she knew, she was in the raider's gateway router, a bland, innocent prompt facing her with a pound sign that rang alarm bells so loudly she had to look up to make sure she wasn't actually hearing them in real time.

For a moment she just sat there fingertips resting on her keyboard, letting her heartbeat settle down.

Okay. Dar took a deep breath. From where she was she could do damn near anything, far more in fact than the hacker could have done to her network if he'd gotten as far as she had.

It seemed a perfect opportunity. She could find out where this guy was from and what were his motives. Maybe turn the tables on him? He'd been pretty confident he'd get to her. Now she could chase him down to his very desk and...

Paybacks? Dar drummed her fingers, feeling a rising instinct that she knew from long experience to ignore at her own peril.

Carefully, she screen capped where she was, then very deliberately she clicked the X box on her command window and took herself out of the alien gateway.

If she could set up a trap, so could he, and the stakes were a lot higher for her if she was caught snooping inside someone else's network. If Mark had done it, well...he was her security chief. But to have the CIO of ILS get caught red handed breaking in?

No. Much as her fingertips itched to do it, that open router with a pre-set enable password...that was just too easy.

"Guess I'm really not that hotshot punk anymore." Dar announced to the blinking routers. "Ah well." She sighed.

Then she sat back and pulled her bag over, taking a swig of her drink and pulling out an apple. She set it on her lap and pulled out her pocketknife, slicing the apple in half. With one eye on the monitors, she pulled out a tube of peanut butter and squeezed a blob onto the apple, taking a bite of it as she freed her other hand to type in a command.

Now, she could find out more about the hacker. She had a spoofed IP he'd been using, but the router she'd dropped into had a real one, and finding out who owned that was a relatively —

Dar blinked at the screen. A square was blinking in the center of her screen, with a simple, red heart in the middle of it, beating slightly.

Then a message appeared. Okay, so it's not Gopher Dar, but it gets my thoughts across, right?

Dar clicked on it, and answered back. Definitely. Where are you?

In my meeting. We're getting a price list together.

Dar watched her trace finish, and then exhaled, her eyes narrowing. Well, Telegenics just tried to send a hacker in here.

Big surprise. Kerry's snort could almost be heard.

No, it wasn't, but it was definitely a two edged attack, Dar realized. If they were coming after her and, as she suspected, trying to lure her into a trap—what would happen if they realized she'd already laid one for them?

Hey, Dar?

Dar took another bite of her apple, and typed a one handed reply. Yeah?

Mark says his alert monitor is going bonkers and no one can get into the master router. You got any ideas what's up?

Oops. Tell him to relax. I'm doing something. Dar put the apple down and rattled the keys, resetting the router security and giving access back to the automated systems. Better?

A few seconds of silence, then He's not hyperventilating anymore. Must be. Can you take a break and come up just to hear the recap?

Dar drained her Yoohoo, looking thoughtfully at the question. Yeah, be right up.

She needed to think about what she'd just seen, anyway.

"WHAT DID YOU think?" Kerry asked, as she and Dar walked down the hallway toward her office.

Dar glanced at her. "About your presentation skills, the plan, or how cute you look in that outfit?" She asked, with a rakish grin.

"What," Kerry sighed in mock exasperation, "am I going to do with you?" She shook her head, giving a wave to Mayte. "Get in here." She added pulling the door open and standing back to let Dar pass.

"Or?" Dar sauntered by, and waited for Kerry to close the door. "You going to spank me? Should have done it out in the hallway. That'd keep the rumor mill going for weeks." She walked over to the small couch in the office and sat down, letting her elbows rest on her knees.

"You're such a little devil sometimes." Kerry walked over and sat down next to her, preferring the couch's soft confines to her lonely desk chair. "And no, I meant the plan. I already know what you think about those other two things." She nudged Dar's shoulder.

Dar wiped a bit of router room dust off her fingertips. "I like it."

Kerry waited. Nothing else followed. "And?"

"And?" Dar reached down and retied the shoelace on her boot. "I think you've come up with a solid proposal. The one question is gonna be the cost."

"Well, sure." Kerry agreed. "But you think the way it's laid out, it'll work?"

Dar leaned back and crossed her arms, giving her partner a sideways look. "Can I ask something?"

Kerry also sat back. "Sure."

"You've done, easy, four dozen accounts without my help," Dar said. "So why do you think you need it on this one?"

Hmm. Kerry crossed her own arms and stared thoughtfully at the carpet, giving the question its due deliberation. Finally she just shrugged. "I don't know." The admission surprised her, possibly more than it did Dar. "Maybe because I know how important this is.?"

"They're all important." Dar unfolded her arms and laid her right one over Kerry's shoulders. "Just run with it, Ker. Don't worry about what I think. Just do what you think is right."

Kerry's index finger traced a light pattern on the denim covering Dar's thigh. "Easy to say, harder to accomplish." She smiled briefly. "So, anyway...what were you doing in the closet?"

"I've never been in the closet." Dar deadpanned, accepting the change of subject. "But I'm glad you asked. C'mere." She got up and led Kerry over to her desk, sliding into the chair and giving Kerry's trackball a roll. "Maybe I'm nuts. But I think I got out of a trap by the skin of my teeth."

"You?" Kerry leaned on the desk next to her. "Trap set by whom?"

Dar looked at her, and smiled grimly. "Someone who'd love to embarrass the hell out of us and plaster it all over the trade press. Look." She called up the screen on her own laptop, which she'd locked in the closet. It still had the screen captures she'd done on it, and her notes.

Kerry bent close, leaning on her elbows as she read, her lips moving slightly. She was aware of Dar's close presence, her breath warming the skin on the outside of Kerry's arm. "Wait, you got right in there?" She said. "Into that router? Holy pooters!"

"Uh huh." Dar rumbled softly.

"Wow. Bet you wanted to go right in there and smack 'em." Kerry mused. "I might have. How did you guess it was a trap? What if it wasn't? What if they're really that stupid?"

"Ker."

A sigh. "Yeah, I know. I just can't help it." Kerry flicked her fingernail against the monitor. "I can't even believe I'm suggesting that. I think my business ethics got chucked in the dumpster when it comes to those two f'ing bitches." She gazed down at her desktop. "Maybe that's why I'm all off balance on this thing, Dar."

"Mm." Dar glanced up as Kerry's intercom went off.

"Kerry?" Mayte's voice broke in. "I have that Michelle Graver person on line one." Though polite, Mayte's voice had a definite tinge of disapproval to it, much like the one her mother's had when necessary.

"Am I in?" Kerry swiveled around and laid down flat on her back, her legs dangling off the edge of her desk. "I have to ponder that for a minute. Tell Michelle to hold on." She turned her head and gazed at Dar.

"Sure." Mayte clicked off.

"Is it unprofessional of me to just want to keep her waiting for the hell of it?"

"No." Dar rested her elbows on the desk and leaned forward, tilting her head and gently exploring Kerry's lips with her own. "On the other hand..." She kissed her again, this time for a longer period. "Making her wait for this is highly unprofessional."

"Oh." Kerry folded her hands over her stomach and let her eyes flutter closed briefly as Dar continued her extremely unprofessional behavior. "If someone walks in right now, I think we'd both deserve to be fired," she finally said, with a small sigh.

"Probably." Dar agreed. "But I'd have to fly Alastair in to fire us, and by the time he got here, something would break and he'd just be asking us to come back."

Kerry's eyes twinkled, but she made a face as she reached across to hit the intercom. "Okay, put her through, Mayte."

"Okay." Mayte responded. "But are you sure? I think the music is very enjoyable for her.?"

Dar chuckled softly. "Mayte, you're sounding more and more like your mother every day." She added watching Kerry's eyes crinkle at the corners as she grinned.

"Thank you." Mayte said. "Mama will like that you said that, I am sure."

"Go ahead and connect her, Mayte," Kerry said. "I wouldn't condemn even Michelle to much more Muzak regurgitated "Nine Inch Nails"."

Mayte clicked off, then after a second, a soft buzz replaced her.

Kerry reached over and hit the answer button. "Operations, Stuart."

"Hello, Kerry." Michelle's voice was a mixture of cordiality and veiled frustration. "Sorry to disturb you."

Dar reached over and traced the edge of Kerry's ear, watching it turn pink after a few seconds.

"Ah, no problem. What can I do for you?" Kerry gamely replied. "Or are you just calling to insult me a little more? It's been a slow morning." She ignored the tiny mewing sounds from very close to her ear.

An audible sigh came through the phone. "Actually, I'm calling you to eat crow, which I know you'll enjoy, and ask how much you want for your blackmail circuit."

Kerry wiggled a little on her back, doing a small victory dance. "To be honest, Michelle—"

"Oh yes, I know you'll be that."

The mewling had altered, growing into a low growl. Kerry glanced at Dar, not surprised to see the pale blue eyes narrowed into slits. Experimentally, she reached over and touched Dar's lip, lifting it to inspect a well formed canine tooth just underneath.

Dar cocked an eyebrow at her, and stopped growling.

"Pass through cost plus five percent." Kerry said. "Take it or leave it." She drew a line up the center of Dar's nose, watching her eyes cross as she tried to follow it, and smiled as she imagined she could hear Michelle?s teeth grinding together on the other end of the phone.

"Fine." Michelle answered, clipping the word short. "What do you need to get it done?"

"A check and a circuit terminus." Kerry replied. "Just have someone see Mark Polenti at our office in Pier 10 tomorrow. He'll take care of it."

"Fine." Michelle said again. "Thanks. Bye."

The line went dead. Kerry exhaled. "Well, boss, we made almost four percent profit on that insurance policy. Not bad, huh?"

"Brilliant." Dar blew in her ear. "So brilliant, I'm going to leave this other little problem in your hands because when I backed out of that router I didn't want the CIO of ILS to be caught hacking. I remembered I put an industrial spy in Telegenic's camp. What happens if that comes out?"

Kerry eased herself upright, her back not particularly appreciating the hard surface of her desk. It gave her time to think about Dar's question, and consider the impact of it. "Well." She hopped off the desk and walked around in front of it. "How would it come out? It's not like he's not just doing a job, right?"

"Mm."

"Shari never met him, I guess, or she'd be a long squashed mango on I-95 by now." Kerry went on. "So unless he—"

"Hears them talking about us," Dar got up and ran a hand through her hair, "and behaves like he usually does, we're safe. Right?"

"Oh boy."

Dar headed for the back door to the hall that connected their offices. "Worry about it when it happens." She waved a hand at Kerry. "Meanwhile, I'm going to see if I can't find a way to turn the tables on our little bucket of chum."

Kerry sat down in her chair, the leather holding a hint of Dar's scent that surrounded her as she leaned back. What would really happen, she wondered, if Andy was found out? Would it be viewed as a scandalous criminal act, or just a smart piece of business? It wasn't as if, as she'd said to Dar, that Andrew had gotten the job on false pretenses.

He was qualified and more to do what they were paying him for. If he did the work, then what could anyone say, really?

Kerry felt the irony, though. She knew this was something her father would have done in a bare instant, and in fact, he'd readily approve of her tactics.

She grimaced.

That sure wasn't a nice feeling. Yet Andrew hadn't seemed to object to the task either. He'd agreed readily and seemed to think it was a good idea.

So where was the "right" in all this? Kerry opened her drawer and removed a piece of dried apricot from the bag there, putting it into her mouth and chewing it slowly. Was there any right?

Hmm.

KERRY EDGED THROUGH the construction zone in the middle of the ship, and looked around. She spotted ILS's senior electrical contractor near the other end of the space, and hastened to where he was standing surrounded by ship staff. "Jack.?"

The man turned and saw her. "Ah. Ms. Stuart. Glad you're here." He waited for her to join him. "We seem to have a problem here."

Only here? Kerry allowed her public, diplomatic cloak to settle over her shoulders. "What seems to be the issue guys?"

"Are you in charge of all this?" One of the men standing around asked her. "I am hearing this person say he needs to turn off power to several decks of the ship."

Kerry eyed him thoughtfully. "Well, sure," she said. "He has to do that to put in more power, and the cabling we need for the new computer systems. He can't do that with the power on."

"What are we supposed to do?" The man asked. "We live here. Would you like to be in this damn heat with no power?"

"I was, just a little while ago, matter of fact," Kerry said. "No, it's not pleasant. But it's the only way we can get the job done, so what do you think we're supposed to do? I'm sure Jack will work with you and shut down a section at a time, not all the decks at once." She turned. "Right?"

Jack hesitated, and then nodded. "Right."

"But we've got jobs to do too." The man continued arguing. "I have people to administer, services to fulfill. I can't be without power."

"We can move you to someplace that has it," Jack said.

"Certainly not! I have far too many important things in my office!" The man stated flatly.

Kerry folded her arms over her chest. "Okay." She looked him right in the eye. "I understand."

"Good." The man smiled.

"Just give me your name, so I can go back to Mr. Quest, and tell him why we can't proceed with his project." Kerry smiled back at him. "I'm sure he'll understand, too."

The man blinked in shock, then stiffened. "I didn't say you couldn't proceed!"

"Sure you did. You said you can't be without power. We have to turn the power off to go forward. So if you can't be without power, and you won't move to where power is, then we can't go forward."

The rest of the staff seemed content to watch, their eyes shifting between the man and Kerry as though watching an exciting ping-pong match. They all seemed to be deferring to the argumentative man, whose bearing indicated he was used to obedience and authority.

That was all right. So was Kerry, but in a different way. "So, can I have your name?" She asked gently. "Because Jack and I both have other things we could be doing if we're not going to be able to start up here."

"Right you are, ma'am." Jack stuck his thumbs into his jeans pockets, and rocked on the heels of his work boots. "Plenty of projects lined up.?"

"Unless maybe we could work something out with you–maybe we could have our guys move your stuff when we needed to." Kerry read the man's body language and decided giving him an out was a good idea. "We'd be glad to do that."

Jack scowled.

The man snorted, and lifted a hand. "Fine." He relented. "If you have to, you have to. But you must come to me before you turn off anything, so I can make sure nothing gets disrupted."

"Sure." Kerry said. "Jack, can you assign someone from your office to liaise with—" She looked at the man questioningly.

"Pieter Oshousen." The man supplied. "Staff Captain." He gave them all a nod, then turned and walked off, his back stiff.

"Right." Kerry watched as the rest of the staff dispersed also, their attitudes half amused and half disgruntled. "Oh, this is going to be so much fun." She added, once they were gone. "It's like being in an inhabited construction zone."

"Got that right." Jack sighed, scratching his head. "Where in the hell do we start? Every time I try to put a plan together, I keep running into these roadblocks."

Kerry shook her head. "Yeah, I know. C'mon, I think I found us something we can use for a central core, since my first choice just isn't going to fly." She led the way to the stairwell, and started down. "They don't like this idea either, but it takes space away from passengers not crew, so at least they won't stand in our way, and the overall ship management approved it."

Jack snorted. "Figures." He followed Kerry down the steps, and then though a series of doorways until she stopped in front of one. She pushed it open and stood back pointing inside. With a doubtful look, he stepped past her and entered the space. "Ah."

Kerry entered after them. "Yeah."

Jack turned around. "This is a cabin."

"It is. But it's an inside one and they've actually given me two of them." Kerry agreed. "This one and the one next to it, which is through this connecting door." She shoved the inner door open and looked through.

Both cabins had seen far, far better days. The carpet was an indiscriminate color, perhaps it had once been aqua, and the walls had peeling laminate of an equally grayish hue. There were no beds, but on one wall, a pull down bunk was clamped.

It smelled horrible.

"We'll have to strip both rooms, but I think it's workable, and this wall," Kerry walked over and slapped the inner partition, near the bunk, "backs onto the elevator shaft and all the conduit track ways."

Jack looked measurably happier. "Eh? Do they? Now that's workable." He walked over to inspect the wall, then reached up to push at the ceiling. It gave under his touch, the panel lifting up and showering them both with debris best left undescribed. "Uh...sorry."

Kerry plucked her shirt out, scattering the gunk, and ran her fingers through her hair to send more flying. "No problem." She responded. "Anything up there?"

Her companion flipped a flashlight up and peered into the space. "Lucked out." He grunted. "Not a firewall. This is an easy punch." He turned his head. "Good pick, ma'am. We can work with this."

"Thanks. Now," Kerry put her hands on her hips, "you can start laying cable in, while I get a general contractor in here to make this space livable. I can't even put a rack in here until we put down a substrate and extra AC."

"Yup." The electrical contractor nodded. "I'll get my fiber guy in here, and the cable people. You pick where you want the access closets, or is that a fight too?"

Kerry sighed. "What do you think?"

"Need to know that, 'fore I can have the fiber feller quote the job."

Jack sounded apologetic. "I was going around the decks before you got here. I thought I saw some electrical closets up there you could mount a switch or two in, and they can't use 'em for storage."

"Really? Show me." Kerry followed him out the open door and down the hallway. Could she get that lucky? Electrical closets already had ventilation, and naturally they had power—could she get away with not having to fight the already hostile staff for yet more precious space?

They started up the forward stairs wincing a little as their shoes stuck to the treads. Workmen dressed in ship jumpsuits brushed by them going the other direction without giving them a second glance, but just seeing them made Kerry suddenly wonder about something.

Andrew was in Shari and Michelle's ship. What if they'd put someone in hers? How would she tell? She looked around at the workmen, all of whom looked more or less alike, and most seeming to look right through her in return. Well, she could request all their employment details and have checks run, but?

"Here." Jack led her off one of the stair landings into a side corridor, with cabins on either side. He found one unmarked door and yanked it open, to reveal a small, poorly lit closet with a large breaker box and other electrical piping inside.

It was small and dirty, but Kerry pulled out a tape measure and found a relatively clear spot on one wall of the closet. "We can squeeze a half rack in here," she said. "How many of these are there?"

"Two on each deck."

Kerry snapped the tape measure shut. "Sold." She tucked the tool away. "Put an extra one percent on your estimate, Jack. You solved a huge problem for me. To retrofit space for these things would have cost me a bundle."

A big smile crossed the contractor's face. "Y'know, that's what I love about dealing with you. I never feel like it's always one of us taking, one giving, or turn around." He held a hand out. "Makes my life easier too. I've already got a lot of conduit up there I can use."

Kerry solemnly shook his hand. "Okay. Give me an eight-strand fiber core to each closet, terminating in our snazzy cabin digs, and cable runs to all the places on the blueprints. When can I expect a quote?"

Jack chuckled, as they went back down the hallway. "Tomorrow, maybe. Hey, one thing though, this electrical mostly isn't up to code. Not your gig, but the stuff I have to put in will be. What about the rest?"

Good question. She wondered if that had been part of Quest's plan, since the construction would have to pass local inspection at some point. "I don't know. How about I put you together with their admin people. Maybe they'll let you quote it, if they don't have a contractor already."

"I'd appreciate that." He grinned at her.

Yeah, bet you would. Kerry muffled a smile. She liked Jack but she knew he knew where his best interests lay. However, it certainly wouldn't hurt to have him get more business, and maybe he'd agree to adjust his costs if he could get a bigger volume.

Business was like that. You did a favor, sometimes you got a favor. Sometimes you didn't, but she'd learned that despite what Dar often said and did, you really could get more with honey than vinegar. "Okay, I'm off to go call Roberto. See you later, Jack." She waved at the contractor as they returned to the main deck.

"Oh, Ms. Stuart."

Kerry stopped and turned as she saw the chief purser headed her way. In contrast to the hostility the day before, the woman now seemed anxious to be polite to her. Hmm. Kerry waited for her to catch up and wondered if her fencing with the staff captain had gotten around. "Hi."

"Hi." The woman smiled at her. "Listen. I just wanted to apologize about yesterday. I know you're just here to get a job done, and I was totally out of line going off like that."

Uh huh. "No problem." Kerry replied. "I really do understand how strange it must be for you to have us come in here and just start doing things. We really don't know much about how you run everything." She shifted her body language taking a more casual stance. "And now that I've been around the ship, I can see how tight everything is."

The woman relaxed and her smile widened. "Wow, I'm glad you understand. I hear you found another spot for your stuff. Is it going to be okay?" She edged around a little. "Listen, we've got some coffee over in the mess, can I get you a cup?"

Well, when it came to gift horses, the heads were definitely better than the tails. "Sure." Kerry agreed, allowing herself to be lead on by her new friend. "Maybe you can fill me in on how things work here, you know? So we can all get along better."

"Ah. Glad to." Drucilla seemed far more confident. "You just stick with me."

Uh huh. Kerry produced a grin. Let's see where this goes, because sometimes you just never know.

Chapter Four

THE CONDO WAS very quiet as Dar slipped inside, too quiet, until Chino came sliding out of the bedroom barking a greeting at her. "Hey girl." She set her briefcase down and knelt to greet the dog and ended up sitting on the floor with Chino climbing all over her. "Hey, hey, hey."

"Growf."

"Hang on." Dar managed to get to her feet and headed for the back door followed by an ecstatically prancing Labrador. Chino stopped halfway, though, and looked back over her shoulder as though missing something.

"Yeah, I know. It's just me." Dar told her, opening the back door to the small garden. "Kerry's not here." She watched the dog trot outside whisking through the evening sun still splashing through the trees. Kerry was at the ship working on her project.

Dar had almost gone there too, but she stopped herself with a stern reminder that she'd turned the damned thing over to Kerry and she needed to butt out already. So instead, she'd just gone home.

And here she was. Dar leaned against the door jam and surveyed the quiet kitchen. Usually she and Kerry came home together, but occasionally Kerry left before she did, and whenever she did, Dar always came home to something nice like dinner, or a waiting hot tub or...

But she had no idea when Kerry was coming home. A note sent earlier had gone unanswered, and so now Dar was at a bit of a loss. She removed her PDA and scribbled a second note, sending it on its way before she turned and headed off toward the bedroom.

Inside, she paused a moment tugging her shirt from her waistband and unbuttoning it before sitting down briefly to remove her boots. She removed the shirt and then her jeans folding them both neatly and putting them on the dresser.

Chino bounded back in and came over to her, wiggling happily against her knees. Dar played with her for a few minutes, and then she got up and retrieved a pair of shorts and a t-shirt slipping into them before she went back out into the living room.

She could watch television. Dar studied the blank screen, and then moved past it. She could go for a swim, or a walk with Chino, or go to the gym.

Or sit in the hot tub.

She went to the kitchen and closed the back door. She could do some work or play with her models. With a sigh, Dar went to the refrigerator and got some milk, leaning against the counter to sip it as she considered all of her various options.

None of them really appealed to her, so she went into the living room and sat down at the dining room table sorting through the basket of mail placed there by the island staff.

No bills, because they handled all theirs electronically. A few bits of junk mail, mostly related to software upgrades or offers of new computer hardware. Dar tossed all these to one side and pulled over a diving magazine that spurred a bit more interest.

She checked her PDA after a few minutes, finding it still silent, and then gave up on the mail. "Hell with it." Dar tossed the magazine and got up. "Okay, Chino, wanna come to the gym with me? You can help me lift weights, okay?"

"Gruff."

"Okay." Dar put on her sneakers, then headed for the back door pausing only to scribble a note on the small white board just to one side of the refrigerator. She'd spend an hour or so at the gym, then see if Kerry was home and stop at the club for dinner on her way back.

Satisfied with her plan, Dar headed off down the path to the gym with Chino trotting along after her. With the sun having set, the heat was dissipating and the breeze off the ocean was almost comfortable. She watched as Chino retrieved a tennis ball from somewhere and raced back to her with it. "Gimme that."

She threw the slimy ball across the beach and kept walking as Chino chased it down. Several tosses later, they were at the entrance to the gym, and Dar cheerfully ignored the glares from two other residents as she held the door open for Chino to trot past.

They'd had a problem with that since they'd started bringing the Labrador to the gym. At first, Dar had been delivered with six or seven letters of objection from the condo association over her practice, and she'd even been served with an official summons from the Island's legal office.

Unfortunately for all of them, she had Aunt May's original copy of the bylaws, and nowhere in any of them did it say you could not bring dogs into the gym. It hadn't made her popular with a few people, but Chino was well behaved, and she'd won over most of the residents after a while. "C'mon, Chi."

Unlike Dar herself, apparently. She gave the other two residents a charming smile, and went inside the inner door that lead to the dressing rooms. Inside, she went to her assigned locker and opened it, removing a towel and a pair of weighted gloves that she slipped over her hands and fastened.

They weren't that heavy, only two pounds each, but she found they gave just that little extra bit of punch to her workouts and she'd noticed a bit more definition appearing in the muscles of her upper arms from using them.

Or, well, she hadn't exactly noticed that. Dar went over to the weight bench and settled herself on it. Kerry had noticed, and commented on it in the shower the other day. Then, she'd just laughed, but now she had to sit here and acknowledge just how much she liked having Kerry notice things like that.

Total ego. Dar did a quick couple of sets with a relatively light barbell just to warm up. Total ego, and on the fringes a haunting insecurity she tried very hard to pretend didn't exist. She liked Kerry paying attention to her, and probably that was why she felt so out of sorts having two messages ignored so far today.

Stupid, really. Dar got up and moved to a leg press station sliding a pin into place and waiting for her body to settle into position before she started the exercise. Chino stood up and licked her arm, sliding up and down as she tried to keep her balance. "Chi, down." Dar muffled a chuckle. "Lie down."

Reluctantly, the dog obeyed, seating herself on the rubberized floor at Dar's side.

Kerry was probably busy doing what it was ILS paid her for — taking care of details and putting her plan into effect with her typical detail oriented style. While it never matched her own, Dar appreciated her partner's very disciplined operating mode.

It matched her usual schedule in the gym. While Dar tended to wander from machine to machine, using whichever one struck her fancy at the moment, Kerry always followed one or two or three routines, studiously using all the machines in it until she either finished or exhausted herself.

Dar kept the image of her partner in her mind as she got up off the leg press and switched to an abdominal machine, lying flat on her back and taking hold of the handles before she started her sit ups. She enjoyed the exercise, though this one was a little harder for her than it was for Kerry due to her longer torso.

For a while after they'd gotten together, Dar had strongly suspected that Kerry was doing gym work more to fit in with her lifestyle than because she really enjoyed it, and it had made her feel a touch guilty even though she'd called Kerry on it more than once.

After all, Kerry had been forced into doing things she didn't really want to do for so long, was it fair that she escape from her family life only to feel obligated to change again to meet what she felt were Dar's expectations?

Except they really weren't her expectations. Dar didn't honestly care if Kerry worked out or not, and she'd tried really hard to convince her of that until Kerry finally just told her she really liked it. Or, actually, she didn't fanatically enjoy it, but she very much liked the results so she was willing to put the work in to get them.

Dar paused to add a little more weight to the machine's resistance and continued her sets. That had finally made sense to Dar, since taking control over her looks had been a big part of Kerry shrugging off her past.

Of course, now it meant that for the first time in a long time, Dar was concerned about what her body looked like, but it seemed a small enough price to pay for having found the most amazing love of her life.

Probably, though, Dar almost chuckled at herself, Kerry would tell her she didn't care what Dar looked like just as insistently as Dar had told her. Both of them probably wondered if the other really meant it, and neither wanted to find out for sure.

So her life was now complicated. Dar exhaled and let her eyes close, her thoughts wandering elsewhere as her body went through the motions. But it was a nice kind of complication and she had no desire to get rid of it, so hell with it all anyway.

Instead, she imagined herself underwater, in the peaceful blue of a dive doing lazy somersaults as Kerry floated nearby taking pictures of sea urchins. She loved watching Kerry take pictures because she'd get herself into the nuttiest positions doing it, usually standing on her head to be closer and get a tight focus on the tiny creatures.

Her hair would float around her head in a halo and she'd cross her ankles, her fins fluttering lightly to keep herself in position. Dar would sometimes get herself horizontal in the water and rest her chin on her clasped wrists, just hanging there and watching the show.

She could almost hear the bubbles of her own breathing.

So a warm, solid weight settling over her lower body nearly scared the shorts off her until she managed to get her eyes open and her hands untangled from the machine and found Kerry sitting on top of her dressed out for the gym and looking amused. "Bah!" She yelped in surprise, dropping flat on her back again.

"Hi there." Green eyes twinkled. "You didn't wait for me, you punk!"

Dar blinked, trying to get her tongue to work properly after having bitten it. "Abu." She cleared her throat. "Wait for you when? I had no idea you were coming home this fast." She protested. "I thought you'd be later at the port." Jerked so quickly out of her peaceful day dream, her body now didn't know whether to jump or completely relax and she felt like hiccupping.

"I answered your last note." Kerry replied. "I didn't realize when I was in the bowels of the ship my signal was cut off. I got topside and saw I had messages from you." She wiggled the fingers she had laying on Dar's stomach, giving her a friendly scratch. "So I answered them right there on the gangway, and annoyed the heck out of some really big guys trying to move wood onboard."

"Oh." Now that Kerry was here and more than paying attention to her, Dar felt a little abashed. "No problem. I figured you got tied up in details. Thought I'd come over here for a while then grab us some dinner." She looked around. "My PDA's in the locker."

"Details." Kerry eased herself up and off her living bench. "Oh, my god did I get details. I got introduced into the world of people who live on ships." She paused and adjusted one of her wristbands. "Please, please don't tell me the Navy is like this, because if it is, I can't believe your dad survived in it as long as he did."

"Eh." Dar watched as her partner went to the first machine, the bicep curl, and sat down in it, carefully adjusting the weight stack before she fit her hands to the handles and began her exercise. "People. Politics. Can't have one without the other. You know that."

"Hmm." Kerry grunted a little with the effort of bringing the weighted bar up. "More I see people, more I love Chino."

"Gruff." Chino trotted over and licked her knee.

Dar got up and decided she'd had enough of the crunches. She went over to the pull down machine and sat under the bar, sticking the pin into a fairly significant amount of iron plates. Fitting her hands over the handles of the bar, she carefully pulled it downward, wedging her knees under the supports as she tested out how her shoulder was feeling about the weight.

So far so good. Dar flexed her arms slowly and brought the bar down, glad the ache had finally faded from her injury. It had taken a long time, though Kerry had probably been right in telling her it would have been shorter if she'd done the physical therapy she'd been told to.

"How's that feel?" Kerry asked.

"Good." Dar straightened her arms and let the weight up. She pulled it down again, a little faster this time.

"You look great when you sweat."

Dar opened one eye and peered at the triceps machine. Kerry winked at her, and stuck her tongue out. "Everything going alright at the pier?"

"Yeah, it's coming together." Kerry straightened her arms out, forcing the machine lever down. "You find the hacker?"

Dar grunted, and released a little snort. "No, but if he comes back, he'll have a surprise waiting." She said. "But I spent some time in our gateways today and I gotta admit, Ker. I'm a little worried."

"Yeah?"

"Yeah."

Kerry sighed. "Well, to be honest, I'm a little worried about how I'm going to pull off this project competitively, so we're even."

They were both silent for a few minutes, concentrating on their respective exercises. Finally, Dar let her bar up and sighed. "Know what I think?"

"What?"

"Ice cream." Dar got up from her bench and picked her towel up, extending a hand toward Kerry. "We can finish this later."

Kerry got up and took her hand without hesitation. "You're on. Let's go." She followed Dar out the door, not giving the room a single backward glance.

ICE CREAM ACTUALLY turned into dinner on the beach club's ocean facing deck. A nice breeze made it very comfortable sitting outside.

Kerry let her head rest against one of the roof supports, her eyes lazily taking in the waving palm fronds down the beach. "I don't know, honey," she said, "maybe it's a blessing in disguise. If you hadn't issued that challenge, you'd have never found the weaknesses you just told me about."

"Maybe we—maybe I—should have been looking for them before now." Dar was also leaning against the wall supports, one long leg slung over the chair arm.

"Dar, you're the chief information officer of the company. I think a lot of other people, like Mark, should have been looking for this stuff. Not you." Kerry replied honestly. "It's ridiculous that you need to be sitting on the floor in some closet trapping hackers, you know?"

A slightly stronger breeze made itself felt, whipping their hair around. Some sea grape leaves blew across the tile floor, one of them ending up on Kerry's foot. She reached down and picked it up, twirling it in her fingers. "Kinda windy."

Dar leaned to one side and looked out at the sea, spotting whitecaps. One eyebrow hiked up. "Don't tell me another damn storm snuck up on us." She checked her PDA, but there were no ominous looking messages on it.

"Mm." A slightly dreamy smile crossed Kerry's face. "Oh, man, I'd love it if it did."

That made Dar smile back, a frank grin of appreciation that lightened her entire face. "I'll take that as a compliment."

"It was." Kerry impulsively reached across the table and fit her hand into Dar's. "Want to go down to the cabin this weekend?"

Without even thinking, Dar nodded agreement. "Yeah."

"I have a meeting on Friday afternoon. How about we do this..." Kerry's mind raced over the details, thinking about their dual schedules. "How about we ride together Friday morning, and I get a ride over to the port, then you can pick me up and...vroom."

"Absolutely." Dar agreed instantly. "We can stop for dinner on the road somewhere and watch the sunset."

Kerry glanced at her watch and sighed mournfully. "It's only Tuesday."

Dar's cell went off before she could suggest something crazy like going after dinner. She took it out and checked the caller ID. "Uh oh." She opened it. "Yeah, Mark. What's up?"

"You in the building, boss?"

Dar glanced around her. "Me? No. I'm home. Why?"

"Shit. Someone's messing around in here and I thought it was you...looked like what was going on this afternoon." Mark cursed. "Okay, thanks. Lemme get back to you. Hey you like...locked that door, right?"

Dar's gaze went inward briefly, as she carefully traced her actions from the afternoon. "Yes. I went up to a meeting on fourteen, then came back down and did a few more scans. I left the closet around four. Shouldn't have been any access after that."

"Gotcha. Bye." Mark hung up hastily, cutting off a yell in the background, and the sound of a buzzer going off.

Dar looked at her cell, looked at Kerry, and then they both got up and headed for the condo at a run.

DAR COULD HEAR the beeping of the alerts as she cleared the doorway into her office and put her hands on her desk, vaulting over it to land near her chair on the other side. "Son of a bitch!"

Kerry forced herself to slow down enough to close the door behind them, making sure not to slam it on Chino's tail as the Labrador bounded in after her, tongue lolling out. She hesitated, then grabbed her briefcase from the dining room table where she'd left it, carried it into Dar's study and took possession of the couch.

As she hit the leather, it started raining, and for a brief second she had a flashback, startling and vivid, of the first time she'd been in the room. But it only lasted that one second, because then she was yanking her laptop out of its case and opening it, waiting impatiently for the machine to boot up. "What's going on?"

"Fuck if I know." Dar's fingers were nothing but a blur on the keyboard. "Something's loose in the network. Jesus Christ I hope I didn't do something stupid and leave something open today."

"The door?" Kerry was rapidly logging in.

"No...no, that I know I shut. Something in the router...I was doing those changes so damn fast." Dar's brow was furrowed. "When I was talking to you, when Mark was seeing the blocks."

"Oh." Kerry called up her network monitor and keyed it, sitting there for a minute as it started registering and lines began blinking red across the screen. "Holy cow." She looked quickly at Dar, seeing the tension scrawled across her face.

Dar hesitated, her fingertips flexing above the keys, undecided on what to do. She hated not understanding what was happening. As far as she could tell random data was flooding the network and she could not find the source of it.

She could shut everything down, and by definition that should stop the flood, but it also would take down everyone and everything using their network including the remote monitoring consoles.

Kerry watched the emotions cross her partner's face, and decided

she should do something more productive. She started up her analyzer
and grabbed the main switch, opening up the data stream and focusing
her attention on what it was showing her.

A lot of garbage. Kerry flipped to her filters and cut off the
standard network traffic, keying back to see what was left. "Dar."

"Uh?"

"It's not coming from outside."

"What?" Dar got up and sprawled on the couch arm to peer over
Kerry's shoulder.

"It's coming from inside the office." Kerry traced a line with her
finger. "Look. Here. I don't know what that is."

Dar blinked slowly, exhaling a little. "Neither do I." She admitted.
"Worm? Better tell Mark."

Kerry hit enter on the text message she'd already been composing.
"Done. Dar, what would put out that kind of traffic?

Dar slid back into her seat and continued her scanning, slamming
filters into place on interface after interface, attempting to staunch the
flow of traffic. "Son of a son of a son of a..."

Kerry got up and peered over her shoulder this time, her machine
telling her nothing new other than the traffic was continuing to build.
"That must be pretty damn close to the core, Dar. You want me to start
shutting down the building floor by floor?"

"Might have to." Dar felt herself starting to sweat. She could
imagine the calls beginning to come in to the ops center, and speculated
on how long it would take before her phone, and Kerry's, started
ringing. "What if it's directly in the core?" She pulled up another access
list reviewing the results. "God damn it, where is this thing!"

Kerry slowly backed off then went to her laptop, acting on a hunch.
"What switch is the conference center in, Dar?"

"Conference center? Ten. Why?"

"Let's just say I smell rotten fish." Kerry logged into the switch
and checked the top traffic port. One switch out of twenty seven in the
building. What were the odds? "Dar."

Dar scrambled out of her chair and nearly crawled into the seat
next to Kerry, her eyes avidly searching the screen. "Bingo. Shut the
damn thing off."

Kerry rapidly disabled the port, as Dar jumped up onto her desk
and swung the monitor toward her, watching the read-outs in tense
silence. The signals jumped for a moment more then slowly settling
down to a more even keel.

Dar slapped the desk, and turned her head toward Kerry. "Talk to
me."

"Okay." Kerry felt her heart rate slow down, though her fingers
were still shaking a little. "Inside the office."

"Yeah."

"Security audit just completed two weeks ago, and it was clean. No new hires since then."

"Right."

Kerry got up and went over to sit in Dar's chair folding her hands together on the desk. "I think this is my fault." She paused, then looked right up into Dar's eyes. "Because I'm the jerk who had four competitors sitting in our conference center with laptops and gear, and didn't ask for a security scan afterward."

Dar's face remained absolutely still for a very long instant. Then she slowly released her breath, her shoulders relaxing as she leaned on one elbow. "Quest's meeting."

Kerry nodded.

"There was a lot going on then, Kerry."

"Don't make excuses for me," she replied. "There is no excuse for that, Dar, and we both know it." She watched her partner's expression carefully, a little surprised to see the strong planes relax, and a faint, almost sheepish, smile cross her lips. "Don't we?"

Dar traced a random pattern on her desk surface with her finger. "I'd like to agree with you." She finally said, in a quiet voice. "Except that I'm finding it hard to forget what you were being distracted by the most."

Mm. Kerry nibbled the inside of her lip. "Well."

Dar's cell phone rang. She picked it up and opened it. "Yeah?"

"Did you do that? You stopped it? What was it? Where is it? What'd you do?" Mark's words spilled out so fast and so loud Dar almost dropped her phone. "C'mon, Boss! Don't tell me it just stopped, please?"

Without answering, Dar just handed the phone over to Kerry. "Have him find whatever it is, and secure it. We'll do an analysis tomorrow."

Kerry took the phone as she watched Dar get up and wander out of the study into the living room. "Hi, Mark." She finally sighed. "I...um...found the problem. It's in the number ten switch, blade six, port thirty."

Rattling keys. "It's disabled!"

"Well, yes."

"That's the big conference room. I'll get some techs down there. What ya think—the projector system go nuts again?" Mark's voice sounded utterly relieved. "Son of a hoota...that scared the crap out of me. I thought we were getting slammed."

"We were." Kerry hardly knew how to feel inside. "I think we might have gotten something planted on us during that meeting we had here in the blackout. Remember?"

Silence. "Oh, man!" Mark nearly howled. "I had that on my schedule. I had a damn sticky note here to check... oh, crap. Crap. I'll go check it myself. Crap. Sorry, Kerry."

"S'allright."

"Call you right back." Mark hung up the line, still obviously very upset.

Kerry folded the phone shut and sat there for a moment. She heard a sound and looked up to see Dar standing in the doorway, leaning against one edge of it in almost the same pose she'd seen her in the very first time they'd met. "Did you ever think we'd come to a point where we both needed to quit?" She asked.

Dar pushed off the door jam and came over, flopping down in the couch and patting the seat next to her. Kerry got up and settled onto the cool leather, hitching one leg up over Dar's left knee. "You thought it was your fault, I thought it was my fault, Mark thinks it's his fault? The hell with it, Dar. Let's just all go open a taco stand down on Card Sound road."

"You like tacos?"

Kerry leaned against her partner. "Not particularly. I like fajitas better but a taco stand sounded easier and more fun."

"Would we have to get a Chihuahua?"

"No, but Chino would have to wear a hat." Kerry appreciated the quiet humor very much. She was upset at herself, but like Dar she was finding it very hard to regret her choices and so indulging in their light banter at least distracted her mind. "You think she'd like wearing a hat?"

"Sure." Dar leaned closer and gave her a kiss on the cheek. "Don't beat yourself up, Ker."

Kerry sighed.

"Did I ever tell you about how I found out about the outage the night you ended up coming over and helping me fix it?"

More banter. Kerry gave in and snuggled up. "The night we kissed?"

"Uh huh."

"Mm...only thing I remember about that whole thing is opening the door, seeing you in your pajamas, and forgetting what my name was."

Dar chuckled softly. "Well, the ops center called me, and told me the whole damn network was down. You know what I said to them?"

"What?"

"No problem, guys. Just go on home."

"Oh, you did not." Kerry started laughing, despite herself. "C'mon, Dar. I know you're trying to make me feel better, but really."

"Really." Dar went nose to nose with her. "I told them to go home, no sense in them sticking around if everything was down, right? Made sense to me at the time."

"Really?" Kerry tried to imagine that, and just started laughing again. "Oh my god."

Dar gave her a hug. "Let's wait to see what Mark finds, and instead of beating ourselves up, figure out how we're gonna get even."

Would they? Kerry wondered seriously if they should. Oh well.

Tomorrow would be yet another day.

"HEY UGLY!"

Andrew looked up from the crate he was methodically ripping apart; correctly assuming the voice was addressing him. "Yeap?"

The supervisor hurried over to him. "Hey listen...remember that thing you told me about those invoices? You got any more tricks like that?"

Andrew leaned on his crate and considered the man, eyeing him with shrewd thoughtfulness. "Maybe. You got something better for me to do than mess with these here boxes?"

The man chewed his lip. "Well, I could...I'd hate to lose you out here because you're the only guy I got who doesn't bitch all the time, but I could do like a half day here, and half day in the office, how about that?"

"They got coffee inside there?"

The man chuckled. "Sure."

"All right." Andy nodded. "Saw them big trucks coming in this morning."

"No kidding. All that damn high tech crap with ten thousand little pieces and no manifest. C'mon." The supervisor motioned him to follow. "Let's see what we can do so it doesn't become a cluster."

Andrew followed him willingly, leaving behind his crate full of bolts and nuts and emerging from the dockside warehouse into the sun. It was early yet on Wednesday morning, but he was glad to get out of the noisy, chaotic building with an opportunity to do something more interesting.

Not that he'd never unpacked boxes. He'd unpacked more boxes than Dar had brain cells, but the action had limited opportunity for mental exercise though it did provide plenty of physical work.

They went into the trailer being used as an office. It was small and only barely cooled by an overworked wall air conditioner, and the four men sitting at old, scarred wood desks inside it were sweating as they worked.

"Hey, Brady, gimme that file." The supervisor held a hand out, and when the tattered manila file was put in it, he promptly turned and gave it to Andy. "There...see what you can do with that stuff. Most of it's Greek to me. I know carpet, hammers, and machine parts. This stuff is just garbage."

Andy opened the folder and studied the first page. "Wall." He sniffed reflectively. "Mah kid's one of them geek types. I think ah can figger this stuff out."

"Yeah?" The supervisor sounded interested. "He want a job?"

Pale blue eyes looked up at him. "She's got one already, thanks for askin'." Andy moved over to a chair near the side of the trailer sitting down and putting the folder on his knees. What he had here, he realized after studying the papers for some minutes, was all the stuff he'd heard Dar and Kerry talking about putting in their ship. So it was a sure bet the two people working against his kids had come up with their own list and here it was. "First off." He looked over at the supervisor. "Better make up some copies so I can mark on 'em."

"Right over there." Brady, the heavyset paymaster, pointed at a paneled wall without looking up.

Andrew got up and went around the wall, finding a copy machine there. With a satisfied grunt, he set the stack of papers down on the top sorter and punched the number 2, then copy.

The super poked his head around. "Listen, I cleared off the end of the table in there. You can use that to work on, okay?"

"All right."

"Great!" The man disappeared, leaving Andy to stand and watch the copier do its work. He bounced up and down on his heels a few times, whistling softly under his breath until he heard the door slam open.

"Where the hell is that asshole?" A woman's voice rasped.

Andy's eyebrow quirked as he recognized one of the two targets he'd heard the previous day.

"Pardon me?" Brady asked in a bored voice. "You'll have to be more specific, lady. There are a lot of assholes around here."

"Heh." Andy chuckled silently. "Ain't that the damn truth?"

"Don't give me that...oh, there you are. Where's our gear?"

There was a scrape and a thump as the door to the trailer's bathroom was closed, and heavy boots crossed the floor. "We're working on it, ma'am. I got my best guy sorting all the deliveries right now."

Andy's eyes twinkled wryly, and he shook his head. "Lord."

"That doesn't help me. I need to know what's here and what's not." The voice snapped back. "We don't have time to waste on your stupidity."

Andrew took his pile of copied papers and sorted them into two piles. He looked up as the super came around the corner. "Sounds like someone's got a bee in their buttocks." He drawled softly.

"Jesus." The super rolled his eyes. "You think you can get me a list of all this stuff?"

"Yeap." Andy allowed. "'Bout an hour, something like that."

"Great." The man ducked back out. "Ma'am, we'll have something for you in about an hour. We just got the invoices in now."

"You'd better, or else your company's going to explain to me why you can't even keep truck deliveries straight." The voice faded, then vanished as the outside door slammed shut.

"What a bitch." Brady snorted. "Sounds like she needs a good screwing."

"You can have her. Not my type." The super also left, closing the door more gently behind him.

Andy went to the small window and looked out, spotting the stocky form of the bigger woman retreating from the trailer. He watched her disappear into the pier building, then he returned to his task, picking up the stacks of papers and going back into the main room.

The other men in the room eyed him, then went back to their work as he took a seat at the end of a long banquet table. He set the papers down and picked up a pencil lying on the table, examining the first page thoughtfully.

When Dar had taken an interest in technology, he'd made a point of going out and reading up on the stuff she'd decided to make her living from. Most of it wasn't that much different from some things he'd encountered in the Navy, but it had its own language.

Since he'd retired, he'd taken the opportunity to delve a little deeper into the subject, and he felt he was almost at a point where he could at least have a somewhat all right discussion with his kid about it. So when he looked at the pages and pages of parts, at least the names and descriptions were somewhat familiar to him.

It seemed like they'd been shipped without any mind to what went with what though. Andy scratched his head and frowned. He knew the names, but had to admit that the functions of each of the gizmos were somewhat foggy, and he really had no way of guessing which part went with the next except by actually guessing.

Darn it.

"Wall." With a shake of his head he started sorting out the bits by the maker, figuring at least if he put all the ones from the same place together it was a start.

"That's a mess, yeah?" Brady looked over at him. "What a bunch of morons shipping that stuff."

"Yeap." Andrew scribbled some notes down. "Pain in mah butt, tell you that. Don't know what them folks was thinking."

Brady got up and looked over his shoulder. "Weren't." He commented briefly. "You got a background in this sort of thing? Thought you were just a loader."

"Done some stuff." Andy answered. "Spent thirty years in the Navy, had to learn something."

"Wow." Brady's attitude altered abruptly. "Really? Were you out on the ships?"

Pale blue eyes peeked up at him. "That is what the Navy does," he replied. "But ah tell ya what, someone be this disorganized on a carrier, they'd be pitched overboard or sent shoreside fastern' you could spit at 'em."

"Yeah." The paymaster agreed. "They don't seem to know what they're doing, you know. Like everyone's doing their own thing, and nobody's coordinating. Then you get those bitches like that one coming in here and thinking they own the joint."

"Woman did have her an attitude." Andy nodded. "Ain't a way to get things done."

"Yeah." Brady said again. "Maybe we should stop jumping when she barks. That way she'll back off."

"Could be." The ex-SEAL agreed mildly. "I sure wouldn't be saluting her, that's for damn sure."

Brady wandered off, going over to the other table and leaning over to talk to two of the men sitting there working. Andy peeked over at him, then put his head back down with a smile, continuing his sorting.

DAR PUSHED THE door to the computer center opened with a stiff armed motion, almost hitting one of the techs on his way out. "Sorry."

The tech jumped out of the way and stammered own apology, then slunk out past her as she walked on by. Dar went past the MIS command desk and headed for Mark's office, where she could hear voices already raised in excited conversation. "Hey."

Mark's head jerked up as she entered. "Oh, hey, boss." He greeted her. "Check this out!"

Dar obligingly circled his desk and focused her attention on the small, silver gray box sitting on top of it. "I'm checking. What is it?"

Mark turned it over and displayed a circuit board. "Integrated unit, plugged into our extra port for the projector down there, and get this..." he slid a small panel aside, "cellular."

Dar peered at it. "No kidding?"

"No shit, "Mark said. "They dialed in and activated it, sent the worm in over the cell link, then had it refocus out the network port. If Kerry hadn't found it...Jesus."

Dar picked up the device and studied it closely. "Damn."

"Yeah."

"That's pretty sophisticated." Mark's assistant, the lanky Peter, spoke up. "I checked it out on the web last night. That's like...black bag stuff."

"Mm." Dar nodded in agreement. "It sure is." She looked up. "So, tell me why we didn't catch a rogue MAC on the network?"

Peter stuck his hands in his pockets. Mark cleared his throat.

"Will you excuse us, please?" Dar looked at Peter. "And close the door on your way out."

The tall man escaped gratefully, shutting the door and leaving them alone in the office.

Mark gave her a look that could easily have been one of Chino's when caught stealing cookies from the closet. "It's not an excuse." He temporized. "But it's that damn projector. We've had it fixed like six times in the last four weeks."

"And?"

"So the guy told me last time he thought it was the MAC blocking that was making it freak out." Mark admitted.

"So you turned it off."

"For that port, yeah." He agreed. "It fixed the problem."

Dar folded her arms, then she walked over to Mark's office window and looked out. "That's a breach of our security policy." She remarked quietly, keeping her eyes focused outward as there was no answer behind her. "Here I have Kerry beating herself up for not asking for a scan, and the fact is the room was left deliberately wide open."

Mark shifted in his chair, the leather squeaking softly. "You want my resignation?" He asked, in a somber voice. "It was my screw up, Dar. I took the security off that port, not one of my guys."

Dar found a small boat to watch as it skittered across the water. "What I'm more interested in right now is who knew you did it, other than you and the projector tech."

Mark remained silent for a few moments. "I don't know, boss. I didn't tell anyone here."

Dar turned and leaned against the window. "So then either someone here just happened to see the change in the switch and got bought...or we have a problem with a vendor, because whoever put that..." She pointed viciously at the device. "Sure knew it."

Mark relaxed just a trifle. "You think it was one of those Telegenics goons, right?"

Did she? It was tempting to. They were in the room and no doubt about it, they had a motive. And yet... "That's more tech than Shari's capable of, and damn it, I think Michelle's too ethical for it."

"Huh."

"But you never know. Let's start hunting." Dar decided. She headed for the door, stopping as she reached it and turning. "No, I don't want your damn resignation. I screwed up, Kerry screwed up, you screwed up...that's it. We've exhausted our once in a blue moon big time. No more screw ups."

She walked out and shut the door behind her, leaving a slightly stunned Mark sitting at his desk in silence. After a moment the door cracked open again and Peter stuck his head warily inside. "You okay?"

"Yeah." Mark finally let his held breath out. "I think so. She's just really pissed." His brow creased. "I think."

"You think?"

"Yeah." Mark rested his chin on his fist. "But I can't really tell who she's more pissed at, the joker who stuck this on the network, or herself."

Peter looked confused then he slowly withdrew his head and shut the door again, leaving Mark to ponder the question alone.

"KERRY?" Mayte stuck her head around the corner of the door. "I have a fax for you."

Kerry looked up from her pile of paperwork, one blond eyebrow cocking. "Nifty. I needed more paper on my desk. Bring it over."

Mayte walked into the office and put the thick stack of paper down. "It is from the port, but I do not understand what this is."

Kerry glanced at the cover sheet, and saw a somewhat crude rendition of a seal scrawled on the page. "Ah." She tossed aside her current list of ordering and pulled the stack over. "I do, and boy, we sure did nail down which of her folks Dar gets her doodling from." She flipped through the pages, leaning a little closer to study the details. "Ah." She repeated softly. "Interesting."

"Kerry?"

Kerry looked up again. "Sorry Mayte. Was there something else you needed from me?"

Her assistant fiddled with her hands, then she sat down in Kerry's visitor chair. "Is it all right if I ask you something that is a little personal for me?"

Uh oh. "Sure." Kerry pushed aside the fax and focused her attention. "What's up?"

"Did you...I am sorry, this is very embarrassing, but...did you know right away when you were liking La Jefa?"

Liking? "Um...well, not really." Kerry replied very slowly. "If...I mean, Mayte, are you asking me when I knew I was in love with Dar?"

Mayte turned brick red, even under her already well tanned skin. "Si." She answered in a whisper.

"Boy, that's a tough question." Kerry frowned. "Because we came together in such an odd way—with work and all. But, you know, I will tell you this. I felt something in here," Kerry touched her chest, "from the very minute I set eyes on her. I just didn't know what that something was for a while."

Mayte nodded slowly. "That does make very much sense."

"Are you...uh..." Kerry hesitated. "Someone you're interested in?" She finally asked then they both looked up as Kerry's inner office door opened and Dar entered.

The blue eyes flicked to both women, and Dar paused. "Sorry. Didn't mean to interrupt," she said, retracing her steps.

"No no. I was just leaving." Mayte jumped up and raced out, closing the door quickly behind her.

Dar looked at the door, then looked at Kerry. Both eyebrows shot up.

"Beats me." Kerry shook her head. "She was just asking me about how to know when you're in love."

"Uh oh." Dar advanced again. "Someone catch her eye? Maria hasn't said anything to me at any rate."

"I got the feeling yes." Kerry pushed the fax over toward her.

"Look what Dad sent, and did you talk to Mark? He gave me a rundown on the thing he found. Holy cow, Dar."

Dar flipped through the pages, then looked up at Kerry. "What did you tell her?"

Green eyes blinked in confusion. "Huh? What did I tell who?"

"Mayte."

"About what?"

Dar glanced out the window. "About how you know when you're in love." She peeked back at Kerry's face, with a half abashed grin. "Or did I interrupt that part?"

"Oh." Kerry leaned back. "Yeah, I think you sorta did." She pondered, twiddling her thumbs together. "Probably a good thing...I don't think my going into racing heartbeats and sweating palms would do anything for our professional rapport."

"Probably not." Dar's face eased into a smile.

"Though I did tell her I knew the second I met you." Kerry smiled back. "I'm not sure why she ran out of here like that, though." She idly stifled a yawn. "Was it something I said?"

Dar took a seat on the edge of Kerry's desk, regarding her with a faintly amused expression.

"Stop it." Kerry punched her in the leg. "Don't start with that crush stuff again, Dar. The last thing on earth she'd be asking me if she really had a crush was the question she just asked. Right?"

The taller woman shrugged one shoulder.

Kerry made a face. "You really think so?"

"I really do," Dar replied. "But I don't think you've got much to worry about. She knows you're taken."

Kerry's eyes that twinkled. "Now that's the truth." She leaned her head back against her leather chair. "I'm looking forward to class tonight. You going to be out of your meeting in time?"

Dar had been studying the fax. Now she dropped it lightly onto Kerry's desk and stood. "Yep." She indicated the papers. "Not sure what that gets us, besides what they're paying for the standard gear. Nice of Dad to send it though. Wonder why he had them?"

"Yeah." Kerry twiddled her thumbs. "At least I know we're paying less than they are. Volume has to count for something, eh?" She pushed the fax with her index finger. "What did you think of that thing Mark found?"

Dar had wandered over to the window and was gazing outside. "Slick."

Kerry waited, but Dar offered nothing else on the subject. "Okay." She leaned forward and went back to her mail, recognizing a rebuff when she felt one. "Guess I'll leave that in your ballpark. Mine's busy." She put her head down and concentrated on the screen, trying not to become hyper aware of the figure standing behind her.

She knew Dar was looking at her though. She could feel it, feel the

impact of those blue eyes on the back of her head even before she heard
the soft rustle of fabric as Dar turned. She heard the light scuff of her
footsteps against the carpet, and against her will, she found herself
straining to figure out if they were coming closer or leaving.

"I really don't know what to think." Dar's voice sounded
unexpectedly loud in the office.

Kerry continued typing. "Well, I'm sure you'll handle it."

Dar resumed her perch on Kerry's desk, making it very difficult to
continue to ignore her. Kerry tried, but after a moment she felt a nudge
against her shoulder, and it was either look up, or really escalate her
miffed feelings into a fight.

Did she want a fight? Kerry swiveled a little and rested her chin on
her fist, gazing up at her partner. No. She never really did want to fight.
It was just that sometimes their differences pushed them in opposite
directions until they clashed. "Yes?"

"Was I being a bitch?" Dar asked.

Kerry shrugged one shoulder.

"I wasn't trying to be," Dar admitted. "That thing Mark found has
got me confused."

"Why?"

Kerry?s phone rang, and she gave it an evil look. She hit her
intercom button. "Mayte, can you get that please? I'm in an important
meeting right now."

"Si, of course." Mayte answered back promptly then clicked off.

Kerry returned her attention to Dar. "What's confusing you,
honey? Was it more than you expected it to be? Mark showed me the
details. It was pretty sophisticated."

Dar sighed. "It was pretty sophisticated," she admitted, running
her fingers through her hair in some distraction. "Ker, I know you want
to think it was Shari and Michelle, but I..."

"You don't think so? Really? C'mon, Dar. Who else could it be?"
Kerry almost laughed. "I mean, let's be real. We have our worst enemies
right here in the building, I leave them unsupervised for a half hour,
and a couple days later we get hit with an internal probe." She put a
hand on Dar's leg. "Honey."

Her partner exhaled. "So now you know why I didn't want to talk
about it." She got up and headed for her office, shaking her head. "Just
forget it. Yeah, it was probably them."

"B...? Kerry got up and chased after her. "Dar! Wait a minute?" She
caught up to her at the inner door and gently took hold of her arm.
"Hey, hey...hey —"

Dar stopped, but there was a perceptible pause before she turned,
and when she did, her expression was dour. "What?"

As their relationship progressed, Kerry had learned bit by bit just
what worked with Dar and what didn't. She had no idea what the heck
was going on with her, but she knew enough to know that attempting to

placate her at this point would do exactly jack squat. "Okay."

"Okay what?" Dar repeated, but in a slightly modified tone.

"Okay, we've both already cycled this month, and it's not a full moon. So let's blow this office and get some lunch." Kerry said. "Somewhere outside this building."

Dar hesitated, then she wrinkled her nose up and clucked her tongue. "I'm in a really pissy mood. You don't want to have lunch with me. Maybe I should just go to the corner and get a hot dog." She said. "Last person I want to wrangle with is you."

Kerry bumped her gently. "C'mon." She replied softly. "We'll talk about the new fish tank." She looked up into Dar's eyes, watching the strong planes of her partner's face shift a little as some of the storm clouds faded. "I'm sorry if I rubbed you the wrong way, I didn't mean to."

Dar scowled, but it was one of her more engaging ones. "S'allright. I didn't mean to be a touchy, whiny ass this morning." She eased closer, exhaling as her body relaxed. "Lunch sounds great. You can try and talk me into those boxing crabs." She gave Kerry a gentle pat on the side. "Let me go close my machine down and we can take off."

Kerry stepped back and watched as she left, her own body relaxing from the tension she always felt in the times when they disagreed. "Thank god it doesn't happen often." She turned and went back to her desk hitting her intercom button as she sat down. "Mayte? Was that anything critical? C'mon in."

After a moment, the outer door opened, and Mayte poked her head in and entered, crossing over to Kerry's desk. "It was Mr. Jose. He has a gigantic problem with something in Los Angeles." She handed over a piece of paper with some notes. "I wrote down what it is he said, but he wants to talk to you."

Kerry reviewed the notes. "Well, he's going to have to wait until after lunch." She decided. "Dar's in a mood, and I'm going to work on getting her out of it. Let him know I'll be up to his office when I get back."

Mayte blinked at her. "Si." She agreed softly. "I will do that. And thank you before, Kerry, for your advice. It is appreciated."

"No problem." Kerry smiled. "Good luck."

Mayte smiled back, then left.

Kerry leaned back and studied the closed door. "Nah." She shook her head. "It's not me." With a click, she locked her computer screen, and headed off to wrangle fish.

Chapter Five

"OH, SHIT!"

It was like something exploding against her head. One moment she was spinning into a defensive kick block and the next the world was turning over around her and the floor was coming up way too fast at a very wrong angle.

"Ker!" Dar dropped her hands and bolted ducking under the arm of her startled sparring partner. Kerry's body had barely hit the mat before she was dropping to a knee at her side, reaching for the arm Kerry had curled around her head.

"Jesus! I'm really sorry!" Kerry's sparring partner also knelt, looking mortified. "Man, I didn't mean to kick you like that!"

"Ow...not your fault." Kerry hissed. "I stepped into it. Damn...that hurt." She half rolled over, recognizing the arms closing around her. "I'm used to someone taller."

"Easy." Dar pulled her hand away. "Let me see."

"Ahh, Dr. Dar." Kerry turned her head slightly, her face only half visible under her foam protective gear. "I think his boot..."

"Got you right in the eye." Dar winced.

Several other students gathered around with concerned expressions. The teacher came over, crouching down next to them with a frown. "What happened?"

Dar eased the head protector off, pushing Kerry's sweaty blond locks back to reveal an angry, red patch starting above her right eyebrow and extending across her eye to her cheek bone The eye itself was closed, moisture leaking from the inside corner. "Oh, boy."

Kerry reached up, then let her hand fall when Dar gently took hold of her face. "We were going through that new roundhouse kick, and I turned the wrong way," she said. "Ow."

"That's gonna bruise." One of the other students said sympathetically. "You should get some ice on it."

"Yeah." The instructor agreed. "I think you should, too." He glanced across the training room. "We're done here, anyway. I was about to call practice."

"Me, three." Dar responded promptly. "C'mon, Ker."

Not really wanting to be picked up and carried, Kerry carefully rolled onto her side, then got her knees under her. She was glad of Dar's steadying hand, though, because when she tried to open her eye, the stinging tears made her promptly shut it again.

It hurt like hell. She got to her feet, with Dar's hands firmly grasping her wrist and upper arm and stood a moment, getting her balance. "Jesus, that hurts."

Dar made a small noise, which Kerry recognized immediately. She took a deep breath and steadied herself, straightening up and giving her partner a pat on the side. "Okay, give me a second to catch my breath, then we can head for the icebox."

"I think we should detour." Dar said, tilting Kerry's head up to the light and looking at the forming bruise. "I'd like Dr. Steve to take a look at that."

"Dar..."

"That's a very good idea." Don, the instructor, interjected. "I think Dar is right."

"God, I'm so sorry." Kerry's sparring partner repeated. "Kerry, I don't think you moved wrong, I think I did. I was supposed to go right."

Kerry felt a headache coming on, and her eye was stinging badly now. She didn't want to have to go to the doctor, but she didn't want to stand there arguing either. "Okay." She nodded. "Let's go." She let Dar guide her to the locker room, and sat quietly as her partner unlaced her gloves and removed them.

"That's gonna hurt." Dar muttered. "Son of a bitch."

"He didn't do it on purpose, hon." Kerry felt the headache getting worse, and she didn't object when Dar took her by the shoulders and eased her up onto her feet, so she could strip the workout gear off her body. "I'm going to have a black eye, aren't I?"

Dar cupped her face in both hands. "Oh yeah." She informed her regretfully. "Can you open that eye?" She watched as a sliver of very bloodshot white and a bit of green appeared. "Can you see?"

Kerry closed her other eye and blinked a few times, then nodded. "Yeah, it just hurts." She reassured Dar. "I think I just need a cold compress." She paused. "Or maybe the old fashioned cure—a chilled piece of roast beef."

Dar managed a short laugh. "I think it's supposed to be raw sirloin." She tossed Kerry's gear into her locker, and handed her a t-shirt. "Slip that on. Let me get this junk off me."

Kerry eased the shirt over her head as Dar stripped out of her own gear and rid herself of her sweat drenched shirt, pulling a gray heather tank top over her sports bra. "Hey, Dar?"

Dar turned and faced her. "Hmm?"

"You're really sexy when you're grubby. How do you do that?"

Dar carefully looked around and then back at her. "Are you trying to distract me from taking you to the doctor?"

"Me?" Kerry eased her small duffel over her shoulder. "Would I do that? No. I was just making an observation." She meekly followed Dar from the locker room, tangling her fingers in the waistband of Dar's shorts as the throbbing in her head intensified.

Maybe going to the doctor wasn't a bad idea after all.

"LOOK UP, KIDDO."

Kerry did her best, squinting at Dr. Steve through her half open eye, now puffy with swelling and very tender.

Dr. Steve clucked his tongue. "I don't know what I'm gonna do with you kids. Can't you take up something like bowling? What's all this chop socky stuff, anyway?"

"It's more fun than bowling." Kerry protested faintly. "Honest. I don't usually get my noggin kicked."

She was lying on her back on the examining table, still fully clothed due to the office's chill. Dar was huddled on a stool next to the foot of the table, her arms leaning on the leather as she watched Dr. Steve like a hawk.

"Uh huh. Likely story," the doctor said. "Except I've been patching up old blue eyes down there since she was a tot, and she still doesn't have the sense to take up croquet after all these years." He touched the side of Kerry's face gently. "Well, chipmunk, you've got a real nice bruise there, but it doesn't look like anything's permanently broken."

"Mmph." Kerry grunted in some relief. "My head hurts."

"I'm sure it does." Dr. Steve chuckled. "You were lucky you had you some Styrofoam over your face, or you'd have broken that cute little nose, I'm thinking. As it is, you just need a bag of ice, and some TLC." He turned and looked at Dar. "You'll take care of that, right?"

Dar propped her chin up on her fist, and managed a half grin. "Yeah, I think I can handle that."

"You think?" Kerry nudged her with one knee. "Tell you what, you can walk around with me at work and explain why I look like I had a run in with the ultimate fighting squad tomorrow. Otherwise I'll have to wear a sign around my neck."

"Sugar, if you still got that headache, stay out of that office tomorrow." Dr. Steve advised. "You didn't break anything, but if you hang around in there getting your blood pressure up, it'll just make for a worse bruise." He leaned on the table with both hands and studied Kerry. "Speaking of which, let me get a check on that little old thing."

Kerry tried to relax her body fully as she waited for him to come back with the pressure cuff, not really worried, but not really confident either. She'd been watching herself lately, making sure she lay off the salt, and avoiding too much caffeine, but she wasn't sure the recent aggravation wouldn't show up on Dr. Steve's annoyingly accurate cuff meter.

She'd been borderline on her last examination, much better than before she'd gone on vacation, but still not in a range either the doctor or she felt comfortable with for a normal baseline. Now, after having to go through the stress of the bid, she was sure it was going to be at least as bad.

Hopefully not worse. With a little sigh, she glanced down at Dar. The taller woman was looking back at her with wry sympathy, and they exchanged brief grins.

She felt Dar's fingers curl around her lower leg, and a gentle stroking start up on the inside of her knee. A surprising tension eased from her, and she watched in almost benign regard as the cuff was fitted around her arm and the tension increased.

It tightened further, held, then relaxed after a few seconds. "Very nice." Dr. Steve pronounced. "You've been being a good girl, I see."

Faintly surprised, Kerry managed a nod. "Trying to." She agreed. "Glad it's working."

The doctor patted her shoulder comfortingly. "You keep it up, Kerry. I don't want to have to be your whiny, old doctor too frequently." He turned and glanced at Dar. "Okay, take this little prizefighter home and put her to bed."

Dar unwound her long legs from the stool and stood up, visibly relieved. "Don't worry, I will." She promised. "Anything we can do for that except ice?"

"Nope." Dr. Steve turned and studied the X-ray he had taken of Kerry's skull, reviewing it one last time. He ran a finger over the bony ridge around Kerry's eye and leaned closer. "It's fine, honey. Just a black eye that's gonna drive her nuts for a few days."

Dar sighed.

"I'll live." Kerry sat up and hopped off the table. "Hey, I've never had a black eye before. Have you?" She asked her partner.

"Yes." Both Dar and Dr. Steve answered at once. Dar gave her old family friend a slit eyed look, but then just chuckled and shook her head.

"This scrappy little thing had more fights as a tyke than a Chihuahua in a pack of Dobermans," Dr. Steve said. "Wasn't a week she wasn't in here with something or other—broken arm, broken ankle...cracked skull, you name it. Ran out of lollipops one week when she'd been here three times."

Dar put her hands on her hips. "C'mon. I wasn't that bad."

"Honey, your files are right in there." Dr. Steve pointed. "I don't make this stuff up."

Kerry put her arms around Dar and gave her a hug. "C'mon. You can tell me all about your fearless battles while I put that steak on my eye."

Dar returned the hug, kissing the top of Kerry's head affectionately, then pausing in mild embarrassment as Dr. Steve chuckled and shook his head. After a moment's frown, she shrugged one shoulder and hugged Kerry again, patting her back gently. "How about we get that steak cooked, and use my gel pack instead. It's less messy, and Chino won't be trying to eat it off your face."

"Okay." Kerry agreed. "Whatever you say, babe. You're in charge."

Dr. Steve walked them out to the front room, where the lights were mostly out and the building silent. When they reached the door, Dar clapped her old friend on the arm. "Thanks for meeting us. I appreciate it.?"

"Any time, Dar." The doctor patted her on the back, and carefully ruffled Kerry's hair. "You take care of her, okay?"

"Always." Kerry answered before Dar could. "Thanks, Dr. Steve." She released her partner, and gave their doctor a brief hug. "Take care."

"You too, Kerry." The older man responded, holding the door open for them. "Drive safe, eh?"

"I will." Dar promised, as they walked out into the tropical night, and headed for home.

NOT LONG AFTER, Kerry was laying on their leather couch with the promised gel pack draped over the side of her face as she listened to Dar accept their dinner delivery at the door. Her head was still hurting, but the pain had at least reached a plateau, and the rest of her body was far more comfortable, nestled into the the couch.

She'd never had a black eye before, and from her brief glimpse in the mirror before Dar pointedly steered her toward the couch, she'd certainly started off with a doozy of one. The bruise extended all around her eye and halfway across her cheekbone, and it was a little scary looking.

She wasn't looking forward to explaining it to everyone. It reminded her suddenly of a classmate of hers in college, who'd gotten involved in some chancy business her boyfriend was doing and went crossways of him.

Sarah, her name had been, Kerry recalled. She'd come to class one day with a huge black eye, and explained it away with a laugh, as an accident that occurred when she'd been taking something out of the refrigerator.

No one had believed her. Everyone thought the boyfriend had beaten her up. Kerry sighed, and shrugged a shoulder. At least everyone knew she did martial arts, so it would be more embarrassing than anything else especially since she didn't have a criminally inclined boyfriend.

"All right." Dar settled next to her on the edge of the couch, setting something down on the table. "How's it feeling?"

Just an endearingly overprotective spouse. "Ucky." Kerry responded honestly. "Dar, I look like a poster child for the anti-boxing league." She reached up to touch the ice pack. "Freaky."

"Nah." Dar unwrapped their dinner.

"Yes, I do." Kerry draped one hand over her partner's thigh. "What'd you get?"

"Open up and you'll find out."

Obediently, Kerry opened her mouth and waited, biting down instinctively when something was placed inside it. She chewed and swallowed, then smiled. "Mm. Orange chicken." She was happy to taste a favorite of hers.

"Yeah, I figured it would be easier for you to chew than a sirloin." Dar touched the side of Kerry's face gently. "You said it was a little sore here."

"Mm." Kerry moved her jaw from side to side slightly. "Yeah, it is. What else you got?"

Dar lifted the cool pack momentarily, then set it back down a little to one side. Despite her casual dismissal, the bruise did look horrific, and the green eye under the compress was swollen almost shut. "Green beans and chipotle polenta."

"Ah, Spicy grits." Kerry started to ease up onto her elbow. "My favorite."

"Lie down." Dar took hold of her shoulders and pressed her back down. "Let that ice pack do its thing." She waited until Kerry complied, then went back to arranging the plates. There was no real easy way for her to accomplish her task of getting her ailing partner fed, but then, she was never much into doing things the easy way, so improvisation was in order.

Carefully, she lifted the plate up, then hoisted herself up and over Kerry's legs to settle between her partner and the back of the couch.

"Mm." Agreeably, Kerry squirmed over a little, giving Dar more space as she felt the plate settle on her stomach.

"There." Dar propped her head up on her hand, working the fork with the other as she selected a piece of chicken. "How's that?" She rumbled right into Kerry's nearby ear.

Kerry merely grinned as a response. She'd taken some ibuprofen and she had her ice pack, but there was something about having Dar this close that beat both of those. She accepted the chicken, and sighed. "I still can't believe I was that stupid."

"Ker."

"Well, I was."

"He moved wrong, you didn't." Dar argued.

"You're just saying that." Kerry picked up a green bean and nibbled it. "You didn't even see it happen, did you?"

Dar scowled.

"See?"

"I know you didn't do it wrong." Dar stubbornly insisted. "That guy's a nitwad. He's got the reflexes of a gumby." She grumbled. "I should have kicked his ass in the last round, and maybe..."

"Dar, Dar, Dar." Kerry tapped her partner on the head. "Stop that." She dropped her hand to Dar's neck and kneaded the back of it. "Tell me about how you ended up in Dr. Steve's office so much, huh? Take my mind off this."

Dar offered her a forkful of polenta. "I scrapped." She admitted briefly. "I fought with anything that got in my way and it didn't matter how much bigger than me they were." Her eyebrows twitched a little. "And I was a little accident prone."

"You?"

"Uh huh."

"I find that very hard to believe. You're disgustingly graceful."

Dar chuckled wryly. "Now, most of the time, sure," she said. "But I grew six inches between sixth and seventh grade. I gave myself concussions just getting in and out of the damn truck." She offered another green bean. "Wasn't pretty."

"Hmm." Kerry regarded the long body fitted against hers. "I guess sometimes short has its moments. I think the most I grew in any year was about an inch, maybe." She reached up and traced Dar's cheekbone. "But I bet you were pretty anyway."

Dar shook her head negatively.

"Yes." A thumb traced across the well shaped lips. "I've seen pictures, Dar. Don't give me that icky face."' Kerry remembered one in particular, a full length shot of Dar at thirteen or fourteen, in shorts and a dirt covered t-shirt, long dark hair half obscuring her face, but not the sharp blue eyes peeking out or the hesitant half grin that surely identified the camera holder as her father.

Gorgeous. Even then, Dar's face had been distinctively unique and the smudge of mud across her cheek only amplified the character of it.

"Kerry?" Dar whispered into her ear. "Hello? Earth to Kerry?"

"Sorry honey." Kerry felt the pounding in her head beginning to subside. "I just so absolutely love you I can't help drifting off into dreamy hazes sometimes." She turned her head so her good eye could meet her partner's.

Dar was blinking at her, an expression of somewhat puzzled pleasure on her face. "Really?"

Kerry traced her fingertips over Dar's lips again, and nodded. "Thanks for taking care of me." She felt a smile tug at her mouth. "And I think you're right. He did go the wrong way. I just wish I could have stopped in time so I didn't hit his foot."

Dar lifted the ice pack, and leaned forward, brushing her lips over the injured area before she replaced the gel again. "I'll kick his ass for it next week." She promised solemnly. "And then I'll teach you how to duck."

Kerry exhaled in satisfaction, putting her accident behind her for the moment. "Hey. I've got an idea." She burred softly. "How about I wear a patch over my eye tomorrow, kinda like a pirate?"

Dar chuckled soundlessly.

"Arrrr... Avast ye mateys!"

DAR DROPPED INTO her seat, glancing at the clock on the wall in some mild embarrassment. She shook her head, then leaned forward and hit the intercom. "Maria, what the hell's on my schedule today??"

"Uno momento, Dar. I will be right there." Maria answered promptly.

"Hope it wasn't anything that started at eight." Dar remarked to the empty office. Both she and Kerry had fallen asleep together on the couch and woken abruptly at eight, realizing they'd forgotten any kind of alarm.

Kerry's ice pack was a sloshy, warmish pack by then, and it had slipped down off her face, revealing a still swollen and tender area underneath. Her eye was mostly closed, and Dar didn't have much trouble in convincing her to stay home and relax once she'd seen her reflection in the mirror.

So here she was at just past nine, trying to collect the scattered threads of her day after its late start and hoping she hadn't missed anything really critical. Dar folded her hands as Maria entered, carrying a pad of paper, and gave her assistant a wry grin. "Morning."

"Good morning, Dar." Maria sat down. "Is Kerrista all right? Mayte said that she would not be here today."

Dar sighed. "We had an accident at kickboxing class last night. Kerry got bopped in the head, so I made her stay home. It's not that bad, but she looks like she was beaned in the eye with a baseball."

"Dios Mio!" Maria exclaimed. "That poor thing!"

"Yeah." Her boss agreed. "Wish I was..." She paused awkwardly. "Anyway, what's on the schedule? Did I miss something already this morning?"

Maria smiled at her, and looked down at her pad. "Ah, no, no. There is a meeting after lunch today, with the gentleman from AT&T, and a conference call for you at four for the international."

Rats. Dar sighed again. The four o'clock international call tended to last forever, and she... "Okay." She cut off her thoughts abruptly, reminding herself she was actually a corporate officer here. "Thanks, Maria. Let me get to work on the damn inbox. Tell Mayte to forward any calls for Kerry over here to me."

"Yes, I surely will." Maria stood up. "Would you like some coffee, Dar?"

"Do I look like I need it?" Dar replied with rakish grin. "Yeah" sure."

"I will be right back," she said. "While you are getting your things ready."

Dar watched her leave then she gave her trackball a spin bringing up her inbox in the hope it would keep her occupied and not wishing she was at home.

One note caught her eye, and she opened it, scanning the contents quickly. Her fingers drummed lightly on the keys, then she hit reply and answered. She hoped Kerry would forgive her for it.

THERE WERE A lot of things Kerry knew she could be doing. However, she was curled up in their waterbed with the blinds drawn, listening to an audio book playing softly in the CD player instead. Her eye was still swollen shut, and trying to read anything, much less her laptop screen just wasn't working for her.

So she'd retired to their bedroom instead of her office, keeping her laptop nearby for mail purposes, but she simply laid there in the comfortable air conditioning with her other eye closed as well.

It felt good to just chill out. Kerry felt a little guilty as well, but not enough for her to get up and do anything about it.

Chino came over and rested her jaw on the edge of the waterbed, snuffling at Kerry's slack hand until she reached over to scratch the Labrador's head. She licked Kerry's fingers, then hopped up onto the waterbed, making the surface move as she picked a spot and curled up against her owner's body.

Kerry sighed contentedly, taking in a breath and catching Dar's scent, still clinging to the pillow her arm was wrapped around. She was a little surprised when the phone rang, but reached over and snagged it, cradling it between her shoulder and ear. "Hello?"

"Hey, Ker!" Colleen's voice sounded through the phone. "You there?"

"Um." Kerry cleared her throat. "You called my home number and I answered, didn't I?"

"Ah, heh. Yeah." Her friend said. "So, what's the deal? I heard you got hurt?"

Kerry snorted softly into the phone. "Yeah. I was a klutz last night in kickboxing class. The guy I was sparring with slipped and kicked me in the head."

"Oh, Jesus!" Colleen blurted. "So it was some guy? Not Dar?"

"Dar?" Kerry chuckled. "Of course not. She's got more control than the damn instructor." She paused. "Why?"

"Well, that makes more sense." Colleen replied. "No, it was just how I heard it. For some reason it sounded like it was Dar who'd been involved. Boy, she must have been pissed."

"To put it mildly." Kerry felt her brow crinkle as she reviewed her friend's words. "She took me to the doctor, had my head x-rayed, cursed the dumbass who clocked me, and then rocked me to sleep on the couch last night. I can only imagine what she'd have done if it'd been her."

"Aw." Colleen's smile could clearly be heard through the phone. "She's such a sweetie."

Kerry relaxed. "Yeah." She sighed. "So, anyway, I've got this black eye and I can hardly read a screen. Dar made me stay home."

"Darn right." Colleen stated. "You need anything? I've got to go pick up my car so I'm leaving early. I could stop by."

"Nah, I'm fine." Kerry reassured her. "Listen, do me a favor? Make sure whoever's talking about what happened gets the story straight. If Dar hears people thinking it's her, she's going to have a heart attack."

"No problem, girl," her friend said. "You leave it to me."

Kerry sighed. "God damn it."

"What?"

Her temper flared. "Why in the hell would anyone think she'd done it? That really pisses me off."

The phone crackled a little as though Colleen had shifted or moved. "Hey, hey, relax." She said, in a lower tone. "Listen, I don't think anyone though it was on purpose, Kerry. Just an accident, you know?"

"Bullshit." Kerry rolled over and scowled at the ceiling.

"Kerry." Colleen replied. "Would you take it easy? Honest, no one was mean. It was just...I don't know, I guess people thought it was kind of funny that..."

"Funny?" Kerry growled. "There is nothing funny at all about it. Even if it had been Dar, it wouldn't have been funny. People getting hurt is funny? Me getting hurt is funny? Wow. Nice."

There was no answer for a few seconds, then Colleen sighed. "That's not what I meant."

Kerry plucked at the soft down comforter draped over the bed. "Yeah, I know. It's not your fault." She admitted. "I just really hate when people talk bull, especially about her."

Colleen cleared her throat, then chuckled. "Well, I do know that Kerry, me lass. That's how I knew you were falling for her way back when. You nearly took my head off when I dared to call her a rude name."

Had she? Kerry studied the plaster ceiling, a faint smile tugging at her lips. Yeah, she had. Even at the very beginning after she and Dar had bumped heads just once or twice, she?d started defending her. Many of her co-workers had thought, and probably still did, that she was just sucking up.

Maybe even she thought that, back then, or maybe it was just survival. But the instinct to protect Dar had kicked in very, very early. "Yeah," she said. "Sorry, Col. It's just a button of mine." She continued. "And it really hurts, especially after how sweet Dar was last night. I felt like I was being swaddled in silk. Don't even get me started on this morning."

"No problem, girl." Colleen sounded happier. "Listen, let me go finish up a report I've got due. I'll give you a buzz later, okay?"

"Sure." Kerry agreed. "Thanks for calling, Col." She hung up the phone, her relaxed mood gone despite her reassuring words to her friend. "Man that does really piss me off." She reached over to scratch Chino's ears. "Why do people do that, Chi? Why can't they just be nice?"

"Growf." Chino licked her fingers and snuggled closer again.

Kerry regarded the ceiling for a few moments more, then she

reached over and hit the speakerphone, dialing Dar's private office number without looking. It was answered after two rings. "Hey."

"Hey." Dar's voice sounded reasonably chipper. "How are you feeling?"

"Like a grumpy warthog," Kerry said. "What's going on there?"

A soft creaking came through the phone, surely Dar taking a seat in her leather chair and leaning back. "I'm going to be interviewed in about a half hour," she said. "Mark's still trying to track down that damn device, we've been hit by a dozen more attacks, and we're out of milk in the cafeteria." She paused. "So, how's your day been so far?"

Poised on the verge of spilling her concerns, Kerry hesitated, hearing the stress in her partner's voice. "Boring," she said instead. "I can't really use my laptop, so Chi and I are just lying in bed, listening to Modern Trends in Network Design."

"Ah. Light reading." Dar chuckled softly under her breath. "You could go watch Animal Planet. How's your headache?"

"Better." Kerry felt slightly foolish at bothering her busy partner. "Listen, sorry to interrupt. I was just...um..." She paused. "Anyway, why are you being interviewed?"

"Ah." Dar grunted. "Fallout from that goddamn Telegenics glory hunting with Discovery Channel or whoever the hell that is. Now this woman from the Washington Post wants to talk to me."

"Oo. Make sure she takes a pretty picture for the front page." Kerry teased. "Given what they usually have to put up, getting their hands on you will definitely be a pleasant change.

"Pfft." Dar made a rude noise.

"Same to you." Kerry replied. "Hey, let me let you get back to work. I'm going to laze around here for a while, then maybe catch some sun outside on the porch." She stretched a little. "Talk to you later?"

"Absolutely." Dar answered warmly. "And you weren't bothering me. I'm glad you called."

Kerry smiled as she hung up the line, but the smile faded after a moment and she rolled up out of bed and sat on the edge of it, leaning her elbows on her knees. After she stared at the floor a minute with her good eye, she pushed herself to her feet and trudged into the bathroom.

She didn't really want to look in the mirror, but she did anyway, watching her face twist into a grimace as she examined her reflection. Around her eye, almost in a perfect circle, was a dark, mottled bruise that would have almost been comical if it hadn't hurt as much as it did.

Her eye was puffy and half closed, but that, at least, was an improvement over what it had been last night. With a sigh, Kerry used the restroom then wandered into the living room as Chino jumped off the couch and joined her.

Now that she was stirred up, the thought of lying in bed was almost intolerable. Instead, Kerry went into the kitchen and made some herbal tea, stifling a yawn as she opened the refrigerator to find herself something to nibble on.

Removing a bottle of juice, she poured herself a glass and replaced it, turning in surprise when she heard a soft knock at the door. "Now, who the heck could that be?" she asked following Chino into the living room as the Labrador bounded ahead to guard the door for her. "Oh, pooters. Must have forgotten to tell Clemente not to come in today."

She went to the door and opened it, not bothering to check the peep hole first. "Oh." She blinked in surprise, finding not the stocky hospitality manager, but Ceci outside. "Hi."

"Hi." Ceci had her hands behind her back, and was looking quite diffident. "Can I come in?"

"Sure." Kerry backed up and let her past. "Sorry, I wasn't expecting anyone, but you're always welcome."

"Mmm hmm." The diminutive woman strolled past. "Remember that after you find out why I'm here."

"Uh, oh." Kerry half chuckled. "Want some tea?"

Dar's mother nodded. "Love some. Nice shiner you have there." She came closer and examined Kerry's face. "Don't suppose I can talk you two into croquet or something equally benign instead, huh?"

"Ah. So you know all about what happened, huh?"

"Mmm hmm."

"Dar send you here?" Kerry hazarded.

"Mmm hmm." Ceci nodded. "Me being the only mother she knows in the area, yes. She asked me to come over here and practice my non-existent maternal skills on you." She gave Kerry a wry grin. "So why not let me get the tea, and you rest your head so I can say I tried. Hmm?"

Kerry walked over to the couch and sat down extending her legs along its length. "Sure," she agreed amiably. "I'll get her back later."

Ceci gave her a big thumb up and disappeared into the kitchen.

"You little stinker wench." Kerry addressed the ceiling. "I will get you later. Just wait." She reached for the remote control and flipped on the television, picking a channel at random and settling back to watch.

Ah well. It could be worse. Kerry eyed the door to the kitchen. It could be my mother.

THE REPORTER ENTERED behind Maria and followed her over to Dar's desk. She was a tall, poised black woman with striking good looks, and she met Dar's firm handshake with one of her own before she took the proffered seat.

"Thanks, Maria." Dar returned to her chair and dropped into it. "So, Ms. Cruickshank, what is it you'd like to talk about?" She leaned back and steepled her fingers, watching the reporter as she settled herself in her chair and took out a notepad.

Notepad. Dar's eyebrow twitched. The last few times she'd been interviewed, it'd been with at the very least, a tape recorder. It was interesting that the reporter had chosen to stick with the basics in the local headquarters of one of the most highly technical companies in the world.

"What would I like to talk about?" The reporter repeated, in a quietly cordial tone. "Well, Ms. Roberts, as you may know, some of my colleagues are working very hard to make a documentary about Peter Quest's effort to re-establish American cruising." She studied her pad and then looked up at Dar. "Everyone keeps trying to cast you as the bad guy."

Dar smiled cheerfully at her.

"Are you the bad guy?" She asked. "From the research I've done, your image wanders from Cruella deVil to Joan of Arc, depending on the time of day and phase of the moon or who I've talked to." She leaned forward a little. "So what's the real scoop?"

Joan of Arc? Dar's eyes widened a trifle. "I'm not sure there is a scoop," she replied. "I'm just here to do a job. I don't employ any bizarre tactics, just decent business sense, and the time I invest in acquainting myself with the newest technology."

Cruicshank scribbled a note. "Well, let me tell you what I've got here on you, and then you can tell me if you still think you're not a news item." She flipped a page over. "You're a Florida native."

"Mm." Dar gave an agreeable grunt. "That's pretty newsworthy, I guess."

The reporter smiled. "So I hear. You grew up on Navy bases, right?"

Dar nodded.

"You've only worked for one company, that being this one and you joined ILS when you were...fifteen?"

Dar nodded again. "I think that makes me more boring than scoop." She remarked. "I never saw any reason to change companies. I just kept changing jobs within this one."

The reporter made another note. "Do you like your job?" She studied Dar's face. "The one you have now, I mean?"

For a moment Dar almost considered answering honestly, then she reviewed the issue and realized there were some things even she couldn't get away with. "Most of the time, yes." She finally responded. "I can do without publicity seeking monkeys trying to make me look bad every couple of hours, but in general, yeah. I like what I do."

Cruicshank looked intrigued. "Is that what you consider your competitors? Publicity seeking monkeys?"

"Well," Dar met her gaze squarely, "I can tell you I've never asked a news crew to hang off my ass during any of my business deals. I've also never rigged a convention for failure so I could come in and save the day to make press, or tried to bug my rivals."

The reporter straightened up and looked really intrigued. "Some people would say that's just smart competition."

"Some people are morons." Dar replied. "I find it easier just to be very good at what I do, and save the fun and games for the weekends."

They looked at each other for a moment then the reporter grinned. "You know what, Ms. Roberts?"

Dar raised her eyebrows in question.

"You're my kind of bad guy." She told her. "Can I buy you lunch?"

Dar was peculiar about lunch. She liked to either grab something at her desk, or if Kerry was there and not busy, have lunch with her. It was a chance to wind down for a few minutes in either case and de-stress in the middle of the day.

However, since Kerry wasn't here, and this was at least an opportunity to make an impression, Dar decided she'd make an exception. "Sure." She agreed. "You'll get out easy. The rest of your bunch has to spend whole days with my competition."

The woman chuckled. "Now, as a professional journalist, I have to keep neutral, Ms. Roberts, so I certainly can't pass along to you any of the comments of my colleagues." She paused, and let the words simply saunter off with their meaning fully intact. "But I'm sure we can find something else to discuss."

Dar checked the time on the computer screen. "Probably, but it needs to be now, because I've got conferences starting in an hour and a half." She got up, pausing only to type a quick message and send it. "What's your poison?"

"Anything." The reporter responded promptly.

Dar looked up, with a devilish grin and watched the woman wince.

"Oh, I should not have said that." Cruicshank mourned. "I just know I'm going to end up regretting it. The one thing everyone agrees on is that you have a very twisted sense of humor."

"Nah." Dar gestured toward the door. "Most people think I don't have one at all." She locked her PC and came around the desk. "There's a sushi place next door that's fast and something less than noisy."

"Phew." The reporter followed her out. "I decided to try a little place near my hotel yesterday and boy did I end up regretting it. I think the grease inside was older than I am."

Dar held the door then went out after her. "Sounds like a place I'd love." She cheerfully stated giving Maria a brief wave. "Lunch."

Maria waved back, then cleared her throat a bit. "Dar, by any chance did you speak with..."

"Yes, she's fine, she doesn't need anything, she wishes she were here, and I sent my mother over to keep her company." Dar rattled off on her way to the outer door. "But if you want to send her chocolate ice cream, go for it."

Maria covered her mouth to stifle a laugh, as she watched them leave. She shook her head, then turned to flip through her phone directory until she found the number she was looking for. Just as she was about to dial, the outer door opened again and Mayte slipped inside. "Bueno. I am glad you are here. Please pay attention, so you know the next time what to do, yes?"

Mayte came around the desk and knelt down, watching obediently. "Mama, Kerry's friend, Colleen, just came to the office and said to tell everyone who is talking that Kerry did not get hit by Dar. Did you know that?"

Maria stopped in mid dial and clicked the phone off. "Did I know that it was not so? I never once even thought that it was. Was there people saying that?"

"She said that there were, but I did not hear anything like that," Mayte said. "People do not say such things to me, I think, because they are afraid you will hit them."

"Good." Maria nodded briskly. "I will send a note to Conchita and Rose, and those others so whatever they are saying, they will stop. I have got them good chained."

"Trained, mama." Mayte murmured. "But I am glad it is not true. I would not like to think Kerry could get hurt that way."

Maria leaned on her desk. "I will tell you something. Dar may be many, many things and some people may think she is tough, and mean, and would do something like that. But I know in my heart that before she would do any little thing to hurt Kerry, she would faster jump off the building."

Mayte nodded. "I think so too." She hesitated. "But mama, I did hear something that really bothered me just before. Some people are saying that they are going to break up, and they have heard Kerry talk about leaving. Do you think that's true?"

Maria turned in her chair and stared at her daughter. "Como?" She said, astonished. "They told you that? Who told you that?"

Mayte shook her head. "No, they did not tell me, Mama, I heard. It was in the bathroom. They did not know I was there." She explained. "One was the woman who works over near the little room with all the books here, and the other I did not know."

Maria was quiet for a brief time, as she pondered what to do. "Mayte, no, I do not think that is true at all." She finally said. "But we must find out who is saying these things, and why they are saying them."

"Okay." Her daughter agreed. "Then we can throw food at them, yes?"

"Tch." Maria gave her a look. "That was not funny."

"Mama, yes it was." Mayte told her. "Kerry said it was very funny. She is so sad there are no pictures." She got to her feet. "But, yes, we should find out who is being so mean, and make them stop it. I know it would hurt Kerry very much if she heard someone say that. I think she really is very devoted."

"Si." Her mother agreed. "First, let me do this thing I want to show you. Have you gone for lunch yet?"

Mayte fidgeted a little. "I was going to meet someone for lunch, Mama."

Maria looked at her, then made a clucking sound. Mayte blushed, and shrugged. "It is not that person with the pins again, is it?"

Mayte shook her head.

"Dios Mio." Maria dialed the phone. "Please god, that you find someone nice like Kerrisita who I don't have to worry about being a pincushion."

Mayte sighed. "It would be nice if Kerry were twins." She admitted mournfully.

Her mother paused, and gave her a look.

"Don't you think so?"

"Dios Mio." Maria glanced at the ceiling, then looked down as the phone was answered. "Hello, Senor Clemente? Si, this is Maria. Yes, I have something I need for you to do for me."

ANDREW LOOKED UP as the door slammed, recognizing one of the two women in charge of the computers. She stopped and looked around, then headed determinedly toward him. Since he was the only one left in the trailer, it wasn't unexpected, so he turned and faced her waiting in neutral silence.

"I'm looking for the crew chief," the woman said, stopping in front of him.

Andrew rotated his head and looked round the small trailer. "He ain't here." He drawled politely.

"I can see that. Where is he? I need to speak to him right now." Shari snapped.

"Wall." Andrew sniffed. "I do believe he said he was goin' to get him some lunch."

Shari looked at her watch. "When?"

"'Bout half hour past."

Visibly disgusted, Shari turned and regarded the trailer. "Did he say where?" She turned again and stared at Andrew. "With all this going on, how could he have just left?"

"He was hungry?" Mild, blue eyes blinked back at her. "Feller's entitled to have him some lunch."

"Not on my dime." The woman paused. "Did I meet you somewhere before? Or are you just from around here?"

A corner of Andrew's lip twitched. "Ah do believe we have never met. I surely would have remembered it."

"Whatever." Shari turned and headed for the door. "When he gets back, you tell him to call me. Otherwise, I can arrange for him to find another job." She turned, pausing on the steps out. "Sure you can remember all that?"

"Ah do believe I can," Andy said. "If that there feller does come back, ah will surely tell him."

Halfway out the door, Shari stopped. "If?"

Andy got up and stretched, his hands touching the roof of the trailer as he shook the kinks out of his tall frame. "Yeap. He done took all that there paperwork with him, and ah figure he probly headed back to his office or something."

"Shit." Shari slammed the door and stomped down the steps making the wall of the trailer shake.

Andrew lowered his arms and chuckled, half turning as the back door opened and the supervisor returned wiping his hands off on the tails of his shirt.

"Hey, did I hear that woman in here?" The super asked.

"Yeap." Andy nodded. "I done told her you took off for the day."

The super started laughing. "You did?" He walked over and slapped Andrew on the back. "Damn, I like you Ugly. I'm gonna give you a damn raise." He went to his desk and looked out the window. "There she blows...I mean goes...what'd she want, anyway?"

Andrew returned to his sorting task, making marks on a sheet of paper. "Ah do not know," he answered honestly. "Just wanted to talk to you."

"Ahhh...it'll wait." The super sat down at his desk. "Last thing she asked me to do was submit one of her orders six times. What kind of bullshit was that? Must be nuts."

Andy's eyebrow lifted. One thing he was fairly sure of was that whatever the woman did, it was for a purpose, and the purpose was probably something he wasn't going to like.

Just like he didn't like the woman herself.

"WHAT?" Kerry frowned, listening to Mark's voice on the cell phone. "Tell me this again?" She glanced up as Ceci re-entered the living room. "They said what?"

"It's a crock, boss." Mark sounded more than peeved. "Son of a bitch. I called them to find out a ship status on the order, and they told me it was on hold because they were out of stock."

Kerry's one good eye narrowed. "You didn't hear that when you placed it the other day?"

"Nope, I had a seven day delivery quoted," Mark said. "So I called our rep, and he said there wasn't anything he could do–out of stock is out of stock— but he could get us hooked up through a distribution channel provider."

"At list price," Kerry said.

"Yeah."

"Problems?" Ceci sat down on the love seat and picked up her teacup, sipping it as she watched Kerry's face. Her usual good humor had vanished, and the gentle planes had hardened into a much sterner profile.

"Bastards." Kerry murmured. "Mark, that can't be an accident. We're all using the same gear. Someone got to someone."

"That's what I thought." Mark agreed readily. "But the rep won't budge, said someone above him released the shipment, some big customer apparently."

Kerry folded her arm over her stomach and stared past the glass doors. "We're big customers, Mark."

"That's what I told him. And told him. And told him," Mark said. "I don't think there was squat he could do, Kerry. I even asked to talk to his boss and got told he was out of the country."

"Pfft." Kerry snorted in derision.

"So what do you want to do? Go with the distribution order? Maybe we can shave off some costs somewhere else?"

Kerry exhaled, wondering really what her options were. If they lost the advantage their discount gave them, could she make it up somewhere else? The project was so important, could she risk it?

What would Dar do?

Kerry turned her head and focused her vision on the picture just to one side of the television, the one where Dar was looking right at the camera, and seemingly right into her eyes.

Hmm.

"Mark?"

"Still here, boss." Mark spoke through the ever present rattling of keys. "You got any great ideas? I was even surfing around our inventory to see if we can pull from stock, but we just don't have enough units for the full order."

"Call that jerk back up, and tell him that I said if he doesn't shake that order loose, we're going with another vendor's gear."

Silence. "Um...okay." Mark hesitated.

"Company wide."

Longer silence. "You're kidding, right?"

"Nope," Kerry said. "They want to lose a top tier partner? Fine. I'll get two other infrastructure companies in here giving me bids by the weekend, and believe me my friend, they'll be more than happy not only to give us better prices, but tell the press all about it as loud as they can."

More silence.

"You want me to call him?" Kerry asked.

"No, I'll do it." Mark recovered hastily. "No problem, matter of fact, I'd enjoy the heck out of it. Lemme call you back after I talk to him, okay?"

"Okay."

Kerry folded the phone up and laid it on her stomach letting out a long breath before she glanced over at Ceci. "Sometimes, you just have to be a bitch."

Ceci leaned on the arm of the love seat, her gray eyes wryly twinkling. "Kerry, don't take this the wrong way, but you'd have to channel the Wicked Witch of the West with terminal PMS to come off as a really good bitch. You're just too cute."

Her guts still churning in side, Kerry nevertheless managed a wry grin. "Yeah. I know. Dar says the same thing." She admitted. "Even my getting a tattoo really doesn't up the intimidation factor."

"You?" Ceci sat up. "Got a tattoo?"

"I sure did." Kerry got up off the couch and walked over, crouching next to her mother-in-law and pulling her t-shirt down off one shoulder. "See?" She watched the puzzled, then charmed expression cross Ceci's face and smiled as their eyes met again.

"What did Dar say when she saw that?" Ceci asked. "It's absolutely gorgeous, by the way. You found a great artist."

"Mm." Kerry relived the warmth of the moment. "She didn't say much. But she liked it." She got up and plopped back down onto the couch.

"I bet she did," Ceci said. "What made you decide to get that done? I never figured you for the pain loving type." She settled back in the love seat and tucked her bare feet up under her, leaning on the arm as she watched Kerry squirm around on the couch.

"Well," Kerry stretched out, resting her head on the thickly padded arm, "I'm not. I hate needles almost as much as Dar does."

"That's saying something." Ceci commented wryly. "I always timed her checkups for when Andy was home, because he was the only one who could hold her down long enough for them to inoculate her."

Kerry spared a moment to imagine that. Her partner had a considerable amount of strength, and she could easily imagine her terrorizing the nurses. "Well, considering what happened to her in the hospital that one time, I can't say I really blame her. I know I was an adult when I had my one horror show and how it affected me, so..." She glanced up at Ceci, who now had a pensive look on her face. "Anyway, it was when Dar was in New York. I finished boxing class, and I guess that, plus talking with the guys, plus the smell of a new Harley...I don't know. I think I just went nuts for the night."

"Ah." The older woman nodded.

They were both quiet for a brief time. Then Kerry sighed. "It was just something I wanted to do," she said. "And you know I was worried about what Dar would say."

"About that?" Ceci's eyebrows popped up like a surprised meerkat.

"About me doing it." Kerry turned and grabbed her cell phone again as it rang. "Yes?" She answered it, pushing her disordered hair out of the way. "Hey Mark. What's up? Did you get through to that guy?"

Mark sounded as though he was out of the office for a change, traffic sounding behind him instead of the usual humming bustle of the MIS center. "I did, boss. He's gonna call me back." He told her. "He was not a happy guy."

"I'm not a happy gal," Kerry retorted, "so we're even. Did he really think he'd just get away with that game that easily?"

"I dunno." Mark sighed. "I'm just grabbing something for lunch. I passed DR heading to the sushi place with that reporter. Glad she wasn't there when this hit the fan."

Mm. Sushi. Kerry stifled a grin, recalling the little place she'd found that had been there for years and escaped Dar's notice somehow. It was small, but the service was good and they had a table in the back where the little waitresses always recognized them. "That reporter's connected with the ship bid." She told Mark. "Guess they didn't antagonize Dar too badly, if she's eating with them."

"Yeah." Mark agreed. "She looked nice enough, not like that scruffy guy who came in here last time." A siren blared. "Well, soon as I hear back on our order, I'll give you a buzz, okay? I'm almost to the pizza place."

"Right." Kerry agreed. "Have a good pizza, Mark." She hung up, and felt her nostrils twitch just a trifle as she acknowledged a brief pang thinking about Dar having lunch with another woman. It was extremely unclassy, and stupid, and pointless, so she just waited it out and after a second it passed, and she could mentally roll her eyes at herself.

If there was one thing she knew she could trust completely, it was Dar in that regards. Heck, Dar had turned away offers even before they were barely friends, much less involved with each other. She was steadfast and honest, and it bothered Kerry to even have the littlest of reactions to the thought of anything otherwise.

Ah well. She released a long sigh, and dismissed the thought. "So anyway, that's how I ended up with a tattoo."

Ceci had been quietly watching her. "Did Dar mind you doing it? I don't really think she'd object. I know she really wanted one when she was younger, but her father and her own dislike of the apparatus dissuaded her."

"No." Kerry shook her head. "I don't think she minded at all. She thinks it's kind of...um..." She blushed slightly. "Well..."

"Well, it's her name on your chest." The gray eyes twinkled. "So I'm sure it's quite sexy."

"Yeah." Kerry's blush deepened and she scrubbed one hand over her cheek. "But it's not just that, I think? I think it means something else, too."

Ceci pursed her lips. "I think it means for her the kind of permanence she was always looking for." Dar's mother spoke up unexpectedly. "I didn't understand that for such a long time."

Kerry nodded, a lump rising in her throat. "That's what I wanted it to mean." She could hear the husky note in her voice, and she stopped speaking to let it clear.

Ceci fiddled with her cup as the silence lengthened. "Want more?" She offered. "I'd offer to bake cookies, but we both know how that's going to turn out."

Kerry smiled. "Sure. How about you get some tea, and I'll bake the cookies? I've got a black eye, not a broken leg." She got up from the couch, suddenly wanting something to do. "Besides, I know they won't go to waste later on if we have extra."

"Eh." Ceci amiably joined her. "That's for sure."

"Hey, any chance of Dad stopping by after work?"

"With cookies in the offing? Absolutely."

Kerry chuckled, putting aside her worries for now. There would be time enough to worry about them later.

Chapter Six

"OKAY. SO NOW I have some questions." Pat Cruicshank said, as the waitress set down two tiny cups of tea. "You ready?"

Dar was in the back corner seat one arm spread along the bench back and her legs extended almost into the aisle imperiling the service. "You can ask," she said. "No guarantee I'll answer." She picked up the small cup and set it down in front of her, adding a packet of sugar to it before daring a sip.

"Question one." The reporter went on gamely. "How come you go to a sushi restaurant, and don't order any sushi?"

Dar's eyebrow quirked. "Any raw sushi, you mean?"

"Yeah."

"I've swam in the water they pull those fish from," Dar replied, with a brief flash of white teeth. "Take mine cooked, thanks."

Pat pondered that, then made a face. "Do you have any idea what you've just done for my love of raw tuna?"

"You asked," Dar said. "So let me ask you something."

Cruicshank looked slightly dubious. "Okay."

"What's your angle in this? Just an opposing viewpoint?" Dar watched the reporters face without seeming to, propping her head up with one hand. "I'm fed up with the games, and that includes the scruffy little reporters they keep sending to bother my staff."

The black woman looked down at herself, then back at Dar, her eyebrow lifting. "You talking to me?" She indicated her chest with her thumb.

Dar's lips twitched. "Your predecessors," she clarified.

"Well." She folded her hands on her pad. "Yes, it's an opposing viewpoint, and that's useful for the story."

"Ah." Dar felt faintly disappointed. She'd been hoping the filming team had started to see through Michelle and Shari's façade of noble underdogs. "Yeah, I guess someone has to interview Goliath and get his perspective."

Cruicshank chuckled a little. She glanced up as the waitress returned, bringing them plates of various pieces of sushi. "Thanks." She looked at her tuna, and then looked at Dar.

Dar popped a piece of well cooked egg on rice into her mouth and winked.

The reporter left her plate for a moment and concentrated on her table mate. "But you know I had to pull all kinds of background video and all that on you for the story, since you were cast as this big, old villain. All I could dig up just showed you as this lady knight in shining armor saving everyone's behind on national television."

Dar chewed her sushi and kept a straight face. "There's film of me eating kittens, but they won't release it to the press. Too disturbing."

Another chuckle. "No way because if it existed, trust me, those gals at Telegenics would have already had it up on a poster." Cruicshank disagreed. "So here I was having to reconcile what I was seeing with what I was hearing. I decided to come and see for myself."

"Uh huh." Dar munched steadily through her meal. "Better eat that before it swims off."

The reporter gave her a mock evil look, but picked up her chopsticks and bravely doused the fish in soy sauce then took a bite of it.

Dar took the opportunity to remove her PDA and glance at it, then flip it open to scribble a short note before she sent it out. She laid the unit down on the table and picked up another piece of sushi. "I'm not the one you should be talking to."

The reporter blinked. "Excuse me?"

Dar swallowed. "I'm not in charge of this project. The only reason Telegenics is focusing on me is for personal reasons. It's not my bid."

Cruicshank put her chopsticks down. "It's not?" She asked. "I don't understand. I thought..."

Dar managed a mildly amused expression. "I'm the CIO of the company. I do actually have more important things to do than baby-sit what is, on our level, a midrange contract being handled by our VP Ops. Who, by the way, has already done more than a dozen of them this year."

"That would be...Kerry Stuart?" The reporter asked. "She is your operations vice president, right?"

Dar nodded.

"And..."

"And my partner." It didn't even give her a twinge to say it, just a sweetness that she could taste on the tip of her tongue as the words rolled off it. "So, if you want a real perspective on the bid, you need to interview her."

The reporter scribbled a note and then sniffed reflectively. She went back to her lunch plate and took another bite of sushi before she continued her questioning. "All right. I'll do that," she said. "You're very open about your relationship, aren't you?"

"No point in being anything else," Dar answered.

"Does that bother your co-workers? Must be a little awkward sometimes."

Was it? Dar neatly bit a piece of shrimp in half and chewed it. "Not anymore" She shrugged. "At the beginning it took a while for everyone to get used to it, but now...eh." She picked up a rice grain and ate it. "Biggest problem Kerry has now is all the people who hang around her trying to get her to get me to do things because they're too chickenshit to ask."

Cruicshank burst out laughing. "Oh, that puts a different perspective on it. You know, my colleagues asked your counterparts about that, and they said they just treated each other as business associates at work."

"That explains a lot." Dar drawled. "I don't stop loving Kerry while we're in the office, why would I act like I did?" The words came out almost in a rush, and after she said them, she found herself somewhat shocked that she had.

The reporter was a little surprised also, but she covered it up by writing several more notes. "Well, they seem to think it's more professional," she said. "What do you think about that? Do you think they're right? After all, there are a lot of people who have to deal with you both on a daily basis, and maybe they don't feel that comfortable knowing about your relationship."

Ah. Good question, Dar admitted to herself. In fact, this woman was full of surprisingly good questions. "I think at first a lot of people had a big problem with it." She answered honestly. "But then, ninety percent of the company had a big problem with me to begin with. I think having Kerry as a buffer has far more helped than hurt. We...we tried to keep it out of the office at first, but you know how offices are. Every time we passed in the hallway, it would make the weekly newsprint."

"Uh huh." Pat nodded in complete understanding. "I work in an office with forty other thirty and forty-something's and believe me, there's always drama everywhere. That's why I asked. Because my boss got involved with one of our top reporters, and for a month, it *was* the news."

Dar chuckled under her breath.

"And it was hard, you know?" Pat went on. "Everyone was tiptoeing around the subject and it made life real hard for a while."

Dar grasped her last piece of sushi between her chopsticks and neatly positioned it, then dunked one end into her soy sauce. "You break up after that?" She asked casually, glancing up at her tablemate as she took a bite.

The woman's expression confirmed her guess in a heartbeat.

"So yeah, eventually everyone got over it." Dar continued, breaking the silence. "Now we only get the odd remark from clients in the bible belt." She finished her lunch and took a sip of the now cooled tea, picking up her PDA as it beeped.

"You know what? You are just too damn sharp, Ms. Roberts." The reporter sighed, after a few more stunned moments. "Here I thought I was being so slick and you just see right through it."

Hey sweetie! Are you sucking up more fame again?

Dar smiled and scribbled a reply. That's me, Fame-Sucker. How's your head?

There was a brief pause before the answer came.

Spinning from your mother's jokes about how much

chocolate I put into your chocolate chip cookies. Other than that, I'm fine.

Ah. **Dar just kept herself from licking her lips.** Well, I'm going to keep that afternoon conference call short. I don't think my reporter friend will be sticking around much longer. She might want to talk to you tomorrow or sometime though.

Is she nice?

Dar glanced at her lunch companion, who was taking advantage of her tapping to finish her own lunch. Very nice and pretty sharp. Not like the last one.

Kerry's rolled eyes were almost visible in the reply. About time. I figured she must be okay if you had lunch with her.

Dar read that response twice, then hit reply. Eh. Slim pickings since you're not here.

No, I'm here baking with your mom. Why don't you get hold of Dad and bring him home with you?

Dad, cookies, Kerry...maybe she'd stop for flowers. Dar paused in her thought, and then rewound it. Maybe she'd stop for a bottle of wine. You're on. See you later—don't burn yourself.

Heh heh. Yes, mommy Dar. Have a cup of tea for me.

Dar closed her PDA and slipped it into her pocket leaning back again as her table companion finished up her lunch and wiped her lips. "Sorry if I shook you up a little. If it's any consolation, I've been there." Dar told her, with a faint grin.

"You certainly did shake me up." Cruicshank agreed ruefully. "Or was that a very clever way to get me to stop asking questions?"

Dar's eyes twinkled. "Maybe it was just a way to get enough time to finish eating."

The woman held one hand up. "Okay, touché." She looked up as the waitress came over, and neatly plucked the check from the woman?s hands. "I'll take that, thanks."

Dar poured herself another cup of tea, drinking it slowly as the reporter settled their bill. It hadn't been a bad interview, she thought, but it hadn't really given the woman anything concrete to use either.

Had it?

She frowned, having the distinct feeling suddenly that she'd gotten more personal than she'd intended. What if the reporter chose to slant the story that way and it ended up as part of the show?

Kerry wouldn't like that. Dar was pretty sure. She'd had to face the press with that front and center more than she'd ever wanted to and hated every moment of it. Maybe she should have discussed the whole thing with Kerry before agreeing to the interview?

But how was she to know the reporter was going to ask that stuff?

"Well," Cruicshank folded her credit card receipt and put it neatly into her wallet, "okay, so I have to talk to Kerry Stuart about the ships, but one of the things that most caught my eye about the information I gathered was the way your company responds to a crisis."

Eh? Dar watched the train she'd thought they were riding on take a flip. She raised a polite eyebrow in question, but remained silent.

"The most spectacular thing I saw was the ATM outage on the East Coast," the reporter said, "played out on national television. I'd like to talk to you about how that all went down, if you don't mind."

That seemed harmless enough. "Sure." Dar got up. "I've got about forty five more minutes."

"I'll try to make them count." Cruicshank promised. "Is there some place we can pick up a cup of coffee on the way back? I'm still on west coast time."

"We have some inside the office." Dar led the way out of the restaurant, giving a casual wave at two of the marketing regional managers who had just sat down to eat. "Unless you'd like to try Cuban coffee."

"Cuban coffee? Okay, sure. How bad could it be?"

Dar grinned evilly and pushed her way out the door.

"WELL?" KERRY ANGLED the phone against her ear as she mixed items into a mixing bowl. "What's the scoop?" She'd given Mark three hours to hear back from their vendor, and her patience was wearing thin. "Listen, if he won't talk to you, Mark, I know who he can talk to."

"Relax, Kerry. He just called." Mark sounded much happier. "He's pissed. Really, really pissed, but they put the order through. He said he's in a lot of hot water."

"Tell him he could be in boiling. I was going to sic Dar on him. Can you imagine what she'd have said?"

"Um...yeah." Mark chuckled wanly. "Actually, I can. But whatever, he caved. So we're cool. I was just gonna call you."

Kerry felt her shoulders relax. Despite her fierce words, she knew damn well they didn't have time to spec out a new vendor's gear and if their current partner hadn't given in, she really didn't have much of a backup plan to replace them.

Dar, of course, was in reserve, but Kerry really hated to pull that card out unless she really had to. It made her feel like she wasn't capable of doing her own job if she had to go running to her partner for help all the time.

She felt good that she'd been able to resolve this problem by herself. "Okay, so when can we expect delivery?"

"Monday." Mark sounded a touch smug. "I think you scared the crap out of them. Maybe they went and bought those units at distribution, and just resold 'em to us at our price."

Kerry chuckled. "Whatever it takes," she said. "We've given them so much business they've got nothing to gripe about." She pulled out a baking tray and set the fish fillets she'd just coated onto it's already lightly oiled surface. "Okay, thanks, Mark. I'm going to set up a touch point meeting tomorrow afternoon for the whole team, just so we can see where we are."

"Gotcha."

"See you tomorrow."

Mark almost hung up, and then paused. "Hey, Kerry?"

"Mm?"

"Are you feeling better?"

Kerry blinked her bad eye, which had pretty much opened fully during the course of the day. The swelling had gone down, and now it was merely tender to the touch. "I feel a lot better, thanks." She told Mark. "At least I can see out of both eyes now and I just look like half a raccoon."

"Cool deal." Mark replied. "I was wondering because I just saw big D, and she looked real antsy so I was hoping it wasn't because you were feeling bad."

"Ah." Kerry pondered. "Well, we're having a family get together tonight."

"Oh. Um..."

"I'm cooking."

"Oh!" Mark's tone altered to one of understanding. "Cool! Hey, have a great time, okay?"

"Thanks, we will." Kerry hung up. She scattered a handful of crushed pistachio nuts over the filets, then covered them and set them in the refrigerator.

She was alone now, Ceci having headed back to her boat home to pick up a few things for the dinner. Chino was curled up on her bed in the corner of the kitchen, and Kerry had a soft new age CD playing in the living room.

It was quiet, and peaceful, and it smelled like freshly baked cookies. Kerry leaned against the counter and gazed out at the pretty sunlit ocean and indulged in a brief moment of mindless observation.

She went to the refrigerator, removed a bottle of ice tea, then headed to the sliding door and slipped outside into the warm air. It smelled like warm sand and salt outside, and she sat down in their swinging chair with a sense of satisfaction.

Chino had scuttled out after her, and she stood up on her hind legs and put her front ones on the porch rail, gazing out at the sea with an intelligent expression.

"You like that, Chi?" Kerry sucked slowly at her ice tea, swinging back and forth in the chair. "Want to go for a walk on the beach? Just you and me? We can find some sticks for you to bring back to mommy Dar, how about it?"

"Growf." The dog dropped down and came over to her, licking her knee affectionately and sitting down next to the swing chair, her tail sweeping the stone tiles rhythmically.

"You're so cute." Kerry scratched the dog's soft ears. "You know what, Chi? We're going to the cabin this weekend. How do you like that?"

The tail swept faster, as the Labrador recognized a word she knew.

"You like the cabin, right? I like the cabin too. I think I like it better than even this place." Kerry confided. "How about I teach you to ride on the back of the motorcycle, hmm? Would you like that? Your ears all flying back?" She tugged one ear.

"Growf!" Chino wiggled her entire body back and forth.

Kerry chuckled. The sun was already behind the line of the condos, so the porch was in shade. A cool breeze came up off the water, and she squirmed into a more comfortable position, and exhaled in contentment.

Okay, so where am I at the moment? She let her eyes follow a lazy white cloud as it drifted overhead. I've got my project going, the equipment's ordered, my people are in place, and the wiring is going. I'm doing good.

She nodded once or twice.

It's a good plan. I know the technology works. So the only question left is — how do I price it so that it comes in under what that low balling bitch Michelle comes up with? "I know she's going to lie, Chi."

"Rowf?"

"She's going to low ball that bid, sure as I'm sitting here just like she did everything else. But I don't want to fall into that game."

"Rr." Chino rested her chin on Kerry's knee.

"I don't know what I'm going to do about that." Kerry told her pet seriously. "I want to win this one, Chi. I really do." She ruffled the dog's fur, then she let her head rest back against the chair, simply enjoying the lazy moment.

DAR OPENED THE door to the condo, poking her head inside and listening to a surprising lack of sound. "Ker?"

When she wasn't answered, she entered and stood aside to let her father come in behind her, then shut the door and glanced around curiously. "Maybe she took Chino for a walk."

"Fuzzball likes that." Andrew allowed.

With a faint shake of her head, Dar ducked into her study and dropped off her laptop case, then went toward the kitchen. She paused as she spotted a Labrador tail outside on the porch, and changed direction. "Ah. Maybe not."

She slid the door open and looked out, then emerged onto the porch with a grin as Chino scrambled up to greet her. Kerry was sleeping soundly on the swinging chair and only slowly stirred as she heard the noise their pet was making. "Uh?"

"Hey." Dar managed to get past the canine roadblock and sat down on the chair next to her partner.

"Oh...bwah." Kerry blinked herself awake, her hands reaching out instinctively to wrap themselves around Dar. "I fell asleep."

"Really?"

"Uh huh." Kerry stifled a yawn, and then rested her head against Dar's shoulder. "I didn't mean to do that. I was just going to relax for a minute, then take Chi for a walk on the beach." She gave her partner a little hug. "But I guess waking up to find you here is a pretty good substitute."

"You guess?" Dar reached over and tilted Kerry's head up a little to study her injured eye. The swelling had gone down quite a bit, returning a more normal shape to her face, and the bruise seemed a little less lurid. Two pale green pupils looked back at her, rather than the morning's one eye, and she smiled in reaction. "I missed you today."

Kerry grinned, her eyes lighting up from within. "How did your meetings go?"

"Pretty good." Dar leaned back and braced her foot against the rail, rocking them both gently. "Hacking calmed down today. I only saw three attempts, and they were all pretty lame."

"Think you scared them off yesterday?"

"Maybe." Dar said. "Dad's inside. Mom go back to the boat?"

Kerry nodded. "Guess we should go inside and be sociable, now that you woke me up and all." She nudged Dar affectionately. "I need to go put some water on my face. I could go right back to sleep."

"C'mon." Dar stood, lifting her up at the same time. "That's a cute apron. I like the pocket."

Kerry looked down at herself. "Ah." She studied the position of the single, centered pouch, featuring a saucy looking gopher. "I wonder why, Gopher Dar?"

Dar pushed the sliding door open and entered the cool of the condo where her father had taken over the loveseat with Chino in adoring attention. "Look who I found outside."

Andrew looked up. "Hi there, kumquat." He greeted Kerry. "Spiffy looking battle wound you got there." He got up and came over to meet them, peering curiously at Kerry's face. "How in this earth did a feller kick you in there with all that stuff you put on your head?"

"Just bad timing." Kerry released her partner. "The toe of his boot caught me right in the gap here." She touched the front of her face. "It happened so fast, all I knew was one minute I was turning, the next I was on the mat. Boom."

"Wall." Andy turned her face to the light a little. "Ain't a patch on what Dardar there used to get. Should be all fixed up in no time." He patted her cheek gently.

"That's what I hear." Kerry grinned, ducking past him and heading for the downstairs bedroom. "Be right back."

Andrew settled back down on the couch, and Dar took a seat across from him on the larger one. "Been a hell of a week." Dar said, with a grimace. "How's it going on your end of things?"

"Wall now." Andrew spread both long arms out across the leather surface, and extended his legs, crossing them at the ankles. "Ah do believe I have been of some use to you ladies during this here week."

"Yeah?" Dar half grinned.

Kerry poked her head out of the bedroom. "Yeah?"

"Yeap." Andy looked pleased with himself. "Soon as you come on out here, kumquat, I'll tell all about it."

Hmm. Kerry patted her face dry. Maybe it'd been a better day than even she realized.

HALF AN HOUR later, the fish were in the oven, Ceci had returned with a bucket of vegetables and dip to snack on. They were all enjoying a beer as the few lines of sunset peeking between the condos painted the beach outside a coral pink.

Dar was sprawled in one corner of the couch with Kerry next to her. One of Kerry's legs was slung over hers, and she was happy to sit there and listen to the conversation as she slowly sipped at her drink.

It was times like this when she understood the measure of change she'd experienced in the last few years. Aside from having a partner, someone to share her everyday life with, she'd also regained a family that had been lost to her.

It was almost as though she were a completely different person sometimes. Not inside, because Dar knew she herself hadn't changed any, but outside, where other people saw her. Instead of being a loner, mysterious and threatening, she had become someone who even her co-workers treated as one of the corporate family now.

As though falling in love had made her much more understandable to them.

This was odd because it had made her much less understandable to herself sometimes. Dar gazed quietly at the tan thigh covering hers, half smiling as she slid her fingers over Kerry's skin and savored its warmth.

Kerry flexed her leg in response, rubbing the inside her heel against Dar's calf, while she kept on talking, explaining what she'd been doing on the ship.

"So, we finally got everyone to agree to what we wanted to do and give us space." Kerry said. "But I tell you, it wasn't easy."

"Naw." Andrew shook his head. "Nobody likes to give up a nickel's worth of space on board one of them there things, kumquat. Every squinch is worth the earth," he said. "Though them folks should count their blessings. Worst I saw in there was five bodies bunking up together and them's with their own bathroom."

"Oo." Ceci chewed on a celery stick. "Luxury." She poked Andrew in the ribs. "More than six inches of drawer space and I bet they don't hot bunk."

Kerry paused, looking at them. Then she turned and looked Dar questioningly.

"Remind me to take you on a tour of an aircraft carrier next time we're near one." Dar told her.

"O...kay." Kerry amiably returned her attention to her in-laws. "So you're saying they've got it pretty good, compared to what sailors in the service have, right?"

Andrew shrugged one shoulder. "Get used to anything." He commented.

"Yes." Ceci interpreted. "The first time Andy took me to see where he lived on a ship; I nearly took a header overboard. Twelve stories up. Horrific."

"Wasn't that bad."

"Oh, yes it was. Nobody was more relieved than I was when you got your officer's promotion."

"Was it that bad?" Kerry whispered to her partner.

Dar pondered the question, as she watched her parents playfully arguing across from her. "To be honest," she whispered back, "it was the one single thing I knew would keep me out of ship duty."

"Really?"

Dar nodded. "A rack is a six inch foam mattress, with a space underneath to store your stuff. It's got a curtain across it so you can sleep in the daytime, and they're stacked three atop each other."

Kerry's eyes widened.

"Hot bunking is two or three guys sharing the same bunk in turn."

Kerry's eyes nearly came out of her head.

"Hey, beats a foxhole." Dar grinned slightly. "And the food's a lot better."

"Brr." Kerry shuddered. "Well, to hear those guys talk, you'd think I was trying to take away their Christmas presents. But we worked it out."

"Yeap." Andrew nodded. "Heard them hollerin' about the same thing over on the boat I'm at. Don't think they worked out the same deal you did...they were still hollerin' this morning."

"Heh." Kerry smirked a little.

"Them women running that thing don't know much about getting folks to cooperate." The big ex-SEAL continued. "All they do is run to and back making a lot of noise." He folded his arms over his chest. "Ah do not like them."

Dar sighed inwardly. She hadn't expected her father to like them, and it made her wonder how, once upon a time, she had.

Youthful dementia?

"They're not too fond of us," Kerry said. "I thought Michelle was going to chuck up a kidney when she had to call and ask me for that circuit." She leaned back against Dar. "Thanks for sending those pricing lists over by the way."

Dar wrapped her arm around Kerry's waist and rested her chin against her partner's shoulder. "We know for sure they're paying more than we are." She agreed.

Andrew shifted and took a swig of his beer before he answered. "Wall now, something funny's going on there," he said. "Either them women are just nuttier than a squirrel, or I don't know what. They put that damn order in six times, and not one body there can figure out why."

Dar cocked her head in confusion. "Huh?"

Kerry's eyes narrowed. "Six times?"

"Yeap."

"Must be some kind of mistake," Dar said. "How did you know? You got six copies of the invoice?"

Her father nodded. "We figured first it was one big truckload of that stuff you all use, but I was sorting the pages, and they just kept..." He made a rotating gesture with one hand. "Didn't make much sense."

"Oh no." Kerry said. "It makes perfect sense."

Everyone looked at her. Dar blew gently in her ear. "It does?"

Kerry turned her head and her eyes almost crossed. She blinked. "I got a call today from our infrastructure supplier. Seems that all the stuff we need suddenly went out of stock."

Dar's eyebrows hiked right up.

"Do tell?" Andy murmured. "Wall then."

"Hmph." Ceci felt she understood enough of the conversation to contribute at least a token noise of disgusted agreement. She had no idea really of what was being discussed, but the expressions on both Kerry's and Dar's faces clued her into the fact that neither was happy.

"So you think —" Dar paused.

"Do you seriously think it was coincidence?" Kerry replied.

"No." Dar shook her head. "So what's the plan?"

Kerry felt that little tingle inside whenever she had to put her business skills out on display for Dar's perusal. She was good and she knew it, but she also knew Dar was more than good and no matter how long she worked with her, she never got over that little internal squiggle. "I had Mark call them, and tell them either they coughed up our order, or we'd switch vendors company wide."

Dar's eyes widened a little, more white showing around the deep blue centers.

Andrew whistled.

"My." Ceci murmured. "For some reason I'm getting the feeling that meant more to them than me threatening the same thing to Publix."

Dar cleared her throat. "And?"

"They caved. It's on the way." Kerry replied matter-of-factly. She exhaled in satisfaction. "And now that I know who paid those little buggers off, I almost wish they hadn't."

Dar digested the information briefly, and then smiled. "Nice." She gave Kerry a squeeze. "But what did you have in mind if they said no?" Threats aside, specing brand new gear they had no experience with in that time frame wasn't a realistic solution and she knew Kerry knew that.

"Oh, I was going to throw you at them." Kerry assured her. "I was just seeing what they were made of, and it turned out to be Swiss cheese." She patted Dar's muscular leg. "So it turned out okay, but now — now that makes sense, Dar. Don't you think? That has to be why they did it."

"Unless it's a mistake." Ceci commented mildly. "Someone hit the fax key too many times."

There was a brief moment of relative silence. "That could be." Dar said slowly. "But given what Kerry said about the vendor's reaction, I'd have to say it's not a mistake. If it was, they'd have just called and corrected it. I'm sure when they got the purchase order six times, someone said something."

"Well..." Kerry rolled her eyes.

"True enough, Dardar," Andy said. "Someone surely did say something, but someone was told to mind their own business."

So Dar felt angry, but more comfortable with this bit of business behind the backstabbing. The cellular transmitter was beyond Shari, but this kind of bullshit certainly wasn't. "Better keep an eye on that shipment." She warned Kerry.

"Ah surely will." Andy replied, with a half grin. "Since them fellers picked me to be in charge of that there part."

"Heh." Kerry picked up Dar's hand and kissed the knuckles, then got up and headed for the kitchen. "A tisket a tasket two bitches in a basket..." She warbled as she disappeared.

Dar chuckled and shook her head. "Damn, this just gets screwier and screwier." She sighed. "You having fun there, Dad?"

Her mother laughed.

Andrew gave a dignified sniff. "Ah do like to think ah am providing a useful service," he said. "And it surely is a good thing to know that general civilians are a damn sight dumber than most of the people I done worked with in blue and white suits."

They all laughed, and Dar relaxed into the couch again, letting the tensions of the day seep from her. Things were looking up she decided. She'd had a good interview, Kerry had handled a sticky problem with panache, and her father was having a kicking good time making trouble for her adversaries.

Life was good.

"Hey, Dar?" Kerry called from the kitchen. "Can I get a hand with all this?"

Life was very good. Dar launched herself off the couch and headed for the scent of baking fish and cookies. Things were working out nicely all around.

She only hoped it kept on going that way.

"MORNING MAYTE!" Kerry felt in a more than usual cheerful mood, and it showed as she sauntered across her outer office. "Did I miss any disasters yesterday?"

Mayte looked up in surprise. "No, not that they told me about," she replied. "Are you feeling better today?"

Kerry stopped at her inner door and looked back at her assistant. "Other than looking like an outclassed prizefighter, I feel great." She indicated her eye, which still sported a distinct bruise. "But Dar says I have to start wearing a helmet in practice from now on."

Mayte laughed. "Like a football one?"

"Exactly." Kerry agreed. "Dar's mom and dad were over last night, and they were goofing around with me, trying to figure out how to build one so I won't just keel right over with it on." She chuckled. "They're so funny. Mom kept trying to convince me to switch to Tai Chi."

"They are very nice people."

"Very." Kerry said. "And it's so funny, because they're a blast to hang out with. I could never imagine ever being that comfortable with any of my family. Drinking beer with my father? Good lord." She gave her head a little shake. "Anyway, so it was quiet here?"

"Si." Mayte nodded.

"Figured it was, if Dar went out for lunch." Kerry turned to enter her office. "Can you schedule me a project meeting for ten? I want to make sure we're all on track."

"Sure."

Kerry turned. "And if anyone wants to meet with me tomorrow, it has to be early. I'm taking off a little early to go down south."

Mayte cocked her head slightly in question.

"I need some time out at the cabin." Kerry grinned. "So nothing past 3 p.m., okay?"

"I will make sure." Mayte scribbled a note on her pad, and turned to her email as Kerry disappeared into her office. After a moment, she looked up, with a wryly impish expression, as she heard a delighted laugh coming from behind the door.

"CLEAR MY SCHEDULE." Dar paused just in front of Maria's desk. "I'm going to be in the closet all day."

Maria paused in mid type and looked up at her boss. "Como?" She peered at Dar with interest. "I did not think you were one to be in a closet Dar."

For a moment, Dar simply stared at her, and then she broke in to a grin, and let out a burst of laughter. "Oh, hell, you got that right Maria." She chuckled. "I never even knew what the term meant until after I left college and picked up a gay magazine in an airport somewhere."

Maria also chuckled. "You have always been right in the front of everything about how you are. It is a nice thing. I do not like people who make themselves different in their face from what is real."

Dar considered that for a minute, and then she nodded. "I don't like those kinds of people either. I think that's one of the things I always appreciated the most about you."

The older woman's eyes lit up.

Dar smiled, and turned to head for her office, opening her door and entering before Maria could really collect herself to answer. She walked over to her desk and set her laptop case down, then sat down in her chair and let her hands rest on her thighs.

She was in a very good mood for once. They'd had a wonderful time last night, and this morning she'd woken early, lying quietly before dawn thinking of her security project while she held Kerry in her arms. Somewhere in all that, whether from the peace or the simple pleasure, she'd suddenly had a breakthrough in the design.

A piece had fallen into place that she'd been missing, and now she had a new direction to go in the intricate programming latticework she was painstakingly putting together.

With a pleased chuckle, she took out her laptop and opened it, spurning her desktop since she knew she had to take the fledgling program down to the closet to test it out. She rubbed her hands together and waited for the machine to boot, and then she tilted back in her chair and set the laptop on her lap.

After another moment, she put her booted feet up on her desk and relaxed, glad beyond measure that she'd found yet another excuse to wear jeans in the office. She flexed her fingers, and started typing, humming slightly under her breath as the lines of code seemed to flow effortlessly.

"I LOVE IT." Kerry circled the new addition to her office, a weighted boxing dummy in the front corner where a big empty spot had been previously. Originally a work group desk had been there, but Kerry had it removed when she decided meetings would be held in meeting rooms and she hadn't really found anything to replace it with.

Hanging around its neck was a pair of boxing gloves that she took off and slid on her hands. The figure had a bland, wide-eyed face and a business suited body. She jabbed at it playfully, socking it in the nose and making it rock back and forth. "God, I just love it."

The door opened and Mayte poked her head in. "Did you say something?"

Kerry turned and held up her gloved fists. "This is spectacular."

She pronounced. "Who did it? I know it wasn't Dar...she can't keep a secret from me for beans anymore."

Her assistant blushed. "It was me." Mayte confessed. "Mama said for you to get chocolate, but I think this will be more useful, no?"

Kerry boxed at her with both hands, jiving a little with her body at the same time. "Mayte, you rock. I absolutely love this." She pointed a fist at the younger woman. "But I'm absolutely positive I'm not going to let you pay for it. I know what these cost."

"You do?" Mayte made a wry face.

"Almost got one for Dar." Kerry winked at her. "So either you cough up the receipt, or I'll just start stuffing bills in your purse until you scream for mercy."

Mayte appeared exquisitely pleased, but she shyly shook her head anyway. "Please, Kerry, you have done so much for me. It is a gift to me to be able to do something for you in return."

Kerry planted her fists on her hips, or at least as nearly as she could wearing boxing gloves. "Mayte..."

"Please?" Mayte begged. "It really was not so much. My uncle is the boxing instructor for our YMCA. He helped me to get it."

"Hmm..." Kerry produced a mock scowl, then relented, and let a chuckle escape instead. "Oh, all right." She moved forward. "C'mere."

Mayte entered the office and shut the door, walking over to Kerry and smiling as she was enveloped in a hug. "It is better than chocolate, right?"

"Well, chocolate is pretty good." Kerry gave her a last hug and stepped back. "But this lasts longer, and it can be just as much fun." She tapped her gloves together. "You want to try it?"

Mayte indicated her chest with her thumb. "Me?"

Kerry slid off the gloves and offered them. "Sure."

"Oh, no, no." Mayte grimaced wryly, holding her hands up in a warding off gesture. "Please, Kerry, if my mother ever knew I even put those on, she would go crazy!"

Kerry looked at the gloves, and then looked down at herself, before returning her gaze to Mayte's face. "Just what exactly does she think boxing turns you into?" She queried. "I'm not a candidate for a freak show...or at least I wasn't the last time I checked."

Her assistant turned a deep shade of coral. "No...no...it is not that,? she said. "It is just not what is considered proper in my culture."

Kerry had to laugh. "Mayte, it's not considered proper where I come from either. I have to admit if my mother ever saw me put these on, she'd just keel right over and we'd have to call 911." She winked at Mayte. "But you know what?"

"You do it anyhow."

"Uh huh." Kerry tied the gloves together and hung them back over the dummy's neck. "So if you ever get the urge—go for it." She headed back for her desk. "I won't tell anyone."

Mayte gazed at the dummy, and then she grinned. "Okay." She sidled back toward the door. "I am glad you like it." She disappeared, closing the door and leaving Kerry in peaceful silence.

"Oh, I really do." Kerry grabbed her mug. "I really, really do." She walked toward the door, punching at the air in the direction of the dummy all the way.

DAR RAISED HER head at the knock on the door. She was a little surprised since she'd given instructions not to be bothered. "Yeah?"

Mark entered and crossed the floor to sit down opposite her. "Hey, DR."

"Hi." Dar cracked her knuckles. "I'm in the middle of spawning an app. Is this important?"

Mark blinked in surprise. "Oh, sorry." He started to get up. "No, it's just about that thing in the conference center...didn't realize you were coding." He paused. "Man, been a long time since I've had to say that, huh?"

Dar's lips twitched, and then curled into a grin. "Yeah." She waved him back down. "But I can take a break."

Mark sat back down. "Good news and bad news." He paused. "Bad news first?"

"Always."

"It's an unreleased beta rig from Taiwan."

Dar scowled. "So no tracing the purchaser, is that what you're saying?"

"Yeah." Mark nodded. "I contacted the place where it was built...they've been going nuts because it's missing, and man, they were crawling all over my ass right through the phone trying to find out how I got it," he said. "If they were Star Trek fans, I'd have had them beaming right onto my desk, hands grabbing for sure."

"Ah."

'They want it back, big time."

"Uh huh. Bad enough to give us an exclusive license on it?"

Mark grinned like the pirate he was. "Man, you are so psychic." He sighed admiringly. "That's the good news. They want to do a deal with us. One of their guys is heading over here."

Dar sighed. "Doesn't help us figure out who it was." She nibbled the inside of her lip. "And if it wasn't who everyone thinks it was, then it could be someone who's on the inside here."

Mark frowned. "An employee?"

Dar nodded. "Yeah."

"That would suck."

Dar drummed her fingertips on her keyboard. "Yeah."

KERRY TUCKED HER notepad under her arm and prepared to leave the conference room. Her team was still milling around, discussing some of the items they had pending, but it had been a good meeting and she was pleased with their progress.

Mark walked over and perched on the edge of the conference table. "Did you hear from the wiring guy?"

"This morning." Kerry nodded. "He's started, but he says it's like trying to wire inside the New York subway system. Tough going."

"I bet." He nodded. "Hey, that shiner doesn't look that bad. The way DR was talking yesterday, I thought your eyeball was hanging out of your face."

Kerry winced at the visual. "The way she was treating me I thought the same thing." She admitted. "She's such a nanny sometimes. You'd never expect it of her." She indicated the door. "C'mon. I've got lunch lined up and it's about that time."

They walked together out of the conference room and down the hall toward the elevators. The tenth floor was somewhat more crowded than the fourteenth, and they had to dodge a stream of bodies, some of whom paused to greet them briefly.

"Hey, Kerry." One of Eleanor's assistants waved. "How's the head?"

Kerry paused and turned, stepping out of the path of traffic for a moment. "Ah, it's not too bad." She indicated her eye. "Just embarrassing, really."

"Yeah." The woman looked sympathetically at her. "Hey, Joyce and I are heading down for lunch...you want to join us?"

Kerry smiled and started to edge away. "Thanks, but I've got a date. Catch me some other time?" She continued toward the elevators, then paused seeing the crush of bodies around them waiting to go downstairs.

"Oh yeah, reclaiming your territory." The woman called after her. "Gotcha. No problem, Kerry."

What? "Heck with that." Kerry turned and pushed open the stairwell door, starting up the steps at a brisk clip. About at the twelfth floor, she heard footsteps coming down the other way, and looked up to find Mariana headed in her direction. "Hey there."

"Morning, Kerry!" Mariana greeted her warmly. "How's the eye?"

Kerry stopped in mid motion and gave her a look. "Was it such a slow news day yesterday that my darn eye had to be the center of *everyone's* conversation?"

Mark had slowed down behind her and was now standing with a martyred look on his face. "I told you sending that email out was a bad idea," he said to Mariana.

Kerry turned. "Email?"

Mariana nibbled a fingernail. "Well, it seemed like a good idea at the time." She mused. "Maria thought so."

"Maria?" Kerry repeated the name and then she held up both hands. "Excuse me. Could someone please rent me a clue here?"

"Whoops...I'm late for a meeting." Mariana skirted Kerry and skipped off down the stairs. "Catch you up later, Kerry...okay?" She waggled her fingers and popped through the door on the next landing, leaving Kerry to turn slowly and look at Mark.

Mark hesitated and then managed a weak grin. "I'll forward you a copy. It was no big deal, Kerry. It was just that everyone was kinda talking about how something had happened to you and she just aum..."

"Talking?"

Mark prudently didn't answer seeing that one blond eyebrow lift up sharply, uncannily like Dar's when she wasn't pleased about something.

"Colleen mentioned that too. Isn't everyone over using us as discussion fodder by now?" Kerry's voice deepened a little in anger. "She told me people thought Dar did this." She pointed at her face. "Is that true?'

Mark looked suddenly way out of his league.

"Screw you all." Kerry turned and abruptly left him standing there, taking the rest of the steps two at a time until she reached the fourteenth floor and shoved her way through the door, slamming it behind her.

Mark released a breath after a few moments. "Shit." He climbed slowly after his boss.

DAR RELAXED IN the lobby, sucking at the straw in her smoothie as she waited for Kerry to join her for lunch.

She leaned against the wall, crossing her ankles and letting her thoughts wander briefly, going over the design she'd left sitting on her laptop up in her office. Most of a module was finished, and almost ready for testing, and Dar found herself looking forward to the trial with a giddy sense of anticipation.

If it worked...

Well, it would not work at first. No program did, Dar acknowledged, mentally preparing herself for it, but if she tweaked it, and got the logic right, and it worked...

It would be an amazing breakthrough ironically spurred on by her own lack of good judgment.

Life was just so funny that way sometimes. Dar idly let her eyes wander over the lobby, and then she straightened up a little as she spotted Kerry coming off the elevators.

Uh oh. Kerry never threw her arms around or otherwise projected her anger, but Dar could always tell by her body posture when she was pissed off. Her hands would clench up, and her head would tilt forward a little, along with the point of her jaw.

She was pissed off now. Flicking her mind over the events of the morning, Dar decided it wasn't anything she'd done that had caused it, so she pushed off from the wall to go meet her ticked off lover, and see what she could do about fixing whatever was making her so mad.

Kerry spotted her approaching, changed course and headed for Dar, reluctantly grinning as they met near the center of the large space. "Hi. Sorry I'm late."

"Hi." Dar gracefully circled her and gestured toward the outside doors. "No problem. I just got down here myself. C'mon." She draped her arm casually over Kerry's shoulders as they started off, and immediately felt the stiffness in them relax. Okay. So she knew for sure it wasn't her Kerry was annoyed at.

Direct, or non-direct? "How'd your meeting go?" She decided on non-direct for now.

Kerry sighed. "It went fine. The project's on track, though John's having some problems in the wiring. I might have to run down there tomorrow and see if I can smooth things out for him."

"Cool." Dar replied. "My program's close to test state."

Kerry perked up a little. "Yeah? That was fast. You said the other day you were a little stuck." She circled Dar's waist with her right arm and bumped her hip lightly. "What changed?"

"You inspired me this morning." Dar told her, as they walked out the front door and into the heat of the day. "Me?"

"Yup." Dar bleeped open the doors of her car and steered Kerry toward it.

"I thought we were walking?"

Dar opened the passenger side door, and indicated the inviting leather seat inside. "I feel like wings."

"Wings?" Kerry climbed inside, reaching over to open Dar's door. "Are we going to Bayside?"

"We are." Dar got in and started the Lexus, adjusting the air ducts to dump a larger volume of cold air into her lap. "I'm not in the mood for Cuban, and I had my fill of sushi yesterday."

"Mmph." Kerry settled back in her seat and watched the heat simmer off the tarmac as Dar pulled out of the parking lot. "Well, if we eat at Hooters, you can bet there won't be useless little catty do-nothings from our office sitting at the next table."

Hmm. Dar made the turn onto Biscayne Boulevard and watched her partner out of the corner of her eye. "Y'know, Ker, you shouldn't let all that bullshit bother you so much."

"I know." Kerry acknowledged readily. "But it does. I can't help it."

The traffic was light, and Dar made quick work of the drive from the office to the trendy shopping mall, driving under the parking garage to find a spot somewhere out of the sun near the entrance. They got out and she locked the door, joining Kerry for the short walk into the mall's confines. "So what was it this time?" She finally asked. "I didn't hear any chatter today, and I usually do, from Maria."

Figures. Kerry paused to window shop, spotting a pretty dress in a nearby window. "Oh, everyone's just buzzing about my war wound," she muttered. "Mariana felt the need to put a damned email out about it."

Dar peered at the dress. "You'd look good in that." She pointed out.

"Mm. I like it." Kerry said, before she turned to continue down the walk. "Why should anyone care about what I do in my off hours, Dar?"

Dar shrugged. "It's human nature," she said. "What'd they all think, that I clocked you?? She watched Kerry's reaction, the sudden shift of her features and turn of her head giving her the answer before she even spoke. "Figures." She chuckled wryly. "If I'd have tried that move it would have gone right over your head, and you would have slapped me in the ass on the way around."

Kerry's entire face twitched. "You know something?" She stopped and faced Dar. "You know why I was so pissed about all that?"

"Because they're idiots?" Dar offered.

"Because I didn't want you to hear all of it and feel bad that people thought that." Kerry put her hand on Dar's belly, giving her a little scratch. "It really bothered me."

Dar bumped her toward the sidewalk again. They walked together along the shops, pausing to peek inside the windows from time to time. Kerry paused to plaster herself against one pane of glass, spotting a Ski-Doo inside. "Oooo...you know, Dar, that's just like a..."

"Motorcycle for the water." Dar agreed, with a grin. "Much as I hate to dodge them on the water, they're a lot of fun." She paused, watching Kerry's face intently. "Want to get a couple for the cabin?"

"Mmm..." Sorely tempted, Kerry unstuck her nose from the window. "Let's think about it." She took Dar's arm and they strolled on, passing a Sharper Image and, by common consent, not even peeking inside. They had to get back from lunch at a reasonable hour, and if they went inside not only would they not get back, but they'd end up spending a fortune on enticingly useful, but less than critical, items to boot.

Shopping together was always dangerous but fun. They both tended to trigger spending splurges in each other, and when they were together, it sometimes got ridiculous. It wasn't as if they couldn't afford it, but really, did they need more colorful wooden parrots for the house? Or hand painted ceramic dog bowls?

"Hey look." Dar pointed. "Hermit crabs."

Kerry kept walking, making sure she had a tight hold of Dar's arm. "No."

"But they're cute...look they painted their shells." Dar walked backwards, peering at the vendor stand. "And they have little coconut shell houses...it'd look great on your desk."

"Nonononono." Kerry pulled harder. "Wings...wings, c'mon, forget the crabs."

Dar chuckled, turning around and steering Kerry up the escalator. They dodged a few confused tourists at the top trying to take the upstairs down, and circled the upper deck to end up at the door to Hooters.

Kerry was right about one thing; Dar had to agree as she followed her to an empty table near the window. No one, absolutely no one, would either expect to see them here, nor be found dead eating lunch here themselves because of what people would say about it.

"Hi!" A pretty, red haired girl in criminally short shorts and a cutoff white t-shirt approached. "How are you guys?"

"Hi, Cheryl." Kerry greeted her with a smile. "How's the classes?"

"Driving me nuts." The woman shook her head wryly. "I have three advanced biochemistry labs this semester, and every time I see a plate of wings, I keep expecting them to twitch. You want the usual?"

"Sure." Dar settled on her stool and hooked her feet into the rungs. Aside from the visuals—which she wasn't too proud to admit to enjoying—she liked the restaurant because it lacked the usual lunchtime crowds more common near their building.

"So," Kerry fiddled with the table tent, "did I overreact to all the BS talk?"

Dar rested her chin on one fist. "Did Mari really put out an email?"

"Yeah. It wasn't...I mean, she didn't get into any details. She just said I got nicked by the guy I was sparring with in karate class."

"It's not karate." Dar frowned.

"No, but it was worded cleverly." Kerry admitted. "I don't know, the more I think about it, the more I think I really did just blow up for nothing." She sighed. "Especially at Mark, who didn't deserve it."

"Tell him." Dar suggested. "He knows you did it for a good cause."

Pale green eyes lifted and studied her and a gentle smile appeared on Kerry's face. "What makes a difference for me is that you know I did it for a good cause."

Cheryl returned, setting down a pitcher of ice tea and a couple of glasses, along with plates and a new roll of paper towels. "So, what's up with you guys?" She asked. "I saw a couple of your techie guys here yesterday. They said they were working down at the port?"

"Yep." Kerry answered, while Dar busied herself pouring them some tea. "We're working on those ships over there." She pointed toward the port, even though not much of it could be seen except the top decks. "Our guys ended up here? Oo...wait till I tease them." She chuckled.

"Uh huh...and you're going to explain knowing that how?" Dar handed her a glass, and winked at Cheryl.

Cheryl winked back and sauntered off to get their wings.

"You and your logic." Kerry felt a lot more relaxed now. The worst of it, she realized, had been how afraid she'd been of Dar finding out about the rumors. Now it seemed like Dar just thought they were stupid, so she was free to feel the same way.

Did she?

Kerry sighed, wishing she did and could dismiss it. But she didn't, and it still ticked her off. Now she just had to decide what she was going to do about it. Then a thought occurred to her, a memory of earlier that day. "Reclaim my territory?" She asked aloud, giving Dar a puzzled look.

"What?"

"Nothing. Just something someone said..." Kerry's voice slowed, and trailed off. She sighed again. "Just more crap."

Dar reached over and ruffled her hair. "Thanks for your outrage on my behalf, Ker. But the only opinion in that building that means jack to me is yours." She gave Kerry a smile, and then her eyes slipped past her partner as a motion caught them. "Son of a biscuit."

"Now what?" Kerry turned her head, almost chucking her ice tea when she spotted who Dar was looking at. Shari and Michelle, along with a very smug looking Peter Quest had just seated themselves at an outside table. "Oh, poop."

"I don't think they can see us." Dar observed. "Let's see how much I can offer Cheryl to do a Maria."

"Oh god." Kerry covered her eyes.

"Or maybe just listen in." Dar continued, in a softer, more calculating voice. "After all, last place they'd expect to find the competition would be here, eh?"

"Mm." Kerry felt a tickle of apprehension in her guts. Or maybe it was just the thrill of it all. "Last place they'd think of."

But at what point, she wondered, did they just become what Shari and Michelle were? Were they already? Kerry picked up her tea and took a sip. "I'd rather we just ate." She finally said, looking Dar in the eye. "And just ignore them."

Cheryl came back and put down two plates of crispy hot wings in front of them. "Here you go guys. Anything else right now?"

Dar selected a wing, and saluted Cheryl with it. "Nope. We're just fine."

Kerry picked up a wing of her own, and waited for the waitress to leave before she spoke. "Thanks."

Dar winked, and munched on her wing, apparently unconcerned. "Your wish is my command." She announced. "Besides, the best we could find out is what we already know."

Kerry took a bite, satisfied with the answer. At least for now.

Chapter Seven

KERRY LEANED BACK in her chair, balancing her keyboard on her lap as she typed out a spurt of emails dealing with two of the minor projects she was supervising along with the ship one. In the time since she'd gotten back from lunch with Dar, she'd gotten a lot done as well as felt her earlier aggravation dissipate.

She had noticed recently that Dar's presence tended to do that to her. It wasn't anything her partner did or said, particularly, but if she was angry or upset, hanging around Dar just made her feel better. Even when she was hurting; if she had a headache or a bellyache, she'd curl up with her head in Dar's lap and it would all just go away.

Why was that? She wondered idly. It had been really noticeable that afternoon when she'd come down for lunch. She'd been steaming as she stepped off the elevator, but when she spotted Dar heading her way, her blood pressure had dropped and the knots in her gut had eased the minute they came together.

Ah well. Kerry shook her head a bit, and went back to her typing. Certainly, Dar wasn't around to make her feel warm and fuzzy right now. Her partner was stuck in the downstairs closet again, testing her new program.

Which reminded her. She hit the button for a new message and addressed it to Mark.

Hey—Dar's testing some new code downstairs. So if you see freaky things, it might be her.

She hesitated a minute, then continued.

Sorry I went off today. I should be used to the talk by now, but when it comes to Dar, I never am. Thanks for letting me know about it.

K

She hit send.

A small box popped up in one corner. *Hey.*

Kerry grinned. *Hey.*

Do we have marshmallows at home?

Marshmallows? Kerry nibbled her lower lip thoughtfully. Marshmallows had never been a particular favorite of hers, since she found them relatively tasteless and preferred to squander her calories on something more appropriate such as chocolate. *I don't think so. Why?*

There was a faint pause before the answer, and then it popped up. *I want rice crispy treats.*

A new message popped into her inbox. Kerry clicked on it while she considered how she should respond to that request.

Hey, Kerry -
No problem, I know big D's A number 1 on your list.

Thanks for telling me she's down in the dungeon - I haven't
seen anything yet but with her you never do until it's too
late.

Oh, that's not really true. Kerry shook her head back and forth.
Sometimes she's just very, very obvious.

Anyway, sorry all that stuff got dredged up. People just
talk shit because it's how they make themselves feel better
about not being you guys.

Kerry read that last bit a few times, then shrugged. Personally, she
just viewed the talk as venal human nature. It was easy for her to
rationalize it that way, but far more difficult for her to ignore it when it
was directed at Dar, and not at her. For herself, she'd been talked about
since she was old enough to realize what that meant.

She keyed the instant message box and typed a reply. *If you swing
by Publix on the way home, I'll make you some.* She hit enter, and then
typed another message. *I hear they're really good when you dip them in hot
fudge.*

The answer came back immediately. *Why not? You are.*

"Yerk." Kerry muffled a squeak. *You are such a punk. They could be
random logging this, y'know!*

And?

*Yeah, and? What are they going to find out, we're lovers? Whoohoo...
news flash...call Panic Seven.* Kerry wrinkled her nose and grinned again
in acknowledgment. *How's it going?*

Good. You?

Kerry reviewed her inbox and sighed. There were a number of
mails backed up waiting for her attention, and she knew she had to
plow through them if she wanted any chance of getting out of the office
early the next day. *Eh. I'll be here a while.*

Surprisingly, an answer came right back again. *Me too. How about
we meet for a romantic dinner over a pile of cable later on?*

She simply regarded the note for a while, a fond look crossing her
face. *I love you.* She typed back, hesitating, and then just hit send.
Really, was there anything that needed to be added to that? She clicked
back on her mail and continued to type, justifying for the nth time why
new computers had to be budgeted for and not just plucked out of a
non-existent IT genie bag.

"Keeeeeeerrrrry."

She jumped, and then looked at her screen. Gopher Dar was back,
peeking around her email program and waving. "Oh, my god, she got it
to talk! C'mere, you little rascal." Her mouse pointer chased after the
critter, and she poked him in the tail a few times. "Aggghhh...gotcha!"

Far from being disturbed, Gopher Dar turned and waggled his
behind at her, then somersaulted over and ended up sitting down. "I
lloooooooooovvvvvvveeeee youooo..." He warbled. "Youurrreee the
best!"

"Oh, my god." Kerry repeated, biting her lower lip. "You are so amazing sometimes." She continued, in a softer voice.

Her office door opened, and Mayte poked her head in. "Did you call for me, Kerry?"

"Shh." Kerry admonished Gopher Dar. "No, I was just talking to myself." She directed her attention to Mayte. "Sorry. I'm trying to get some of this mail cleared up. Did you need me for something?"

Her assistant entered and walked over to her visitor chairs sitting down on the left hand side one. "I have a little question for you." Mayte said. "I really want to understand more about what we are doing so much of the time. Could I ask you which class I can take? In my school, we did a lot with software, and programs. We did not do so much with the networks."

Ah. Career advice. Kerry gladly turned her attention from her mail, though reluctantly from Gopher Dar, and focused on Mayte's slim form. "Well, I can fully appreciate how you feel, Mayte. I had some experience with infrastructure before I started here, but it's been a learning curve for me too. The best person to really ask about that is Dar. She's the expert."

Gopher Dar chittered softly. Kerry clicked on him. "You hush."

"Excuse me?" Mayte gave her a puzzled look.

"C'mere." Kerry motioned for her to come around the desk. "Want to see something really cute?"

Mayte willingly got up and circled the desk, peering over Kerry's shoulder. "What is that?" She asked, as Kerry chased the little critter around the screen. "Oh, look! Que Linda!"

"This is Gopher Dar." Kerry pinned him down by the tail, and watched his tiny feet scrabble. "He was talking a minute ago."

Mayte gave her boss a faintly skeptical look. "Si?" she asked. "But what is it? Where does it come from?"

Gopher Dar sashayed across the screen, doing a little dance. He had on a tank top and shorts, and incongruous rubber boots today. "Keeeeerrrrry..." He warbled.

"Oh!" Mayte covered her mouth.

"He comes from Dar," Kerry explained. "It's a program of hers that she works on when she's not doing anything else, and every so often she sends this little guy over here to interact with me."

Mayte leaned a little closer. "Wow."

Gopher Dar waved at her. Then he did another little dance.

"He really cheers me up most of the time. "Kerry smiled. "And it's an amazing program. It's different every time. She puts different clothes on him; he does different things...her talent as a programmer is amazing."

"He is blushing." Mayte noted, with a grin. "So cute."

"So, anyway, as I was saying, Dar's the expert on what makes this place tick. But I think she'd agree that you should take a basic class on networking fundamentals to start with, and get the terminology down."

Kerry flipped over to a different screen, and called up a browser window. "We've got classes internally...here. Look at this set first." She pointed.

"Ooooo..." Gopher Dar warbled approvingly. "Gooooooddd."

They both started laughing. "Kerry, that is so adorable," Mayte said. "And it is nothing serious — it is just for fun, yes?"

"Sure." But Kerry suddenly wasn't so sure about that. Gopher Dar had started making more and more frequent appearances lately, and she wondered if working with the little guy wasn't Dar's way of exercising her programming chops to ease her growing restlessness. "Is that not clever, or what?"

"Absolutely," Mayte agreed. "I wish I had one! It is like a little friend. I think my cousin found a little cat program something like this, but it was not nearly so smart. It went to sleep, and it made a purr, and that kind of thing."

"I've seen that." Kerry said. "They have a puppy, too. But nothing like Gopher Dar."

Gopher Dar had lain down on his side, and was simply gazing out at her. Kerry resisted the urge to reach out and scratch his nose. "So. Does that answer your question about classes?"

"Si, yes it does." Mayte eased out from behind Kerry's chair and came to stand in front of the desk again. "I will look at that website and sign up for one today. Is it all right if I make it at the end of the day, and go after we are done here?"

"Sure," Kerry agreed. "But think about it — sometimes people do class better in the morning." She paused, and a wry grin appeared. "Not that I was one of those people, but you know what I mean."

"Yes, I know." Mayte agreed mournfully. "Mama has to pull me out of my bed in the morning. So I think the afternoon is better." She turned to go. "Thank you, Kerry, and also for showing me your very cute friend. It is a very good program."

"I think so." Kerry gazed affectionately at the little creature. "I work on him a little sometimes and every once in a while I send him back over to bother Dar. She gets a kick out of it." She looked up. "But I'm not in her league when it comes to that."

"She is very talented." Mayte smiled. "You are very lucky, I think."

"I'm very lucky, I know." Kerry gave her a little wave, as she left. "I do know that for sure." She returned her attention reluctantly to her mail, almost hoping that Gopher Dar would come up with something else to distract her.

Which sucked, actually, since she had to get her damn mail done. Kerry frowned, focusing on the next page of complaints.

Hey, Ker?

Ah. An even more welcome distraction. *Yes, Gopher Mom?*

You tied to that desk?

Kerry drummed her fingertips on her keyboard. *You got a network connection for my laptop down there? Say yes and I'll go keep you company in your pile of cable.*

Gopher Dar got up and started scooting around the corner of her screen, beckoning her to follow. Kerry clicked on him, waiting for the message to come back.

C'mon. I've got a nice dusty piece of concrete with your name on it right next to me.

Ah, it just didn't get any more romantic than that. Kerry closed her mail and stood up. *Be right there.* She typed into the screen, before she closed down the desktop and grabbed her brief case. "But you know," she remarked to the empty office. "Only love struck nitwits with zero sense would trade a nice comfortable leather chair for a piece of dusty concrete."

She shouldered her laptop. "One nitwit, en route." Kerry headed for the door, giving her new boxing dummy a wink as she scooted out of the room.

THE SOFT SOUNDS of new age echoed against the concrete walls interrupted erratically by the patter of keystrokes on two keyboards.

Dar was seated on the ground between two tall racks, her long legs extended under them as she leaned back against a third. Kerry had taken a position right next to her, sitting cross-legged on the hard concrete with her laptop balanced on her knees.

Neither of them was talking. Both of them were concentrating on what they were doing, and yet the atmosphere in the small room was one of total absorbed contentment.

Kerry clicked send on her mail, and reviewed her inbox. The stack of messages she'd needed to take care of had decreased by over half in a surprisingly short amount of time, and she was beginning to see the light at the end of her email tunnel. "Know something? We should work down here more often."

Dar finished typing a line, and grunted. "Uh huh." She compiled the program she'd just finished, and opened a run window, starting the program and watching the results as it executed. "Ahhhh?"

Kerry rested her cheek against Dar's shoulder and peered at the screen. "Working now?"

"Uh huh. Hang on to your socks. I'm gonna run it against the backup router." She clicked over to a different screen and pulled it to one side, adjusting a monitoring parameter until she was satisfied with it. "Okay."

It was fun and interesting watching Dar work. Kerry waited for her to start the program again, and then switched her attention to the monitor. The gauges jumped and fluttered, indicating *something* was going on, but it was hard to tell what effect the program was having.

So, she remained quiet and waited for Dar to comment on it. She'd been acceptably competent at the programming she'd done in school, but it had never been a passion of hers, and this was not only complex, it was cryptic in a way that only Dar could be.

"Eh." Dar folded her arms and regarded the screen.

"Is it doing what you want it to?" Kerry hazarded.

"No." Her partner replied. "But it's doing something useful, which I hadn't anticipated."

"Hmm. Is that good or bad?"

Dar rested her head against Kerry's. "I don't know yet. Give it a few minutes." She studied the screen. "See here?" She pointed with one long finger. "I wanted it to analyze the headers and determine multiple instances of same sender, but what it's actually doing is logging out of sequence packets."

Kerry looked at the screen, then at her partner. "That's useful?"

Dar nodded. "Yeah, because that's a symptom, sometimes, of a dictionary attack—something just throwing guesses at the router and masking its own IP."

"Ah hah." Kerry murmured approvingly. "So that's progress."

"Mm. At least it's not crapping out every six seconds now," Dar agreed. "How's your mail coming?"

Kerry snuggled a little closer. "Fine," she said. "I knocked out a lot of it. It's really nice and peaceful down here. I can see why you decided to do the test this way."

"Mmm hmm." Dar nuzzled her hair a little. "And it's perfect now."

Aww. Kerry figured if she had a tail, it'd be wiggling big time. Ridiculous really, since they were sitting on a dirty concrete floor surrounded by humming network gear in a room that stunk of damp stone and electrons.

But who cared. "So, what's next?"

Dar left her program running while she called up her coding screen and made a few corrections. "Take another baby step, that's what." She cleared her throat a little, and continued pecking away.

"Mm." Kerry shifted and set her laptop aside. "I'm going to get a soda. Interested?" She waited for Dar to nod, and then she got up and stretched, reaching down to ruffle her partner's dark hair. "Be right back." She stepped carefully over the cables on the floor and pulled the door open, escaping from the small room into the hallway that led to the lobby.

It was after five, and the building was quieting down. The café on the ground floor was closed, and the cleaning people were beginning to pop out like night owls, starting the task of cleaning the place. Kerry walked across the mostly empty lobby toward the ground floor break room, giving the guard a wave as she passed his desk.

"Hey, Ms. Stuart." The man waved back. "You still here? Thought you were gone for the day. Michael passed by your office and said it was closed up."

"Nope." Kerry shook her head. "I'm working on a project in the main telco room." She pointed back the way she'd come from. "Probably be there a while yet. Was someone looking for me?"

"Yeah. Matter of fact a lady came to the front guard desk over there and wanted to talk to you. That's why Michael went up." He got up and met Kerry as she slowed down. "Here. She left a card."

Kerry took it, cocking her head a little puzzled over the name. It wasn't one she recognized, and she certainly had no idea what a real estate agent would want with her. "Um...okay." She half shrugged, and stuck the cardboard slip into her back pocket. "Thanks. I don't think I'm in the market for what she's selling, but who knows?"

The guard shrugged also. "Have no idea, ma'am." He cleared his throat. "Ah, do you know if Ms. Roberts is here too? I saw her car still outside, but her office is closed up."

"She's here." Kerry turned to continue her task. "We're working together on this project. You need her?"

"No ma'am." The man shook his head. "Is that the security zone in the inside corridor?"

"Yep." Kerry started to walk off. "We'll be there if you need us." She continued across the marble tile floor and into the inner hallway, pushing open the non-descript door and crossing from public splendor to linoleum tiled plainness in the space of a step.

It reminded her of the ship, a little—the difference between the passenger areas and the crew. Kerry stopped in front of the big soda machine, reviewing her choices. "Ah." She popped some coins in and selected a button, waiting for the bottle to drop before she added more coins, and made a second choice.

The bottle rattled down, and she opened the bottom flap to retrieve Dar's YooHoo and her own root beer. Whistling softly under her breath, she headed back out to the lobby.

DAR HAD SET her laptop down and now she was walking around, stretching her body out and easing the stiffness from sitting on the ground for so long. Above her head, the cable ladders stretched to either side, bearing their bundles of multicolor strands.

Experimentally, Dar reached up and grasped the ladder bars, pulling her body up and letting the metal take the weight of her body for a short time.

Satisfied the structure wasn't going to collapse, she took a better hold, then lifted herself up again and got her legs up over the top of the ladder, hooking them securely through the rungs.

Then she released her arms and hung down, letting her spine relax. "Ahh." She let her hands dangle as she flexed them, feeling the soft pops as her vertebra eased into place. It felt good, and was something she hadn't done in a long, long time.

Since the weekend she'd spent in this very room upgrading every piece of equipment in it, in fact. Dar swung back and forth a little, enjoying the motion and the memories. She'd just been a tech then, before she'd decided to move into management.

Looking back along that curve now, Dar found herself wondering a little if that move had been the right one after all. Here she was, years later, right back in this closet doing something she could have easily paid an entire roomful of programmers to do instead of getting involved.

So why was she doing it? Just to have something to do and stay out of Kerry's way? Dar grimaced. Oh that was an attractive thought. Maybe she'd let herself be promoted past her competency, like she was always accusing Jose of.

Ah, Dar. She sighed at herself. You can't really complain, can you? After all, if you'd stayed a grunt, chances are you'd never have met Kerry, right?

No, probably not. Dar swung back and forth a little more, and thought about how much more she'd gotten done after Kerry had joined her today. She'd been less restless, and more focused, and suddenly it occurred to her that the more she separated herself from her partner and her projects, the more antsy she tended to be.

It was so obvious, once she'd thought of it, that she almost slapped herself on the head. "Damn." In her efforts to distance herself from Kerry's efforts, and let her partner fly on her own — was she sending herself down the stupid path?

Didn't they really work better as a team?

Didn't they?

The outer door opened, and she was graced with the sight of her lover from an interesting perspective. "Hi."

"What are you doing?" Kerry walked in and set the sodas down before she came over to where Dar was hanging like a bat. "You have no idea how funny you look."

"Just stretching." Dar said. "It's good for your back." She reached out and gave Kerry a poke in the belly. "Join me?"

Kerry studied her, and grinned. "If you say so, honey. I'll take your word for it. Last time I did that I fell out of a tree and my mother nearly had me hogtied for a month. Wasn't a pretty sight."

Dar reached up and caught hold of the bars, reversing her position and letting herself down onto the ground again. She reached around Kerry to pick up her Yoohoo bottle, ending up in an intentional hug as Kerry bumped up against her. "You're always a pretty sight."

Kerry wrapped her arms around Dar and gave her a powerful squeeze. "And you're the best thing my ego's ever, ever had." She sighed. "Dear god, you make me feel ten feet tall sometimes, Dar."

Dar nodded a little to herself, and accepted the fact that her judgment had been off. It happened sometimes, but in this case, she had an idea of what to do to correct it.

"Mm." Kerry hesitated. "Dar..."

"I think I like it when we work together." Dar commented casually. "Even when we're not on the same project I like having you here."

Unexpected, but startlingly identical to the words running through Kerry's mind as well. "Wow." She murmured. "I was about to say the same thing." She let her hands rest on Dar's waist. "You know something? I think that's why I've been so rattled over this ship project." She looked up. "Dar, I don't need you holding my hand on it." A sigh. "But I want you there. I want us to beat them. Not just me."

"All right." Dar leaned her forearms on Kerry's shoulders and touched her forehead to Kerry's. "And I want you guiding me on this security package. I need your judgment."

The concrete and steel suddenly became magic, framing the moment indelibly. Kerry felt an impish grin forming on her lips, smothered a moment later when Dar kissed them.

She sincerely hoped there weren't any cameras.

"URGF." Kerry took a breath and continued her sit ups, the roll of thunder percolating into the island's gym. Behind her, she could hear the soft clank as Dar did leg presses. She resisted the temptation to move from her current exercise to that one.

Sit ups were definitely not her favorite things. They made her back ache, for one thing, and since she was now using an incline board, they were just plain hard to do.

Still, she kept them up, resolutely closing her eyes and concentrating on the positive results she knew she'd get by completing her self-imposed sets.

The rain outside had canceled their morning run, and they'd decided on a work out to replace it—possibly suffering from some mutual guilt brought on by consuming an entire baking pan full of rice crispy treats the night before.

With fudge. Kerry blinked her eyes open, scattering a fine mist of sweat as she regarded the stolidly boring ceiling. She let her back rest against the padded surface, breathing deeply as she waited for the burning ache to dissipate from the muscles that lined the front of her stomach.

"Ker?"

"Uh?" She grunted.

"You okay?"

"Just resting." Kerry extended her arms over her head and stretched her body out. Her bare legs were hooked around supports at the end of the board holding her in place, and she flexed her thighs a little, watching the skin tighten and relax.

"Thought you didn't like doing those." Dar commented.

"I don't. But I do like having a six pack." She patted her belly. "Do you know how horrified my family would be if I told them I did?"

Dar merely chuckled.

"When I went home the first time," Kerry said, "I took my shirt off in front of my sister, and she started teasing me about being She Ra. You remember She Ra, Dar?"

"Bwahhahahaha."

"Uh huh. I used to have a plastic sword, and everything." Kerry chuckled. "Until my parents found it and threw it out."

They both stopped chuckling. Dar cleared her throat. "I think...I first started to be aware of the way I looked when I was around thirteen or fourteen or so."

"Mm?" Kerry took another breath, and started in on her sit ups again. "Puberty?' She grunted.

Dar got up and went to the free weights, picking up a triceps bar and starting some curls as she walked over to be nearer to Kerry. "Yeah. Killer growth spurt. I grew...almost five inches in a year and my whole metabolism went nuts."

"Uh huh." Kerry agreed in sympathy.

"I started eating like a horse, and figured if I didn't start working out, it was all gonna stay on me like it was on a lot of my classmates." Dar related. "So I did."

"Sensible decision."

"Yeah." Dar chuckled. "Except I went to the base gym, and worked out with all the guys. I didn't know I wasn't supposed to use the same weights they were using, and my mother walked in on me one day while I was dressing and nearly had a fit at what I looked like."

Kerry snickered, but kept crunching.

"Hey, I thought it looked good." Dar mused. "And the guys all sure respected me."

"I bet." Kerry finished her second set and pulled herself off the board, escaping gratefully to the lat pull down machine. It was angled perfectly so that she could see Dar while she was doing the exercise, and she studied her partner's body as she started the new routine.

Dar had definitely grown into her height. Her shoulders were broad, and rounded with muscle, and that extended down her arms to corded wrists that were currently tensed as she did her curls. Yet, her skin fitted over her body in supple curves, never giving the impression of a bodybuilder's starkly ripped muscularity at all.

Kerry liked that. She liked the impression of strength Dar had without looking at all masculine, and she'd consciously or unconsciously patterned her own aspirations in the same direction. She'd first started noticing a difference a few months into their relationship, before she'd moved in permanently with Dar.

It had all started with a shirt. She'd been dressing for work one day, half in the dark of a very early morning when she'd pulled on a silk blouse she hadn't worn in several weeks and found the sleeves binding uncomfortably around her upper arms and shoulders.

"Huh?" Kerry turned to the mirror in her bedroom and flipped the light on, giving herself a puzzled look in the reflection. Sure enough, the fabric was pulled taut over her upper body, the length draping down over her half bared torso still unbuttoned.

"Great." She sighed, apprehensively reaching for the lowest button, and matching it with its hole on the other side. To her mild surprise, it mated easily around her waist, easing her sudden fear that her recent change of habits had added more pounds to her frame than she'd realized. "So, what the heck?"

With a touch of impatience, she stripped the shirt off, and let it fall to the dresser, studying her body in the mirror with a very critical eye. What she saw surprised her, and she straightened up a little, squaring newly broadened shoulders and holding her arms out, turning them a little as she flexed her muscles.

Holy pooters. Kerry exhaled. Under her skin she could now see visible power, bunching and moving in the lamplight as she shifted. Her shoulders had gained a cap of sinew over them and she could see the beginning shadow of an arch that extended from the points of her shoulders to her neck.

It felt very strange, and for a moment, she felt a little scared of the changes. She'd kept an image of herself in her head for so long, hammered in by her parents that this shift was almost as intimidating as the twenty pounds she'd carried home after her first year in Miami.

That had merely ended up being embarrassing. Kerry spread her arms out fully, and almost shook her head at the new shape of her outline, the widened shoulders giving her body a very pleasing taper she hadn't really anticipated.

"Wow." She finally said, letting her hands drop to her sides. "You know, I think I like this." She met her own reflection's eyes and grinned. "Wonder if Dar's noticed?"

A wink of dawn light peeked through the blinds and she put her hands on her hips, turning her attention to the problem of dressing for work. She walked back to her closet and reviewed her options. The skirt she'd intended on wearing hung there, but she pondered now what top she would go with it.

Her eye fell on a simple, tailored linen shirt with crisp lines and a conservative cut right up to the point where it became sleeveless. "Hmm." Kerry removed it from its hanger and slipped it on, the whispered chill of the air conditioning feeling slightly illicit on her bare shoulders.

She put on her skirt, tucking the ends of the shirt into the waistband and buttoning it. She buckled the slim leather belt, then removed her linen jacket from its hanger and put it on. Facing the mirror she observed the effect.

Businesslike and conservative. Kerry gave herself a brief nod, and then she let the jacket slip off her shoulders and looked again.

She grinned and put the jacket back on and headed off to work.

"What's so funny?" Dar inquired, pausing in her curls. "Am I making faces again?"

Kerry chuckled. "No, I was just thinking of something." She stood up and let the pull down bar return to its resting position. "Hey, let me ask you a question." She let her arms rest against her thighs.

"Hmm?" Dar cocked her head in inquiry, the muscles in her arms jumping as she brought the weighted bar up.

"Do you think I look too butch?'

Dar paused in her upswing, the bar ending up pressed against her breastbone. Her nostrils flared, and she made a small snorting sound, attempting to stifle a laugh.

Kerry put her hands on her hips. "What was that supposed to mean?" She cocked an eyebrow at her partner.

Hastily, Dar put down the barbell and walked over, wiping her hands on the towel she had tucked into her shorts. She cupped Kerry's chin and tilted her head up, regarding her with serious affection. "You don't look at all butch."

"I don't?"

"No."

"Not even with these?" Kerry lifted her arm and tensed her biceps.

"No."

"Really?"

"Really." Dar said. "Just incredibly sexy." She paused. "Why? Do you want to look more butch?" She asked curiously.

Kerry shook her head. "No, not really. I was just remembering something someone told me right after I first moved down here, about not falling into the typical gay routine of becoming a...um..." Her face scrunched a little. "Um..."

"Baby butch?" Dar inquired. "Well, I don't know...you looked great as a Revolutionary." She chuckled softly, giving Kerry a pat on the cheek. "But I love the way you look, no matter what it is, Ker. You know that."

"Mm."

Dar gave her a one armed hug, and then she went over to the incline board, and took Kerry's place on it. She adjusted the length, and then settled herself in to start her own set of sit ups, the motion relaxed and easy.

Kerry watched her a moment, then sighed enviously and got up on the stair climber. "What do you think...another twenty minutes? We should leave a little early in this weather."

"Yeah. Sounds about right." Dar had her arms crossed over her chest, and was moving up and down steadily. "You said you had to go over to the pier today?"

Kerry increased her pace. "Yep."

"How about we go there, and then take off." Dar said. "If you drive, I can get the revisions done on my program, and I won't feel guilty all damn weekend."

"Sounds like a plan."

They were both quiet for a few minutes, concentrating on their exercising. Finally after several sets, Dar let herself down on the board and gazed up at the ceiling, sweat dripping liberally across her body. "Hey, Ker?"

An equally dewy blond head lifted. "Hmm?"

"Any time you want to quit this and become couch potatoes, just drop me an email, yeah?'

Kerry chuckled, as she straightened on her machine and took a swig from the water bottle hung by her wrist. "You got it, baby. You got it."

They both started laughing, the noise echoing softly off the ceiling of the gym.

"ALL RIGHT." Dar motioned Mark to follow her into her office. "Let's see what you've got." She walked across the carpet and changed direction at the last minute, going to the small worktable in the corner of her office instead. "Here."

Mark followed her and put a cardboard box on the desk. "Sorry to grab you so early, DR, but I heard you were taking off today so I figured I'd better do it when I could."

"No problem." Dar perched on one of the two stools behind the worktable. She opened the top of the box and peered inside, reaching in to remove the cellular gadget along with several other miscellaneous bits of hardware.

"Going down south?" Mark asked.

"Yep." Dar set the cell unit down and leaned forward, removing the battery pack and examining the inside surface. "We're taking off after lunch. I'm going with Ker down to the boats, and then we're outta here for the weekend."

"Ah." Mark picked up a second bit of hardware and showed it to Dar. "This is the remote interface. I took it apart. It's got a circuit card in it to mask its internal ID."

"Huh." Dar took it.

"So, I guess after all that crap you guys needed some time out?"

Dar glanced up. "Not really. We just decided to go down. Why?"

Mark looked distinctly uncomfortable. "Just some stuff I heard." He knew better than to dissemble in front of Dar. He could get away with it with Kerry on occasion, but those icy blue eyes lanced right through him as Dar's expression changed.

"Now what?" With a look of disgust, Dar dropped the part on the table. "C'mon, spill it. What bullshit are they passing around this time?"

Mark studied the table, wondering for the nth time how he let himself get into situations like this one. Stolid loyalty to Dar? Maybe. "People are saying you guys are having problems."

"Problems?" Dar's tone sounded honestly puzzled. "Mark, we always have problems. Our whole damn job is nothing but problems."

Mark looked up. "No, not here." He took a breath. "Like, between you." He watched Dar's face, feeling a sense of weird relief at the expression of mild confusion that appeared there. "It made like, no sense to me, you know?"

Dar crossed her arms over her chest. "Is this..." She fished for an explanation. "Having something to do with her black eye? I'd heard rumors some idiots think I did that."

Dar's reaction wasn't what he'd been expecting. Mark fingered the piece of gear again. "No, um...it was more like that Kerry's mad at you and thinking about moving out," he said. "And that, yeah, I guess you guys were fighting, and that's how she got a black eye."

"That's ridiculous."

"Well yeah, I know," Mark said. "I don't know where this crap comes from."

Dar sighed, tossing the bit of hardware away from her. Then she paused and considered what she was feeling—impatience, annoyance? "Maybe we should put on a boxing exhibition," she remarked, with wry humor. "Or...I know. We'll put on a kissing exhibition in the lobby. How's that? Think anyone will catch a clue we're not breaking up?"

Mark blushed. "Um..."

"I just don't get it." Dar gazed thoughtfully at the other side of her office. "We've both been hurt before. Hell, we've spent weeks in slings since Kerry's started working here. Why all this crap now?" She rested her elbows on the table and shook her head. "Hope Ker doesn't hear all of it."

"Me either," Mark said. "She's got a mean temper."

The words made Dar smile a little. "Anyway." She picked up the cellular device. "Talk to me about this thing. When are its owners coming after it?

Mark gathered his wits and accepted the change of subject. He'd half expected Dar to fly off the handle, or react in some way, so the almost benign indifference she was exhibiting puzzled him. It wasn't as though he thought the rumors were true—after all, he interacted with his two bosses on a daily basis, and neither of them was great at hiding even minor spats.

Kerry got all nervous when they were disagreeing. She was restless as hell in meetings and she lost her usual even tempered patience when dealing with the staff or the daily problems they often faced. Luckily it never lasted that long, but it was easy to spot.

"I think they'll be here Monday," he told Dar. "But the basics are—it's a remotely accessed cell device."

"I got that far on my own." Dar cocked an eyebrow at him.

Now Dar, on the other hand, she'd pull back into her shell, glaring and snapping at everyone. Nobody liked dealing with her when she was like that, but Mark could also remember that before Kerry had entered her life nobody had much liked dealing with Dar even when she wasn't angry or upset,.

So he usually knew when they were squabbling. Just looking at Dar's relaxed body posture reassured him that nothing like that was going on, so now he considered her previous words and wondered himself — yeah, why now?

Why now? "It doesn't ring like a cell; it just picks up and makes a data link." Mark went on. "It's pretty sophisticated." He picked it up and looked at it. "I was trying to think of what the hell legitimate purpose it had for those guys developing it."

Dar snorted.

"Yeah, I thought that too."

"No wonder they're coming out here." Dar got up off the stool. "What you're telling me is that this thing was designed to bust networks from the inside."

"Yeah." Mark agreed. "Pretty much. The slickest thing is, it pops up on the network, listens for a real MAC address, and then spoofs it, so if you have MAC security turned on, it bypasses."

"Hmm." Dar juggled the device. "What about these things?" She pointed at the smaller pieces of technology, as she turned her hand and checked her watch. Almost lunch time. "Anything to tie them back to who planted the damn things?"

Mark got up and paced around a bit. "Boss, you sure this isn't from those Telegenics guys? I mean, the time's right, you know? I checked with the projector people, and the tech they sent out here is a guy who's worked for them for like twenty years. He's pretty clean."

Dar put the phone down and leaned back. "It's not them."

"Boss, c'mon. They were the only ones in there from outside the company in weeks." Mark coaxed. "I know it sucks to think they got one over on us, but chasing the cleaning people kinda sucks too."

Dar crossed her arms and glared at him.

"Y'know, it does." After so many years, he knew pretty much what he could get away with. "If we know it's them, maybe we can do a jive on the guys coming over here, and get them to spill."

"It's not them," Dar repeated stubbornly. "I don't give a damn how much sense it makes. I'm telling you it's not them. Find another possibility." Part of her acknowledged that Mark was right — believing it was Shari and Michelle burned her guts. But another part of her, the instinctive part that understood people at a base level, was telling her that someone smarter than either of them was behind it.

Was it just wishful thinking? Dar got up and went to her desk, dropping into her chair and putting her booted feet up on the desk. She was dressed down, glad of the excuse of the pier visit to be wearing her broken in jeans and short topped hiking boots.

"Okay." Mark gave in gracefully and collected his techno bits. "I'll see what else I can find out." He started to back away toward the door. "Sorry about all the talk and crap."

"Not your fault." Dar picked up her keyboard and put it on her lap. "Just tell everyone from me they're full of shit."

"Will do, boss." Mark disappeared and closed the door behind him.

Dar pecked out a few words, and then paused. She half turned in her chair as the inner door slammed open and Kerry strode in, green eyes snapping, hands half clenched, and for all intents and purposes it seemed like a thunderstorm was on its way to happening. "Hi," she greeted Kerry apprehensively. "What's up?"

"Stupid, mother mphfing, sons of pooters," Kerry spat out. "Do you want to know what kind of horse manure I've had to listen to for the last twenty minutes?"

Kerry was adorable when she was mad, just so long as it wasn't Dar she was mad at. "Let me guess." Dar put her keyboard down. "I hit you. We're breaking up, you're moving out, and maybe...the sky is falling?"

"Augh." Kerry sat down on Dar's desk. "I am so pissed."

"I can see that."

"Aren't you?" Kerry frowned. "Dar, this is bullshit!"

Was she? Dar leaned an elbow on Kerry's leg, and wondered about that. "It's bullshit," she agreed. "And I know it's not true, so while I'm aggravated that people are wasting their time, I'm not going to waste mine by blowing my top."

"I know it's not true also." Kerry growled. "But I want to boot these people, Dar. They have no right to talk about us like that. It's insubordination."

True enough. "Do we know who it is?"

Kerry got up and paced around Dar's desk, still visibly upset. "No one. Everyone." She groused. "It's cowardly! No one has the guts to say something to my face, it's all damned whispers."

Dar rounded the desk and intercepted Kerry, laying her hands on her partner's shoulders. "Ker, take it easy.

"I'm not going to take it easy," Kerry shot back. "I'm sick and tired of people just...just..." She let the words trail off. "Heck!" She pulled a square of cardboard from her pocket and tossed it on Dar's desk. "See that? Some freaking real estate agent was just in my office, saying she heard I was looking for a place."

Dar's eyebrows lifted.

"Augh!"Kerry balled her fists up fully and shook both of them. "Dar, I am so pissed!"

"Shh." Dar put her arms around Kerry and hugged her. "Take it easy."

"Grrrr!!!

"We'll figure out what's going on."

Kerry allowed herself to collapse against Dar's warm body. Her entire insides were tensed in knots, and her anger really had no place to go. "Goddamn it." She felt the knots ease, as Dar's hands rubbed her back. "Someone's trying to get between us, Dar."

"Yes."

Kerry took in a breath. "And you're not upset?"

Dar heard the catch in her voice. "Of course I am."

"You're just not freaking out," Kerry exhaled, "like I am." She leaned against Dar and let her breathing settle. "Sorry." She felt the gentle pressure as Dar kissed the top of her head, and felt very tired as the anger drained away.

Jerks.

Just...Jerks.

KERRY WAS STILL unsettled as they walked across the parking lot toward the ship buildings. She'd considered putting out a scathing memo, but Dar had convinced her not to, reasoning with her that making a big deal out of the whole thing would just cause more talk.

She knew that was true, but she didn't have to like it. Kerry booted a small rock across the parking lot, glad of her heavily tinted sunglasses protecting her eyes against the glare. The late afternoon thunderstorms hadn't built up yet, and the sun was beating down on them as they walked, making even her light cotton shirt feel like it weighed a ton.

"You all right?" Dar asked.

"Yeah," Kerry replied. "Just thinking."

They both stepped over a parking bumper in unison, and then continued on. Dar looked between the buildings to where the ships were moored seeing a great deal of activity around them. Cranes had been set up as well, and men were working all over the place. She could hear rivet guns, and the sound of saws and sledge hammers beating away at the aged metal hulls.

There was a scent of ozone in the air from the welding torches being used, and as they moved closer, they could hear the rough voices of the workers calling out. Kerry resolutely pushed her lingering unsettledness back, and turned her attention to the project hoping their wiring team had been able to make some progress. "Looks like a mess."

"Mm." Dar stepped around a jagged pothole in the road and produced her identification as they approached the door to the pier building. The guard barely looked at it, and then just stepped to one side so they could walk inside.

"Warm and fuzzy," Kerry muttered.

"Right there with you," Dar agreed, taking off her sunglasses as they entered the gloomy building. She could hear raised voices from the back office, and headed in that direction with Kerry at her heels. They rounded the corner and saw two men at the door to the office facing off against their security guard and the office manager Kerry had assigned to the building. "What's going on here?" Dar asked crisply.

The two men turned, and the two ILS employees' faces brightened when they spotted Dar and Kerry. "Ma'am, I'm glad you're here," the guard addressed Dar. "These gentlemen are demanding we give them access to our switches in here."

Kerry removed her sunglasses and gave the men a direct stare. "This should be good. For what?"

The two men appeared caught slightly off-guard. "We had a report someone in this office was trying to hack in to the port's network," the man nearest Dar said. "We need to check it out."

Dar looked him up and down. "Buddy, if I was hacking into your network, you'd never know it," she said. "You don't get access to anything. You have a problem with that, have your boss call me." Digging in her wallet, she pulled out a business card and handed it to the man. "Now, excuse us."

The man looked at her card, and then gave Dar a dour look. "Lady, we don't need your permission to go anywhere on this port. I was just being nice. I'm going to stop being nice now."

"I'm going to call the police now," Dar replied, "since this space has been bought and paid for, and isn't part of the port for the time being."

Kerry removed her cell phone and dialed it, content to let her partner exercise her kickass gene. "Hello, yes. Can I speak to someone about intruders on my property?"

The man pointed Dar's card at her. "I'll go get our security and be right back. Don't go anywhere, lady." He brushed past Kerry and walked out, followed by his silent companion.

Kerry waited for him to turn the corner, and then she folded her phone shut. "Hmm."

Dar edged past the guard and headed into the office. "I'll check the damn thing. With my luck, it's in a loop and the bastards think it's trying to attack them." She headed for a nearby workstation, sitting down in front of it and keying in her own login.

"Hi, Cheryl." Kerry stuck her phone back on her belt. "So, other than the goon squad visiting, how are things going?"

Cheryl had perched on the corner of one of the gray laminate desks they'd stocked the office with. She was a good looking woman of perhaps forty, with ginger colored hair and gray eyes. Dressed in jeans and a neatly pressed, floral shirt, she appeared comfortable, if a bit harried. "Oh, well, actually, things are going pretty good, ma'am."

"Ahem."

Cheryl smiled slightly. "Sorry, Kerry." She cleared her throat. "The wiring guys have been killing themselves to get work done. They've turned off most of the AC inside the ship and the other vendors have been giving us a very hard time."

Kerry entered the office and leaned against the wall. "Deliberately?"

"No, I don't think so. It's just very close quarters, and everyone wants to get their part done and get out of there. We're fighting with the electrical and air conditioning people right now."

"Ah."

Dar half listened to the conversation, as she poked around inside the switch they'd installed in the office. The inoffensive green box was mounted in a rack near the back of the room, with a locked door and sides around it. Dar scanned the box's contents, then abandoned the device and switched to their router instead. "I don't know what the hell those guys are talking about. We're not even touching their network."

She checked the router's interfaces just to be sure. The piece of gear had been a spare in their office, and only two of the interfaces were in use, but she investigated the others to make sure they were properly turned off, and that no one had plugged something into them they shouldn't have.

Everything appeared clean. Dar got up and went to the rack, opening its door with the universal key she kept on her ring. She checked the cables on the front then went around to the back and stuck her head inside the cabinet, a warm gust of vented air blowing against her face carrying the distinct scent of electrons.

"Anything?" Kerry peeked in the front and peered between the switch and the router at her, the edges of the gear framing her sea green eyes.

"Nah."

"Should we call the cops, Dar? I don't think those guys are going to take no for an answer again, even from you." Kerry lowered her voice. "I really don't want to be involved in a dockside brawl."

Dar rested her chin on the switch. "We could call my Dad. Then you could just watch a dockside brawl instead of being in one." She removed her head from the cabinet and closed the door, locking it carefully. Walking around to the front, she pulled Kerry from the rack and shut the front panel as well. "Now that I'm sure we're clean, maybe I'll be nice and let them look. But don't count on it."

"Huh." Kerry leaned against the rack. "What would make them think something was coming from here, then?"

Good question. Dar bit the inside of her lip gently. "Did we have the circuit pinned down right into here?"

"Yes." Kerry nodded. "I could have had it into the central telco closet, but I elected to pay the extra bucks and have it drop directly into this room." She pointed to a locked, gray box on the wall. "There."

"Nice." Dar said approvingly.

"Kerry, we did get this today." Cheryl came over and offered Kerry a fax. "It's the pre-order shipping list for the network gear."

Kerry studied the paper. "Good. Do we have a completion yet from the wiring guys?"

"No." Cheryl shook her head. "And my problem is, if this stuff shows up before they're done, we're going to have to find someplace to store it all. I don't think it'll fit in here."

Kerry looked around at the interior of the somewhat dingy office. She'd had a cleaning service come in, but the walls really needed a coat of paint instead of the scrubbing they'd done, and she could still smell the sharp scent of new office carpet underfoot. "We'll need some place to set the gear up before it goes on the ship, too."

"Yes."

That meant she had to rent more space. More expenses to charge against the project, which was already expensive and she was under pressure to deliver a price to Quest that was bare minimum. Kerry sighed. "I'll see what I can do."

Footsteps made them all look up, but it was only John, the wiring contractor, who entered. "Afternoon!" He noticed Dar near the rack and grinned. "Should have put in ten percent just for aggravation. My god, those people are a ratchety bunch."

"The ship people?" Kerry was mildly surprised. "I thought we ironed things out with them?"

"Ah." John went to the small refrigerator in the back of the office and removed a soda, popping it open and taking a swallow. "It's the engine guys. They get their pusses into everything in there—want to know what I'm doing, where I'm doing it, what kind of cable—for the love of god, what part of shielded twisted pair are they not getting? Damn chief engineer made me give him a sample this morning."

Dar and Kerry exchanged looks. "Well, after we arm wrestle the pier people we can go talk to the captain," Kerry said, with a sigh.

"Good idea," Dar agreed. "Ah, here comes the goon squad now." She watched through the open office door as a group of men rounded the corner and headed in their direction. The two men they'd chased out earlier were in the lead, with three other men, big guys in jackets, coming after them.

"What the hell's up with that?" John wondered. "Who are those guys?"

Kerry moved to stand shoulder to shoulder with Dar in front of the network rack. If she stopped to think about it, the entire situation was almost sublime in its ridiculousness. Intelligent human beings did not put their bodies on the line for enterprise switches, no matter how expensive they were.

Dar folded her arms and fixed the men with a cool, blue glare.

On the other hand, Kerry smiled inwardly, smart guys didn't mess with Dar, either. Watching the group approach, she had to acknowledge that she could almost smell the stupidity in the air.

Her nose wrinkled, and she hoped Andrew had gotten her note.

THE SCENT OF acrid, hot oil attracted Andrew's attention as he crossed over the gangway into the ship. He stopped midway and leaned over the rail, peering down at the green water with a frown. The surface appeared clear, but the smell continued, and he stepped back off the gangway to walk along the edge of the pier.

With all the construction going on around, there were chemicals and stinks everywhere. But to someone who had spent as much time as Andrew had on ships, certain smells always meant trouble, and diesel oil was one of them.

He walked along the ship, pausing to look down between the hull and the water, until he was halfway down. Then his eyes caught a multi-color reflection on the surface that caught the sun in a bad way. The smell was much stronger, and as he knelt down and examined the slick, he also heard a faint grinding sound from inside the ship.

"Wall." Andy sat down on the concrete and let his legs dangle over the side. "That does not sound like any good thing."

The surface of the water was shiny with oil, and the slight current was taking the slick forward of the ship heading out the cut and toward the sea. Boats discharging into the ocean weren't a rare thing, but he knew cruise ships were watched closely and fined if they were found doing it.

He kicked his boots against the seawall regarding the slick. If he looked all the way down the channel, he could see the oily reflection extending past the ship he was working on, past the space between the piers, and on toward the ship Dar and Kerry were taking care of.

Andrew's brow creased a little. He pushed himself to his feet and walked toward the other ship. The sun revealed the slick extending to the rear of it, as he'd suspected, but as he closed in on the other vessel, he could see that an oily residue seemed to be seeping from it, as well.

Midway between the ships, Andrew stopped and put his hands on his denim clad hips. Several workmen passing by looked at him, but none spoke. He stood there regarding the water, considering his options. "If I saw this here stuff, sure as hell everyone else did too."

"Hey, Ugly!"

Andrew turned, to see the supervisor near the gangway of his ship. He pondered a moment longer, then turned and headed toward the man, ambling along with deceptive speed until he caught up. "Lo."

"Hey, what the heck are you doing out there, looking for fish?" The supervisor asked. "I thought you were supposed to be checking in that new order."

Andrew leaned on the gangway railing. "This here ship and that one down yonder are leaking oil." He said. "Them uniforms gonna bust someone up for that?"

The supervisor jumped off the gangway and went to the side of the pier, looking over. "Shit." He glanced both ways. "I told those guys — Man, if the environmental people see this they're going to pitch a fit."

Andrew's pale blue eyes rested briefly on the supervisor's face, then drifted off again to the water. "Yeap." He agreed. "Them gov'mint types too."

"Nah." The other man shook his head. "They got that paid off...but if one of those mangrove huggers sees it...well, crap. Let me go make a phone call. You go get that box unloaded before those damn women show up again."

Andrew watched him walk off. "Huh." He slowly started across the gangway again. "Paid off them gov'mint types, 'magine that." His pocket started beeping and he stopped, tugging the cell phone out of his pocket and opening it.

Rather than ringing, it was displaying a symbol he'd never seen before. After a moment's thought, he punched the buttons over the flashing icon, and was rewarded by text scrolling across the phone's screen. "What'n the hell is..." The words penetrated, and he turned around, heading off the gangway as he stuffed the phone back into his pocket. "Ah swear them little girls get into more hellfire trouble than a Humvee full of wet swabs."

"Hey!"

Andrew heard the hail, but paid it no mind. He broke into a loping run, picking up the pace as he headed for the port buildings.

Chapter Eight

"ALL RIGHT, LADY. I don't know what you think the rules are here, but let me let you in on a little secret." The biggest of the port security men addressed Dar. "You don't own this place. We do. So step aside and let this guy do his job, okay?"

Dar didn't budge. "No." She stated flatly. "I don't own this place, but I own this gear, and you're not touching it."

"We are going to touch it, and you're going to just move aside and let us." The security chief stepped toward the equipment in question, clearly expecting both Dar and Kerry to move aside. Cheryl was already standing near the wall away from them, and the security guard from ILS was behind them.

"Kiss my ass." Dar suggested. "And make sure your lawyer's on speed dial."

The security officers shifted and looked at their leader. Dar was standing in front of the equipment rack, leaning against it in fact, and showed no signs of moving. Kerry was standing next to her, also clearly challenging their authority with her hands balled into fists and planted on her hips.

"C'mon, we need to get this done." The port technician said.

"I don't really see what your point is." Kerry said. "There's no attack coming from here."

"Not according to this." The tech held up a sheaf of papers. "There's a probe coming from this location, and frankly, I don't give a shit what you think my point is. I think we should call the cops and just have you thrown out and shut down. This is a security area."

"Is that what you want, lady?" The security chief asked Dar, as he stopped within reach of her. "Why not just move, make it easy for all of us?" He suggested. "Because the fact is, this is government area, and I can throw your asses out of here if I want to."

"You can try." Dar warned, in a soft voice.

"Excuse me." Kerry finally felt her interjection would be appropriate. "I tell you what. We'll let you look at our equipment..."

Dar gave her an outraged look. "Kerrison."

Kerry reached out without looking and put a hand on her partner?s back. "If you can explain to me how it can be affecting your systems when there are no wires connecting us to you?" Kerry finished.

The security officials turned and looked at the technicians.

"Can you explain that?" Kerry gave Dar's back a little scratch, feeling the shift as her partner relaxed a trifle.

The security chief turned to the port tech. "Can you?"

"Sure they'd say there's no connection." The port tech laughed.

"They're not stupid." He held up the papers. "This trace shows it as coming from this location. Can you explain that?"

Kerry stepped forward and reached out for the papers. "Let me see them."

"No way." The tech jerked them back.

The security officer turned to Kerry. "Can't you just let him look?" He asked. "It's almost quitting time, lady. I don't want to be filling out paperwork all night, y'know?"

"No." Dar reasserted herself. "This is a secure network. Nothing goes on it that isn't our hardware."

"Okay, then you're admitting to hacking us. That's pretty clear. So get them out of here, and let's do what we need to do," the tech said. "We're wasting time."

"Our time," Dar said. "But if you throw us out of this room, you'll be wasting more than that. Your boss better be ready for a very expensive lesson." Instead of standing back, she now advanced on both the tech and the security guy. "And your boss, if you decide to put a finger on anyone." She warned the bigger man. "Because I don't give a damn what rules and what regulations this damn piss poor port runs under, I guarantee if I go high enough up in the chain around here, someone's going to get FIRED." Her voice rose with each word until the last one was a shouted bark. "Now get the hell out of here!"

Kerry planted herself squarely behind her partner, her heart beating fast as she hoped the men would back off. Not that she doubted Dar's threats were real — after all, she knew darn well they were in the right — but the men looked like they were used to getting their way, and she didn't want to see Dar hurt.

"Wall." A new voice interrupted the chaos briefly. The men turned as Andrew slipped into the room, ducking around the desk to end up next to Dar. "What's all the hollering about, Dardar?"

Kerry relaxed against the rack, reassured now they weren't going to get bruised in any way. The ILS security guard, apparently emboldened by the new arrival, also came around the desk and stood facing the bad guys as well.

Cheryl slipped around and came up next to her, wide eyed. "Jesus." She whispered. "What in the heck's going on around here?"

Good question. Kerry observed the bristling antagonism in the room, and felt compelled to try and circumvent it again, though her first attempt had been a dismal failure. "Okay, folks." She edged around Andrew's bulk and got in front of him. "Tell you what. This is going nowhere. How about you show me what makes you think anything's coming from here, and if it's our stuff, we'll let you look at this end."

Dar actually growled, low and deep in her throat. Kerry decided to pretend she didn't hear it, and waited for the technician to answer. "It's the best deal you'll get. Otherwise, I think we're really talking police here, because without seeing that, I agree with Dar. You're not getting access to our corporate systems. No way."

The security chief decided to take control now. "Give me that." He reached over and grabbed the papers from the tech, who squawked in protest. Shuffling them, he handed them over to Kerry, holding out a hand to stop the tech from advancing. "Stop it. I'm not missing my beer because of you."

Kerry glanced at the trace, her eyes flicking over the details as she moved closer to Dar. "Here." Dar put a hand on her shoulder and read the page as well. "What do you think?"

Dar's brow creased. The trace without a doubt contained one of their addresses, but...she leaned closer. "That's not our router." She indicated the resolved name. "Someone's spoofing us."

"Oh, sure."

"It's an MCI router." Kerry told him. "The building's lit with Bellsouth. You should know that."

The tech grabbed the paper back and looked at it. "No way."

Dar shifted her position and now leaned her arm on Kerry's shoulder. "Sorry. She's right."

"Someone making trouble for you all?" Andy asked his eyes fastened on the techs.

"Shit." The tech put a fingertip on the paper. "That's the damn Seaport center router."

The other tech looked at it then silently shook his head, his expression altering to glum.

"You couldn't have checked that before you dragged our asses over here?" One of the other security men asked. "That lady spotted it in a half second."

"I wasn't looking at that, I..." The first tech was turning red. "We just ran a check on that IP and it was assigned to them." He pointed at Dar. "And they just put up an office here. What would you think?"

The security chief now appeared impatient and bored, rather than impatient and menacing. "Okay, so it's not them. Let's get out of here, and you can figure out who it is, right?" He edged away from Dar. "Sorry about that, but you know security's a touchy subject around here. We got a lot of merchandise going through the port."

"Uh huh." Dar snorted. She reached over and grabbed the papers back. "Give me that. I've got a lot better chance of finding the damn pirate than you do." Inside, she was rattled. Seeing their own IP structure in the trace had made her heart race just long enough to make her lightheaded before she realized the source wasn't inside their network.

Someone was taking a lot of time and effort to cause trouble, all right. Question was, who? Was it hackers still trying to embarrass her, or... Well, hell, what were the chances some hacker would pick this particular target?

"You can't have that, it's restricted information." The tech protested.

"Yeah, well, she sure looks like she can do more with it than you can, buddy. Move." The security chief knew when to cut his losses. "Next time you call us, try to have your act together, huh?" He and his men herded the techs out of the office. "Sorry again."

"Jerks." The second security guard muttered, shaking his head. "Get us all tangled up for no reason."

Dar folded the paper in her hand in half, sharpening the crease with intense, precise motions. She waited for the men to leave and disappear around the corner before she half turned to look at the rest of the people in the room. "Hi, Dad," she murmured. "Was I yelling loud enough for you to hear me outside?"

"Naw." Andy retrieved his cell phone and held it up. "Kumquat sent me a note thing."

Kerry sat down on the edge of the desk. "What the heck was that?" She looked up at Dar. "Can you trace it from those notes?"

"I don't know." Dar half shrugged. "But I guess I'll find out." She added, "I'm sure someone was trying to make it look like we're doing something wrong."

Kerry's eyes darkened. "Oh, I can't imagine anyone would want to do that," she replied sarcastically. "But Dar, who says they won't try it again? This location's so vulnerable."

Cheryl sidled up, with a worried look on her face. "She's right about that." She gave the security guard an apologetic look. "No offense, Charles, but you wouldn't have stopped those guys if they'd charged in here."

The guard didn't look embarrassed. "No, ma'am." He agreed. "But I would have called the police. We're not bouncers." He looked at Dar and Kerry. "Ah, not that?"

"Why not? I've got a black eye. Maybe we moonlight." Kerry remarked dryly.

Andrew chuckled under his breath. Dar gave him a look, then folded the paper into quarters and stuck it in her back pocket. She walked past them to the rack, circling it as she considered her options. The box on the wall was connected to their gear by a set of conduits running through the drop ceiling.

Dar walked over and grabbed a chair, dragging it behind her until it was behind the rack. She climbed up onto it and punched the ceiling panel up, shoving it up and into the framing as she stuck her head up into the dark space.

The rest of the room's occupants looked at each other. Cheryl gave Kerry a slight shrug, and then she went back to her desk and sat down. The security guard sidled back out to his station in the hallway, leaving Kerry and Andrew standing in the center of the space.

"Long as there ain't no more hollering, I'm going to get back to mah work." Andrew said. "Them fellers don't much like when folks wander off."

"Thanks for coming over Dad," Kerry told him. "I just wasn't sure what was going to happen."

"No problem, kumquat." Andy told her. "You find anything up there, Dar?"

"Dust bunnies with fangs." Dar sneezed. "Thanks for asking," She looked down for a moment, "and thanks for coming over to make sure we weren't in trouble."

Andrew patted her leg. "No problem, squirt. See y'all later." He headed for the door, giving Cheryl a brief nod as he passed her. "Lo."

"Hi." The office worker waggled her fingers at him. "Bye." She waited for Andrew's tall form to disappear beyond the door before she looked at Kerry in question, her brows lifting. "Dad?"

Kerry nodded. "Hers, not mine unfortunately." She pointed at Dar. "He's doing some work on one of the other ships."

Cheryl peered at the now empty door. "Is he working for them?" She indicated the next pier.

"He's working for us."

"Ahhhh." The office manager smiled, giving Kerry thumbs up. "Nice."

Dar put her head back up into the ceiling, her eyes tracing the conduit. It moved in an unbroken curve from where it dropped down to her rack, up through the drop panel, bracketed to the concrete true ceiling, and dropped back down through the panel to the box on the wall.

No taps, no junction boxes. Dar felt better. She tugged the ceiling panel back into place, then pulled her way along the drop ceiling as she balanced on the chair, it's wheels squeaking in protest.

"Dar!" Kerry popped up off the desk and grabbed hold of the chair back as it threatened to squirt out from under Dar. "Careful!"

"Ah, with any luck, I'll fall on my head." Dar now carefully examined the box on the wall, unlatching it and swinging it open. With a satisfied grunt, she closed and latched it. "Put a lock on that," she ordered Cheryl, as she turned and hopped off the chair. "No one goes near it, no one touches it, no one does anything to that unless I'm standing here watching. Got me?"

"Yes, ma'am." Cheryl nodded.

Dar dusted her hands off, her eyes falling on Kerry as she reached for the chair to move it back. Kerry had her fingers resting on the rack, a look of quiet pensiveness on her face.

Sensing the attention, Kerry looked up. "Maybe we should stick around here this weekend?" She suggested.

Perhaps they should, Dar acknowledged silently. There was too much going on, too many loose ends for them to just take off out of town. She could see the agreement in Kerry's posture, the slight relaxing of her shoulder muscles that almost, but did not quite seem like a slump. "No." She was surprised to hear herself saying. "We've got a line at the cabin and our cell phones. C'mon." She tapped Kerry on the arm and pointed to the door. "Let's go onboard, and get moving."

Without further argument, Kerry simply nodded, and headed for the door. Dar followed her, wondering if that decision, too, wouldn't come back to bite her in a bad, bad way.

"C'MON, CHI...IN you go." Dar held the door to the cabin open, allowing her family to enter before she stepped over the threshold and followed them inside.

It was dark, close to ten p.m., and later than either of them had expected to arrive after traffic and a stop at a tiki hut. But it had been a nice drive even so, and Dar didn't regret it as she detoured toward the wall switches.

Ah. She turned the lamps on and gazed around appreciatively. *Definitely worth the trip.*

Kerry dropped her overnight bag on the couch as she headed for the cabin's kitchen, putting down the bags she was carrying on the stone countertop just inside the door. She whistled softly under her breath as she put away the supplies they'd picked up, listening to Dar ramble around turning on the air conditioning and flipping on the lights.

It felt very good to be here. Kerry opened the cabinet after she finished, taking out a coffee filter and going about the task making coffee. The cabin was now finished, and she leaned on the counter as the hot beverage brewed, looking out over the interior with a sense of pleasure.

The living area had a long couch against the wall, its ends curving around to make a huge seating pit across from a wood enclosed television set. The furniture was overstuffed and comfortable, butter soft green leather that blended with the stone floors and wooden walls.

There were richly woven colored carpets scattered around, and in one corner a large round dog bed that Chino was busy scratching and snuffling. On the walls were a few pictures, one piece of Dar's mother's art, and some of Kerry's photography.

Overall, the impression was one of a richly appointed, if very small, hunting lodge, except it had no tacky animal heads on the wall and there was a distinct lack of testosterone.

Kerry turned around in the kitchen. It had stone countertops of polished and cool granite that framed the gas stove, brushed stainless refrigerator, and blue shutters that closed over the window above the sink.

Rustic. Except that there were wireless access points mounted on the walls near the ceiling. The television was a flat plasma display, and the entire cabin was hooked up to a remote monitoring system that could have let her turn on the air and the coffee from the car on the way down, if she'd really put her mind to it.

But she hadn't. Kerry smiled as Dar appeared from the bedroom, having already traded her jeans and crisp cotton blouse for a pair of shorts and an old, ratty t-shirt. "Know what?"

Dar walked over and leaned on the other side of the counter from her. "You're glad we're here," she said. "So am I."

Yes, she was glad. Kerry sighed happily. It felt so calm and peaceful here in the cabin. The sound of the ocean was audible through the sliding doors that opened onto their big porch — which was a little funny, because their condo on the island was equally quiet, and had an equally close relationship to the sea — and yet, she always felt different when she was here. "I am very happy to be here, yes," she said. "But what I was going to say was, how about a bowl of designer popcorn and a movie?"

"You don't need to ask me twice," Dar replied instantly. "Tell you what; I'll fix the coffee while you go change."

"You don't need to tell me twice." Kerry said doing a little dance as she exited the kitchen, bumping hips with Dar on her way to the bedroom. "Pick something gory."

"Only if you promise not to use that red candied apple stuff on the popcorn." Dar took her place in the kitchen, taking down a set of mugs and putting them down on the counter. "Gave me nightmares the last time."

Kerry chuckled as she entered their bedroom, smiling as she bypassed the neatly made waterbed and the mahogany dressers that held the clothing they now left at the cabin all the time. They'd picked ocean colors for the bedroom — blues and greens, with the odd punch of color, fiery orange and red, as though tropical fish had made an unexpected appearance. On both sides of the floor to ceiling windows were stained glass panels, throwing warm bars of color when the sun slanted through them.

She loved this room. Kerry unfastened her jeans and slipped out of them, folding them neatly and putting them on the shelf inside the closet. She put her hiking boots next to them, and then removed her shirt, hanging it up as she traded it for a shirt of Dar's that hung down halfway to her kneecaps.

Chino trotted in to find her, tail wagging as she spotted Kerry and rushed over to bump her knees. "Hi, sweetie. Did mommy Dar send you in here after me?"

"Growf."

"Okay, well here I am." Kerry reached down to pat the dog's head. "Are you glad we're here too?"

Chino wagged her tail even more furiously. The Labrador enjoyed the cabin almost as much as her owners. Her favorite activity was chasing the crabs down the beach just outside.

Kerry gave the soft ears one more scratch, then she patted her leg and headed back out into the living room. Dar was just coming out of the kitchen with the coffee cups, and she paused to put them down on the counter as Kerry passed her. "Ker?"

Willingly, Kerry detoured, swinging around and coming nose to nose with her partner. "Yes?"

Dar leaned forward and kissed her gently on the lips. Then she rubbed noses with her. "I love you." She rested her forehead against Kerry's. "Do you care if it rains tomorrow?"

"Hell no."

"Me either."

Kerry leaned in for another kiss, then reluctantly backed off and ducked into the kitchen. "How do you feel about milk chocolate and caramel?" she asked, removing a package of popping corn from the refrigerator.

One of Dar's eyebrows waggled. "Lose the corn, shorty." She drawled, in her sexiest voice.

Kerry started laughing.

"Wasn't the reaction I was going for," Dar complained.

"Harumph." Dar took a sip of her coffee.

Kerry looked at her and left her corn to pop as she climbed up onto the counter and leaned across it, capturing Dar's lips just as she managed to swallow. "You can drizzle me whenever you want, my love." She leaned even closer, whispering in Dar's ear, "But caramel hardens in really, really awkward places."

Now it was Dar's turn to laugh, almost making her coffee spill.

Satisfied with the reaction, Kerry got down off the counter and retrieved the small containers of sweets, sticking them in the microwave to heat up as the corn started popping in the popper. "You know, I'd love it if it rained tomorrow. I would absolutely adore a day to just lie around and be a complete bum."

"You can do that if it's sunny." Dar walked around the counter, handing Kerry her coffee.

"Nah. If it's sunny, I just have to be outside messing around on the beach, or in the water, or on the bike..." Kerry demurred. "I feel so guilty being a couch potato when it's pretty out."

"Eh." Dar had no such problem, having learned to take her slothdom where she found it. "Well, if it's nice out, I'll fish for dinner. How's that?"

Hmm. Kerry removed the corn from the popper, putting it in a huge round bowl. She drizzled her additives over it and tossed the corn. "I think that sounds spectacular." She looked over her shoulder at Dar and grinned.

Dar grinned back. They took the corn and the coffee and curled up together on the couch. Kerry leaned back and felt the aggravation of the week dissolve as Dar wrapped both arms around her. Even the tension of the ship, where the wiring had slipped behind schedule, eased into that place she reserved for things she had limited control over.

John was going as fast as he could. The conditions in the ship were hellacious; there was intermittent power and no air, and even Dar had come off the vessel shaking her head.

Kerry could not change the conditions. All she could do was press John to meet his commitment because time was running short and she had a deadline herself.

Here, she could release all that, putting it aside until Monday. Even in the condo that was hard to do because all she needed was to walk outside and she could see the ship from there. In the cabin, there was only peace, the sea, and the warmth of Dar's body pressing against hers.

She picked up a piece of popcorn and offered it to Dar, who accepted it, licking the chocolate drizzle off her fingers as she took it between her teeth. "Can I ask you something?" She looked away from the opening credits of the hack and slash movie her beloved partner had selected and peered back over her shoulder.

"Sure." Dar opened her mouth and poked her tongue out, looking inquiringly at the bowl.

Kerry placed another corn on her tongue and watched it disappear. "I was a lot more pissed off about all the bullshit talk at the office than you were."

"Was that a question?"

"Erm...no. I guess I was just..." Kerry paused. "I guess you're just used to it, huh?"

Dar's hold tightened. "No." She gazed reflectively past Kerry's shoulder. "I just knew none of it was true, so I didn't care."

Kerry's brow creased.

"The last time I heard stuff like that, it was," Dar clarified quietly, "And the time before that, and etc." Her shoulders moved in a faint shrug. "All I felt was just this sense of relief, honestly. As long as you know the truth, nothing else matters."

There were faint reflections in the depths of Dar's eyes. Kerry disregarded the movie and the popcorn, half turning to lay her hand gently on Dar's cheek. "Nothing else does matter," she said. "I never thought about that, you know? About how it was before for you."

"Mm." Dar blinked peacefully at her. "It sucked," she said, "especially the last time. Everyone took a..." She paused a second, "certain glee in our very, very public breakup."

Kerry rubbed the side of her thumb against Dar's skin. "Well, if I'd been there..."

"If you'd been there, it'd have been a moot point."

"Okay, well, if I'd been there and we hadn't been together..." Kerry restarted.

"You think that's really likely??"

Kerry shifted her hand to cover Dar's mouth. "Let me finish my over the top declaration, please," she scolded. "If I'd been there, and we hadn't been together, and we were just friends, I would have taken the biggest mallet I could find, and gone around whacking all those bastards on the head like moles." She removed her hand and leaned closer. "Do you believe that?"

"Oh yeah," Dar agreed instantly. "You have the staff scared spitless. They'd rather spill gossip to me than dare to tell you about it."

Kerry's eyebrow cocked. "Really?"

"Really." Dar kissed her. "So yes, Kerrison, I believe that with all my heart."

"Oo." Kerry nibbled a piece of corn. "I feel like such a mercenary." She let her head rest against her partner's. "Grr. You bring out the beast in me."

Dar eyed her, a grin surfacing immediately. "I'd buy that a lot faster if you didn't have that cute smile, Ker."

Kerry solemnly stuck her tongue out, then licked Dar's nose with it.

Dar reveled in their closeness, feeling a simple happiness not only in having Kerry in her arms, but in being here in this place that was so much a part of both of them. The troubles at work niggled at the very periphery of her conscience, but she ignored that, leaving the potential issues for the daylight.

Tonight didn't belong to work, it belonged to them. Dar poked her tongue out for more popcorn, and they then settled in to watch the mayhem.

AS IT HAPPENED, it did rain the next day. Kerry was in her glory, lounging in her pajamas on the couch watching luridly violent, yet curiously satisfying, cartoons. Dar was stretched out facing her, the length of the furniture explicitly planned so they both could relax on it at the same time.

"Mm." Kerry wiggled her toes against Dar's, grinning as she responded. While purchasing leather furniture didn't usually involve measuring for footsies, in their case they'd decided to make everything in the cabin fit them—even the chairs on the porch. Hers was a little smaller with a shorter seat, and Dar's was long enough to fit her legs perfectly. A bit pretentious, perhaps, but as Dar had said at the time, they could afford it and it lasted longer than an ice cream cone so why not?

At least they hadn't had the towels embroidered with Hers and Hers. "Find anything yet?" Kerry asked.

"Nope." Dar had her laptop balanced on her thighs. "So far, nada. That MCI router exists, but they swear nothing in it has got our IP."

"Uh huh." Kerry put her head down on the plush leather couch arm. "You think they're covering up, or just clueless?"

"Eh. Let me threaten more people. I'll let you know."

Sounded like a fine idea to Kerry. She stifled a yawn as she watched the animated characters thrash and dance their way across the screen, reminded suddenly of her little friend Gopher Dar. "Are you messing with that program a lot more?"

Dar's fingers stopped moving, and she peered at Kerry over the top of her laptop screen. "That program." She repeated. "You mean..." She made a face, and chattered.

"Yeah."

Dar continued typing for a bit in silence, thinking about the question.

"I thought maybe you were getting a little bored," Kerry suggested. "So you were using that to keep yourself interested."

"No." Dar shook her head. "Actually, I think I've just been lonely."

Kerry rolled over and looked at her in surprise.

"That's my way of hanging out with you when we're both busy." Dar had most of her concentration focused on her screen, and was unaware of Kerry's rapt attention. "I'd be sitting in my office — c'mon, you bastard — and I'd be on this stupid, pointless conference call wishing I was out on the boat with you instead, and all of a sudden some new idea for the damn thing would occur to me. New t-shirt, new dance...I finally got the vocal program working the other day."

"I noticed," Kerry replied quietly, now understanding the message it had conveyed.

"Anyway, it's more interesting than listening to people bicker about their budgets."

Kerry studied Dar's angular face, watching the pale eyes flick over the screen with restless energy. "Dar?"

"Hmm?" Dar looked up.

"Do you...not like what you're doing now?"

Dar's brow creased. She thought for a moment, and then cleared her throat a little. "I don't know, really. It's not so bad most of the time."

Kerry got to her knees and scrambled forward, sprawling over Dar's legs to get closer to her. "You liked what you were doing before though, right?"

Dar shrugged. "Yeah, I guess."

"I took your job."

Dar chuckled easily. "No you didn't. I horse-wrangled you into the position over your protest, if I recall correctly." She set the laptop aside. "Besides, you do it better than I did."

Kerry crawled up further. "That's not the point, Dar." She objected. "Not if you're not happy because of it."

"Happy?" Dar took hold of her and pulled her up further until Kerry was half lying on top of her, their limbs tangled in a warm mess. "I have never in my life been happier."

Kerry rested her chin on Dar's shoulder. "That's not what I..."

"I know. But it's the truth." Dar nuzzled her hair.

Perplexed, Kerry fell silent, not really sure what to say next. Maybe, as Dar had hinted, it was time for her to change and move on to do something else. The thought made her anxious, though, and she had to admit, if only privately, that the last thing she wanted from a professional standpoint was Dar leaving the company.

Maybe they should both leave. Kerry liked that idea better. They'd talked around the idea of forming their own business for the longest time. Maybe it was really time to get off their butts and do something about it.

She put her arm over Dar's stomach and squiggled down between her and the couch, liking the view from this end better anyway. She thought for a bit about her own job, and whether or not she liked it as much as she had when she'd started.

It was okay, she finally decided. The one big problem with it was that it never really allowed a sense of completion of anything. It was always one situation after another, after another, after another. There was never really any time when she could sit back and feel satisfied with where she, and by extension the company, was.

Would that ever change? Kerry doubted it. She was about to mention her revelation to Dar, when her cell phone rang, as though punctuating her thoughts with eerie precision. With a sigh, she took the phone from Dar, and opened it. "Hello?"

"Ms. Stuart?"

"Yes?"

"This is Justin in operations, ma'am," the voice replied. "I'm sorry to bother you on the weekend, but I had note in the log about a file transfer on the financial lines?"

Kerry glanced up at Dar, who was now listening. "Yes. Is it happening again?"

"Well, I'm not sure, ma'am. I'm just seeing a lot of traffic on that line, and it's sort of unusual for a Saturday, you know?"

Dar picked up her laptop as Kerry straightened to give her room.

"Yes, I understand," Kerry said. "Okay, we'll take a look at it, Justin. Thanks for calling me. Did anyone from the bank contact you?"

The tech sounded surprised at the question. "On a Saturday? No, ma'am. They sure didn't," he said. "I've notified my boss, and he's checking it out too, but he thought maybe you'd be interested in hearing it also."

Dar switched off the program she'd been using and opened up her network systems instead. "Got that right."

"Your boss is spot on," Kerry told the tech. "Thanks for calling me, and let me know if anything changes, okay?"

"Yes ma'am, I sure will." Justin promised.

Kerry hung up and squirmed around so she could see the laptop screen. "I am getting really freaking annoyed at all this crap, Dar."

"Mm. Sorry." Dar was typing quickly. "My stupid fault." She

accessed the circuit in question and reviewed it. "Damn it, he's right." She sighed. "Same crap as before. I'm going to just cut it off."

"Don't you want to try and trace it?"

Dar's fingers hesitated. "I don't think we can risk it," she admitted. "I don't know what this is, Ker. It's too dangerous on the bank lines." She typed in another command. "I'll grab what I can, then dump the connection."

Kerry watched in silence as she completed the action, and the activity in the monitors fell to normal levels. "Why didn't Mark do that?" She asked, curiously. "Was he trying to track it down?"

Good question. Dar keyed up her messaging program and typed in a question, then hit send. She reviewed the logs of the router, checking the address sources still held in its memory. "Hmm." She frowned and reviewed them again, then copied and pasted them to her desktop. "Ker?"

"Yeah?" Kerry peered at them. The list of addresses was mostly of no interest to her, save one. "Isn't that one of ours? Is that you or maybe Mark coming in remote?"

Dar checked her laptop's configuration. "Nope not me." She probed further. "I don't think it's Mark."

"Another spoof?" Kerry leaned even closer. "But wait, that's from..."

"Inside our network." Dar completed the sentence unhappily. "Now I hope it's Mark. It's gone already." She searched, but found no trace of the offending station. Her machine beeped, and an answer came back from Mark.

I was trying to get a dump. Got a partial.

Dar typed back a question.

No, that's not me, I'm on the protected security range. Mark typed back. *That's one of the pool addy's.*

"Shit." Dar sighed again. She typed back. *Then we need to find out why one of those pool addresses was inside the bank router. Because it's one of the sources of that data parse.*

The screen was briefly silent. *That sucks.*

"No kidding." Kerry felt a sick sensation in her guts. "Someone inside the company is doing this? Is that what we're looking at, Dar?"

"Maybe."

Well, ulterior motives didn't usually show up on the security checks. Kerry thought back over the recent new hires in their division. "Dar, we haven't hired anyone for three months. Are you saying someone might have been here for that long, just lying low?"

"Doubt it." Dar put a series of controls in place. "If it's a pool, it might not be from IT." She debated a moment, then exhaled. "I'm going to put my program in all the border routers."

Kerry winced. "Is it ready?"

"No. But it's better than nothing." Dar called up the utility and started transferring it from her laptop to the remote devices. "Worst it will do is crash the whole net."

"Dar..."

"I know, hon, but we've got very few options." Dar replied gently. "I'll take responsibility for it."

"That's not my issue." Kerry protested. "It's just really hard to fathom having to explain to a zillion customers that they're down because you crashed us."

Dar chuckled without humor. "I'll take the calls if it happens." She finished transferring the program to the first router, then activated it. "I built the network, I can wreck it, I guess."

Kerry hid her face in Dar's shirt. "Can you program it to scream if it crashes? At least we'll get warning — "

"Hopefully..." Dar finished her work. "Okay, it's in the number one pair." She monitored the devices with some anxiety, despite the confidence she had in her own skills. You just never did know when something you never anticipated would interact with a program, and send everything all to hell. "I think it's okay."

Kerry peeked at the screen. The gauges were steady, but with the same odd flutter she'd seen the last time Dar's program had run. "Can you dump the warnings here?"

Dar drummed her fingers. "Yeah, I better. Ops has nothing set up to receive them." She keyed in the programming change carefully. "Okay...let me get that on the rest of them."

Dar!

"Whoops...should'a warned him." Dar glanced at the message. *Sorry. I'm putting my new code in.*

Hey, that address was from inside the office! The server issued it at 2pm. I'm calling security to find out who's in.

Kerry reached across Dar's forearms to type on the keyboard. *I want to see that list! KS*

Dar glanced at her, a grin twitching at her lips. "Should I get the mallet?"

"This is not funny." Kerry growled. "Dar, if someone inside the office is responsible for that, we need to call the police."

"I know." Dar answered. "Let's just find out what's really going on before we jump to conclusions though." She typed further. "Not that there's any legitimate reason for anyone in our office to be in that router, but I do like to have the facts."

"Grr."

"Then we can whack 'em."

Kerry put her head down on Dar's shoulder to wait, watching the screen with impatient eyes. Someone inside. Her eyes narrowed. Didn't that just suck?

ANDREW PUT DOWN the crowbar he'd just been using, and lifted the cover off the crate in front of him. The hold of the ship was thick with workers despite it being a weekend, and he was careful to prop the cover up against the bulkhead out of the way.

It was hot in the hold, and he had to pause to wipe the sweat off his brow. He was glad he'd picked a tank top to wear to work. The sky was becoming overcast and the breeze had dropped, promising rain later but doing nothing to dispel the mugginess.

He hadn't expected to be called in today. The supervisor had been a touch mad at him for running off the previous day, and Andy had half expected the man to punish him by giving him a few days off without any pay.

That would have been just fine, from his view. There was a nice big ocean right out there waiting for them to be driving over it. Sitting at the helm of their boat was a sight nicer than unpacking boxes inside an old metal sauna box.

But the super had gotten a call, and everyone'd been told to come in the next day. So here he was. A quick look over the side of the ship had confirmed that the ship was still leaking oil, and he was pondering what do about it after Ceci had nearly scared most of the fish out of the harbor when she'd heard about it.

Sometimes, he did forget his wife was one of them environmental types. Andrew scratched his jaw, then shook his head, scattering a few droplets of sweat over the box. Ah well. He'd figure something out.

With a low, melodious whistle, he picked up a shipping invoice and then peered inside the crate, glancing at the sheet for confirmation. The box was alleged to contain boxes for cash registers, and as he pulled aside a thick wad of cardboard stuffing, the corner of stacked gray boxes were revealed. "Yeap."

A yell outside the ship made him look up, and he heard the sound of air brakes releasing and catching just outside. "Now what?" He muttered, going to the hatchway and looking out.

An eighteen wheel truck was parked outside, its driver arguing with one of the guards. Andrew glanced inside, watching the crew around him gathering around the coffee pot for a break. He stepped out onto the gangway instead, and crossed over to the road to listen in.

The trucker was a big, tall, man wearing cowboy boots, a big buckle belt, and with a hat to match, as much a stereotype as Andrew had seen recently round these here parts. Feller even had highway patrol sunglasses on.

"Listen, buddy." The trucker pointed past the guard. "There ain't no gate down there big enough to pull this rig in. I just need to go over there, so get outta my way, okay?"

The guard shook his head. "Sorry, buster. My boss said no one goes through here to that pier, period."

"What's the big deal? It's just a damn road."

"Not to that pier. They don't want anyone going through this pier or to that pier for deliveries. Forget it. So just take off."

"This stuff's got a rush delivery!"

The guard, a young man in his mid-twenties, smirked. "Rush? I don't care. My base said no one, and that means no one. Guess they're just out of luck," he said.

No deliveries to Dar's boat, huh? Andrew ambled closer, leaning against a stone post near the truck. "Now, that don't make much sense." He drawled. "Feller's just looking to pull on through."

The guard looked at him. "Shut up, old man. Get back in there to work. No one asked your opinion."

No one, least of all Andrew, expected what happened next. The trucker, standing within arm's reach of the guard, dropped his clipboard and lashed out, slugging the man across the face with one gloved fist, and sending him sprawling to the ground. "Know what I hate worse than a pissass little punk?" The man growled. "It's a pissass little punk disrespecting people."

Andrew snorted, covering his mouth with one hand.

The trucker stomped back toward his rig, grabbing his clipboard on the way, shaking his head and muttering as he walked. "Ain't got the balls to stop me going where I want to go, that's for damn sure."

The guard got to his feet, and wiped a bit of mixed blood and spit from his face, then removed the baton from the ring on his belt and took off after the trucker. "Son of a..."

"Wall, now." Andrew shoved away from the stone pylon and intercepted the guard in two long strides, catching him by the arm and swinging him around. "Son, don't be a jackass."

"Let the fuck go of me!" The guard squalled, lashing at Andrew with the baton. "I'll kick your ass!"

"Boy, don't you do that." Andrew warned, reacting out of instincts honed during many years of experience.

The trucker turned, to see his erstwhile attacker being bent into a pretzel as Andrew put him in a restraint hold and lifted him off his feet. He put his hands on his hips and just watched, as the uniformed man was shaken like a rat, bits of his guard accoutrements bouncing off the pavement and rolling under the truck.

"Ah told you, don't be a jackass." Andy told him firmly. "That there feller's just going to drive that truck over you and make you flatter than a pancake."

"Let go of me!" The man struggled to no avail.

Andrew walked over to the waterside with him, and held him threateningly over the edge of the pier. "Ya like salt?" He inquired. "No? Then just shut your mouth up." He looked over at the trucker, who had climbed inside his rig and started the engine. "Now, don't you be speeding on this here dock, young feller." He cautioned the driver, getting a grin in return.

The trucker honked his air horn in appreciation, giving Andrew a big thumbs up as he drove past the ship toward the next pier.

Andy waited for the truck to clear their space, and then he released the guard giving him a healthy shove across the dock to prevent any errant stupidity.

The guard caught his balance, and turned, starting back toward Andrew with an angry expression on his face. "You are in so much trouble, old man."

"Ah am not in any trouble, son." Andrew merely sat down on the pylon and waited for him, relaxed and calm. He made eye contact with the guard and held it steadily as the man advanced on him, years of facing danger lending a sheen of ice to his composure. "But surely you will be." He added, in a soft tone. "If you keep on keeping on."

The guard slowed as he approached, and then halted uncertainly. Then he backed off, sticking his baton back into his belt. "I'm not going to bother with you."

Andrew smiled.

"I'll just get my boss to get your ass fired." The guard gathered the shreds of his dignity and stalked off toward the small guard house, leaving Andrew in peace on the side of the dock.

Thunder rolled overhead, making him look up at the sky. "Ah do think ah just like trouble." He remarked. "Lord knows mah kid got that from some damn place, after all." After a brief moment, the ex-SEAL got up and headed back across the gangway, chuckling softly under his breath.

DAR REACHED OVER and picked up her cup of coffee, taking a sip before she offered it to Kerry. They were still squished together on the couch, after an hour of tense work on the laptop had at least given them a measure of security over the situation.

"How long does it take security to figure out who is in that building?" Kerry groused, handing the cup back after taking a swallow. "What did they do, call out the dogs to sniff the Xerox supply rooms?"

Dar watched her gauges, her fingers twitching above the keys. "It's a big building."

"Not that big." Kerry listened to the thunder, and then she returned her head to Dar's shoulder. "You know, it's a pity we can't work like this all the time."

"From the cabin or from this couch together?" Dar asked.

"Yes."

"I have a couch in my office."

"It's not as comfortable as this one." Kerry objected, reaching over to type in a few lines, and hit enter. "And there is just no way I could wear my jammies there, Dar."

Dar cocked her head and regarded Kerry's dress that featured adorable little cart wheeling piglets all over it. It consisted of a nightshirt that was just barely legal, but also had a pair of bottoms Kerry seldom wore. "I could post a policy change just for you."

"Uh huh. I can just picture me running meetings like this."

Dar chuckled. "Not a goddamn thing would get done," she said. "Ah...here we go. All right. Now that's looking better." She was at last satisfied with how her program was behaving. "Okay, I think it won't crash now."

"Phew."

Dar now switched to her mail, clicking on a late arrival. "Here's the trace Mark got." She reviewed the results. "Encrypted."

"Can you un-encrypt it?" Kerry asked. "I can't even read the header."

"Hmm." Her partner drummed her fingers on the keyboard. "Not without the..." She hesitated. "Let's wait to see if Mark finds the machine it was coming from. It'll be easier with the key. I might be able to crack the encryption, but it would take me forever."

Kerry typed on the keyboard. *Mark – what is taking so long for the security report?*

Dar slipped her arm over Kerry's shoulders, and rubbed her back gently. "This is going to be a big issue. I better warn Alistair."

Freaking all of sales and marketing is here! Mark's answer came back, brimming with disgust. *The whole damn floor is packed with them, and they've been sucking DHCP addresses all morning.*

"Oh. Crap." Kerry sighed. "That sucks."

Dar considered the screen. "Maybe...maybe it doesn't." She said slowly. "I wonder how many new people they've brought on in the last month."

"They turnover like..." Kerry started to say then her voice trailed off. "But Dar, whoever did this was technically very savvy."

"Uh huh. Where better in our company to hide then, hmm? Last place I'd look for a nerd is in those groups." Dar's tone was grim. "And you know what else?"

Kerry stared at the screen, then up at Dar. "They're all around the presentation rooms."

"Exactly."

Exactly.

Chapter Nine

KERRY GUNNED THE engine of her bike, looking both ways before she eased out onto the still damp road and headed south. The sun had reluctantly made an appearance on its journey to the west, and she decided it was a good time to buzz off down to the market and get something for dinner.

The roads were still wet and she was careful to keep her speed down. Being dumped on her butt on the road wasn't something she was willing to experience, even if Dar had patiently taught her how to right the bike if she did get overturned.

It wasn't easy even though she was stronger than most women her size. Kerry shifted gears and headed through a green light—one of the few traffic stops in the general vicinity. The quiet nature of the town was one of the things she liked most about it and even now on the weekend, there was little traffic to impede her passage.

The market was just up on the right hand side, a low, wooden building with sun-faded paint and crushed shell pathways leading from the scrubby little parking lot to the door. Kerry pulled into a shady spot near the door and shut the bike's engine off, swinging her leg over the seat and removing her helmet.

She tucked the safety gear under its bungee and headed for the doors, the still damp breeze brushing over her bare shoulders. Pushing the left door open, she entered the pleasant chill of the air conditioned room and removed her sunglasses, tucking them by one earpiece into a belt loop. "Hi, Bill."

The man behind the meat counter looked up and waved. "Hi there, neighbor." He greeted Kerry amiably. "Didn't know you were down here this weekend. Thought the rain would keep folks up north."

"We came down on Friday night." Kerry picked up a basket and started browsing up and down the aisles. "But it looks like it's clearing up now. How's Martha?"

"Oh, she's doing fine." Bill said. "Hey listen, I just got in some fresh snapper. You want a couple pieces?"

Snapper. Kerry cocked her head slightly. Both she and Dar were quite fond of fresh fish, and a nice broiled filet sounded pretty good to her. "Sure." She agreed, detouring to the vegetable section and selecting a couple of Yukon gold potatoes, some green beans, and two ears of white corn.

She also added a quart of strawberries and carried the lot of it up to the counter. She could have gotten stuff for tomorrow also, but she preferred to let whimsy control what she picked rather than planning things out too far in advance. "Wow those do look nice." She commented on the fish.

"A cook would know that." He chuckled. "And I know you're the cook in that house."

Kerry accepted the brown wrapped bundle with a slight grin. "I guess Dar's habit of only buying ice cream, milk, chocolate bars and bananas sort of clues that in, huh?" She handed over her credit card. "But I like cooking. It's fun."

"Me too." Bill pushed the credit card receipt her way for signature. "I get kidded about it by the boys, though. You know how it is."

Kerry signed her name in a neat script hand and gave it back to him. "Well, not really." She admitted. "Usually girls are expected to know how, and to like cooking." Her face creased into a smile. "I've never had anyone look crosswise at me for that. For other things..." She waggled a hand.

"Like that pretty tattoo?" Bill asked, with a grin of his own. "It's new, yeah?"

"Yeah." Kerry glanced down at the half visible mark, peeking out from around her tank top strap. "I got it a few weeks back. Like it?"

Bill leaned closer, raising his glasses slightly to get a better look. "Nice work." He complimented her. "I've got a pair of dolphins, myself, but it'd take a pair of speedos that I'd die before wearing, to show 'em to the world."

Kerry chuckled. "That was my second choice of locations." She picked up her packages and the keys to the motorcycle. "But I think I really wanted people to be able to see it." Her eyes strayed, for a moment, to the mark and the letters of Dar's name visible, before she turned and headed back toward the doors. "Have a great day, Bill."

"You too, Kerry." Bill replied, sitting back down on his stool. "Drive careful now, it's wet out."

Kerry lifted a hand in acknowledgement as she slipped through the door, reaching hastily for her sunglasses as the glare outside made her blink.

"Excuse me...are you Kerry Stuart?"

Kerry pulled up short and turned, finding herself the focus of a well-dressed black woman, and a man with a camera. The woman didn't look unfriendly, but the light was on the camera, and Kerry hadn't grown up in a spotlight for nothing. "Yes." She answered slowly. "Can I ask why you want to know?"

"Great. We found you." The woman smiled. "We're doing filming as part of the special on the new American Cruise line project, and I'd like to ask you some questions."

Kerry squared her shoulders, shifting her packages carefully to one arm. "Our office is in Miami. Is there some reason you came looking for me here?" She kept her voice even, but there was little warmth in it.

The reporter looked warily at her. "Well, someone tipped me off you might be down here...so I thought I'd take a chance. Since the other teams are up at the port working, it seemed a little...unusual that you'd leave the city."

Anger started to bubble inside Kerry's stomach. "Well, I guess you just wasted a trip then. I've got nothing to say at the moment. It's my time off." She turned and headed for her bike, her ears catching the whine of the camera behind her.

"Wait..." The reporter came after her. "Ms. Roberts talked to us."

Kerry put her packages into the small storage area in the back of the bike and got on it, shifting it over its center of balance and putting up the kickstand. "In the office." She started the engine, and revved it, the low throaty roar making speech momentarily impossible.

"You don't think it says something about your company, to have you down here on vacation while everyone else is working?" The reporter queried. "Maybe my source was right after all."

Kerry put her helmet on. "The only thing it says about our company is that we trust our staff to do what we pay them to." She backed the bike and prepared to leave the lot. "Excuse me." She tried not to look directly at the camera, the blank gray eye following her every move.

"Is Ms. Roberts down here too? Maybe I can talk to her." The reporter persisted. "Maybe she can explain it to me since you're unwilling to."

Answering didn't seem wise. Kerry gunned her engine and headed out onto the road, shifting through first and into second gear as she glanced behind her to see if the woman was following. She was caught between outrage and worry, wondering briefly if she should have played the reporter's game and just talked to her for a few minutes.

Dar had, as she'd noted.

Ah well. Kerry shifted into third gear and picked up speed, anxious to get back to the cabin and get the bike under cover before the woman could find out where they lived. Would she knock on the door? The thought made her angry, and she felt somewhat invaded by the idea.

This was a haven for them. To have the reporter come here and shove herself into this part of her world bothered Kerry more than she liked to acknowledge, and she resented it hugely. She leaned into the turn that would take her toward home, and panicked for a moment as she felt the bike start to slide out from under her.

Her body reacted uncertainly, not used to the motion and she leaned back the other way out of pure instinct. For a second, it was riding the line, the tire skidding against the wet pavement for an eternity before the traction caught again and she brought the motorcycle back under control.

"Jesus." Kerry felt her heart pounding in her chest, as she slowed down, ready to make the turn into their driveway. To her surprise, Dar was out in the yard heading for the road, and she jumped the fence as Kerry pulled to a stop in the soft gravel. "Hey."

"Hey." Dar joined her, laying a hand on Kerry's arm. "What's up? You okay?"

"Yeah. Almost laid the bike down." Kerry admitted. "Let's get it in the shed. I had a very unpleasant encounter with your friend from the filming people at the market."

Dar blinked. "My friend?"

"The reporter?" Kerry got off the bike and started pushing it toward the shed.

"How'd she find you down here?" Dar helped, getting her hands between Kerry's. "What the hell did she want?" Her voice sharpened.

Kerry got the door to the shed open, and they pushed the motorcycle inside. She pulled the door closed, just as the sound of tires on the road sounded loud in their ears. They both stood together and listened as the car slowed down outside, then, after a long and still moment, drove on past. "Son of a bitch."

Dar's jaw tightened. "They get you on camera?" She asked, as Kerry moved to take the bags from the back of the bike.

"Yeah." Kerry turned, letting her sunglasses slide down a little and peeking at Dar over them. "Don't worry, though. There's no way anyone's going to believe Roger Stuart's kid with a tattoo on her chest is riding a bike down in the sticks. I'll just say someone was impersonating me."

Dar's lips tensed, then relaxed into a faint grin.

"What are we going to do if she shows up here?" Kerry went on, with a grimace. "It won't take much, Dar. We're in the local phone book. All she has to do is look and she'll have the address."

"Not to mention my car's outside." Dar remarked dryly. "Let's worry about it when it happens. Did she say what angle she was after?"

"Oh yeah." Kerry picked up the parcel, and nudged Dar toward the door. "ILS snooty sloths snuggle while minions slave away." She sighed. "And I joked about it, but I think I just sunk my image big time."

"Hell with 'em." Dar led her back toward the cabin. "If they show up here, I'll just toss them in the salt. Besides, we are working." She peeked inside a bag. "Mm...strawberries."

Kerry allowed herself to be distracted as they walked over to the cabin, and slipped inside. She had a distinct feeling, though, that the reporter wasn't going to give up that easily, or be dissuaded by even Dar's rejection.

Not to mention what it all would look like to anyone viewing the film.

Kerry sighed. *Muskrats.*

THEY WERE BOTH surprised when the rest of the afternoon proved peaceful and reporter-less. Kerry retreated into the kitchen to make dinner, while Dar huddled with her laptop, obsessing over the results of her program.

"Hey, with this filming stuff," Kerry positioned the snapper filets on the broiling pan, dusting them with her jealously guarded mixture of spices, "don't they have to get our approval to show any of it? I mean, it's not a news program, right?"

Dar stretched, lifting her arms over her head and popping her shoulder joints. "Good question," she said. "I should probably send a note to legal and ask, huh?"

"Might be a good idea." Kerry put a final swipe of herbed oil on the fish and prepared to put them in the broiler. She glanced up as Dar entered the kitchen, circling around her and settling her arms around Kerry's waist and observing as she put dinner up.

"Mm." Kerry leaned back a little, savoring the solid warmth of her partner's body. She felt Dar rest her chin on the top of her head and they simply stood together for a bit in silence, swaying lightly to some far off music only their souls could hear.

"Keeeeerrrrry." Dar warbled, in a high tone that mimicked her gopher's. "I llooooooooovvveee you."

Kerry felt like she was going to dissolve into a puddle of blond goo. Slowly, she turned within the circle of Dar's arms and looked up at her. "Can I tell you something?"

"Could I stop you?" Dar leaned forward a little to rub noses with her.

Kerry tilted her head and they kissed, as her arms slid up and clasped around Dar's neck. She caught Dar's lower lip between her teeth and then released her with a soft chuckle. "Well, Paladar, as a matter of fact, yes, you could." She drawled softly. "Just like that, in fact."

Dar chuckled along with her, lifting a hand up to brush Kerry's cheek. "You're so easy to distract sometimes."

Kerry leaned into the touch, pressing her body against her partner's. "Depends on the distraction." She smiled. "But what I was going to say before I was so pleasantly led off course was..." Her eyes gentled and warmed. "You're the best part of my life."

"I am?" A charmed look appeared on the Dar's face. "Even better than ice cream?"

"Much better."

"Aw." Dar hugged her, tucking Kerry's head against her shoulder and giving her a healthy squeeze. "Likewise, sweetheart."

Kerry closed her eyes, and exhaled, welcoming the sweet affection in Dar's tone. After all the chaos of work and the aggravation of meeting the reporter, she wanted this.

Needed it. She slid her arms around Dar's waist and returned the hug, and then ran her hands along her partner's spine giving her a light massage. "I looooooooovvve you too." She warbled softly. "My little gopher."

Dar snickered.

They walked into the living room with their arms wrapped around each other, and got halfway across it before they heard a knock on the door. After sharing a dour look, Dar removed her hold and dusted her hands together. "I'll go take care of this. Stay here."

Kerry debated briefly, and then uncharacteristically obeyed, flopping down on the couch and extending her legs along its length as she watched Dar stalk toward the back door.

She didn't envy the reporter, if that was who it was. Dar could, and often was, rude and nasty when she felt the need to be and being on the receiving end of that was really no fun. Not that Kerry herself knew that from personal knowledge, even when she and her beloved partner disagreed, Dar never went past blunt with her.

In fact, Kerry knew she herself had been by far the nastier of the two of them when they'd first met. She wiggled her toes reflectively, her ears cocked as Dar opened the door.

"Yes?" Dar peered out into the late afternoon sunshine, her body blocking the door open just to her shoulder width.

"Well, hello there, Ms. Roberts. Remember me?" The reporter smiled at her.

"Yes." Dar responded. "Anything else you need? No?" She started to close the door.

"Wait...wait...I really need to talk to you." The woman put her hand out to keep the door from shutting. "Please?"

Dar stared steadily at her. "I'm not on the clock." She let her eyes drift past the woman, but the camera and its operator were nowhere in sight. After a moment, she focused back on the intruder.

"Well, no, but I'm here, and you're here, so..." The reporter persisted. "It'll only take a minute, really."

It all sounded so reasonable. Unfortunately, Dar wasn't feeling very reasonable at the moment. "No." She stated. "I don't appreciate people who invade my private life. So I'd get my hand off the door if I were you, unless you want a broken wrist out of this."

The woman took a step back. "Now, I don't really think we're invading..."

"Did I give you my address here?" Dar asked pointedly.

"Well, no, but —"

"Did you ask if you could do an interview with me during off hours?"

"That's not the point, here —"

"It's exactly the point." Dar started closing the door again. "And damned unprofessional if you ask me. I think I need to make a call to your production office on Monday."

The reporter put her hand out again. "Whoa whoa...wait a minute, are you the same person I interviewed a few days ago? What happened?"

"You screwed up." Dar pulled her head in and pushed the door closed, getting her weight behind it just in case the reporter got any stupid ideas to stop her. "Jerk." She started to walk away, only to stop when a knock came at the door again.

She put her hands on her hips and looked at Kerry. Kerry shrugged sheepishly. Dar narrowed her eyes and turned, going back to the door and yanking it open. She drew back her other hand near her ear and curled her fingers into a fist, cocking it meaningfully. "I am not playing games with you."

The reporter stopped in mid speech and blinked at Dar in surprise. "Are you going to hit me?" She asked in an incredulous tone.

"Yes." Dar said.

"You're crazy."

"No, I've just had my privacy invaded and it's ticking me off." Dar narrowed her eyes. "And we have a law down here that lets me protect my property with pretty much any show of force I want."

"I don't get it. You were just the friendliest thing in your office. What's up with that?" The woman said.

"I'm not in my office."

Kerry got up and walked over, standing behind the door out of sight and pressing her back against it as she listened.

"Okay, so, how does it hurt to talk to me for a minute?" The reporter said. "What's the big deal? We had lunch, remember? C'mon."

"If you want to discuss something, call me during working hours." Dar kept her patience with great effort.

"Or is it that you're with your girlfriend now?"

Dar merely stepped away from the door, and allowed Kerry to slam it shut for her. She loudly threw the deadbolt, then turned her back, waiting for Kerry to join her before they made their way toward the couch again.

"If she knocks again, I'm going to go Republican on her." Kerry commented. "You actually had lunch with this person?"

"That's what happens when you leave me to my own devices for a meal." Dar paused, glancing over her shoulder. "Hell, now I better send legal a note. I can just picture how we'll come off in their little script."

Erg. Kerry trudged back into the kitchen. "Should we have been less rude?" She asked.

Dar picked up her laptop and brought it over to the counter, setting it down and seating herself on one of the wooden stools. She rested her head on one fist and studied the screen. "Screw it."

Kerry turned on a front burner and set a pan over it, putting a little peanut oil and butter in the bottom. As it heated, she removed a colander of green beans from the sink and set it down next to her, grabbing her wooden stirring spoon as she listened to Dar type.

"She was a lot nicer at lunch."

"Uh huh." The green beans were sacrificed into the pan, releasing the scent of spices and garlic as Kerry stirred them. "Like she was on your side?"

Pale blue eyes peeked over the laptop screen at her. "Yeah."

Kerry's lips quirked slightly.

"Did I get scammed?"

Kerry flipped the beans in the pan expertly, remembering the lectures of her childhood. The press, she'd been taught, were not ever, ever your friends and they never were on your side. "Well..." She hesitated, not wanting to insult her lover. "Dar, I'm sure she's very slick. Probably. She might have fooled me too."

Dar sighed. "I thought she was nice." She admitted. "She did say a lot of things...well, anyway, I guess I took her at face value." She saw an email arrive, and clicked on it.

```
Hey Boss -
Got the list, here it is, but everyone and their mamma is
on it. You want me to pull their security scans? I sorted 'em
by hire date, but there's no one in there less than three
months. I don't know what the hell's going on.
Mark
```

"I don't know what's going on either." Dar admitted, with a sigh. "You know what, Ker? I really don't know what the hell's going on. I'm losing it."

Prudently, Kerry merely murmured in sympathy, as she finished the beans and turned off the fire. She got two plates ready, opening up the broiler and retrieving her snapper filets. "I'm not sure I know what's up either," she said, sliding a filet off onto one of the plates and adding some beans along with a baked potato and half a corn.

Dar sat there swinging her legs for a minute, and then she got up and came around into the kitchen, reaching around Kerry to take possession of the plates. "Mmm."

They walked into the living room and sat down next to each other on the couch as Dar set the plates on the burled mahogany coffee table.. "Oh, hang on." Kerry put hers down and got up again, walking back into the kitchen to get them both a drink.

Dar used her fork to separate a bit of fish and tasted it. "Mm." She waited for Kerry to return and sit down again. "Good stuff."

Kerry bumped shoulders with her. They ate quietly, both apparently lost in deep thought.

ANDREW SLUNG HIS tool belt over one broad shoulder and headed off the ship. The sun was blotted out by dark clouds, and there was a heavy smell of rain in the air. Even the usually calm waters of the cut picked up a little chop that washed against the hulls of the ships lined up against the pier.

He was halfway across the open space when the door to the guard hut opened and a man emerged heading in his direction with a distinct sense of purpose. Given the man's bad taste in suits, and the badge holder hanging from his belt Andrew reckoned he might be his guard friend's boss, but he waited until the man was obviously intersecting him before he turned his head and made eye contact.

"Hold up there." The man lifted a hand. "You Roberts?"

Andy slowed and halted as he came even with the man. "Yeap."

The man had thick, slicked back dark hair and a trimmed moustache, a bad complexion, and watery gray eyes. They now fastened on Andrew's face with a cold, stern glitter. "I understand from my man you caused some trouble today, mister."

Behind him, Andrew could see the punk guard, peeking out from behind the shutters in the little guard shack. He shifted his gaze to the man in front of him. "Do ah look like a feller who'd cause trouble?"

The security manager looked him up and down. "That's no answer."

"Young feller there was fixing to get hisself run over by a truck," Andrew said. "Ah just stopped him."

The other man looked down the pier to where Dar's ship was then he looked back at Andrew. "I had orders not to let any trucks through there. How do you want me to explain why one went through? I'm not taking the heat for it, buddy. I'll get your ass fired."

Andrew shrugged. "Ain't made no sense to me. What in hell's the difference if a truck goes on down there?" He figured if he was going to get fired, might as well get any information he could first.

"Doesn't have to make sense to you. I got my orders." The man turned as a yell sounded over the docks. "Shit. Now there's the one giving the orders. You stay here; let me see what they want done with you."

Andrew looked over the man's shoulder to see Shari approaching, an angry look on her face. "Wall." He exhaled. "Don't that figure. That there woman's more trouble than a hemorrhoid in a bucket."

The man swung around and gave Andrew a startled look, an almost smile twitching at his lips. Then he went to intercept his unwelcome visitor.

Andrew hesitated, then he ambled after him catching up as they met Shari halfway across the dock.

"I just got a call, saying you let a delivery go through. I told you no trucks! What's wrong with you, are you stupid?" Shari yelled at him.

"Wait a minute, lady..." The security chief held a hand up.

"I'm not waiting for anything. I gave a direct order." Shari overrode him. "I want your boss's name, right now. I'm not putting up with any more of this horse crap." She pulled out her cell phone. "Give me his number."

"Just hold on a minute..." The security chief looked around as Andrew shifted. "Roberts, I told you to stay back there." He said.

"Damn it!" He returned his attention to Shari. "Now look, lady. It wasn't my fault. This guy here got in the way of my guy doing his job and...lady?"

Shari had stopped in mid motion, and was looking at Andrew with a suddenly suspicious expression. She closed her phone. "Roberts?" She asked, gritting her teeth.

Ah well. Busted. Andrew produced a wicked grin.

The security chief looked from one to the other of them. "You know this guy?" He asked Shari. "He's the one who distracted my guy and let that truck through."

"I just bet he did." Shari's eyes narrowed.

"Sir!" The young guard was calling, from the gate. A group of men and women were standing there, looking impatient. "Sir, you need to come here, please, sir!"

If anything, the chief looked relieved. He edged past Shari and headed for the gate with a muttered apology leaving the two of them facing each other.

"Didn't realize Dar had a brother." Shari snorted, in a disgusted tone. "But now it all makes sense. Let me get that damn stupid supervisor on the phone and get you out of here first."

One of Andrew's grizzled eyebrows hiked up. "She don't," he rasped. "Save yer breath. I'm leaving." He shifted his work belt to his other shoulder and started to walk around Shari.

"Oh no, you're not just waltzing out of here. I'm calling the police." Shari reached out to take hold of his arm. "Have you arrest..." Shari stopped as a hand far larger than hers closed around her wrist and removed her grip. "Let go of me."

Andy stared steadily at her. "If you had any smarts, woman, you would count yerself lucky to just turn round and walk away from here." His voice was soft, but firm. "Mah daughter is real special to me and ah do not take kindly to folks who done messed with her."

"D..." Shari's eyes widened. "Oh shit."

Andrew grinned again, narrowing his eyes.

"Captain! Captain! Get over here!" Shari yelled out in panic. "Help!"

Andrew looked over her shoulder and saw the guards fully engaged with the new visitors, who were pushing their way onto the pier and forcing the two watchmen back. He released her arm, and wiped his fingers off on his jeans as Shari backed away from him.

She swung around, and spotted the guards busy with the gate, and then she headed for the guard shack, leaving Andrew behind without looking at him.

"Have a nice day." Andrew drawled, as he headed for the gates. As he got closer, he could hear the people arguing with the guards, and the word 'oil spill' echoed out of the babbling. "Uh oh." He edged carefully around the man in front, a tall, gray haired tower of indignation and escaped out into the front of the pier.

A pickup truck was waiting for him, conveniently enough. He opened the door and tossed his tool belt behind the seat, sliding in next to Ceci and shutting the door after him. "Just got me fired."

"Really?" His wife inquired.

"Yeap. That there woman fin'ly figgered out where she done knew me from. But ah think them folks right there are gonna be more trouble than me."

Ceci peered past him. "Ah. The EPA." She nodded solemnly.

"You figger?"

"I sent them." Cecilia gave the chaos a supremely satisfied look as she put the truck in gear. "C'mon, sailor boy. Now that we've caused this much trouble, let's go paint the town red. It's Saturday night."

Andrew stretched his arm across the seat and leaned back as they drove away from the port. He wasn't sure Dar would like the results of the day, but he also knew sometimes you just had to take what you got.

Life sometimes did give ya lemons. Smart fellers learned to take a shining to lemonade.

BY THE TIME the last rays of sunset were pouring through the windows, strawberries were at hand and problems set aside for another day. Kerry settled onto the two person bench swing with Dar and pushed gently against the porch support moving them back and forth.

The surface of the sea lapped invitingly in front of them, bringing a soft swishing roar and the faint tinkle of shells being moved under the waves. "Wanna swim with me tonight?"

Dar blew gently into her ear then leaned over to nibble the edge of it. "Sure." She breathed barely audible. "We can do that too."

Kerry gave a low, throaty chuckle.

The air was almost blue with twilight, warm and rich with moisture but lacking the oppressive heat of the day. Seagulls were circling lazily over the water, several landing on the dock which usually held the Dixieland Yankee when they came in by water.

It was quiet, and very peaceful. Kerry leaned against Dar, accepting the berry her partner was holding out before her lips. "It turned out pretty tonight."

"Mm hmm." Dar settled the bowl of fruit in her lap and extended her arm across Kerry's shoulders. There were still clouds across the horizon, but they only served to make the sunset glorious. It was pretty indeed, and now all the more so when she considered how their relationship had opened her eyes to the beauty of the world around her.

She'd always found the ocean pleasing, and enjoyed being at the shore in the salt breeze. But she'd never really just sat and watched a sunset until Kerry had come into her life.

The office was quiet, most of its inhabitants already gone home for the day. Dar packed up her laptop and got ready to leave herself, hesitating without really knowing why after she put her case on her desk.

Just another day, right? Nothing to really hang out here for.

Dar drummed her fingers on the desk, then she bowed to the inevitable and headed for the back corridor, intending on simply saying goodnight to her new assistant. It was only the polite thing to do, after all, and Kerry made a point of poking her head in every morning to say hello so...

She walked down the corridor and paused beside the door to Kerry's office, aware of the gentle tickle of anticipation in her stomach. It had been a long time since she'd felt that and the speeding up of her heartbeat as she thought about those kind, green eyes looking back at her.

She knocked, but there was no answer. Dar felt an immense bit of disappointment, surprised to find herself hurt that Kerry had left without saying goodnight.

Piqued, she opened the door anyway, her mood brightening when she spotted Kerry's briefcase on her chair. She entered the office and circled the desk, her sensitive nose picking up with ease the scent of Kerry?s perfume.

There was a cup on the desk, and as she brushed her fingers over the side of it. She found it still a quarter full with warm tea. So, Kerry couldn't be far off, could she? Dar headed for the front door and slipped out of it, looking both ways down the empty corridor.

Right? Left? Dar went left then turned left at the major intersection that went to the elevators, crossing past them to the other side of the building. Then she paused and pondered. To one side was marketing, to the other, accounting.

A cleaning woman pulled a garbage bin past her, giving Dar a polite smile as she stood there in the middle of the hallway. "Jefa."

Dar focused on her. "Did you just come up on this floor?" She asked, in Spanish.

"No." The woman shook her head. "I have just finished this side. Did you need something done for you?"

Dar looked around carefully, her voice lowering a little. "Did you see a blond woman, about this high?" She held her hand up at shoulder level. "Around in there?"

The woman also looked around before she answered. "Si, she is out on the patio over there, but she told me to say nothing!"

Ah. "Thanks." Dar headed off down the corridor arriving at the sturdy glass and steel doors that blocked off the west side viewing platform. Looking through them, she spotted Kerry at once, leaning against the railing and just looking out into space. "What on earth is she doing?"

She pressed her nose against the glass and watched as the breeze blew Kerry's pale hair back and fluttered her silk blouse tight against her body. The tickle in her guts became a burn, and she felt a little short of breath as she shoved the door open against the wind and emerged onto the patio. "Hi."

Kerry turned. Her expression altered from surprised to muted delight in an instant, and she smiled as Dar walked over to her. "Oh, hi."

"Whatcha doing?" Dar leaned on the railing next to her. Her eyes casually met Kerry's and held there, as the sunset gilded her profile.

"Um...not much." Kerry laughed softly. "Just watching the sun go down." She indicated the orange orb, which was painting the western sky every shade of bad sherbet imaginable. "It's so pretty from up here, isn't it?"

"Absolutely." Dar said, a moment before she took her eyes from Kerry's face, and glanced at the horizon. To her surprise, the view was more interesting than she'd imagined, and she stood there in silence as the shifting rays constantly changed the vista as they watched.

Kerry leaned against the rail next to her, their shoulders almost touching.

Dar wondered if she yelled loud enough, would the world stop turning so she could enjoy the moment just a little longer? It certainly beat the quiet, lonely drive home.

"Um...did you...need me for something?" Kerry asked suddenly, hesitating over the words. "I...I mean, were you looking, uh, or were you just..."

Uh oh. Dar felt totally at a loss. Make up a lie? Not answer? Glib answer? Jump over the railing? "I was just..." She finally got out, clamping her jaw shut after that with an audible click.

Kerry looked at her, a tentative grin appearing as she returned her gaze to the sun. She cleared her throat after a moment. "You know the pre-registration for the networking convention opens up tonight. I was thinking of heading down there early to get my paperwork done." Her eyes moved back to Dar's face. "Are you interested?"

A smile formed on Dar's face, as the sun slipped reluctantly under the horizon. "Absolutely."

Ah, sunsets. Dar smiled at the memory, wondering why it had taken her so long to appreciate them.

Possibly because the sun never set over the water where she'd been living. They'd deliberately picked the west side of the island when they'd bought the cabin to address just that subject. Kerry loved sunsets over the water and though it made it more difficult to reach the cabin since they had to go round the key, it was worth it.

The breeze carried a brief wisp of citronella coming from the candle burning near the post and for a brief moment Dar found herself wishing intensely that every day could end just like this.

Ludicrous, she knew. Dar sighed, and picked up another berry. Besides, if they were all like this, how could moments like now be special? She rested her head against Kerry's.

"You know something?" Kerry continued her gentle rocking. "When I was a kid, I used to go down to the lake near my house and just sit there, watching the sun go down. It wasn't nice like this is, but there always was that little peaceful time when it was happening where everything sort of stood still."

"Mm."

"I wondered for a long time if I would ever have anyone to share that time with." Kerry went on in a soft voice. "I was so completely alone surrounded by all those people and my family."

Unsure of what to say to that, Dar took a safe compromise, and reached out to clasp Kerry's hand, twining her fingers with her partner's.

Kerry exhaled, shaking her head slightly. "I am so blessed."

Dar absorbed the words, finding them even warmer than the residual sunlight. "We," she put in a slight correction, "are so blessed."

"Mm." Kerry selected a berry and bit into it. "That we are." She agreed.

They shared a few more berries, and Dar even threw one over to a gull bold enough to traverse the space between the dock and their porch. The bird picked up the offering suspiciously, then bolted it down with a raucous squawk. "Everyone's a critic." Dar commented.

"I don't think they usually eat strawberries, do they? I thought they eat like...dead fish and tormented baby turtles and things." Kerry split a huge berry in half and offered Dar a portion, smiling when it was taken from her fingers and the juice licked off them in the bargain. "Know what I want to do tonight?"

Ah. Easy question. Dar shifted and half turned, curling her arm around Kerry and kissing her on the lips, tasting the sweet tang of the strawberries as their tongues met. "Yes."

"Hmm...I could have meant Scrabble." Kerry whispered, her fingertips tracing the side of Dar's face with a light touch.

"Or Twister." Dar teased, kissing her again.

"We could combine the two and I could stick letters on you with peanut butter."

"Ooo...romance." Dar slid off the bench and rose to her feet, holding out a hand to Kerry. "Mix that with some fudge and we could infringe on Reese's patents."

"Oo." Kerry mimicked. "Now doesn't that sound sexy?" She got up and put her hand in Dar's, muffling a giggle as she was wrapped up in a pair of long arms and hustled toward the doors to the cabin. "Honey, you can infringe on my patent any time you want."

Dar held the door open and they eased past Chino, trading the languid warmth for the pleasant chill of the cabin. She put the bowl of berries down and concentrated on Kerry, running her thumbs down her collarbone before lacing her fingers behind her neck.

Kerry moved closer, slipping her hands under Dar's t-shirt and sliding it up to expose most of her torso. She angled her head and nibbled the curve of one breast, while she reached around to unhook her partner's bra.

Dar slowly moved them both in a rambling arc heading for the bedroom. She unbuttoned Kerry's shorts and they both laughed softly as the garment obligingly dropped around her ankles, nearly tripping her.

She stepped out of them as Dar eased her shirt up over her head and tossed it on top of the shorts then ducked her head as Kerry removed the t-shirt she was wearing and tossed it even further.

They went through the doorway into the bedroom in each other's arms, Kerry depending on Dar's navigation skills to keep them on course as she lost herself in a moment of passionate head rush. She concentrated on the warm skin under her lips and fingertips instead.

Dar did a good steering job, and a moment later they tumbled into the waterbed. She rolled over onto her back and felt Kerry's thigh slip between hers, their bodies pressing against each other. The surface flexed under them, as Dar ran her hands up Kerry's sides and eased her fingers between them to cup her partner's breasts.

"Grrrwow." Kerry responded, biting her earlobe gently. She nibbled Dar's pulse point then worked her way up over the curve of her jaw to her lips. She indulged in a leisurely kiss as she stroked her fingers lightly down Dar's torso, tracing the bumps and ripples of bone and muscle that shifted under her touch.

The best part, Dar always found, was the look in Kerry's eyes when they were being intimate. There was such a mixture of desire and joy there, passionate yet loving. It made making love the sweetest of confirmations. She let one hand drop down to Kerry's bare hip, her thumb running over the line of her pelvis before sliding lower to tickle the inside of her thigh.

The lips exploring hers parted slightly, a gust of air escaping as Kerry exhaled, then drew in a deeper, faster breath. Her body shifted as Dar tickled her again, and they rolled over onto their sides as they slid against each other.

Lying down, her height disadvantage didn't matter. Kerry felt her guts igniting as Dar teasingly explored her and she reciprocated, working her way down her lover's long body as Dar placed a series of tiny bites across the back of her neck.

Tingles went everywhere over her.

Her hands went everywhere over Dar.

As she felt warm breath heat the skin over her navel, the rest of the world could have separated and spun off into its own orbit and she wouldn't have given one little spit.

"SO, WHAT DO you think?" Kerry was glad the clouds had finally cleared out, exposing a half circle of brilliant stars for her appreciation. "Bear?"

"Hmm." Dar gazed up at the sky speculatively. "More like a pig."

"Pig? C'mon." A wave rippled under them, and they rode it atop the rugged canvas float tied off to the dock. It rested at water level and let the ocean wash over them, but prevented them from being tugged out to sea at night, which could ruin the day of even the most avid of ocean lovers.

The sea was warm and only lightly choppy, bucking them up and down every few minutes in a pleasant rhythm. Dar was lying on her back with her ankles crossed, and Kerry had chosen a spot at right angles to her, using Dar?s belly as an opportune pillow.

"How can that be a pig? It's standing up on its hind legs. Describe to me the last time you saw a pig do that."

Dar sighed. "Well, it's a really fat bear then. Look at its belly." She described an arc. "Must have eaten all the pigs."

"Hmm." Now it was Kerry's turn to ponder. "Maybe it's getting ready to hibernate."

"Eh." Dar pointed at a different set of stars. "I think that looks like a horse," she paused, "with a cart behind it."

Kerry looked. Then she rotated her head to look again. Then she turned and pressed her cheek against Dar's stomach, peering up at her partner. "When was that optometrist's appointment, again?"

Dar solemnly stuck her tongue out. She flexed her body, making the raft ripple and bringing a wash of seawater over them complete with a floating chunk of fragrant seaweed. Dar batted the weed overboard, and exhaled, closing her eyes for a moment.

It was extremely peaceful, Kerry acknowledged, if you could block out from your mind the knowledge that they were floating over thirty or forty feet of water filled with all kinds of critters. Most harmless, a few not, and the truth was she'd never grown to be as comfortable as Dar was at night in the sea.

But the raft helped a lot, and having Dar there made up the difference, so she was able to relax after their swim, and enjoy the pretty sky overhead. "I'm glad it rained today, but I'm even gladder it cleared up," Kerry said. "It's so pretty to look up at the sky like this."

Dar draped an arm over Kerry's body, the edge of her thumb rubbing gently across the fabric over her ribcage. "It is." She agreed. "I could do this every night."

Kerry's eyes flickered briefly closed, then opened again. "Me too."

But not in Miami, she silently added. While their condo was most certainly right on the water, the thought of floating in the sea that close to the port made her grimace.

Dar cleared her throat gently, and took a breath to speak, but then hesitated when the sound of an approaching boat engine caught their ears.

They lifted their heads and looked north, spotting running lights not that far offshore and heading in more or less their direction.

"Would it be outstandingly paranoid of me to wonder who's out there?" Kerry said.

"Mm."

Dar patted Kerry on the stomach and slid out from under her as she sat up. Shading her eyes, she studied the oncoming boat with a frown. It was small, about half the size of theirs, and appeared to be a low profile model without the flying bridge a fishing vessel would have.

Sport boat, at night, wandering around in the Florida Straits. Either he was lost, or...Dar rolled over and off the raft, entering the water without much noise and taking hold of the edge of the float. "Ker..."

"Yeah, yeah." Kerry slid over the side and joined her, peering at the boat over the pontoons that ringed the canvas surface. The water, though warm, was not as warm as the air, and after the long swim and the fact that she'd half dried out made her feel more than a little chilled. "It could just be a party boat."

"Sure." Dar agreed. "Even better reason for us not to be up their lounging in our swim suits." She remarked dryly. "I'm not in the mood to be yelling kiss my ass in three languages tonight."

Kerry edged closer to her, pressing her shoulder against her partner?s as they floated there side by side. The boat meandered around in a circle for a few minutes then approached the shore again, heading directly for their dock. They got close enough for her to see there were three people on board, but it was too dark to see any details beyond that.

Since that meant it was also too dark for the people on the boat to see them, it was a workable trade off. Kerry let her chin rest against the pontoon, the scent of seawater and plastic coming strongly to her nose. "Doesn't sound like a party." She murmured under her breath.

"Nu uh." Dar agreed sinking lower in the water until it just covered her mouth. She tugged Kerry down a little, her partner's pale head far more visible in the low light than her own. "Sure doesn't."

Kerry slid an arm around Dar's torso, glad of the warmth as she pressed against the taller woman. "What in the hell are they looking for?" She whispered into a now conveniently close ear.

"Trouble."

"You really think so?"

Kerry was answered when a bright spotlight erupted from the small boat, throwing a powerful beam of light to explore the dock and the approach up to their cabin. She drew in a breath in a mixture of shock and anger, releasing the air in a stream of bubbles as she ducked lower in the water.

Dar moved lower as well, only her pale blue eyes now showing above the surface, narrowed and glinting in the faint light. The boat moved closer, circling around the raft—its inhabitants paying the floating canvas little attention.

"Ahh, for a spear gun." Dar lifted her mouth clear of the water for a brief moment.

"Ahh, for a bazooka borrowed from your father with live rounds." Kerry uttered back. "Jesus Christ, Dar... who in the heck do these jerks think they are?"

"More to the point, do they realize they're about to trespass?"

They watched the boat approach the dock and pull alongside, one of the figures jumping out to tie a rope to one of the stanchions.

"C'mon." Dar released the raft and started toward them, using a stealthy breast stroke to move herself through the water.

"Wh..." Kerry looked around, then shook her head and followed trying to make as little noise as possible. She wasn't as efficient a swimmer as Dar was, but all the practice she'd gotten since moving to Florida stood her in good stead as she kept up in the mild surf.

A mask and snorkel would have made her life easier. Errant little waves tended to end up splashing her in the mouth, and she kept spitting out sea water, but after a few minutes they were approaching the dock. The other two people had gotten out, and all three were now creeping up the wooden gangway toward the cabin.

Bastards. Kerry felt a flush of anger sweep through her, taking the chill away and replacing it with a fierce heat. The outlines of the three didn't, though, look familiar to her, though she could see two were men, and one was a woman. "Think it's the reporters?" She caught up to Dar as they reached the outer edge of the dock and grabbed on.

"Dunno." Dar pulled herself along the dock until she was just across from the boat, craning her head to see where they intruders were. "Not sure I care."

The tone in her partner's voice alerted Kerry at once. "What are we going to do? Confront them?"

For an answer, Dar swam over to the boat and reached up to grasp the railing, pulling herself up and over the side in a brief moment of starlit muscularity.

"Uh oh." Kerry grabbed hold of the wooden ladder fastened to the side of the dock and got up on the bottom rung, peering over the edge of the boat to see what her partner was doing. "Dar!" She whispered urgently.

For a moment nothing happened, then a dark head appeared over the side, and Kerry saw the boat start to drift away from the dock. "Oh ho." She chuckled low in her throat. "Bad girl."

The craft bobbed closer to her, as the outgoing tide took it gently from its berth. As it passed, Dar stepped onto the side and then onto the ladder, holding something in her hand. She released the wood and dropped into the water next to Kerry, jerking her arm down as she fell.

The boat's engine suddenly roared to life and it veered crazily off, heading southeast at a rapid clip.

They heard a yell from the shore, and Dar swung to the inside of the ladder, grabbing Kerry and tugging her under the dock, a grin visible even in the dim light.

"You are so bad." Kerry snickered, watching the boat disappear into the surf. "God, Dar...what's going to happen to that thing? Someone could get hurt!"

"Nah." Dar nestled her jaw up next to Kerry's ear. "They were about to switch to the other tank. Not much gas left." They both looked up as footsteps pounded on the top of the pier, accompanied by curses. "Now." She uttered softly. "Do we rise up out of the sea and kick their asses, or what?"

Kerry listened to the voices over her head. "It's the reporter, isn't it?" She uttered back.

"I think so, yeah."

Strategy. It was tough to work that out while you were stuck under a dock in the presence of curious night fish nibbling your heels. If they remained quiet, then the culprits had no one to blame but themselves, and nothing to say about Dar or Kerry.

If they confronted the trio, then their complicity in the boat's startling disappearance would be clear, and they would have to deal with the publicity, not to mention calling the police.

It was late on a Saturday night, and Kerry didn't want to spend the rest of the night calling the Marathon County police and explaining the whole shebang.

On the other hand, she really wanted to kick that reporter in the shins. "I think we should go kick their asses." She finally said, hearing the nascent panic in the voices over her head.

Dar merely began swimming to the other side of the pier, tugging Kerry along with her to the ladder on the opposite side. She went first, climbing up to the top of the wooden platform and waiting for Kerry to join her as they stood behind the three intruders.

"Son of a bitch, that ain't stopping," one said. "We better go call the Coast Guard or something...what kinda idiot were you to leave the engine on, Virgil!"

"I didn't!" The other man replied in an exasperated tone. "I told you that ten times already!" He half turned. "Look, Ms. Cruicshank, why don't you just go over there and sit down while we figure out where we're going to go to get a phone and — "

"You could use ours." Dar interrupted this engaging drama, pitching her voice low and projecting it across the dock.

All three intruders jumped, and turned to find Dar?s tall form standing menacingly behind them with Kerry a shorter, more visibly irritated counterpoint to her right. The two swim suited figures were outlined in starlight and threw oddly large shadows across the dock to spill over them.

"Oh...uh...hi." The reporter summoned a weak smile from somewhere.

"You might as well use it before I call the cops." Dar went on. "And then you can explain to them why you're trespassing on private property."

Pat Cruicshank stepped forward. "Okay, okay, just hang on. I can explain this."

Kerry actually just laughed. "So can I," she said, folding her arms across her chest. "And you know, maybe we should call the local paper, too. I'd love to see this on the front page."

Dar glanced at her in some surprise.

"Now, hold on," Pat said. "Tell you what. Let's go up there and we can talk while these bozos figure out how to get their boat back."

"I'm going to call the police." Dar turned and headed for the cabin. "And trust me... I'll press charges." She called back over her shoulder.

"Shit." Virgil sounded panicky. "Man, I told you we shouldn't have done this."

The reporter turned to Kerry. "This isn't what it looks like."

Kerry looked at her, looked at the darkness around them, peered off at the rapidly disappearing boat then looked back at the reporter. Both her eyebrows hiked up. "Okay," she said. "I'm game. Explain to me how three people sneaking up in a boat to a private dock, then creeping toward our house is something other than what it looks like?" She spread her hands out in a questioning manner. "I'm waiting."

Cruicshank hesitated, looking at the two guys with her.

"Okay, never mind. I'm over it." Kerry went to the end of the dock and reached under a bit of rock, removing a small key and opening a locked, watertight box. She lifted the radio receiver inside and keyed it. "Coast Guard, Coast Guard, this is Dixieland Yankee portside, over."

"Wait." The reporter came over to her and lowered her voice. "Listen, I know you've got a right to be pissed off. But would you please just let me explain? This isn't against you. I'm just trying to get some information that will let me work in your favor."

Kerry merely eyed her. "Coast Guard, Coast Guard, come in." She repeated into the mic.

"Please?"

"Dixieland Yankee portside, go head." A man's voice erupted from the radio. "This is Cutter Avalon."

"Avalon, we have a pleasure craft underway without anyone aboard just southeast of us." Kerry unkeyed the radio. "You've got whatever time it takes for the cops to get here. Don't waste it," she said.

"Yankee, we copy, we see it. " The guard officer sounded exasperated. "Good gravy."

"We have the boat operators here." Kerry informed him. "Over."

"Thanks, Yankee. We'll get back with you." The radio fell silent. Kerry put the mic inside and locked the box then turned and headed for the cabin, without another word.

After an awkward moment of indecision, the reporter ran after her.

DAR ENTERED THE cabin shaking her head and muttering under her breath, slamming the door behind her as she evaded Chino's curious snuffling and headed for the phone. Then she hesitated and stopped, putting her hands on her hips. "Chino, if I call the cops, what do you bet it'll be two hours before they get here."

"Gruff." Chino seemed in total agreement.

After a moment's indecision, Dar headed for the bedroom instead, figuring putting on some kind of clothes was probably a good strategic idea before confronting their unwelcome guests. She pulled a shirt and shorts from the dresser and stripped out of her swimsuit on her way into the bathroom, grabbing a towel and drying herself off before she changed.

She glanced cursorily into the mirror. "Ugh." One hand reached up to remove a string of purple seaweed from her neck, and dropped it into the waste basket. "Can't believe I didn't feel that." Pulling on her clothes, she ran her fingers through her wet hair and turned, hearing footsteps on the porch outside.

A single set, and to Dar's ears, a distinctive pattern. She was not surprised when the back door opened and Kerry walked in, her face twitching a little and a stormy look in her eyes. Her hands were half balled into fists, but despite all that, she looked amazingly sexy and Dar couldn't help grinning at her.

"What?" Kerry caught the grin. "Did you call the cops already? I got the Coast Guard."

"Not yet." Dar bumped her toward the bedroom. "Go change. I assume our reporter friend is right behind you? I'll take care of her."

Kerry exhaled, but headed toward the inner door. She paused and turned as she reached it. "Was I doing something funny when I came in? You were grinning."

The door opened abruptly, preventing an answer. So Dar merely looked her partner up and down, and waggled her eyebrows, before she turned to face Pat Cruicshank.

Kerry sniffed. "Ah...hah." She entered the bedroom and shut the door behind her, ears straining as she heard Dar's low rumble start up. "Stupid idiotic son of..." she paused at her reflection in the mirror. Then she sighed. "Dar, you could have told me this damn thing was semi transparent when wet."

At least it had been comfortingly dark outside. Kerry quickly removed the unexpectedly risqué suit and replaced it with a pair of worn denim short overalls, tucking a sedate white t-shirt into them before she buckled one strap over her shoulder.

Impatiently, she flicked her fingers through her hair, and then she turned and marched back into the living room.

"LOOK, I KNOW you're pissed off and maybe you have a right to be." Pat was saying.

"Maybe?" Dar paused in mid motion. She was in the kitchen pouring a glass of milk.

"This isn't what it looks like." The reporter came over and faced her over the counter. "Look, Ms. Roberts, I thought we had an understanding."

Dar gave herself a moment's thought while she drank down her milk. She finally put her glass down just as her partner emerged and braced her arms on the counter. "My understanding is that I am a public officer of a public company, and I perform my public duties during working hours."

"Well, sure..."

"This is not a working hour." Dar cut her off. "I'm not sure why you don't understand that. I am off the clock, out of the office, on vacation, not answering my email. What other—" She slammed her hands down on the counter, with a smack, "way do I have to phrase that so it makes sense to you?"

"But this is not just a working hour's story!" The reporter shot back. "This is about people. It's about people who are in this situation, trying to make something happen. You think everyone else is just taking the weekend off?"

"I don't care." Dar replied evenly. "It's not my problem what anyone else does." She pointed at the reporter. "Why is it a problem to anyone else what I do?"

"Okay, look." The reporter eyed Kerry warily as the shorter woman strode past her into the kitchen, taking the milk jug from Dar's side and drinking directly from the opening. "It's my job to tell the story in this special. Now, I don't mind telling stories, and I don't mind making them up when they're not interesting enough for me." Her attitude was more direct now. "But I also don't like being fed a tale, and you know, I think I'm being fed a tale."

"Okay." Kerry put the milk jug down. "But that doesn't explain why you're here."

Pat looked at her. "Honey, it's you two who are feeding me the tale."

Dar looked at Kerry, Kerry looked back at Dar. They both looked across the counter at the reporter. "What?" Dar's brow creased. "I haven't told you anything." She glanced at Kerry. "Have you?"

"Um...no, I've only cursed at her so far." Kerry shook her head. "What are you talking about?" She asked the black woman.

"Oh, don't play that game with me." Cruicshank said. "You are two smart cookies, and it's way too late to pretend you don't know what's going on." She put her hands on her hips. "So let's drop the act, okay?"

Dar picked up her glass, poured more milk into it, and then wandered out of the kitchen shaking her head. She walked right past the reporter and went over to the couch, dropping into it and extending her legs out across its surface. "What do you think, Ker?"

"What do I think?" Kerry put the milk back into the refrigerator. "I think she got stung by a bunch of jelly fish. Want me to call 911? Hallucinations will be next." She leaned on the counter. "Lady, you're nuts.?"

"I'm nuts?" The reporter's eyes widened.

"We have no idea what the hell you're talking about." Kerry told her in a confidential tone.

Cruicshank looked from one to the other. She pointed at Dar. "You told me from your perspective this whole bid was just business. Right?"

"Right." Dar acknowledged.

"So, then tell me, Ms. Roberts, how professional it is that your father's been working at Telegenic's ship, causing trouble?"

Uh oh. Dar outwardly refused to react, not even to let her eyes flicker over to where Kerry was standing. "My father?" She mused. "My father's a retired naval officer who takes odd jobs on the waterfront to keep busy,? she said. "I find it hard to believe he was causing trouble."

Kerry had to strain not to smile, despite the shock of the words.

"And he just so happened to take one there?" The reporter asked sarcastically. "Just like your..." She turned and looked at Kerry, "assistant just happened to attack your competition at a restaurant?" A snort. "Give me a break," she said. "This is all about personal issues, and you've got as many as anyone else does."

"Actually." Kerry chose her words carefully. "Your friends at Telegenics were trying to get me to come out with them so they could attack my partner here." She circled the counter. "I got called out of town on business." Her smile was icy. "And my assistant was being courteous in letting them know I wasn't going to make it."

"With a chili bowl? I think an email would have been enough." Cruicshank shot back.

Kerry half shrugged. "Your friends were...very professional, sitting in a hamburger shack dissing us at the top of their voices. My assistant took exception to that. I don't blame her."

"Honey, that ain't how I heard it."

"My assistant is eighteen years old, and she was with her mother." Kerry sat down on one of the counter stools. "I believe what they told me." She shrugged slightly. "But for that matter, if Dar and I did react in any way, it was because they were pushing us to the wall."

The reporter looked around the cabin. "I just don't believe that. You know what I think? I think they're right. All those people are up there working their butts off to make this happen, and you two are here in your...love shack."

She turned and walked to the door. "Call the cops. See if I care." Her voice was now cutting. "But let me tell you, ladies, I know exactly how I'm going to play this story, and for you...it's not going to be pretty."

Cruicshank turned and left, slamming the door behind her.

There was a brief silence in the cabin, as the two partners regarded each other. Finally, Dar shifted her position, rolling onto her side and propping her head up on her hand. "Love shack." She mused. "I like it."

Kerry rubbed her eyes. "Dar, this is not funny."

"No." Dar agreed. "But what in the hell are you going to do, Ker? Dad was doing exactly what she claimed, and we're here." One shoulder shrugged. "And the battling burritos did what they did. It's all in the spin, and she's got the turntable."

"Nice." The blond woman trudged over and sat down on the couch next to Dar. She let her hands fall slackly between her knees and extended her bare feet across the carpet. "So, now what?"

Now what. Good question. Dar really had no idea now what. "I just don't get what the big deal is about us being up here. It's not like you and I are running the cables." She temporized. 'What's that all about?"

Kerry pondered. "They're control freaks, so they think everyone else should be too?" She thought a moment more. "And, well, you know hon...I can remember projects where you were a little like that too."

She peeked at Dar to gauge a reaction, but got a mildly bemused expression in return.

"I know." Her partner nodded agreeably. "But I got over it. You helped me, matter of fact. I sniffed around one of yours one time too many, and you told me what I was going to die of."

Kerry's head dropped forward a little. "I did no such thing."

Dar's lips quirked. "Well, not in those words, no." She admitted. "But you did."

"I did?" Kerry thought back, trying to recall the momentous occasion. Had she really told Dar to back off? Then the memory surfaced, and she exhaled, picturing a scene in Dar's office with her pushing a set of colored project folders across her boss's desk. *One of us really needs to own these, Dar.*

Dar had cocked her head to one side, she remembered, and then casually pushed them back across the desk with a smile.

No, not quite in those words. "Okay, you got me." Kerry admitted. "But I don't get why it matters to them. After all, if we're slacking off, isn't that better for their side?"

"Mm."

"And, she told me she had information that would be to our advantage." Kerry suddenly remembered. "Was that just to get inside this place and have her say? I don't get it, Dar. This isn't adding up."

"No." Dar curled her body around Kerry's and wrapped an arm around her for good measure. "I thought that woman had a more balanced viewpoint. Something happened," she said. "Either she bought into Michelle and Shari's pitch, or something else happened that made her turn around. I know she was probably playing me at lunch, but I really..."

"Hrm."

"Really. I didn't get that vibe." Dar shook her head. "I got the feeling she was trying to find the other half of the story."

Kerry sighed. "Wonder how dad got outed? Maybe in retrospect that wasn't the smartest thing we ever did, asking him to go in there."

"Eh." Dar turned her head as her cell phone rang. "That's probably him. I'll ask." She picked it up and answered it, surprised to see the office's caller ID instead. "Uh oh." She flipped it open. "Yes?"

"Oh, Ms. Roberts? Good...this is the security desk." The voice answered, sounding relieved. "Listen, I have the security guy at the pier on the line; he needs to speak to you." There was a click, then another line was connected.

"Hello?" Dar ventured.

"Uh...oh, hi. Is this Ms. Roberts?"

"Yes."

"This is Steven at the pier, ma'am. We've been trying to call Ms. Stuart, and there's no answer. ?

Dar looked inquiringly at Kerry, who sat up and peered around like a startled meerkat searching out her cell phone. "She's here. What's the problem? You need to talk to her?"

"No, well...it's not..." The guard seemed unsure. "It's the port, ma'am. They're going nuts here. There's television cameras and all kinds of stuff all over the place, and I think they're asking everyone to leave."

"Huh?" Kerry took the phone. "Steven, this is Kerry. What's happening? Was there an accident?"

"No, ma'am. But some kind of government people are here, and boy, they've got this place lit up like a Christmas tree for sure. I think they're looking at the ships. Something's wrong, I guess. They won't tell us anything."

Kerry held the phone out a little, and lifted her free hand in question.

Dar was at a loss. "Okay, well?" She rubbed her jaw.

"Did they make all the workers leave the ships, Steve?" Kerry asked. "Are our contractors still there?"

"No, oh, wait. Hang on." The sound became muffled then came back. "Ma'am, one of my guys just came in to relieve me and he said he heard it's an environmental thing."

"Environmental." Kerry repeated. "Okay, but are they asking you to leave the pier?"

"No, ma'am, apparently what some of these people want is for the boats to leave the pier." The guard now sounded much surer of himself. "It's not about us at all."

"Phew." Dar exhaled. "At last, something that has nothing to do with us, for a change."

"Yeah." Kerry agreed. "Okay, Steve, you guys just sit tight near the office, okay? If they make everyone get out, give me a call." She paused, "Wait, give Dar a call because my cell phone's AWOL at the moment."

"Okay, ma'am, will do." Steve replied. "Sorry to bother you."

Kerry hung up the cell phone. She got up and started roaming around the cabin, searching for her own. "Where in the dickens did I put that thing, Dar? I know I had it when we got here."

"Sounds like Quest's got a real problem on his hands." Dar put the phone down and rolled to her feet, joining in the search for the missing cell. "Something he can't blame us for."

"For a change." Kerry paused, then slapped herself on the head. "Damn it, I left it on the bike." She groaned in disgust. "Be right back." She disappeared through the front door with Chino chasing after her.

A knock came at the back door. Dar scrubbed the fingers of one hand through her hair and went to answer it, wondering if it would be their reporter's boatmen, the coast guard, the cops, or the National Enquirer. Nothing would have surprised her at this rate.

She opened the door. "Yes?"

"Okay, listen." Pat said. "Can we start over?"

Well, almost nothing.

PROBLEMS FOR THEM tended to be rated by the number of pots of coffee they required while solving them. Kerry pressed the button to start pot number two while she listened with half an ear to what Dar was saying in the living room.

"Let me get this straight." Dar rubbed her temples. "You came down here because Shari and Michelle convinced you that we were trying to screw up your filming project by deliberately making them look bad."

"Right."

"And we didn't do anything to change that idea."

"No."

Dar folded her hands and rested her chin on her clasped fingers. "So why are you here? Just write your story. They're struggling good guys; we're monolithic bad guys trying to squash them—makes for great television. Go for it."

Pat got up and paced. "You know, I really want to go for that." She used her hands when she talked, her fists clenching and unclenching. "It's a great story, you're right. Make great television. Just what my boss was looking for."

Dar's ears pricked. "Your boss."

Kerry brought the new pot of coffee in, setting it down on the tray quietly and taking a seat next to her partner.

"My boss, really wants this show." Pat agreed. "Something new, you know? Yeah, it's travel related, but it's also got a big human angle, and people like that."

"Mm." Dar nodded. "But?"

"But." The reporter repeated softly. "But you know..." She turned and faced them. "Sweet as this story is, the good guys in it aren't the people I want my boss to see." Hesitating, she finally shrugged and went to the seat across from the couch, sitting down on it. "You're not the only ones with a personal agenda here."

Kerry blinked, positive she was missing something. A quick glance at Dar's profile clued her in to the fact that her partner wasn't.

Dar's head lifted, the entire expression on it shifting from bewilderment to understanding from one breath to another. "You want your boss to see how we work." She indicated Kerry and herself.

Pat nodded. "Yeah," she said. "Because let me tell you, those other two have tried their damndest to convince me that you two are as dysfunctional as they are, and believe me, they're a pair of head cases."

"Dysfunctional?" Kerry frowned then turned her head to face Dar. "We never malfunction, do we?"

A wicked twinkle appeared in Dar's very blue eyes. "Not that you've ever mentioned to me, no." She drawled. "And I've got no complaints."

Kerry looked puzzled for an instant, then she reached over and tweaked Dar's nose. "Wench." She shook her head and faced Pat again. "I don't understand how they'd give you that impression."

Pat's lips twitched. "Whole lot of talk,especially that Shari. She's got a lot to say about you." She looked at Dar. "And it sure isn't complimentary."

"That's just because Dar keeps kicking her butt every time they square off." Kerry snorted. "Shari should learn better business tactics."

The reporter leaned forward and rested her elbows on her knees. "It's not business she's talking about."

"Ah." Dar chuckled shortly. "Let me guess—Shari's painting me as a half unstable megalomaniac with twisted personal issues stemming from my upbringing."

"What?" Kerry barked.

"Who beats her girlfriend," Pat added crisply.

Dar just snorted. Kerry gave an excellent impression of a boiling teakettle without stirring a muscle as Chino trotted over and pushed her head against her shorter mother?s knees. "Boy, does she have her lines crossed." Dar shook her head. "I'm not the Tasmanian devil in this relationship."

"I'm gonna cross her lines." Kerry got out from between clenched teeth. "Has she really been telling people that?"

"Well, she had me half buying it, and to be honest, that's the real reason I came down here." The reporter admitted. "You can act however you want in the office, but like you said, this is not your office, and it's off the clock." She looked around. "And this ain't no movie set."

Dar scratched her nose and produced a brief smile. "No, it's not."

"Dar, do you think that's where all that crap in the office came from?" Kerry turned and looked at her. "From Shari? Is that possible, that she fed all that BS to someone inside?"

"That would be the obvious choice." Dar sat forward and started pouring herself another cup of coffee. She very gently nudged Kerry's bare foot with her own. "But you never can tell. Could be the other way around."

"Ah. Yeah."

"Problems inside your office?" Pat asked alertly.

"Just more of the usual chatter." Kerry shrugged it off. "We had a good laugh about it."

Dar stirred her coffee around counterclockwise just hearing that characterization of her partner's reaction. "So." She set the spoon down and took a sip. "What are you going to do?" Her eyes lifted and met Pat's. "Now that you've achieved your goal and interviewed us today."

Dar's cell phone chose to ring at that moment. With a faint sigh, she leaned over and picked it up, then answered it. "Yeah?"

"Hey boss." Mark's voice sounded aggravated. "Listen, I traced down the IP we saw, and it was one of the Marketing bullpen machines. Could have been any of ten people using it."

"Okay. Get me full scans on those ten." Dar replied quietly. "And put traces on them."

A pause. "All the way?"

"Yes."

"You got it." Mark said. "Hey, you know what? It's been a lot cooler around here since you put that stuff on the big pipes. I haven't had nearly as many alerts."

Inwardly, Dar smirked. "And you're surprised?"

Mark chuckled. "Nah. I knew you hadn't lost your touch. We've only got one little bastard who keeps trying. I'm keeping an eye on it though."

"Good work. Keep me in the loop." Dar said, and then she hung up. "Well?" She turned her attention back to the avidly listening reporter. "Decided what your angle's going to be or what?" Leaning casually back, she stretched one arm across the back of the couch and sipped her coffee, watching Pat over the rim of the cup.

Kerry decided to settle back herself, ending up by design in the curl of Dar's arm, and with one hand resting lightly on her partner's thigh. She recognized Dar's fencing mode, and figured it would be better all-around for her to stay out of the match until she could get more fully clued in on what was going on.

"Well, not yet, no." Pat said. "It's kind of a tough situation, you know? I mean, if Telegenics wins that bid, it's going to be real hard for me to slant my story any way except for what everyone's expecting. We need to have our viewers happy about who comes out on top."

"Well." Kerry pursed her lips. "Y'know, with two sets of dykes in the mix, you probably need to recruit some heteros or you're going to be upsetting most of your viewers no matter what, if either of us come out on top."

That caused a bit of a silence. Dar prudently stuck her nose in her cup and slurped up some coffee, as the reporter merely goggled at Kerry briefly.

"It's true," she said, with a slight shrug.

"Maybe they should back a dark horse." Dar mused. "Knock those lousy lezzies off their pedestal. That'd make a good story, don'cha think, Ker?"

"Mm. I wouldn't watch it, but sure."

Pat shifted uncomfortably. "Are you making fun of me?" She asked, with a slight hesitation. "We don't practice discrimination in our telecasts." She got up. "So that part of your lifestyle never came into the picture."

Kerry got up also, neatly drawing her attention. "How can't it? She asked. "You've got Shari and Michelle, who are very out, and Dar and I, who are also very out. We're competing for the same prize, and we're in a dog fight with all the dirty tricks stops pulled out." She cocked her head to one side. "How do you intend on portraying that without mentioning our sexual orientation?"

"Well, of course we were going to mention it but..."

"Are you saying you weren't going to focus your storyline on that?" Kerry's voice rose a little in disbelief. "Really?"

"Look. This is the Travel Channel." Pat said. "Not E! or Spice. So yes, that would have been mentioned but no, we weren't going to name it the Gay Boat Show."

"Huh." Kerry grunted and shook her head.

"We could always arrange for a Jell-O wrestling match." Dar launched herself from the couch and prowled over to the back window, watching outside and bracing both hands on the window. "That'd get ratings."

"Wrestling." Kerry looked thoughtful. "I'd go for that."

"Wait a minute. This isn't supposed to be about you all fighting each other. Well, not like that," Pat protested. "I mean, yes. We want the personal angle, but it's got to be about the goal too."

Dar turned. "Either you go the personal route, or you don't." She leaned against the window. "If you take that path, you have to deal with the dirty parts. You want your boss to see how we mix living and working? Then you have to show how Shari and Michelle don't, and that means you have the Dueling Dykes show."

"But..."

"She's right." Kerry picked the ball up effortlessly. "Mention why you were here and you have to go over why Shari talks about Dar the way she does. It's not for business reasons."

Pat looked cornered. "Wait a minute..."

"Tell you what." Dar swiped the ball back. "Invite your boss to dinner with us. Save the drama, and stick with the business line on your program. You'll end up with happier sponsors for it."

Kerry chuckled. "At the least."

Pat looked at them both uncertainly. "But the people angle..."

"Find another people angle." Dar pressed her. "Think about it." She turned and opened the back door, gesturing toward it with one hand. "Your boat's ready. I think the Coasties even left your drivers intact."

Slowly, Pat walked toward the door, watching them both until she was in the doorway with her hand on the sill. She took a breath to say something, then she merely shook her head and walked out, without looking back.

Dar swung the door shut. She and Kerry regarded each other for a brief moment then both sighed at once. "This is gonna be a mess if she doesn't take that advice."

Kerry joined her. "You got that right," she agreed. "But, I think it's a mess anyway." She exhaled. "I think we really did mess this one up, Dar."

Dar put an arm around her shoulders. "I think you may be right, Ker." She admitted. "I think we made some bad choices. But we can't change that now, so let's just make the best of it that we can."

"Break out the mops?"

"Yeap."

Chapter Ten

THE MORNING SUN rose gently over South Pointe Marina, gilding the forest of pristine white fiberglass that graced its many slips. Toward one side of the marina, in an area relatively uncrowded in the summer, a sixty foot Bertram yacht rode peacefully within its dock, rocking back and forth slightly as a tall, broad shouldered figure paced across its stern deck.

Andrew whistled softly under his breath as he worked, laying out a new set of white cotton lines for the big boat in orderly loops. His hands worked the rope with almost unconscious skill, fingers half twisting the lines to release the kinks in their new fabric.

It was Sunday, the weather was fine, he had work to do on his boat, and Ceci had promised him a hamburger for breakfast. Life, he reflected silently, just didn't get any better than this — especially given where his life had been not so long ago. He had no doubt at all this was just a gift from God he had no explanation for.

Could'a been a reward, he acknowledged, for the years he'd spent in hell already. Or it could'a been a nod from the feller upstairs over them lives he'd saved getting into all that trouble.

Andy perched on the side wall of the boat and blinked into the sunlight. Maybe it wasn't any of those things, though. Maybe it was just dumb luck, and the payback he'd gotten for pouring his heart into fatherhood.

He exhaled contentedly. Turned out a damn good kid, after all that. It irked him a little that he'd gotten taken out of the ship job. Being Dar's little bit of trouble inside there had been a good thing, and now, them women could be getting up to all kinds of no good without anyone to keep an eye on them.

Not a good thing. Andrew sighed. He hated half-finished missions.

The cell phone clipped to the wooden cabinet near the door buzzed, surprising him. He dropped the rope and walked over to the door, picking up the device and opening its lid. "Lo?"

"Hey, Ugly! Where the hell are you?"

Andrew studied the phone receiver as though it had morphed into a hamster. "This here Bradley?" He queried.

"Sure is! Where are you, man? I told you I wanted everyone working today."

"Wall." Andy crossed his arms and leaned against the cabinet. "Them folks told me not to come back yesterday," he said. "They talk to you? They were pretty fussed up last night."

Ceci emerged from the boat's cabin and cocked her head curiously. "Who's that?" She was carrying a plate containing a cheeseburger, surrounded by a bunch of vegetables and fruit bits. She put it down near Andrew's elbow and leaned next to him.

"Feller thinks he's my boss." One of her husband's grizzled eyebrows waggled, as he covered the receiver with the palm of one large hand. "Ain't figgered out he isn't yet." Carefully removing the burger from its nest of healthiness, he nudged aside a carrot curl threatening to contaminate his breakfast and then bit into it.

"Ah, the mental midget who made your first petty officer look like Einstein. Gotcha." Ceci walked over to the canvas bucket chair on their back deck and seated herself, resting her head against the wooden seat back and contentedly absorbing the early morning sunlight. "Anyone ever tell him that whole Christian Sunday is the day of rest stuff? Only thing in the whole rigmarole that ever made any sense to me."

Andrew reached over to tweak a bit of her hair. "Yeap, ah am still here." He spoke into the phone. "Did you talk to them folks? Got their shorts in a big old twist yesterday."

"Yeah, yeah. I talked to them. Listen, that lady was just spouting some crazy stuff, and yeah, she doesn't want you around here, but I got a spot on that boat behind this one and I really need you to help me out."

"That big blue one with the patches on one side?" Andrew asked.

"Yeah, whatever. The one behind this one."

Dar's boat. Andrew took another bite of hamburger and chewed it thoughtfully. "Hmm."

"C'mon, buddy. I figured you could use the cash, right?" The supervisor sounded a touch desperate. "My guy over there walked out this morning, said he'd gotten a better offer. Tell you what, I'll give you a buck an hour raise."

Forty bucks a week. Andrew mused. Well, it'd pay the phone hook up fee for the month, at any rate. "All right." He agreed. "But I got to finish what I'm doing here right now, so it'll be a bit." He told the man. "Then ah will be over there."

Ceci stuck her tongue out.

"Okay, but not too long, huh?" Bradley said. "This place is a mess. Wait till you hear what happened last night after you left with the government people. It's chaos."

"'Yeap." Andrew agreed. "I do believe the gov'mint usually does cause that. Bye." He hung up the phone and set it on the counter. "Seems like somebody done hired this guys' feller off that boat Dar's working on."

"Oh, really?" Ceci regarded him, a mildly sardonic look appearing on her face. "I wonder if I can guess who that might have been, hmm? My goddess, those women are a pair of hairless Mexican cats." She frowned. "Can they be that desperate, or are they just that pissed off about you?"

"Beats me." Andy finished his breakfast, licking a bit of juice off his thumb. "That was a damn good hamburger, ma'am." He complimented his wife. "Do you want your part of this here MRE?" He handed over the plate of plant matter.

Ceci took a tomato slice and bit into it. "You only wish you ever got these in those." She retorted. "So you're going to go work on Dar's boat now? Doesn't really help much to know what those women are up to."

Andrew shrugged. "Do the best ah am able to. Sides, got me a one US dollar an hour raise out of it."

"Oo. You're taking me to dinner on your paycheck this week, sailor boy." Ceci laughed. "And we're not ending up in that chicken wing place, either." She got up and slid her arms around him, giving his solidness a fierce hug. "I'm glad you're helping out the kids. I think this one's throwing them out of whack a little."

"Ah'm sure they're having themselves a good time down south." Andrew said. "Without none of this here stuff to bother them." He gave her a return hug, then ducked his head and surprised her with a kiss, even though they were standing in what was now broad daylight on the back of the boat.

After a moment, they parted, and Andrew looked down at his wife, his eyes twinkling in the sun. Ceci reached up and stroked his face gently, her fingertips tracing the scars that, though faded, still crossed his skin. "I was looking forward to spending the day with you." She admitted.

"Yeap." Andrew kissed her again. "Me too." He said. "But I told that man I had something to take care of before I went over there."

"Oh, really?"

"Yeap."

"Well then." Ceci smiled. "What are we standing out here for? Unless you want to shock the neighbors." She paused. "Again."

"Nope." Andrew courteously opened the door, then followed her inside.

"AUGH!" Kerry reached for the Frisbee, flying high over her head and knew she was going down. She took a quick breath as she hit the water, then kicked for the surface, her head breaking the waves as she looked around for the bright pink disk. "Darn it, Dar!" She struck out for the toy, swimming quickly toward it before the thing got pulled out to sea.

"Not my fault you're short." Dar bobbed up and down in the surf, not far offshore on the far side of the dock near the cabin. It was fairly shallow there, not like the deep draft they'd had dredged for the Dixie, and the surf was almost calm, perfect for playing Frisbee.

Well, almost perfect. Dar watched Kerry reach the disk and grab it, turning to swim back far enough for her to stand up and throw it back. Chino was racing along the shore barking, frustrated that her owners were somewhat beyond her reach.

"C'mon, Chi!" Kerry got to where she could stand up, and tossed the disk back to her partner. "Come swim."

"Gruff!" Chino bounded halfway in up to her chest, then bolted away as a wave came chasing after her.

"Goofy dog." Kerry shook the wet hair out of her eyes, then set herself as Dar threw the Frisbee back. It was a little high, but not nearly as much as last time and she made a grab for it, pulling it out of the air despite the drag of the water against her body as she moved. "Hah!"

Dar grinned. Kerry always approached the playful sports they engaged in with a healthy dose of competitiveness that at first had surprised her. Then, when she'd learned more about her partner, she'd come to realize that Kerry had been forced to fight for recognition at every turn in her life, whereas standing out had never been a problem for Dar.

It wasn't as though she wasn't competitive herself, in business of course she was. But in her personal life, she'd never really had to do what she often kidded Kerry about — fighting for kibble.

No siblings. No competition. Dar saw the disk headed her way and she lunged through the water after it, uncoiling her body and jumping clear of the surface as she snatched it just before it went sailing on a trajectory that would have taken it under the dock. "Wench!"

"Work for it!" Kerry yelled back, clearly enjoying herself. "Teach you to call me short, huh!"

"If I have to go diving under that dock, you're gonna be more than short, ya little chipmunk!" Dar let fly with the Frisbee, chortling as her partner had to scramble for it, bouncing through the waves and kicking up spray as she went for the catch.

"I'll chipmunk you." Kerry grabbed the Frisbee, and then, instead of tossing it back just headed in Dar's direction, rambling through the water like a miniature freight train. "You're toast!"

Run? Dar considered the effort of escaping from Kerry's evil intentions, and weighed it against the pleasure of suffering them. She grinned, and as Kerry came within range, she dove right toward her, disappearing beneath the waves and colliding with Kerry's legs as she tried unsuccessfully to stop in time.

Way overbalanced, Kerry let out a yelp and tumbled over, landing mostly on Dar and grabbing at her as they wrestled half in and half out of the water. "You...you..."

Dar got a hold around Kerry's middle and then got her legs under her, standing up and hauling her out of the water like a sack of oats. "Yeeeesss?" She purred into Kerry's ear. "Me what?"

Kerry paused to catch her breath from her run through the waves. "You...punk." She slapped Dar on the thigh. "You tricked me."

"Into charging at me like a rhino?" Dar laughed. "Uh okay, honey. If you say so."

"Bah." Kerry let her head rest against Dar's chest. "Where's the Frisbee?"

"Didn't you have it?" Dar looked around. "Oh rats." She spotted the disk floating under the dock. "You stay here, cuttlefish. I'll get it." She released Kerry and headed for the pier, diving under the water as she got close to it.

Neither of them was really fond of swimming right under the wooden surface, since several large sea bass had taken up residence and they loved to nibble intruding humans. At night, the fish were sleeping, but during the day— Dar blinked her eyes open quickly in the salt water then just as quickly closed them. She surfaced and located the disk, swimming over to it and grabbing it just as something bit her foot. "Yeow! Bastard!" She kicked out in reflex then kicked with her other foot just for good measure. She felt a spongy impact then turned and headed out from under the pier.

Kerry was already at the edge of the wood reaching for her. "The fish?"

"God, I hope so." Dar felt a sharp sting where she'd been bitten. "Ow."

"Sorry." Kerry took hold of her arm and started heading for the shore. "I should have kept track of the damn thing."

"Residential hazard." Dar winced, as she hopped out of the water, grateful for Kerry's supportive arm around her waist. "I should have known better..."

"Should have just let the silly thing float off. We have a dozen of them." Kerry muttered as they got on shore, and sat down in the sand together. She scooted down a little and lifted Dar's foot up, setting it on her thigh to look at it. "Let me see."

"Ah ah ah. We don't let plastic into the ocean ecology." Dar peered at her foot, which was covered with an alarming amount of blood. "Wow." She fended off Chino, who snuffled around them anxiously.

"Yikes. We better go inside and clean this off." Kerry leaned closer. The fish had really chomped down on her foot, making a semi-circle of punctures which were liberally leaking blood. "I don't think it's deep, but..."

"But it hurts." Dar observed. "Stings like hell."

Kerry gently wiped the blood away and bent over, kissing the spot. "Let's go. We've got some peroxide in the cabin."

Dar cautiously withdrew her foot from Kerry's clutches. "It doesn't hurt that bad."

"Baby."

"Well, it doesn't."

"C'mon, big baby." Kerry got to her feet and offered her partner a hand up. "Those are puncture wounds, and a very good friend of mine taught me that those have to be cleaned out really well."

"Yeah, well, you shouldn't always listen to your friends." Dar accepted the aid, hopping along the sand over to where the porch steps were. "Look, it's stopped bleeding."

"C'mon."

"Kerry!"

"C'mon, chicken little. What if that was a barracuda?" Kerry took a firm hold on her reluctant damsel in distress and tugged her toward the house. "Bet we've got mercurochrome, too."

"Whine."

Kerry opened the door. "Was that you, or Cheebles?"

IN THE END, Dar gave in gracefully to the attention. She lay down on the couch with her injured foot in Kerry's lap as her partner tended to it. The cleaning hurt, as she'd expected, but it was offset by the look of gentle concern on Kerry's face, and the obvious care she was taking to do the job right.

The punctures were deep. "I know you were kidding about the barracuda." Dar kept her eyes closed the better not to see the holes in her foot. "But you might be on to something there."

Kerry looked up from her task, holding up the cotton swab she'd been using the clean out the punctures. "You really think so?"

"Too narrow a jaw to be the bass." Dar said. "Besides, it's much more macha to say I got bit by a 'cuda than by a poky old sea bass."

Kerry chuckled softly, giving Dar's ankle a little pat. "You realize this means I'm driving home, right?" She painted the top row of punctures with some lurid mercurochrome, admiring the well formed, powerful arch under her hands. "You have such pretty feet."

Dar chortled. "I do not."

"Yes, you do." Kerry traced a line across the side of one. "Have you ever worn toenail polish?"

Dar was quiet for a moment. "Are you suggesting I should?" She wiggled her toes, then wished she hadn't, as the injury protested. "Have you?"

"Me?" Kerry finished the top, and then she shifted to do the punctures on the bottom of Dar's foot, scattered across its ball. "Oh no. The idea of my wearing open shoes in public...I think I'd have had them cut off if I'd tried it. I wasn't even allowed to use anything other than clear or a light pink fingernail polish."

"Did you want to?"

"Yeah." Kerry smiled as she worked. "Bright, flame red." She painted a somewhat deeper puncture. "Oo...Dar, that's a bad one."

"Ow." Her partner sighed. "Well, you could now."

"Could now what?"

"Wear bright red nail polish."

Kerry looked up and over her shoulder at her partner, a quizzical expression on her face. "Do I look like a red nail polish kind of girl to you?" She asked. "I said back then, Dar. Now I just don't consider myself a red toenail type."

Dar studied her back for a moment, wondering about toenail polish among other things. She could honestly say wearing polish of any kind on her feet wasn't something that had ever crossed her mind, since taking her boots off to find that would have caused her merciless kidding probably right up until this very day. "Well." She considered. "I think a nice sea green would be pretty on you."

"Mmm hmm." Kerry agreed absentmindedly. "Probably. You would look good in coral."

"I would?"

"Yeah."

Dar considered further. "Kerry?"

"Uh?"

"Why are we having this discussion?"

Her partner shrugged her shoulders. "I don't know. I'm sitting here playing with your feet, so I guess the thought just came to me. I remember it was the topic of conversation regularly when I was in college." She finished the last bite mark. "There." She studied her handiwork. "I'm going to put a bandage on this. You shouldn't walk on it."

"I'm not walking on it." Dar agreed, wriggling into a more comfortable spot on the couch.

"I meant after you get up." Kerry gently set the foot aside and got up, heading toward the bathroom.

Dar folded her hands across her stomach and relaxed, sure that the worst of the tending was over. The injury now stung more than anything due to the cleaning, and she felt confident that it wasn't anything serious.

She still felt a little stupid, though, that she'd been bitten by a fish underneath her own dock. Dar wiggled her toes speculatively. Maybe she could tell people she'd been bitten by an alligator. That sounded more interesting.

Not to mention, heroic. Maybe Kerry would say she'd rescued her from it.

"What's so funny?" Kerry came back with a roll of gauze bandage and proceeded to mummify Dar's foot with it.

"Nothing." Dar squashed the temptation. "Just wondering what cock and bull story I'm going to come up with for people at the office tomorrow to explain why I'm limping."

"Well." Kerry said. "You could tell them I got revenge for you hitting me by stomping you with a stiletto heel." She suggested.

"Um...

"Or I could tell everyone you saved me from a vicious barracuda." Kerry continued on without hesitation. "There I was, swimming innocently, not realizing a barracuda was about to bite my ass, when you jumped in and saved me at the last minute."

"Hmm."

"Like that one better?"

"You tell good stories." Dar chuckled. "Even if they are completely fabricated."

Kerry finished her bandage, and patted Dar's calf. "Not completely. You'd have done it if it'd really been after me, right?"

"Right." Dar agreed almost without thinking. "Anyone trying to bite your ass has to go through me to get there. No question." She reached over and snagged a finger into the waistband of Kerry's shorts. "C'mere."

Kerry gladly leaned back, stretching her body out next to Dar's on the couch. "Know what I wish?"

"What?"

"I wish we weren't going back tonight."

Dar pondered the thought. "Okay." She agreed. "We won't."

Her partner laughed shortly. "Stop teasing me. You know we have to go into work tomorrow, Dar."'

"I'm not teasing." Dar replied. "I had this cabin installed with the gear I did for the specific purpose of us working down here. So let's do it. We can log in from here, and probably get three times the amount of work done. If we need to conference, we can finally put that god damned expensive teleconferencing center I paid for to work at the office."

Kerry turned over so she was facing Dar. "You're serious."

"As a heart attack."

Should they? Kerry thought about what she had on her schedule. The ops meeting, sure, and fallout from the weekend which had to be handled by conference call anyway. No clients, and the executive committee meeting wasn't until mid-week.

Hmm. "Okay." She sounded surprised even to herself. "Why not" You don't have anything that needs face time tomorrow?"

"Nope. Just more work on my program." Dar confirmed. "Absolutely I'll get more done from here on that, without someone sticking their heads in my office every five minutes." She liked the idea more and more with every passing second. "And, then I don't have to make up a 'no shit I was bitten by barracuda story'."

Kerry had to admit to feeling a little bit apprehensive, only because she knew what the view would be from their co-workers if they both didn't show for work tomorrow. Then she thought about that for a minute, and decided the hell with it. They talked bullshit about them anyway, might as well be doing what they wanted.

Besides, Dar was probably right. She got more done when she was not in the office as well, and she had several prospective client write ups she hadn't had a chance to do the last week that really needed to get taken care of.

Or was that just more self-justification? "What about the ship?" She asked. "You think it's going to be a public relations nightmare with them finding out Dad was working on it, and all that? If we don't show up for work on top of that, it could be a problem, Dar."

"Hell with it." Dar replied obstinately. "What if it's a problem? What if the media comes to interview me on it, Ker? What am I going to say, I didn't know?"

"Ah. Good point."

"I think it's a good idea to let that blow over a little." Dar decided. "In fact, I think the less we get involved in the whole press nightmare the better right now. Let's let our work stand for itself. Get the job done, then they can make what they want of it. The more we play into this, the worse it gets."

Kerry was quiet for a moment, and then she sighed. "We're really good at talking ourselves into things, aren't we?"

Dar had to smile. "Yeah." She sounded a touch sheepish.

"But maybe you're right." Kerry went on. "We've been playing right into their hands, haven't we? Reacting like we have, and getting all into the spotlight. Maybe it's time to lay low and just get the job done, like you said."

Dar kissed the top of her head. "We could even paint each other's toenails." She suggested. "No one has to know."'

Now it was Kerry's turn to smile. "Renegade. Only if I can paint yours freaking scarlet." She relaxed against the leather, though, her entire body reacting to the knowledge that there would be no late night drive home ahead of her at least tonight.

And, who knew? Dar was really a very good strategist, and maybe this would turn out to be another one of her brilliant solutions. It had happened before, and she'd never regretted trusting her partner's instincts yet. "You up for an omelet?"

"Only if the deceased baby chickens don't touch anything resembling a green pepper."

"You're on."

COFFEE AND A hacker for breakfast. Dar rattled the keys on her keyboard, her eyes flicking rapidly over the large LCD screen in her cabin office. "Yum, yum." She murmured, watching the attempts at entry into their systems.

It was quiet inside the cabin, save the rattling of her keys, and a similar, softer counterpoint from the next office over. Outside, the breeze stirred the tree branches, and leaves pattered fitfully against the window. It was cool enough inside for Dar to be wearing a pair of sedate, yet fluffy lambskin booties, one of them cradling her injured foot carefully.

They were perched on her desktop at the moment, and she leaned back in her leather chair, flexing her hands as she pondered her next course of action. The hacker wasn't that effective, and she didn't really think he was any danger, but it was the persistence behind the effort that had caught her eye.

It was almost a robotic sequence. A probe on each port, using each service, over and over and over again. Was it mechanical, or some idiot sitting there typing the same thing over and over? Dar leaned toward it being a script, but someone was behind the script, and she wanted to know what they were up to.

She probed the inbound connection cautiously, capturing some packets and examining them with a knowledgeable eye. The originating IP was spoofed, that she was pretty sure of. Last time she checked, Wal-Mart wasn't a spawning ground of insurgency, though she did appreciate the ghoulish humor.

Chino pattered in, jumping up and placing her paws squarely on the chair arm, licking Dar's arm with enthusiasm. "Hey Chi." She greeted the animal with an affectionate grin. "What are you up to? You want to help me watch this loser?"

"Growf." The Lab inched forward, nuzzling Dar's neck as she wagged her tail.

Dar put her arm around the dog and scratched her around the neck, typing one handed on her keyboard. "So what do you think, Chi? You like it here?" She asked. "Want to live here all the time?"

"Growf!"

"Sounded like yes to me." Dar drummed her fingers on the keys, watching the persistent signal hammering on her virtual front doorstep. "Look at that guy, would you? Just spewing over and over and over again. What in the hell's he trying to do?"

Chino decided Dar's ear would be tasty, and she licked it, making her owner emit a muffled chuckle.

Her mail chimed, and Dar spared an eye for it, clicking over to her inbox and reviewing the newly arrived message. It was from Mariana, and she opened it curiously.

```
Dar -
Heard you were playing hooky today. What's up?
Mari.
```

Well, now wasn't that refreshingly straightforward. Dar hit reply and typed a response.

```
Why? Everyone freaking out?  If you want to know the
truth, I got bitten by a barracuda last night and didn't feel
like lying about it all day long to everyone who saw me.
   D
```

"What do you think, Chino? Everyone freaking?" Dar gave the dog a kiss on the top of her head.

"Freaking about what?" Kerry responded, entering Dar's office and putting a cup of gently steaming, milky tea down on the desk. She had a pair of shorts and a sports bra on, along with a mostly relaxed expression. "The budgets? I told you that you scared them all last week."

"Nah, us." Dar picked up the cup and sipped it. "Thanks. How's the ship coming?"

Kerry perched on the edge of Dar's custom built, cherry wood desk – twin to the one in her own office next door. "Not good." She admitted. "I just talked to John, and he's having a very tough time, Dar. He's only about half done."

Dar grimaced.

Kerry hesitated. "Any suggestions?" She asked. "I've spoken to the people on the ship, and there's not much they can do, they tell me. Everyone's fighting for space and time there. We're all under the gun." She played with one of Chino's silky ears. "Apparently all the ships are. Someone lit a fire under them on Friday, and the schedules have all been pushed up."

"Yeah?" Dar frowned. "You know, we didn't hear from Dad last night. I wonder if he saw any of that."

"I wonder what happened with him that the reporter knew about him." Kerry added, both eyebrows hiking up. "I wonder why he didn't call."

Dar reached over and picked up the cabin phone, hitting one of the speed dial buttons. It rang several times, but there was no answer and it switched over to voice mail. "Huh." She waited for the beep. "Hi Dad. Gimme a call when you get a chance. Thanks."

"Try mom?"

"Ehm." Dar dialed another number, the slip phone at her parent's boat. It rang several times too, and again, went to a polite, mechanical voice mail. "What the heck's going on up there?" She frowned, waiting again. "Hey mom, it's Dar." She paused. "Boy that was redundant. Anyway, give us a call when you get back. Thanks."

She put the phone back down and looked at Chino, who had decided her half standing, half lolling position on Dar's shoulder was the pinnacle of comfort. "Anyway, so they're behind? Can he put more guys on the job?"

"Honestly, Dar, I don't think it'd help." Kerry said. "It's space they don't have. He's trying to put our cabling in the same place the electricians are running new wiring, and the air conditioning people are putting in new ducting."

"Huh. Yeah. I remember doing a favor for one of my dad's skippers." Dar said. "Wanted cable run from the bridge to his cabin so he could monitor everything from there. Damn guy had me doing it the same time they were replacing the comms. What a mess."

Kerry repressed a smile. "My little cable monkey." She glanced at

Dar's screen. "What's all that about?"

"Ah." Dar put her keyboard down and shifted, lifting one leg off the desk and sliding it around Kerry to trap her. "Some jackass hacker not worth five cents." She scoffed. "Idiot's just beating his head against our outer firewall."

Kerry looked at the monitor window. "Why?"

"No clue." Dar laced her fingers behind her head and leaned back. "Just to annoy me, probably."

"Or distract you." Kerry murmured. "It's almost like whatever that is, is just trying to draw attention to itself."

Dar sat up and looked at the screen, and then she looked at Kerry. "A diversion?"

"Do I need to get out of your way?" Kerry hazarded. "But yeah, it seems like that to me. Someone hammering on the front door screaming obscenities at you."

Shit. Dar's mind raced. She's right.

Kerry gently slipped from between Dar's long legs, and removed Chino from her perch. "Well, let me..."

Dar reached out and put a hand on her wrist. "Tell John to reverse his usual route. Have him pull the cable from the jack end. That'll clear the closets, and when he's done there and ready to do the core installs, the other guys'll be out of his way."

Kerry opened her mouth, then shut it again. A rueful grin appeared. "Should we switch projects?" She pondered. "Maybe some fresh eyes do help."

"Maybe." Dar had to agree. "G'wan. Maybe we can alternate. I'm going to go chase down your idea—though why the hell it didn't occur to me before I can't begin to figure out."

"Ditto." Kerry turned to leave. "How's the foot?"

"Hurts." Dar grunted, as she pulled her keyboard back onto her lap. "Maybe I'll go spear fishing later and get that little bastard."

Kerry paused briefly in the doorway to watch her partner, then she ducked through and swung around into her own office where a cup of tea already awaited her. She sat down behind her desk and picked up her cell phone, glancing at her screen as she keyed in John's number.

More mail. She clicked on it as she waited for her contractor to answer, running her eyes over the new arrivals.

"Hello?"

"Hi, John." Kerry scanned a note from the marketing department. "Listen, Dar had a good idea."

"We could use one." The wiring man grunted.

Kerry told him the plan. "Anyway, it can't hurt, and it'll get you out of the middle of that mess for a while. What do you think?" She clicked on her next mail.

```
Hey Ker -
Listen; remember when all those weird rumors were going
```

around about you and Dar? I thought it was just random chatter, but I had a potty encounter today and I'm not sure!

"Yeah, it's worth a try." John said. "All right, I'll pull my guys out. At least they got some new foreman on the loading dock, and I'm finally getting all my stuff. "

"Yeah?" Kerry was completely distracted by Colleen's mail.

"Yeah, here's a coincidence—his name's Roberts, just like Dar's." John chuckled. "Maybe it's in the name. Anyway, I'll give you a call back later."

"Okay."

I was in the necessary doing the necessary when I heard someone come in. She did a stall check, but I was I in the end one and she missed me. Then she made a call to someone and I heard her talking about trying to mess the company up!

This girlie said she'd started telling everyone you two had a big fight this weekend out here, and she was going to do worse! Well, let me tell you I came out of that necessary like the Queen Mary!

"Oh, my god." Kerry murmured.

She ran out—I tried to follow after her, but I got caught up at the door by two of those bloody secretaries trying to get out their bra straps while talking about some television program. I didn't recognize her, but it was right outside Marketing.

So—watch your back, my friend! I'll try to find the little bugger again.

C

Kerry forwarded the mail to Dar, then after a moment, hit reply.

Col -
We stayed down here to concentrate on our projects and not be distracted by jerks! Dar got bit by a fish and neither of us felt like driving back yesterday. Maybe we'll stay down here for a week. I got more done already this morning than I did the last half of last week.

Can you get a description of this person? We had a security breach...

Kerry paused, and backspaced.

We had a problem this weekend and we narrowed it down to Marketing, but they were all in, so we couldn?t pin it down. Maybe it was the same person. Let me know.

K

"Damn it, damn it." Kerry drummed her fingers on the keyboard, then she made a decision and forwarded the message again, this time to Mariana, along with a request to forward the personnel files of anyone who was in the building over the weekend.

It meant a lot of work, and a lot of crosschecking. Kerry took a sip of her tea, the smooth cherry taste of the green tea leaves soothing her. "But I will find you." She promised the tale teller. "I will find you, and baby, I will make sure you regret ever putting one step into that marble lobby."

She took another sip. "That, I promise.

DAR SAT THERE, arms folded, hands tucked under her armpits and stared at the network overview she had up on her screen. The picture showed their entire infrastructure, routers and switches winking a reassuring green at her as she tried to figure out where to look next.

Kerry's remark about a distraction had rung bells with her, but if it was, then what was it distracting her from? Everything else looked normal.

She turned her eyes to a different window, running results from her new program. Every ten seconds, the system reported back to her from each router she had it installed in, a constant running monitor of the traffic it was seeing.

It was rough, and the monitor only a command line, but Dar couldn't help but feel a sting of pride as she watched it go. She knew it had a long way to run before it could be really used in production, but eventually — with a properly written front end and a ton more robustness — this would be a killer app for them to put on the market.

Even now, with just the barest of kernels running, it was bringing back scraps of information from what it was seeing out there that gave Dar insight into what was going on around them.

It was exciting, in a visceral way to her. But she was also frustrated right now because there was a piece missing here, and she couldn't find it. The hacker was still hammering at the front gates, but Dar had scanned each of the border routers, and she could find no other stealthy attempts anywhere on the outside of the network.

Was it just coincidence then? Kerry's suggestion had made bedrock sense when she'd heard it, but... Dar unfolded one arm and gave her trackball a spin, her brows knit together. She rocked forward and braced her elbow on the desk, leaning her head against it as she got closer to the screen.

A message box appeared, nearly startling her half to death. She glanced to one side, then straightened and pulled the keyboard back over to answer Mariana's hail.

Hey.

Mari answered quickly.
You got bitten by a BARRACUDA?
Dar's somewhat ghoulish humor surfaced.
Family reunion. What can I tell you?
She could almost hear the laughter on the other end of the connection, and had to smile herself.
You got kicked out of the barracuda family when you married Kerry, my friend, and you know it!
Eh, that was the truth. Yeah, well, I was chasing a Frisbee at the time. At least I didn't get nipped by a goldfish for it. Her eyes flicked to the monitor, taking in a few minutes of reports and not seeing anything remarkable.
Damn it. She turned her attention back to the instant message box. So is everyone freaking out?
There was a hesitation before Mari answered. Just a little surprise at our level, but I heard talk going around, so I thought I'd better ask. Now that Kerry's sent me the scoop, and the possible culprit, I'll get on it and see what I can find out.
Huh? Dar felt suddenly lost. "Hey, Ker?" She called out. "C'mere."
"Hang on." Her partner replied from the next room. "I'm reconciling a purchase order."
Dar reread the message, then just shrugged. Okay. Have fun. She ventured, figuring it was a safe answer and that she could get clarification from Kerry later. We may be down here for a few days. I'm getting more done without people barging in my office every five minutes.
Mari's response surprised her a little. Dar, take whatever time you need, okay? Let me handle the crap in the office.
"What's up, sweetie." Kerry ambled in and put her arms around Dar, giving her a quick hug. "More problems?"
Dar scrolled back up in her message box and pointed. "What is she talking about?" She asked, just as the screen underneath, her monitor, began to spit out lines in black on white letters, instead of white on black. "Whoops...hold it."
Kerry slid in behind Dar and watched over her shoulder as she typed rapidly. She could see where Dar was going in the system, but she was hitting keys so fast Kerry couldn't read quickly enough to get a sense of what she was doing once she got there.
And then, just as quickly as she'd started, she stopped, fingertips resting lightly on the keys. The monitor appeared normal again. "What was that?" Kerry asked.
"Good question." Dar murmured. "For a minute, it looked like something..." Her brow creased and she leaned forward a little. "Maybe the damn program just stumbled. God knows, there's a lot of rough code in there."
Kerry put her hands on Dar?s shoulders. She could felt he tension beneath her fingers, and out of habit she started a gentle massage.

"What did it seem to be reporting?" She asked. "Was it an attack, or —"

Dar propped her head up on one hand and used the other to scroll the mouse. "No, not...well, it looks like it thought its libraries were being accessed. But that's just a dud error. There's nothing touching them."

"Mm." Kerry knocked a little of the rust off her own programming memories. "Sort of like...someone was also using them? Or...something opened the files?"

"Yeah." Dar agreed readily. "But nothing's accessing them. Nothing we have even knows the program's there."

"Hmm." Kerry kept up her massage. "False reading?"

"Must be."

They both studied the screen in silence for a few minutes. Then Kerry cleared her throat. "Colleen overheard some slimy nitball in the bathroom talking to someone on a cell about screwing us over."

Dar straightened and turned her head to look up at Kerry. "What?"

"Mm." Kerry nodded. "Spreading rumors. So I have Mari sending me all the personnel files of the scumbags in marketing."

One of Dar's eyebrows quirked. "Why not just get the one who did it?"

"Colleen didn't recognize her, and she lost her outside in the hallway." Kerry informed her regretfully. "Anyway...so that's what's going on. Can I go finish my paperwork now?"

Dar tilted her head and kissed the back of Kerry's hand, still resting on her shoulder. "Sure," she said. "Sorry I dragged you over here."

Kerry returned the kiss and planted one on the top of Dar's head. "No problem." She gave Dar a last hug, then turned and made her way out of the office, leaving behind a faint scent of apricot.

Dar sighed and refocused her attention on the screen. The alert was now well and over and no trace was left of the disturbance that had sent her monitor off the scale. She was satisfied with the possibility that it had been a false alarm, but something niggled at the back of her mind anyway.

She went over the log in the router that had triggered the alarm. No attacks had been detected from the outside, and she confirmed again that no unusual traffic had been seen. The only thing in the logs themselves was a —

Huh. Dar cocked her head. TFTP requests weren't uncommon. They had servers that routinely copied the configurations and logs of the devices for safekeeping, but Dar knew something about that which made this one log entry catch her eye.

She checked her watch. It was seventeen minutes past eleven. She'd written that little collection program way back in the days when she'd supervised the ops center. One of her own peculiarities, generated by her years growing up on a military base, dictated that her timed requests always went off on even fractions of the hour.

Eleven, eleven ten, twenty, thirty, but this request was seventeen minutes after the hour.

So Dar examined the entry, and found it coming from one of the administrative servers. Cracking her knuckles, she called up a terminal program and accessed the server, her eyes narrowing slightly as she started her hunt.

Chapter Eleven

ANDY WALKED ACROSS the pier and up the gangway into his new ship. This one was just as threadbare and full of rusty bolts as the other one, but he felt much more affectionate toward it in any case, and gave the side a pat as he walked inside.

The hold was full of boxes, as the last one had been. He noticed one difference, however. On one side of the storage area several pallets were set, neatly laden with boxes of assorted sizes, shrink wrapped, and tagged with invoices. They seemed to be behind a bunch of boxes, though, almost half hidden.

The orderliness of the stack appealed to him. Andrew walked over and scanned the shipping invoices with a knowledgeable eye, catching sight of a familiar company name on the top. "Huh." He studied the paper, noting the 'K. Stuart' referenced on one side. "I do believe I know that little kumquat."

Unlike the deliveries for the women on the other boat, this here pile had an order to it that had Andrew nodding as he reviewed the list of contents. "Ah do not know which of this here is a leg bone, and which is a foot bone, but I figure this here stack probably makes a whole skeleton and don't that make sense?"

"Hey, you there."

Andrew turned to find a scruffy, sweat-shirted man headed his way with a clipboard. He waited for the man to arrive, surprised when the clipboard was held out to him. "What's this here for?'

"You're Roberts, right?" The man asked.

Andrew allowed that he was.

"Great. The man said you'd be in here to take over for that joker. Here's the lading list, and this is the stuff we're expecting in today. Just get it unpacked and moved wherever you can find a place for it, okay?"

Andrew looked down at the clipboard. "Y'all want me to take charge of this here job?"

"Sure, right. Didn't he tell you?" The man seemed impatient. "C'mon, we're behind a day already, and everyone's screaming at me." He pointed to the stacks of boxes in front of Kerry's pallets. "Start with this bunch first and get it out of the way. Guys are in the break room, just go grab 'em when you're ready, which is like now, right?"

"Right."

"Great. Bye."

The man left at an almost run. Andrew regarded his back a moment, then shook his head. "Hell of a crazy damn place this is." He turned and went to the center of the hold, turning in a slow circle, and looking for a suitable place to start.

"Bloody hell."

Andrew turned, but the comment wasn't directed apparently at him. Two men in coveralls were walking from a just opened hatch toward a stairwell. They didn't look happy.

"Now we've got to get that leak fixed, damn." One said. "I thought they'd gotten that covered."

The other shrugged. "Didn't give 'em enough, probably. Always the same. Well, they can say what they want, that hole isn't getting plugged any time soon, not by me."

The two men disappeared into the stairwell, closing the door behind them. Andrew filed the information away for later study, and headed for the break room to find some bodies to shift them boxes like the feller asked.

But of course he'd start with Kerry's first.

"COULDN'T FIND ANYTHING, hmm?" Kerry asked.

"Program put out the TFTP request out of sequence." Dar folded her hands over her stomach. She was lying flat on her back on the padded bench outside on their porch with her head cradled comfortably in Kerry's lap. "Can't find any reason why," she added, "and it's driving me insane."

"Uh huh." Kerry leaned back, one hand idly riffling through Dar's hair. "Could it just be a fluke?"

Dar wiggled her injured foot, which she was putting in the sun for some mysterious and possibly imaginary medical benefit. "I'd rather not think so."

Kerry eyed her, a tiny, knowing grin on her face. "Because it's your program?"

One blue orb appeared, sparkling in the sunlight, and its brow hiked up. "What are you saying? That I'm a snob when it comes to my own work?"

"Mm." Kerry traced the eyebrow with her fingertip, admiring its fine arch. "You're a perfectionist," she remarked, smoothing the thin hairs down lovingly.

For a half second, Dar almost looked like she was going to be insulted, then her face relaxed into a grin. "Well, I picked you, so I guess I am."

A charmed smile appeared on Kerry's face. "I love you too, honey, but I'm not anywhere near perfect." She trailed her fingers over Dar's lips chuckling a little as they were caught and nibbled.

"To me you are." Dar answered simply. "So get over it."

Get over it. Kerry marveled again at just how fortunate she was in life. No matter what troubles they were facing at work, what they had together was, in a word, priceless and she knew it. She'd seen enough of the world to know that the synergy she and Dar shared wasn't common and needed to be cherished, protected, and nurtured.

They needed these moments. Certainly, Kerry savored them, her ego enjoying the gentle burnishing from Dar's regard. "Well, takes one to know one." She sorted Dar's bangs, running her fingers through them and moving them out of her eyes. "Can I interest you in a shrimp salad sub for lunch? I have a conference call scheduled for an hour from now."

"Mm." Dar licked her lips. "It's your shrimp salad, right? Not that mealy mess the store sells?"

"Mine." Kerry smiled. "With real, identifiable shrimp in it, not mushy shrimplets. That all right?"

Dar nodded, closing her eyes and exhaling in contentment.

It only lasted an instant, before her cell phone rang. Dar scrunched her face up in annoyance, but unclipped the phone from her pocket and opened it. "Yes?"

"Roberts, is that you?" Peter Quest sounded harried and upset.

Dar debated on denying it, then sighed. "Yes."

"All right, that's everyone." Quest said, a little more briskly. "I've got you all on the phone, so I only have to say this once."

Dar held the phone so Kerry could hear it, half lifting one hand as Kerry looked at her in question. "All right."

There were soft murmurs in the background, and Dar thought she recognized Michelle's voice in there somewhere.

"Here's the situation." Quest said. "Some asshole called the EPA, who came down and inspected the waterfront. We haven't done anything wrong, but the bleeding heart fish lovers think they see gas leaking, so they're forcing the port's hand."

"Think?" Kerry mouthed. "They've been leaking since they got here."

Dar put a finger over her lips.

"We've got until Friday. The ships have to be finished then."

Kerry's eyes popped wide open and so did Dar's. "No way!" Kerry whispered. "Dar, that's impossible!"

Dar nodded. "Quest, that's insanity."

Two male voices grunted agreement, then Michelle spoke. "It's a lot more possible for those of us who are actually here, thanks."

Kerry grimaced and made a rude gesture at the phone.

"I don't care." Quest dismissed them all. "That's the bottom line. Finish by Friday, and turn in your bids. If you can't do it, fine, but you leave everything in place on board the ships and just walk out."

"Wait a minute!" Mike Eldridge protested. "You can't just ask us to leave all that equipment if we're not going to bid. That's..."

"Then shut up and finish, because that's my deal." Quest cut him off. "And I'll have my security people enforce it. Now, I have to get off this phone and go deal with some whining liberal, so you've got four and a half days. I suggest you get moving, or get leaving. Good bye."

Dar stared at the now dead cell phone for a long moment. "Son of a bitch."

"Shit." Kerry's eyes flicked to the horizon, going unfocused as she thought about the suddenly mountainous obstacles before them. "Dar, there's no way."

"Did the infrastructure come in yet?"

"It was due yesterday, but—" Kerry hesitated. "No, wait...I had a note this morning from the shipping company that it was coming in this afternoon."

Dar had her eyes closed again. "Okay." She paused. "Call John. Tell him to bring in however many guys he can get hold of."

"You can't be serious...there's no way to..."

"Kerrison." Dar looked at her.

"Dar, c'mon now..."

"Hey." Dar reached up and cupped the side of Kerry's face, drawing her chin down a touch so their eyes were forced to meet.

"Darrrr..." A thousand arguments died before the look in those blue eyes.

"Kerrison Stuart."

A sudden flash of a cold rainy night in North Carolina formed in Kerry's mind, and she heard Dar's voice all over again in a cool, angry bark when she'd protested the impossible. This time there was no anger, just a gentle firmness just as effective in its own way. "Sorry." She leaned against Dar's hand a little. "Go on."

Dar understood the doubt she saw. "We don't know we can't do it, because we haven't tried yet." Dar stated. "So I vote we try, and if we fail, we do, but it won't be because we quit."

Kerry also knew the tasks ahead of them, and she knew no matter how much Dar willed it otherwise, they did not have the time to do what Quest was asking.

But...hey. Dar was right, they had to try. Neither of them were quitters. "Okay, boss." Kerry smiled again. "Guess we better get moving, huh?"

"After lunch." Dar said. "I'll call Mark and have him send everyone we have over there. We'll overrun the damn boat with nerds, and maybe everyone in our way will just run screaming."

Kerry cocked her head to one side. "You don't want to leave right now?"

"No."

"Um. Okay."

Dar resettled her hands over her stomach. "Ker?"

"Mm?"

"Trust me."

Kerry covered Dar's hands with one of her own. "Trust you? I trust you with my life, my soul, and everything that I am, Dar. It's not a matter of trusting you; I just want to know what you're up to."

A blue eye appeared again. "When I figure that out, you will."

"Oh."

"Mm."

"HEY THERE OLD MAN."

Andrew looked up from his bottle of pop to find the cowboy trucker heading his way. "Wall. howdy there, young feller." He drawled, exchanging an amused look with the man. In truth, they were probably pretty close in age, and the trucker chuckled as he extended a hand.

"Wanted to come over and say hello after the other day. I was halfway outta the state, when a company rig broke down and they turned me back. More stuff for this place."

Andrew looked around the dock, where there were trucks and men unloading everywhere. The pace on the pier had picked up incredibly, and he could almost sense panic from the workers around him. "Wonder what got 'em all in a hustle?"

The trucker looked surprised. "Did'ncha hear? Gov'mint tossing them outta here end of the week."

"Yeah?" Andy said. "Heard something like that, but I didn't figure they'd really do it."

"Well, if they ain't, no one's told my boss. We got ten more trucks headed this way right now." The man said. "Hope you all got room for it."

Ten trucks worth? Two for each ship more than likely. Andrew shook his head. The below decks area of the ship was a mess for sure, and just trying to keep it all straight had taken most of his day so far. "What you got now?" He asked. "Stuff for this one?" He pointed at the ship.

Obligingly, the trucker handed over his manifest. "You get nailed for messing with that little sissy boy the other day?"

"Naw." Andrew studied the papers, noting again Kerry's name on one side. "Got me moved over to this here tub." He indicated the ship with a motion of his head. "This here all for us?" He asked, flipping through to the last few pages and catching sight of something else. A tiny grin appeared on his face.

The trucker took back the manifest and examined it. "Far as I can tell, yeah." He agreed. "Where do you want it?"

"Right over there." Andy indicated a spot on the dock. "I'll have them boys move it all inside after."

"You got it." The trucker agreed. "Man, they got those people all riled up. What a mess." He watched as a group of ship personnel gathered near the stern of the vessel, along with a couple of suits all pointing and looking at the water behind the ship. "Well, let me get going. Be right back."

"Yeap." Andrew finished up his pop and stood there in the shade, considering what to do next. A motion caught his eye and he half turned, surprised to see Ceci pulling up to the curb in the truck. He tossed the pop bottle in the trash and jogged over, leaning down to rest his elbows on the window sill and peer inside. "Hey there."

"Hi." Ceci reached and handed him something. "You forgot this, and our child has been trying to get hold of us."

"Aw, hell." Andrew took the phone. "You call her?"

"No." Ceci glanced past him at the chaos on the dock. "I'd have to admit to causing this if I did."

"Cec..."

"Yes, I know. Our relationship is quantum leaps past what it was, Andy, but I'd still rather you did it." The slim, fair haired woman said. "Uh oh...I better go. That guy knows me." She set a pair of wraparound sunglasses on her nose, and ducked behind Andrew's bulk.

"Lord." Andy started dialing.

"You knew you married a leftist radical."

"Yeap, I surely did."

"Well, it could have been worse, Andy."

"Yeap. Dar coulda joined the Army."

"Pffft!"

KERRY LEANED BACK in the driver's seat of the Lexus, watching the somewhat boring bushes pass by as they headed north. Next to her in the passenger seat, Dar was rattling away on her keyboard, pausing impatiently as she waited for her keystrokes to catch up with her over the cellular modem link. "What on earth did we do before cell modems?"

"Got lots of speeding tickets." Dar answered absently.

"Did you?" Kerry adjusted the sun visor to block out the blast of golden light from the west.

"Uh huh. For a while I almost gave up living in my place and thought about bunking at the office. There was space under my desk."

"Hmm. Is that why you have a couch in your office now?"

Dar chuckled. "Yes, but not if you ask the majority of the small minded." She eased her leg straight, wincing a little as she banged her foot against the center console. "The sordid events everyone was convinced took place on that couch were legendary."

"Legendary?"

"Uh huh."

"How legendary?"

Dar paused in mid type, her eyes shifting from her laptop to Kerry's profile. She could see the curve of her partner's jaw line, and the slight bunching and relaxing of the muscles there that meant the question wasn't frivolous. "Um..." She tapped the side of her thumb against the wrist rest. "They were all fictional, Ker," she said. "The only person who's ever slept on that couch besides me is you."

"Oh."

Dar muffled a grin of her own and went back to typing.

Kerry's face tensed into a sheepish grin, as she glanced at Dar. "Boy, do I have a green streak a mile wide, or what?" She sighed. "You know, I never really suspected that about myself until I met you."

"Well, given all the stories you've heard about me in that office, I can't say I blame you for wondering." Dar admitted. "But I have to admit that my reputation in that area was way overrated. I think it was easier for me to let everyone think I was out there having a wild and crazy time rather than them knowing the truth."

Kerry thought back to her days in Miami before she'd met Dar. She'd had, she'd thought, a reasonable social life with her friends from the office, and near her apartment. They'd gone bowling, seen movies, played around at Dave and Busters — it hadn't been bad.

Except. "Nights are a lot more fun now."

Dar raised both eyebrows at her.

"No, I mean...I was always busy during the day." Kerry explained, changing lanes to go around a very slow gasoline tanker. "Or around dinner, with the gang. But then I went home."

"Mm." Dar grunted. "Did your couch have torrid tales?" She asked, a little surprised at the fact that not only was it the first time she'd asked, it was the first time she'd wondered.

Kerry pushed her sunglasses higher up on her nose. "You inaugurated that couch," she replied straightforwardly. "I don't think I had done anything more risqué than eat crackers and cheese on it before that."

"Ah."

They were both silent for a while, immersed in their own thoughts while Dar continued pecking away on her keyboard. Outside the SUV, the scrub brush and occasional crab shack slowly gave way to tacky tourist outposts that beckoned the unwary with deals on seashells and cheap t-shirts.

Kerry passed the first few miles of them, then she pulled into one of the next parking lots. "Drink break. Want something?"

Dar put the laptop on the seat behind her. "Stretch my legs." She responded. "I've got a cramp."

"You going to go out there in your little booties?" Kerry asked.

"Sure. They're not white socks with black sandals. No one'll think I'm a tourist." Dar opened the door and carefully hopped out. The bite on her foot was quite painful and somewhat swollen, and she had to limp to keep her weight off it. "At least not a Florida tourist."

"No, they'll just think you're from New Zealand." Kerry got out on her side and closed the door, then jogged over to Dar's side as they walked toward the mini-mart. "How's the foot doing?"

"Sucks." Dar grunted.

Kerry gave her a sympathetic rub on the back as they reached the door and entered. The mini mart was very mini, and not much of a mart, featuring a lonely coffee burner with a pot of burned coffee in it, a single refrigerator with Coke bottles, a rack of gum and bags of one day old doughnuts on the counter.

Without exchanging even a glance, Kerry veered to the refrigerator case and grabbed two bottles of coke while Dar carefully skirted the doughnuts and examined the sparse choices of packaged snacks.

"Hi there ladies." The proprietor of the mart appeared from a tiny back room. "Can I get you something? We got a special on these doughnuts." He nudged one of the bags forward. "They're pretty good."

"No thanks." Dar responded briefly. "We...um..." She paused as Kerry plunked two bottles of coke and two packages of Snowballs on the counter along with a five dollar bill. "have what we need."

The door opened and let in a blast of warm air and sunlight, along with a tall, burly figure. The newcomer paused as the door closed, revealing an intimidating biker image complete with mirrored shades.

The mart owner regarded him warily. "Howdy."

The man, however, was far more interested in Dar and Kerry. He pulled off his sunglasses. "Hey guys! What's the odds, huh?"

"Hey, Tom!" Kerry smiled. "You here on your bike? Dar hasn't seen it yet."

"Sure am. How's the eye?" Their fellow kickboxing student asked her. "What brings you guys down here?" He tossed a five dollar bill down on the counter. "Pump two."

They walked outside together, and crossed the broken tarmac parking lot to the gas pumps. Tom's new Harley was huddling there in the sunlight, and drew an admiring whistle from Dar. "Nice." She complimented him. "I love the fish."

"Me too." Tom agreed, opening the gas tank and inserting the filler. "Some of the guys, though, they were too wussy, but you know what? Chicks dig it."

Well, it was hard to argue on that since both she and Kerry were undeniably chicks, and they both did like them. "Great paint job. How is it to ride?" Dar asked. "I rented one a few months back and liked how it handled, but it wasn't that good long distance."

"I remember that." Kerry murmured.

"Oh, it's great." Tom told her readily. "I thought it was gonna be a little tough on my...uh..."

"Buns." Kerry supplied.

"Yeah, those too. But it's been cool," Tom said. "Sure you don't wanna trade up to one, Ker?"

"Hmm." Kerry regarded the big bike wistfully. "They sure are cool." Her eyes went to Dar's face. "They just really pissed us off when we went to go buy one." She saw the faintest twitch at the corner of her partner's mouth, and sighed as she leaned against the pump.

"Well, you should go get one at bike week, like I did." Tom said. "Hey, speaking of, how'd the tat come out, Ker? Did'ja go through with it?"

Kerry obligingly unbuttoned and pulled down the shoulder of her short sleeve cotton shirt, exposing the tattoo. "I did." She confirmed. "And you were so lying to me, Tom. It hurt like crazy. I think I made the poor guy deaf from my screaming."

Tom examined the tattoo, and then gave Kerry a very respectful look. "Well...uh...mine was on my arm." He flexed his bicep, displaying a beautiful parrot. "I think it'd hurt a lot more right on your...uh..." His eyes dropped to Kerry's tattoo, then averted, as he blushed slightly. "You know what I mean."

Dar reached around Kerry's shoulder and encircled her with both arms as she re-buttoned her shirt. "We know what you mean," she said. "And I'll keep that in mind when I go get mine done."

Kerry turned and looked up at Dar in surprise.

"Anyway, hey, I'm glad I ran into you guys," Tom said. "Something sorta weird happened on Friday, and I don't really know what to make of it." He put the gas nozzle back in the pump and closed the gas cap. "I was at the bar and some women came up to me."

"That was weird?" Dar was aware of Kerry's intense regard, but she merely laid her arm over her partner's shoulders and addressed Tom instead. "Why? You're not that bad looking."

Tom scratched his nose. "Well, this was kinda serious, you know? One of them said they were some kind of reporter or something, and they were asking questions about you guys, or mostly Kerry, really."

It stopped being funny, and Kerry stopped thinking about tattoos, no matter how startled she was. "What?" She turned around and faced Tom. "Questions about me?"

Tom had the grace to look both abashed and embarrassed. "Um...about you and me, matter of fact."

"You and me what?" Kerry spluttered. "You and me in kickboxing class, or drinking beer together?" She was aware suddenly of Dar's close presence behind her, and felt the warmth of her partner's hands as Dar put them on her shoulders.

"They had...you remember when I showed you the bike?" Tom seemed a little uneasy. "And we kinda...you took that picture with me?"

Kerry's eyes narrowed. "Yes."

"I guess I was showing it to the guys at the bar, and I guess..." He cleared his throat. "Anyway, I got it blown up and one of the copies sorta disappeared."

Dar snorted softly, but didn't make any comment.

"Jesus." Kerry exhaled. "Where did the reporters say they were from? Was it the Travel Channel?

Tom shook his head. "No, uh...the Herald, you know? Some kind of story they were doing about the port, and some ships...and I guess about you."

"And they have that picture, right?" Kerry covered her eyes.

"I guess. They mentioned it, so..." Tom shrugged sheepishly. "I mean, no one thought much about it, Kerry. I knew it kinda went walking, but you know, it was a rocking picture, so..."

"Uh oh." Dar said. "How bad was this photo?"

"Me and Tom on the bike," Kerry still had her eyes covered, "with me posing as a biker chick."

Dar sorted through that, and didn't find anything altogether that dangerous in it. "Okay," she said slowly. "So...when was this?"

"When you were in New York." Kerry sighed.

"Uh huh. Same night you got this?" Dar indicated the tattoo.

Kerry nodded.

"It wasn't anything!" Tom spoke up suddenly. "All Kerry was doing was giving me an ego shot on the damn bike. We didn't do nothing!"

Dar looked at him. "I know that," she said. "Question is what is it they're looking to illustrate using it?"

Kerry put her hands on her hips and stared disgustedly at the broken tarmac. "I've had it," she finally said, turning and heading for the Lexus. "I'm quitting and becoming an itinerant poet. Then maybe no one will give a crap what I do." She opened the door and got in, slamming it behind her.

That left Dar and Tom facing each other across the Harley. Dar sighed, and produced a brief smile. "It's been a rough couple weeks," she said. "Last thing we need is to drive back to town and be greeted with a front page story."

Tom stuck his hands into the pockets on his jeans. "Dar, I'm real sorry."

"Wasn't anything you did." Dar shrugged. "What did you tell the reporters, anyway?"

"Not much." He admitted. "I just couldn't get what they were after, so they kinda just left when I wouldn't tell them me and Kerry had been...um...like, hanging out together or whatever."

"Yeah." Dar pushed her sunglasses up on her nose. "Well, thanks, Tom. Nice bike. Don't worry about the picture, okay?" She lifted a hand to wave goodbye and headed for the car. Circling the back of it, she got in the passenger side and closed the door, half turning in the seat to face the huddled, silent Kerry. "Hey."

Kerry sniffled, and wiped the back of her hand across her eyes. "I'm so sick of this."

Dar leaned further over the center console, and gently gripped Kerry's forearm. "Ker?"

Kerry sniffled again. "Yeah?"

"I'm sick of it too."

Kerry took off her sunglasses and looked at Dar with tear moistened eyes. "I know it's chickenshit."

Dar shook her head. "Just human." She slid her grip down to clasp Kerry's hand, then drew the hand up to kiss its knuckles. "Let's just go do what we need to do, then we can sit down and decide where we go from here."

Kerry looked at her hand, now pressed gently against Dar's cheek. She gave the fingers clasping hers a squeeze, and exhaled, nodding a little in answer.

"Want me to drive now?" Dar asked. "I can try it left footed."

"No." Kerry gathered her wits. "Just open my coke for me, and gimme a Snowball. I'll live." She started the car and put it in gear. "Dar, what are we going to do if that does end up on the front page of the Herald?"

"Won't." Dar was busy ripping cellophane with her teeth. "You're not a communist sympathizer. You might make the business page though." She removed the soft, fluffy pastry and handed it over. "And if it does, we just deal with it."

Kerry bit into the marshmallow top, tearing it apart ruthlessly. "How's ILS going to deal with their VP Ops being a biker chick?"

"About like they did with their VP Ops being a gay redneck." Dar took a sip of Coke. "We'll all cope."

Yeah. Kerry settled into her seat, gazing ahead into the slowly fading sunlight. "Know what I'm going to do if it happens?"

"What?"

"Frame a copy and send it to my mother."

"Ouch."

IT WAS DINNERTIME before they pulled into the driveway. Kerry parked the Lexus and opened the door, sliding off the leather seat to the ground and stretching her back out. "Ugh."

"C'mon, Chino." Dar got out on the other side and opened the back door, allowing the Labrador to jump to the ground. She shouldered her laptop and waited for Kerry to join her, then she limped up the steps to the front door of the condo.

They had debated stopping at the port. Chino had tipped the balance, since neither of them wanted to leave their pet in the car while they checked on things and bringing her onboard the ship just wasn?t an option.

Dar keyed the door open and entered, waiting for Kerry to pass her by and then shutting the door. "You want to change, and we'll run over there?"

Kerry dropped her briefcase and overnight bag on the love seat. "You want to hear the politically correct corporately responsible answer or the truth?"

"Me either." Dar limped past her and went into the bedroom. "Is there really a point? We're both fond of saying we can trust our people, aren't we?"

Kerry trudged into the kitchen and opened the refrigerator, removing a bottle of juice and pouring herself a glass. "Good point." She called back into the living room. "How about we commit to being there early tomorrow morning? We can assess what's going on, and decide what we want to do."

"Uh."

Kerry took a sip of juice, and cocked her head. "Did you say something?"

"Uh."

Drawn by this odd utterance, Kerry left the kitchen and entered the living room, finding Dar sprawled on the couch looking at her injured foot with a frown. "What's wrong?"

"That." Dar pointed.

Kerry walked over and sat down, cradling Dar's foot in her lap and examining it closely. "Oh." She grimaced. "Ow."

The foot was swollen and an angry red color. Dar folded her arms across her chest and glared at it. "Stupid god damned fish."

"Let me go get the antiseptic. Or we could go see Dr. Steve."

Kerry slipped into the bathroom and returned, setting the antiseptic bottle and cotton balls down as she prepared to render first aid. Chino came over and started to help, licking Dar's face thoroughly with a serious expression.

"That's it, Chi. You keep mommy Dar busy while I do this."

Dar reached over the dog and picked up the mail on the coffee table, laying it on her stomach and flipping through it to distract herself. A Hammacher Schlemmer catalog caught her eye, and she opened it, browsing the pages idly. "Want a pair of space socks?"

Kerry tweaked one of Dar's toes. "No, honey, I don't." She wiped around the fish bite carefully with her swab.

"Automatic vacuum cleaner?"

"For?" Kerry looked around. "We have a cleaning service, remember?"

Dar sighed. "How about a train set?"

"You just like buying toys." Kerry peered at the bites on the bottom of her partner's foot. "Dar, these really do look bad."

"Great."

"I don't know if Dr. Steve was a horrible idea." Kerry went on, with a slightly apologetic tone. "I know you don't like to, but I'd hate to see these really get infected, you know?"

"I've had my tetanus."

It was one of the few things they consistently fought about, Kerry privately admitted. Dar hated doctors, and Kerry both sympathized, and understood why she did. In fact, she wasn't fond of doctors herself, though in Dr. Steve she'd finally found one she not only trusted, but liked. "Dar."

"Okay."

Kerry paused in mid breath, taken aback by the unexpected capitulation. She looked at Dar in surprise.

Dar shrugged a little. "It really hurts." She admitted. "And you're right—I don't want it to get worse if I have to spend the next week in hiking boots on the deck of some damn half assed cruise ship," she said. "So, if you want to give Steve a call, I'll go feed Chino."

Kerry gave the long leg wrapped around her a gentle pat. "For being such a good girl, I'll take you out to dinner after he's done. How's that?"

Dar produced a charming smile. "Only if you promise to never, ever, ever tell anyone I was either good, or voluntarily went to the doctor."

"Deal."

Kerry got up and edged between the couch and the coffee table, leaning over to give Dar a kiss on the lips. She stayed there almost long enough to get a crick in her back, then straightened up and headed for the phone.

Dar ruffled Chino's fur with one hand, and laid the other across her stomach. Aside from her foot really hurting, she also found herself completely unwilling to argue with Kerry, especially since she knew Kerry was right and she was only arguing because that's what she always did.

She felt a little adrift. She could feel changes coming, and the thought excited her more than frightened. But first, they did have this damn bid to get through, so she decided to focus on that for now. In the meantime, she would go and get her foot fixed up, and keep Kerry from getting any more stressed than she already was.

"You hungry, Chi? You want some dinner?" Dar swung her legs over the side of the couch and got up, going to the kitchen with a very attentive Labrador now glued to her knee. "Let's go get you fed."

"Growf."

DR. STEVE SHOOK his head as he examined Dar's foot. "Munchkin, between the two of you, I swear I should just tie you up in hammocks for a month and not let you outside for a minute."

"Long as it's the same hammock." Dar replied benignly, her eyes closed and her hands folded over her stomach. "I'm cool with it."

Kerry was loitering behind the examination table, leaning on her elbows. "Count me in too."

"Tch, tch. You wild children." The doctor finished his work and turned around to face Dar. "Honey, I'm going to have to give you a shot of antibiotic.?

"Okay."

"Now, I don't want to hear all that guff about..." Dr. Steve paused. "S'cuse me?"

Dar shrugged. "Go ahead. Anything to make that damn foot feel better."

Her doctor and old family friend put his hands on his hips. "Who in the hell are you?" He asked. "You ain't no Dar Roberts I know." He looked over at Kerry. "You get her drunk before you brought her in here?"

"Nope." Kerry idly played with a bit of Dar's hair. "Hasn't had a drop, though that'll change when we get done." She gave the lock a tug, and was rewarded by Dar turning her head and peering up at her. "Dar's just come to her senses, right honey?"

"Right." Dar kept her eyes on Kerry while Dr. Steve prepared the shot, since she never had liked to watch large pieces of sharp steel enter her body and didn't figure on starting any time soon, or now for that matter.

She could sense the doctor's approach. Kerry must have sensed it too, because she slid her hand forward and cupped Dar's cheek, a welcome warmth in the cool air of the office. Dar let herself get lost in the soft green eyes regarding her, and she didn't even feel the prick of the needle.

"Okay, there you go." Dr. Steve wiped the area with a bit of cotton. "I'm gonna give you a prescription, too, you little rugrat. Wish you knew for sure what kind of fishie that was." He patted Dar's leg. "But you should be okay, long as you don't aggravate things."

Obligingly, Dar sat up and swung her legs off the table, leaning her weight on her hands as she watched Dr. Steve writing her prescription. He was dressed in a short sleeve plaid shirt and Bermuda shorts, and hadn't bothered to assume his white coat for his afterhour's patients. "Did you look at Kerry's eye?"

Dr. Steve looked over his shoulder. "C'mere, Kerry."

Kerry walked over to him and stood in the light, as he tilted her face a little toward him and studied her.

"I'd say her eye was green." Dr. Steve announced. "Just like the other one." He grinned at Kerry, who grinned back. "No headaches or anything from it, young lady?"

"No..." Kerry hesitated. "Well, not from that anyway. We've had a tough week."

His eyebrow rose. "It's Monday."

"Exactly."

Dr. Steve patted her cheek. "Well, you take it easy, okay? Nothing in that crazy world of yours is worth getting sick over."

"You got that right." Dar limped over and laid a hand on Kerry's shoulder. "So, take this stuff, and what else? Don't tell me to stay off it

Steve. I've got a damn ship I have to be crawling over the next couple of days."

Dr. Steve frowned at her. "Honey, how do you expect that thing to heal if you're stomping all over with it? Any shoe you put on there's gonna hurt." He pointed out. "Less you want to go barefoot, like you used to."

"Still does." Kerry teased gently. "But I'd never let her do it on that dock."

Dar sighed. "I'll figure something out." She took the prescription. "Thanks. Sorry to pull you out from dinner." She stuck the paper into her pocket as the doctor led them to the back door, opening it so they could get out.

"No worries, rugrat." Dr. Steve patted her on the back and headed for his open topped Jeep. "You take care." He said. "And keep off that foot!"

Dar got into the car, this time Kerry's smaller blue one, and shut the door. She waited for her partner to get in on the driver's side and gave her a look. "I can't not go."

Kerry started the car, then leaned on the steering wheel and regarded her. "Didn't you just agree with him that the job isn't worth your health?"

Blue eyes blinked unrepentantly. "No."

"No?"

"I agreed the job wasn't worth YOUR health."

"Jesus."

"Not hardly." Dar set her sunglasses onto her nose. "C'mon. We'll figure out something."

"Yeah." Kerry put the car in gear, and pulled out of the driveway heading toward the beach. "I'm sure we will."

THEY ENDED UP going by the port anyway. It was near nine o'clock, but the piers were bustling with activity and Kerry had to steer around several groups of rushing workers as she edged her way toward their ship. The air was full of the sound of heavy machinery moving, the clank of cranes, the hoot of warning klaxons as huge pieces of steel swung overhead, and the ever-present hiss of welding torches. "Looks busy," she commented.

"Very." Dar agreed, peering out the open passenger side window. "Are those protestors?"

"Yeah." Kerry nodded. "Looks like it."

"Hmph."

Kerry parked near their terminal, and got out, watching with some slight anxiety as Dar hopped out on her side and shut the door. "You going to be okay?"

"Fine." Dar put cautious pressure on her foot, and immediately regretted it. "Ow."

"Want to stay with the car, and let me run in?" Kerry circled the Lexus and came to Dar's side, resting her hand on Dar's arm.

"No." Dar stubbornly started toward the pier, limping heavily. "C'mon, let's get this over with."

Kerry followed her, trotting to catch up, then walking along at Dar's side. For once, she didn't have to stretch to keep up, and halfway there she put her hand on Dar's back, giving the surface a gentle rub with the edge of her thumb.

"That jerk at the restaurant aggravated me." Dar said, out of the blue.

"Yeah, me too." Kerry agreed.

"He had no right to take it out on that waitress." Dar continued. "It wasn't her fault he split his pants."

"Too true."

"I wanted to kick him."

Kerry patted Dar's back. "I know, honey, and I know you couldn't because your foot's hurt." She sympathized. "Anyway, I'm sure the karma will come back and bite him in the butt someday."

"Hmph."

Kerry chuckled. "You're such a crusader. I love that about you."

"Me?" Dar hobbled up the steps to the terminal and headed for the doors. "I'm nothing of the sort. I just hate jerks."

Kerry swatted her on the butt as she held the door open and let Dar enter ahead of her, glad when the somewhat clammy but welcome chill of the air conditioning beat back the mugginess of the evening air. The interior of the room was far more active than it had been previously, and they both paused in surprise as the chaos resolved itself. "Holy pooters."

The inside of the big terminal had been transformed from a dank, empty space to a bustle of activity, filled from back to front with people and gear they both recognized as belonging to ILS. "Well." Dar exhaled, and started forward, lifting a hand to wave as people began to recognize her. "We did call up the troops."

"Hey boss." Mark appeared from literally nowhere, carrying a spool of cable and a switch on one shoulder. "How's the goldfish nip?"

"Fine. What's going on in here?" Dar asked, looking around. Boxes and boxes of gear were stacked against the walls, most unpacked with humming and blinking boxes propped up on every available surface. "Mark, the network goes inside the ship, yeah?"

"Lemme get rid of this." Mark trotted over and divested himself of his load, handing it off to a harried looking tech. "A ton of our stuff came in, but they ain't got no space for it yet."

"Ah." Kerry walked over to a carton and examined the packing slip. "Yeah, I was expecting this today. Good." She looked over at Mark. "Guess they came through after all, no matter where they got it from."

Mark nodded. "Yeah, I talked to our guy today, just checking on stuff. He's still torked."

"Too bad." Kerry put her hands on her hips. "So, you brought it all in here?"

"Nuh uh." He shook his head. "I got told it was coming in here, and that I was supposed to do something useful with it."

Dar cocked her head. "Who in the hell had the balls to tell you that?"

Kerry was already smiling, half covering her face with one hand.

"Your dad." Mark cheerfully supplied. "I figured I'd better listen to him."

"My dad." Dar appeared to have developed a headache, from the way she was rubbing her temples. "Okay, fine. So you are...?"

"Setting up, burning in, and testing the network here," Mark said. "Configuring it after that, so when they do have someplace to put it, we'll be ready."

Dar absorbed that, then nodded. "Makes sense." She said. "John around?"

Mark pointed toward the entrance to the ship. He watched Dar limp off, then turned to Kerry. "Hey...um...I got something kinda skanky to show you."

Kerry tore her own eyes from her partner's retreating back, and focused on him. "Skanky?"

She followed Mark over to a pallet that was covered with a gray, dusty tarp. Mark took hold of one end of it and pulled it free, exposing a stack of boxes. "Dar's old man dropped this over here too. Said it was delivered to us by accident, but we should just keep it hidden."

Kerry looked at the packing slip. The receiving name was Telegenics. "This isn't ours."

"Yeah, I know." Mark agreed. "It's the same stuff we ordered, but it's for those jerk wads down on the other ship." He pointed. "Got three more pallets full."

"The four orders."

"Yeah."

Kerry walked to each pallet, and examined the labels. They were all identical. Proof of Telegenic's duplicity — or was it? Could that have been done by accident? "Mark, did you ever ask the goofball if they questioned those four orders?"

Mark walked over and leaned an elbow on the boxes. "Yeah, I did. He told me he was told to shut up and mind his own business, and just deliver what was ordered."

And didn't that just sound like Shari? Kerry slowly let out a held breath. "Well, well." She flicked her fingers against the cardboard, suddenly aware that she held the fate of the bids in her hands, at least the Telegenics one. There was no way for them to get replacement gear for anything less than truly exorbitant prices if this batch went missing, chiefly because they themselves dried up the channel.

What goes around comes around. Wasn't that the saying? Didn't it serve Shari and Michelle right to have this happen after what they'd tried to do?

It was just good, hard business sense for Kerry to keep these pallets right here, under cover, maybe filing a mis-delivery with the carrier that would take several weeks to resolve, right?

Absolutely.

"You have a really funny look on your face, chief." Mark commented.

"My head's having a cat fight with my conscience." Kerry let her hand fall. She turned and spotted a cluster of people near the office. "Now what?" She started toward the group, leaving the pallets behind for the time being.

Mark stood by and watched, until one of the techs came up next to him. "Hey." The tech said. "You show her these boxes?"

"Yeah." Mark nodded.

"What do you think she's gonna do with 'em?"

Mark scratched his neck. "I dunno." He admitted. "C'mon, we've got shit to do." He headed back toward the piled gear, shaking his head a little.

Chapter Twelve

DAR LIMPED UP the gangway, wincing at both the pain in her foot and the glaring spotlights surrounding the pier. She could hear men cursing ahead of her, and suddenly in the rumble of sound she caught a familiar drawl.

She stopped at the top of the gangway, unable to go further due to the cramming of boxes, people, gear, and packing material stuffed in the entrance. Briefly she paused, looking for a way around it, then shrugged and tipped her head back a little. "Dad!" She let out a yell.

One hundred percent of those inside the hold were men, and a significant portion of them were fathers. However, only one shouted. "Dardar, that you? Careful of that there mess, will ya?"

"What in the hell is all this crap?" Dar pushed against a box. "You building an ark in there?"

Abruptly a box moved then disappeared, allowing Andrew to stick his grizzled head into the hole it left. "Lord, I will tell you there are more stupid human beings inside this here boat than I met in all mah years in the Navy."

Dar leaned against the boxes. "What are you doing here?"

"Long tale, young lady," her father said. "Anyhow, them folks are trying to get all this here new stuff up one itty-bitty elevator and it ain't flying. You get them boxes inside? That's all your stuff, ain't it?"

"Yeah," Dar said. "My people are setting it all up and getting it ready."

"Yeap." Andy nodded again. "Folks seem like they know what's up inside there."

"Of course." Dar felt a prickle of pride. "Hey, why don't you put some of this packing crap out on the pier? You'd have more room."

Her father gave her a look. "Cause them there folks," he pointed at a sextet of jacketed individuals watching the ship, "do not want no garbage exiting this here vessel."

"Ah." Dar exhaled. "EPA?"

"Yeap."

"How in the hell did they get into all this?" Dar wondered.

Andy cleared his throat. Dar looked at him. They exchanged knowing glances. Dar scrubbed her face with one hand, and mildly resented this additional complication to an already complex and morally questionable series of actions. "Christ."

"Well," Andy sighed, "them boats are leaking."

"I know." Dar leaned against the side of the ship entrance. "But there are so many questionable things involved with this circus right now, if that gets out...I don't' know." She shifted her weight off her injured foot. "It's a mess."

Andrew was watching her like a hawk. "Something hurting you?"

"I got my foot bit by a fish." Dar answered absently, her mind churning over the possibilities.

"How in the hell did that happen?"

"Long damn story." Dar turned and put her hands on the gangway railing. "All right, let's just do what we can, and make the best of it." She looked over her shoulder at him. "Thanks for watching out for us."

Andy regarded her. "You going inside there? Let you know when a body can move inside this place."

Dar nodded. "You need anything? Drinks or whatever? I saw our catering truck outside."

Andy grinned.

"I'll take care of it." Dar turned and made her way back down the ramp, wondering what possibly could happen next to screw up a situation already so screwed up it defied explanation.

Then she figured she'd better stop wondering in case it happened.

KERRY STOOD INSIDE the small office, surrounded by busy people. She had taken a cup of cold water, and she was slowly sipping it as she listened to the many conversational threads around her.

But her mind wasn't really on the business in the room. She rolled the cold, almost tasteless water around in her mouth and swallowed it, feeling the chill slide down her throat and into her stomach.

"Kerry?" Elaine walked over, holding some papers. "Can you just look at this? I think it's all right, but—"

Kerry took the pages and held them in front of her, eyes scanning the typed print without comprehension for at least a minute. Then she sighed and handed them back. "Hold on to this, would you? I need to go take care of something, and I'll check it when I get back."

"Uh...sure." Elaine watched her leave, a puzzled look on her face.

Kerry exited the building on the side near the ship, showing her identification badge to the guard who waved her past wearily without really looking. Given the number of people that must have been traipsing in and out, she could hardly blame him, but the lack of security bothered her anyway.

Ah well. She'd take care of that when she got back. Orienting herself, Kerry headed down the pier, walking past the tall cranes, the small groups of arguing men and the ever present forklifts zipping everywhere.

It seemed like the pier went on forever, giving her far too much time to think about what she was doing. Doubts pecked at her like hungry pigeons, but she kept herself moving across the pavement resisting the urge to stop and go back and—

What was Dar going to say if she asked her? Would she say not to

look a gift horse in the mouth? After all, they hadn't arranged for
Michelle and Shari's gear to be delivered to their dock, now had they?
For sure, for absolute sure, if the positions had been reversed, Kerry
knew the most she'd ever see of her stuff was a box floating past
heading out to sea.

But she wasn't Michelle, and she wasn't Shari. Kerry crossed the
line between the two piers. She wasn't Dar. What had she just been
saying? What comes around goes around?

Well. She squared her shoulders and edged between two tall stacks
of steel, walking into the floodlights around the other ship and spotting
two familiar figures standing near the gangway.

Two cameramen bracketed them, and it was obvious that Shari was
busy holding court for them. She was making grand gestures, and as
Kerry came closer, her words started to become comprehensible.

Well, she could hear them anyway.

"So, gentlemen, you see the obstacles we must surmount," Shari
said. "We've faced sabotage, dirty business tactics, and espionage.
Didn't think you'd be in for that in a simple story about cruise ships
now did you?"

Kerry slowed as she approached, coming up behind the
cameramen.

"But we'll prevail." Shari spoke confidently. "No matter what ILS
throws in our path, we'll get over it. Their dirty dealing will bury them,
mark my words."

Kerry paused, half in and half out of the shadows.

"We're the ones putting in the time, we're the ones here making
sure the job gets done." Shari pointed toward the other ship. "Not them.
You won't catch them here, getting their hands dirty, that's for sure. Go
on, go ask! See where they are right now!"

"No need." Kerry stepped forward into the light, laying her hands
on the gangway railing. The cameras swiveled to focus on her, and she
let the silence extend a moment before she spoke again.

She'd caught them all by surprise, no doubt. Even Shari seemed to
be tongue tied for the time being. She let her eyes wander over all of
them, hesitating again, even now.

"Come to ask for help, or forgiveness?" Shari found her tongue,
and a smirk.

Kerry was very aware of the round, blank eyes turned on her. A
faint smile appeared on her face, and she exhaled, surrendering to her
own nature with only the faintest of sighs. "Neither," she said quietly.
"Some of your equipment was delivered over to us by mistake. If you
send a forklift, I'll have it loaded."

Caught flatfooted, Shari could only stare at her. Michelle, however,
circled the gangway and approached Kerry. "By mistake?" She
questioned suspiciously.

"Apparently." Kerry agreed. "The four orders you placed for

network gear to try and dry up the channel arrived with ours. Good luck trying to return it." And with that, she turned and simply walked off, not looking behind her to see if anyone was following.

"WHERE DID SHE GO?" Dar asked, resisting the urge to pace around the inside of the building.

"That way, ma'am." The guard pointed down the pier. "Just a few minutes ago, in fact. "

Dar went to the door and peered out, shading her eyes from the glaring spotlights. She could see several figures moving between the two ships, but none of them resolved into her partner's familiar form. Why would Kerry go there?

What was she up to?

"Hey, Dar?" Mark walked over, wiping his brow. "I think we got everything unpacked...you think we can hijack a piece of the line in here so I can download configs?"

Dar blinked, spotting Kerry's distinctive outline appearing from between two stacks, heading back toward the terminal with a determined stride. Her body language was a mixture of anger and ferocity, her head held high, but hands balled into fists at her side.

"Dar?"

Dar pushed the door open and limped back outside, heading across the concrete on a path calculated to intercept her partner. She watched Kerry's eyes suddenly track to her, and the alteration in her body's posture now added a touch of apprehension to her attitude.

"Hey." Dar slowed to a halt as they met. "Where'd you go?"

Kerry looked up at her. "To do something you're probably going to think I'm an idiot for."

Dar felt her heart speed up a bit. "Last time you said that, you got a tattoo and it wasn't so bad." She ventured. "You want to go inside and talk about it?" She hesitantly put a hand on Kerry's shoulder. "I didn't know where you went. I just came back and you were gone. The guard said..."

Kerry stared past her for a second. "Did Mark show you the boxes?"

Dar fell silent for a second. "Uh?"

"Okay. C'mon."

They walked inside the building, and Dar silently allowed Kerry to lead her into the back section of the terminal, in the shadows, where she could now see several pallets of boxes under tarps. "What—"

Kerry walked over and lifted the tarp, pointing at the label. She waited for Dar to lean close to read it, aware of a few set of eyes watching them.

Dar straightened up, and put her hand on the boxes. "Well. Son of a bitch."

"Mm."

"So..." Dar looked around, then back at Kerry. "You went to tell them it was here, right?"

Kerry's shoulders relaxed suddenly, and she leaned against the stack. "Yeah."

Puzzled, Dar shifted her hand from the box to Kerry's shoulder, giving her a comforting little pat. "So, what's the problem, sweetheart?"

Kerry scrubbed her face with one hand. "Your father said...I mean, it's a big competitive advantage, you know, Dar? I mean, we keep this, and they're dead in the water."

"Kerry!"

They both turned around and looked, to find several people including one with a still camera in the front doorway. Mark was nearby, waving at them with a dour expression.

"Ker, we keep this, and it's grand theft." Dar captured Kerry's attention, gently turning her head so their eyes met again. "I may be one to take any advantage, but I draw the line in some places, y'know? That includes putting either of us or the company in danger of criminal action."

Kerry looked at her for a long moment then abruptly sagged against Dar, laying her head to rest on her partner's shoulder. Then she straightened and touched Dar's side with one hand. "I need to go sit down. Can you go see what that's all about?"

"Sure." Dar murmured. "There's a chair over there. Let me get rid of whatever this is, and I'll be right back, okay?"

Kerry gave her a brief, but genuine smile, and then she turned and walked over to where a chair was half hidden behind the boxes. She sat down in it and rested her elbows on her knees, gazing at the dirty carpet with pensive eyes.

Dar paused indecisively, considering ignoring the crowd at the door.

Kerry apparently sensed that because she looked up and managed a grin, raising one hand and flicking her fingers at Dar in the direction of the door.

Reassured, Dar turned and started a somewhat dignified marching limp toward the entrance, gathering an annoyed attitude around her until by the time she got there, people were taking tiny steps backwards and gaining looks of alarm.

"Something I can do for you folks?" Dar asked, stopping in front of them and adopting as aggressive a posture as she was currently capable of.

"Hi." The woman nearest her took the lead. "My name is Elecia Rodriguez, and I'm a reporter for the Miami Herald."

"Good for you." Dar gave her no quarter.

"I'd like to speak with Kerry Stuart, please." The woman apparently had faced down unwilling participants before, and her tone didn't alter a whit.

"She's busy."

"She's sitting over there, not looking busy at all. Can I speak with her please?" The reporter replied calmly. "It's really in her best interests."

"No." Dar answered back, just as calmly. "It's in her best interests to just be left alone right now."

The reporter locked eyes with Dar. They stared each other down for a few minutes. The woman was about Dar's height, and roughly her size and Dar wondered for a minute if she was going to make a rush past her toward her quarry.

Several ILS security guards edged up around them, apparently having the same thoughts. Dar relaxed a bit, reassured that the reporter would surely not be stupid enough to risk that major of a scene no matter how juicy the story she was following was.

"Ms. Roberts, you really do want your side of the story presented here." Rodriguez finally said. "I appreciate that there's a lot going on, and you've got no reason to either want or trust the press at this point but we're not part of Mr. Quest's circus. We're local, and you're the local team. Get my drift?"

Dar paused, hearing a thread of sincerity in the statement. The woman was also being neither overbearing, nor craven, instead she was just being very straightforward and suddenly Dar remembered where she knew the reporter's name from. "That was a nice story you did on the behind the scenes of the sports industry down here," she said. "I liked it."

Caught a little off guard, the woman smiled and her body posture altered a bit. "Thanks. You have no idea how much my company hated me for it though. We lost comp tickets to almost every game in town."

Hmm. "All right." Dar paused to think. "If you can rest your laurels a few minutes, I'll see if Kerry's willing to chat with you." She pointed toward the catering table. "Help yourselves."

The reporter didn't really react, but the three men she had with her, including the camera man, lit up like Christmas trees at the sight of free food. Rodriguez regarded them with a tolerant look, then nodded at Dar. "Fair enough, and at least it's air conditioned in here. Take your time while I feed my starving wolves."

Dar gave them all a brief, last regard, then she turned and retreated back toward the shadows.

"Nice." The cameraman complimented his colleague. "Didn't think we were going to get anything there for a minute."

"Me either." Rodriguez sighed, as she led the way past the watchful guards. "But I've done this long enough to know when you're dealing with someone that smart, just drop all the bullshit and let them make the choice."

"Way different than those other guys." The man agreed.

"Way different." Rodriguez agreed. "This is going to be a good one."

DAR CROUCHED NEXT to Kerry's chair, positioning her body so she was blocking the view of anyone watching them. She put a hand on Kerry's knee and squeezed it gently. "Hey."

"Hey." Kerry responded readily.

"You doing okay?"

"My brain hurts."

Dar chuckled wanly. "My foot hurts. We're even."

Kerry reached up to ruffle her partner's hair. "So."

"So."

"You let the vandals in at the gates, I see."

Dar nodded. "It's a reporter from the Herald." She confirmed. "She wants to talk to you."

"Ah." Kerry sniffed reflectively. "Interview with a rebel biker chick on tap, I guess?"

Was it? Dar suddenly gave in to the discomfort of leaning on her injured foot and sat down instead, pulling her legs up crosswise under her. "I'm not sure." She countered. "Sounded like it was a tie in with this whole deal, but I've seen some of the stuff this one's written and it's pretty even handed."

"Hmm."

"Yeah, I thought the other reporter was all right too, I know." Dar admitted. "But I've actually read her articles. She does business angles, and she managed to take sides with Janet Reno and hasn't been ridden out on rails yet."

"Ah." Kerry leaned on her elbows again, her head resting against Dar's, not caring who was looking or not. "I feel really unbalanced right now. I'm not sure talking to a reporter is a good idea."

"Okay." Dar accepted that readily. "I just told her I would ask you." She wrapped her hand around Kerry's leg, stroking her calf gently. She could feel tension there, a rapid flexing and releasing that paid testament to her partner's rattled state. "Want something to drink?"

Kerry twirled a bit of Dar's hair around one finger, remaining silent. She tuned out the rest of the room, and just concentrated on the touch of Dar's hand around her leg, and the scent of hickory smoke that lightly clung to her from where they'd had dinner.

It was hard for her to say, really, why she was so shook up. After all, she'd acted on her conscience, and she'd turned out to be dead on right, even in Dar's eyes. So, what was her problem? "Dar?"

"Hmm?" Dar seemed quite willing to sit there as long as she was required, completely ignoring the room at her back.

""Why am I so freaked out?"

"I don't know, Ker." Dar replied honestly. "You did the right thing."

"I know I did," she whispered.

Dar leaned her chin against Kerry's knee. "Were you freaked out by my father wanting to ditch the stuff?"

Kerry was thoughtfully silent.

"He's not much into playing by the rules," Dar said, after a slight hesitation. "I mean...I guess I mean he's willing to go to any length for what he thinks is the greater good."

"Yeah." Kerry nodded. "Maybe that's it. I knew he wanted to do that for us. But it was just...it was..."

"Wrong." Dar supplied.

"Yeah."

Dar shrugged a little. "Shari and Michelle would have agreed with him in a heartbeat."

Kerry lifted her head and gazed into Dar's eyes, visibly more collected. "Oh, I know," she said. "Hey, listen." She hesitated.

"Want me to arrange to give them this stuff while you go talk to the reporter?" Dar suggested.

"You're reading my mind again." Kerry lifted her hand and rubbed a smudge of dust from the bridge of Dar's nose. "Do you know half the room is watching us?"

"And?"

"I don't care either." Kerry relaxed at last, leaning back in the chair and extending her legs out past Dar's knee. "Okay. I'll go wrangle with the Herald, and you can smirk and make Michelle feel like an idiot while you turn over these boxes. Here she comes."

Dar patted her leg, and got to her feet, catching her balance against the boxes and straightening up as she spotted Michelle's short figure headed in her direction. "Didn't bring her entourage."

Kerry also got up and headed off, giving Dar a gentle slap on the butt as she went by. "Of course not. No fun in being filmed eating crow."

No, of course not. Dar squared her shoulders and waited as Michelle approached, wrestling a deadpan look on her face. "Evening."

Michelle stopped, glancing past her at Kerry's retreating back. "She drops the bombshell; you get to bask in the stink?"

Dar leaned against the boxes. "The only stink around here is coming from you," she replied bluntly. "Where's your box mover? Or are you planning on dragging them back yourself?"

"Don't hold back, Dar. Tell me how you really feel." Michelle countered. "Don't for a minute think I don't know the timing on that little reveal was exquisitely planned."

Dar merely rolled her eyes, and stepped back, pulling the tarp off the first set of boxes. "You're wasting my time. Here."

Michelle stepped forward and examined the shipping label. She pulled a set of papers out from under her arm and carefully cross checked them, ignoring Dar's lounging presence. Finally, she turned her head and looked up. "Trust me when I tell you there'll be an inquiry on how this shipment ended up in your hands. You better hope your lawyers are up to it."

"Sure." Dar smiled. "They'll be glad to stand up and explain why three false and one true order of yours got dropped off here by a trucker who didn't want to take it down to you because he got called an asshole one too many times. No problem."

Michelle turned around fully. "You know something?"

"Pretty much everything, thanks."

"You're a real asshole."

Dar watched Michelle retreat back toward the door, her entire body seeming to shoot off disgusted anger. "Takes one to know one." She called after the shorter woman. "Better hurry up and get this out of here before I charge you rent!"

At the door, Michelle turned and glared murderously at her.

Dar released a wicked laugh. "You want me to be an asshole? You don't know what you're asking for. Now get those men in here or I'll have the stevedores pack it up and send it back and send you the bill for their time."

The stevedores' boss, who had been sitting on a crate watching the action, gave her a big thumbs up.

Michelle exited and slammed the door behind her. Unfortunately, it was held open by an air compressed automatic closer, and it ended up bouncing back open and smacking her in the rear. She lunged forward, going headlong into two men with a hand cart who had been approaching.

The men leaped back, startled, and made a grab for her, but missed and Michelle fell to her knees between them. They helped her up hurriedly, backing off as soon as she was on her feet and dusting her hands off.

Dar chuckled happily, then sighed. "Damn, where's a camera when you need one?"

KERRY TOOK A moment to get composed before she entered the lighted area around the food table, and approached the reporters. She ran her fingers through her hair and settled it a bit, and then she walked over to the small group and made eye contact with the woman reporter. "Hi."

The woman got caught in mid swallow. Her eyes widened a little, then she finished her mouthful and set her cup down. "Hi." She extended her hand. "Elecia Rodriguez."

"Kerry Stuart." Kerry grasped her hand and shook it. "You wanted to speak to me?" Her tone was soft and slightly husky and she resisted the urge to clear her throat.

"Ah, yes, I did. Thanks." The reporter collected herself. "Is there someplace we can sit down? Not that I mind the ambiance out here, it sure beats standing outside, but..."

"There are some chairs over there." Kerry pointed to an unused corner of the terminal then paused as she heard Dar's voice rise up and send echoes to the rafters. Conversation abruptly cut off in the room.

The reporters turned and stared then Elecia looked back at Kerry. "You sure have one heck of a situation here, don't you?" They all stood listening, but the yell wasn't repeated, and voices started up again around them.

Kerry led them over to the seats and took one, sitting down and crossing her ankles demurely as she tucked her feet under her chair. It was a ridiculous bit of modesty given that she was in faded jeans and scuffed sneakers, but old habits really did die hard sometimes. "What can I do for you, Ms. Rodriguez?"

The reporter sat down and composed herself, removing a pad from her back pocket and a pen from behind her ear. "Okay." She eyed Kerry thoughtfully. "Where do I start with you, Ms. Stuart?"

One of Kerry's blond brows rose. "Excuse me?"

The reporter studied her pad. "There are about ten thousand questions I'd like to ask you, starting with what was it like growing up in Roger Stuart's house, to what is it like getting a tattoo, but I guess I'd have to settle with starting somewhere, and where I'll start is, what exactly are you trying to accomplish with this business here?"

Of all the questions she could have been faced with, at least this one was relatively easy to answer. "We're trying to install and configure a computer network for this ship outside of here, to demonstrate our ability to provide those services across Mr. Quest's fleet and give him the most competitive bid so he'll choose us to do that."

Rodriguez nodded. "Okay." She scribbled a note. "So let me ask you this. Do you do this sort of thing a lot?"

Puzzled, Kerry frowned a little. "Sure." She said. "It's what we do. It's what I do for ILS. Integrate and assist in acquiring new business, among other things."

The reporter scribbled another note. "Fair enough," she said. "So, Ms. Stuart, is this process always like a three ring circus? You must have a very entertaining job."

Kerry sighed. "No, it's not," she said. "Most of the time it's a pretty dry, refined process. Someone contacts me, or our sales department gets a lead, and we do an analysis, then present possible solutions and a price tag. There's some bargaining, then either we get a contract, or we don't."

"Uh huh." The woman mused. "That's pretty much what I thought," she said. "So, tell me about this feud between yourselves, and the folks at Telegenics. Where did that come from? I understand business rivalries, but this seems to go beyond that. True?"

"Well..."

"Here." The reporter removed a folder, and opened it. "I've had my ear chewed off by the people on the other side of that pier all afternoon. They want to bury you in the worst way." She showed Kerry not one, but three pictures.

One was the biker chick, which she expected. The other two were of her and Dar, one at a restaurant down by the beach, the other... in the pool at Disney, kissing.

Kerry inspected the photos. "And?" She gave the reporter an inquiring look. "You want me to rate them, or pick the one for you to use in your story?" She asked. "What exactly does any of this have to do with the business we're doing here?"

"Now, that's exactly what I wanted to know, Ms. Stuart," the reporter said. "It doesn't have anything to do with anything here, and that's why I wanted to talk to you. See, your company has been a part of our community for a long time now, and it's done its share of good works — some crappy works too — but it's done its part in employing a lot of folks in these parts."

"That's true," Kerry agreed quietly. "We try to be good corporate citizens."

"So, then what's behind it all?" Rodriguez asked, shifting a little closer. "You're not unknown to us, Ms. Stuart. My paper's been aware of who you are since you joined ILS."

Kerry merely watched her face, aware at the periphery of her senses that Dar was nearby, and also watching.

"We've chosen, or should I say, my managers have chosen not to focus on you, because your company is pretty darn low key. You just do what you do, pay your taxes, and frankly, bring the city a lot more than you take from it." The woman flipped a page. "So, in sum, when some outside folks start gunning for one of our own, we take exception to it, and we want to know why."

"Why." Kerry mused. "You sure you really want to know why?"

Rodriguez's face suddenly shifted into a faint, mischievous grin. "No. I bet I don't, but we got sent this picture, of you on the bike." She held up the picture. "Now that struck everyone as something that was very, very interesting because not many vice presidents of international corporations get their picture taken like that."

"I bet."

"Are you a hell raiser, Ms. Stuart?"

Now it was Kerry's turn to grin, and she did, a smile of genuine amusement that lit up her eyes. "Sometimes."

"Tell me a story, then. What's going on here?" the reporter asked, poising her pen over the page. "Tell me Goliath's side of the story."

Kerry was aware of Dar's watchful eyes, and she knew if she turned her head to the left, she'd see her partner in the shadows standing by if she needed her. "Okay." She agreed. "I'm a little short for Goliath, but I'll do the best I can."

"I'm sure you've got help if you need it." The reporter didn't look at Dar. "I'm not looking to get my butt kicked. Will that happen?"

Kerry smiled. "Depends."

"Thought you'd say that." Rodriguez chuckled. "I'll take my chances."

THEY ENDED UP in the small office, since everyone had migrated outside to have some dinner and relax. Kerry was seated in one of the comfortably innocuous office chairs they'd supplied, leaned all the way back with one sneaker resting on her opposite knee.

The reporter had taken a seat across from her, using one of the desks to lean on in her writing, and they both had cups of coffee courtesy of Dar, who had briefly disappeared after deciding Kerry wasn't in any imminent danger.

"All right, Ms. Stuart."

"Kerry." Kerry interrupted. "I hate being called Ms. Stuart."

The reporter scribbled a note. "Okay, Kerry." She continued agreeably. "So, you were approached in Orlando by Mr. Quest, right?"

"Actually, Dar was stalked by Mr. Quest." Kerry clarified. "He hunted her down in the lobby of the hotel and approached her with the idea."

"Stalked is a pretty strong term."

"Well." Kerry took a sip of her coffee. "What would you call it if someone had pictures made of you and then went searching through a hotel to find you?"

"Hmm."

"At any rate, he pitched his idea to Dar, and she turned him down."

"Why?" Rodriguez asked.

Good question, Kerry reflected. "I think, because she was wary of how he approached her. It seemed to be something that was outside the normal way businesses approach each other," she explained. "It almost seemed underhanded."

"Hmm." The reporter tapped her pen against her jaw. "So what made her reconsider?"

Another very good question and one Kerry was fairly sure she couldn't answer honestly. "She thought about it, and we talked, and it seemed like it might be a good opportunity to at least get a foothold into an industry we weren't a part of."

Rodriguez nodded, and scribbled a note. "That makes sense," she said. "So it had nothing to do with the fact that Telegenics was also one of the bidders?"

Truth? Kerry acted on impulse. "Sure it had something to do with it," she answered back. "We wanted an opportunity to go head to head with them, after some of the claims they'd been making, and also, after they approached our staff at the trade show to try and offer them jobs."

"Uh huh." The woman grunted. "Telegenics claims that never happened."

Kerry chuckled. "Sure it did," she replied. "The problem is, they forgot to brief their technical manager and he had no idea who he was recruiting." She went on. "When we got to the trade show late the night of the setup day, we found out there was no setup crew on duty. So Dar and I helped our staff to set up our booth, and we were two of the potential recruits."

The reporter looked at her, a half grin on her face. "You're kidding."

Solemnly, Kerry shook her head. "They were telling us how we should join their company instead of working for a faceless corporation where their bosses were sitting somewhere sipping caviar and lounging in limos. My guys thought it was pretty darn funny."

"I bet they did." Rodriguez got up and walked around the small office, stretching her arms over her head. "Did that really tick you off?"

"Getting recruited? We laughed," Kerry replied. "But to us, it was one more indication of the fact that Telegenics was coming after us in a very personal way, and neither of us really caught on to why until we left that night and saw Michelle and Shari coming into the building."

The reporter turned. "You didn't know before then they were part of it?" She sounded incredulous.

"No, we didn't." Kerry answered honestly. "Ms. Rodriguez..."

"Elecia."

Kerry smiled. "Elecia, we have a lot of competitors. We do business analysis on them, sure, but we don't go hunting for people who might be holding a grudge in their offices." She glanced past the woman toward the door, where Dar's head was now peering around the corner. "Hey." She bit her tongue on the 'sweetie'.

"John needs to meet with you." Dar said. "Sorry to interrupt."

"Any way I can chat with you for a few minutes while that's going on, Ms. Roberts?" The reporter interrupted smoothly. "I think we're at a logical holding point here."

Kerry got up, relinquishing her chair to her partner with a flourish. "Be my guest. Let me go see what John's...well, I won't say problem because I know what his problem is, but what he wants." She eased past Dar's body, stuck in the doorway, and gave her a pat on the side as she squeezed by.

Dar hesitated briefly, then limped into the room and took Kerry's chair, rubbing her thumbs on the arms still warm with her body heat. "Well?"

Elecia sat back down at the desk and studied her for a moment. "Thanks for taking the time to talk, Ms. Roberts."

Dar nodded briefly at her and waited.

"Anyone ever tell you that you two are real opposites?"

"It's been mentioned once or twice." Dar allowed.

"Okay." The reporter gathered her notes. "Kerry was just telling me that after first declining to participate in Mr. Quest's bid, you changed your mind."

"Right."

The reporter waited, but nothing more was apparently forthcoming. "You have a history with the two gals from Telegenics, don't you?"

Dar half shrugged. "Yes," she agreed. "Michelle was the IT director of a company I worked a contract negotiation for a year or so back, and I've known Shari for many years."

"That sounds so civilized," Rodriguez said. "And yet, from what those gals say, this bid had been anything but. What's your take on that?"

Dar steepled her fingers and rested the edges of them against her lips. She was very aware that this article would end up being a high profile one in the Herald. Granted, the Miami Herald was not the Washington Post, nor was it the New York Times, but in its own way it was a respected dispenser of local news, and she knew whatever the article ended up being, it would be seen by the board of directors who paid their salaries.

So, how to present utter chaos? "It's been a difficult bid so far," Dar answered slowly. "There were a number of things that contributed to that, most of which did not involve any of us or our respective past histories. For instance," She ticked off a finger, "the unexpected move of the project from New Zealand to Miami and the speeding up of the timeline. That put a focus on us that would not have existed there."

"Because you're local."

"Exactly," Dar agreed. "Second, putting the project into the spotlight by the involvement of the Travel Channel and their filming crew. That added to the circus."

"True."

"Third, the confusion over the intervention of the EPA that further truncated the timeline, and turned the bid into something of a frantic horse race."

"Also true." The reporter nodded. "But that's not what I meant, and I think you know that."

Ah. "Does this article have to do with business or gossip?" Dar countered, looking directly at her. "To be honest, sure, we've all been behaving like contestants for a trip to Jerry Springer, but the bottom line is, we need to get this job done and whoever does it right wins the prize."

The reporter's eyes glinted. "So, you're not saying the controversy between the four of you is the real story? It's their opinion that the discord is what is preventing both of you from being able to effectively compete."

Dar remained silent for a moment then she shook her head. "Far as I'm concerned, we're effectively competing. If they let this distract them to the point they aren't, that's not my problem."

Rodriguez scribbled a few notes, and then she looked up again. "Tell me about your father working on the docks. Deliberate?"

Dar allowed a few seconds to pass before she answered. "Sure," she said. "I asked him to get a job down here to keep an eye on things."

"Ah. Did he?"

"He did. He's the one who discovered that Telegenics had placed four copies of their networking gear order to keep anyone else from getting equipment on time unless they wanted to pay through the nose."

The reporter's eyebrows rose. "Did they?"

"Mm." Dar nodded. "Fortunately for us, we had more clout than most, and we forced an order through."

"For that matter, according to them, you all bought up all the circuits to force them to do the same." Rodriguez countered. "Sounds like a tit for tat."

"Except we didn't." Dar half smiled. "Kerry was just hedging her bets, since they wouldn't assign a pier to any of the ships."

"So you say."

"So it is."

The reporter scribbled some more notes. "Did your father sabotage them?"

Dar chuckled. "My father's retired underwater demolition. He's not subtle. If he really sabotaged them the damn boat would be on the bottom of Government Cut." She scoffed. "If anything, he probably did them good by organizing that chaos."

"Mm." Rodriguez nodded. "The pier supervisor said the same thing. He doesn't have a high opinion of Telegenics, matter of fact." She swiveled to face Dar. "So, I'd have to say most of the points on this are on your side, Ms. Roberts."

Dar held both hands out in a plaintive gesture.

Kerry re-entered the office and ambled over to Dar's side, sitting down on the desktop and exhaling heavily. "He's finished pulling cable, Dar."

"That's bad?" she queried.

"They closed the walls up after they pulled all the wires, and he's not sure if anything got clipped or nicked. He suspects some of it might have been, so we need to test before he can go any further."

"Ah." Dar nodded. "Mark's got some network guys here. Send 'em in."

"I did." Kerry acknowledged. "But here's the issue—the electricians need to turn the power off, and it'll be off all night and part of tomorrow. We're dead in the water while that's going on.?

"Shit." Dar rubbed her temple. "Can we install the switches?"

"In the dark?"

"We have flashlights."

Kerry leaned closer to her. "Dar, that's a construction zone, there's no air conditioning, and they're going to be using welding torches in the same spaces we're putting switches into. Do you want to risk it?"

The reporter was sitting in silence, watching in fascination.

Dar considered. "Yes, I want to risk it," she replied. "If we have the switches in place, already configured, and the lines are tested then when the power goes back on we can bring up the core. Otherwise, we're two days behind and if something's screwed, we've got no time to fix it."

Kerry took her turn at consideration. "Okay, but we need to find out where the electrical crews are, and put our people in after they're finished in each closet."

"Good plan," Dar agreed.

"Right." Kerry got up and left, scrubbing her hair with the fingers of one hand as she disappeared.

Dar returned her attention to the reporter. "Where were we?"

"My question to you now is — why are you here?" Rodriguez asked. "Why aren't you in an ivory tower somewhere, eating quiche and wearing a silk suit? CIO's and vice presidents are not supposed to do the work they pay other people to do."

Dar was momentarily silent, having no real answer ready. In general terms, the reporter was right, and she knew it. "I have good people, and they do a good job."

"But?"

A shrug.

"Or does it really all come down to a very personal conflict after all?"

And of course, the reporter was damn right about that too. "It's just how we do things," Dar demurred. "Stick around, and I'll prove it."

Elecia smiled, biting the end of her pen.

"OKAY, WE GOT THE PIPE UP." Mark had his head bent over his laptop, fingers pecking away industriously. "Let me bring these puppies online."

Dar was leaning against one wall, watching the activity. "We're going to need to put full security on this room tonight," she remarked. "I wouldn't put it past our friends down the pier to try and break in here to make some trouble."

"Psht." Mark made a disparaging noise. "Hey boss..." He half turned and looked at Dar. "Did you do a special config for this, or should I just use the standard?"

"Standard," Dar answered briefly. "We can customize it when it's on the ship." She looked around for Kerry, but she was nowhere to be seen, and the reporter had disappeared as well. "How much more do we have to do?"

Mark turned all the way around to face her. "Dar, like, seriously, you don't have to hang out here. We're fine," he said. "We've just got the setup to finish, and some cleaning."

Dar had the grace to look slightly abashed. "I know," she admitted. "I just felt a little bad about wrangling everyone over here last minute."

Mark relaxed. "No prob. To tell you the truth, the guy's have been pretty curious about what's going on over here, and they think the ship's way cool."

"It's a wreck."

"Yeah, but it's something new and different, y'know?"

Dar did, indeed, know. "Yeah." She removed her PDA from her back pocket and flipped it open, tapping out a message as Mark went back to work.

Hey. Where are you?

The machine remained silent. Dar scowled. Then she gave up and limped back to the office, feeling more than just a touch useless out in the busy hall. She took a seat at the desk and slapped the keyboard of one of the office computers, logging in with her login and drumming her fingers while she waited for the system to authenticate her.

Once she'd gotten things set up to her satisfaction, she put the keyboard on her lap and leaned back in the office chair, getting comfortable as she moved the windows around a little to better see them.

For a moment, she let her eyes linger over the network monitor, studying the readouts intently. Everything appeared relatively normal, the one alert showing indicated to her that eight new devices had been added to the network in the last hour.

"Knew that, thanks." Dar dismissed the alert. She logged into the routers and studied her program's results, calling up the program itself on the second screen and preparing to work on it.

What did she want it to do next? Dar hesitated, her fingertips resting on the keys. Something Kerry had said to her before she'd started on the project came to mind, and she thought about how she'd have the program extend itself outside their network and chase down hackers.

That brought her breakfast to mind, and Dar set aside the program briefly as she went to a third screen and checked for activity at their gateway. All was quiet. Apparently her hacker friend had either given up or just gotten bored and found something else to occupy his or her time.

His or her — Dar suspected it was his, since most hackers she'd ever known had been guys. She'd never been really sure if it was just a social thing, or a hormonal one, and she never really thought too hard about what that had said about her.

With a sigh, she typed a few lines into her program, then stopped and closed it. She switched to the network monitors instead, and started browsing them.

Given the hour, it looked pretty normal. Dar clicked and pointed, shifting the monitor from their outer boundary to the inner workings of the main office, drilling down to a department level. "Let's see. Duks must be working his guys' overtime tonight."

She clicked on a message icon, and typed in a note.

Hey, and you call me a slave driver.

Dar chuckled slightly and went back to her browsing. It seemed busy, and she racked her brains trying to think if there was a deadline she'd forgotten about.

Budgets? No, not for another month, and the quarter didn?t close for nearly two.

Her screen blinked, and she looked at it, seeing the message that had come back from Duks.

I? Here I sit alone in my office with just a dust bunny under my desk. Where are you? I was by your office this evening but you were not there.

Dar blinked at the message. Then she removed her cell from its clip at her belt and opened it, rapidly dialing Duks phone number. Her thighs jerked under the keyboard as she waited for him to answer, sending it bouncing slightly as her nerves jangled a howling warning. "Duks?"

"Ah, Dar." Duks sounded completely calm. "How are you?"

"Just listen to me," Dar said. "I'm in the network, and I see a ton of traffic on your servers. Are you running something?"

Dead silence. Then—"I am not."

"Can you check your running jobs?"

A rattle of keys sounded clearly through the phone. Dar waited, knowing if she had to she could have logged into a session herself and checked them, but also knowing Duks would know most intimately what belonged in the system and what did not.

"Paladar, we have a problem."

Dar licked her lips. "Okay," she responded. "What do you want me to do? I can isolate that box, Duks."

"Please do so."

Dar's hands moved in a blur, cutting off the multiple network accesses to the minis. It also cut off her access, of course, but in her mind, that wasn't important. "Okay, done."

"I am going to the computer room now. I will call you from there." Duks voice was quiet, and very, very serious. "Please do not, as of yet, contact anyone."

"Okay," Dar agreed softly. She closed the cell, and left it folded on her leg, while she opened up the monitor screen to its fullest size and stared at it, focusing on small surges here, and there, flickers of pale green against the normal green, completely ordinary to any eyes including hers.

A flashing alert caught her eye, and she clicked over to her router program, blinking at the screen as she read the cryptic results emerging from her own coding. Another warning about being accessed, and Dar almost clicked it closed before she caught a second line behind it, a routine access listing for a remote router that bore an IP not her own.

She dove after it going to the router in question and scoping it out immediately, found the session and captured the address before it could disappear. Then she deleted the session and locked the router down, allowing only her own login to access it.

Breathing a little faster, she ducked out of that router and into the core, searching for the offending IP. Her heart started to speed up as she located it, racing to trace it before it disappeared. She grabbed the Mac address and pasted it into a note pad, then searched it out.

"Ah." She captured the port and pasted that also, then redid the trace. As she'd expected, the address was now gone, but she had the port.

If she had the port, she knew what was on the other end of it. Grimly, Dar opened up her network documentation and pasted the port number into the search field, then hit enter.

Her cell phone rang. She answered it one handed while she stared at the screen. "Yes?"

"This is Louis."

Dar inhaled, making her nostrils flare in reaction. "Yes."

"Some person has been attempting to remove the records in this system that pertains to our customer accounting," Duks stated flatly. "The login that has run these reports belongs to my department, from the senior auditing unit."

Dar waited, but the line was silent. "And you did not ask them to do this?"

"I did not," Duks confirmed. "I am contacting security, and I would appreciate that you send me what data you saw that spurred you to contact me."

"I will," Dar replied quietly. "I may have another problem."

Duks sighed. "Paladar, please. One disaster at a time is all my heart can handle." He exhaled. "I will call you back after I speak with Able Jacobs."

"Okay." Dar let him hang up, satisfied, at least, that Duks had the situation under control. It would do no one any good for her to get involved. Duks was harsher on his own staff and security than she could ever be and she knew finding a data thief inside his department would send her old friend into an overdrive rage.

Now, to her other problem. Dar studied the screen again. The request for her program files had come from a PC on the fourteenth floor, just down the hall from her own office. It was, she recalled, a spare work room that also held two manual fax machines and a copier, and was occasionally used for visitors who needed access to a PC for various reasons.

Dar quickly dialed the phone again. She listened to the ring then exhaled when it was answered.

"Operations, Rosie speaking."

"Hi Rosie," Dar said. "It's Dar Roberts."

The woman's voice definitely perked up. "Oh, hi, Ms. Roberts! What can I do for you?"

Kerry had her admirers in the office, and so, Dar acknowledged, did she. Rosie was one of them. "I have something I need you to do," she said. "You know the computer in the printer room, on floor fourteen near my office?"

"Oh! Yes, ma'am, I sure do." Rosie assured her.

"Okay." Dar said. "I want you to go upstairs, and listen closely, okay?"

"Yes!"

Dar would have rolled her eyes if it had been a less serious occasion. "Rosie, this is very serious," she told the woman. "Someone just tried to access something from that PC that they shouldn't have." She heard the intake of breath on the other end. "So what I want you to do is to take a couple of plastic bags, and go down there. Put the keyboard and mouse in a bag, and take that, the PC and monitor, back to Ops with you, okay?"

"Right away, ma'am." Rosie acknowledged. "Do you want me to call security?"

Dar sighed. "They're busy with something else right now, and I'm not sure exactly what was going on with this PC. So just secure it, and I'll pick it up from you later."

"I'm on it," Rosie said.

Dar hung up, tapping the cell phone against her chin. Her PDA went off at that moment, almost scaring her out of her wits, and she just barely kept from tossing the cell phone across the room. She pulled the PDA out and examined it.

Sorry, sweetie. I was downstairs on the ship. What's up?

Dar wondered where to start. Is the reporter still with you? A couple things just went down I'd rather not expose to the Herald in this lifetime.

The PDA was briefly silent then flashed. *Be right there.*

Dar nodded a little, and then opened her cell phone again and dialed. She waited. "Hi. This is Dar Roberts. I need a list of everyone who is logged into the building right now, and everyone who entered and exited within the last twenty five minutes."

THEY PARKED RIGHT in front of the office and walked side by side to the door. They passed together through the electronic portals, getting a nervous nod from the security guard on duty.

"Evening, ma'am's."

"Evening." Dar greeted him briefly for them both. She followed Kerry across the huge lobby to the elevators and they both went inside. "Jesus."

"Not how I wanted the night to end," Kerry confirmed, punching the button for the tenth floor. "But at least you stopped them, Dar."

"By pure god damned luck."

"Honey, whatever works." Kerry sighed. "I'm just glad you were there."

Dar stared morosely at the closed elevator doors until the conveyance stopped, and they were admitted to the tenth floor. She followed Kerry out and to the right, heading for the operations center.

"Just goes to show you how much we need your program." Kerry went on, with a touch of hesitance, "And you."

Dar paused with her hand on the door latch of the ops center, and cocked her head to one side. "You really mean that?"

Kerry looked right back at her. "If you mean personally, I'm going to kick your ass for even asking."

An unexpected smile appeared on Dar's face. "I love it when you talk to me like that." She opened the door and indicated Kerry should precede her, the wide open portal preventing Kerry from framing a suitable answer.

Kerry stuck her tongue out instead, and walked into the room, where the console operator was already standing up to greet them. "Hi, Rosie."

Dar followed her inside, and gave the woman a nod as well. "Got the PC?"

"Right there, ma'am." Rosie pointed toward a worktable on one side of the operations desk. "I went right out and grabbed it after you called me."

Dar walked over to examine their prize. The operator had certainly taken her words literally, and the computer, mouse, keyboard, and assorted cables were neatly wrapped in enough plastic to cover half the room they were presently standing in. Duct tape secured it, and she suspected it would take the sharp end of her Leatherman tool to free the poor captive. "Okay."

"Did you see anyone around there when you were getting it, Rosie?" Kerry asked. "Anyone in the hall or anything like that?"

"No, ma'am." Rosie shook her head. She was twenty-something, a middling height and hair color kind of woman who often reminded Kerry of a cocker spaniel. "There shouldn't be anyone up there this time of night, and it was empty as a graveyard when I was there."

Dar checked her watch, and decided to leave the wrapped PC where it was. She limped over to the big console desk and picked up the phone, dialing Duks' extension. "You there?"

"I am here." Duks answered. "Are you here?"

"Yeah."

"Good. Now that this important piece of business is concluded, would you come to my office?"

"Right." Dar put the phone down. "Ker let me go talk to Louis. I'll be back in a few minutes.?"

Kerry took a breath, then merely folded her arms. "Okay," she agreed. "I'm going to go upstairs and see what I can sniff out."

"Good idea." Dar winked at her, as she made her way to the door and bumped it open with an elbow. She limped out and the door closed behind her, leaving Kerry by herself with the console operator.

"Ms. Stuart?"

"Hmm?" Kerry had wandered over to examine the PC in its wrapping.

"How come Ms. Robert's is limping? Something happen to her?" Rosie asked.

Kerry turned her head to regard the operator, whose round, innocent eyes gazed back at her with a marked lack of guile. "Matter of fact, she got that saving me from a barracuda, Rosie."

If possible, Rosie's eyes became a lot rounder and a lot bigger. "No kidding!?"

"No kidding. "Kerry turned all the way around and faced her. "There we were, in the ocean, right?"

"Right."

Kerry waved her hands, mimicking a swimming motion. "I was swimming with our dog, and we swam under the dock. I felt something brush against me, then all of a sudden Dar jumped in, picked me up out of the way, and kicked a barracuda that was about to bite me right in the mouth!"

"Wow!"

"Yeah, but she got bit for her troubles." Kerry went on blithely, "But it was very brave of her."

"Sure was!" Rosie agreed fervently. "Wow. Were you scared?"

Kerry stuck her hands in her pockets. "Didn't have time to be."

"Wow," Rosie repeated. "That's amazing."

"Dar usually is." Kerry went to the door. "Well, I'm going to go check out our offices. I'll be right back." She left the Ops center and closed the door, pausing outside to grin and grunt contentedly. "If you don't like the rumors about you, my father always said, start some you do like."

She walked down the hall toward the stairwell. "Bet you never thought you'd ever use any of his advice willingly, huh, Ker?" With a slight shake of her head, she pushed the door into the stairwell open and started up the four flights to their offices.

DAR ENTERED DUKS' outer office, crossing the soft carpet and opening the inner door to an office that pretty much mirrored hers. "Evening."

Duks was behind his desk, leaning back with folded arms. He watched Dar as she took a seat opposite him. "How is your fish bite?"

"Eh."

"I see that you are favoring it."

"Hurts like hell," Dar allowed. "I went and got an antibiotic shot, but I've been running around on it all night."

"And I have made it worse." Duks said.

Dar shrugged.

"We have narrowed this down to four possibilities, Dar." Duks dispensed with the chit chat. "Tomorrow, I will call all of them into this office, and we will find out which one it is."

Dar cocked her head to one side. "You mean none of the four were here when it happened?"

"No. The job was set to run at this time," he said. "I am thinking someone imagined no one would be here to see it and remark on it." He laced his big fingers together and studied them. "It is hard to believe from any of these people. They have worked for me for many years."

Dar knew what he meant. You liked to trust the people who worked for you, but she'd found out the hard way over the years that loyalty really didn't generally exist. "That's rough," she said. "You sure it's one of them?"

He shrugged. "They are the only ones who know this login. It is the one we use to enable the reports to select from all four databases."

Hmm. "Logins and passwords can be obtained," Dar reminded him.

"Dar, what can I say to that? Perhaps it was me, then!" He stood up and paced behind his desk. "Is it not bad enough I have to find one of my most trusted staff is possibly a thief?"

"Hey." Dar held up a hand. "I'm just bringing it up, because it's true," she said. "How many times have we been in Mari's office because one person gave someone else their password?"

Duks dropped into his seat with a disgusted sigh. Then he looked at Dar squarely. "And what of you? Have you done so, my friend?"

Dar didn't even hesitate. "Kerry has all my logins, and I have hers," she replied easily. "Take it easy, Louis. Wait until you talk to these guys, and go with your gut."

"Thank you, Dr. Ruth." Duks gave her a droll look. "It's just infuriating."

Yes, it was, Dar silently agreed. "Least we stopped it." She fell back on Kerry's conclusion. "I'm not really—" She stopped, as a far off yell penetrated the walls of the office. "Shit." Dar bolted from her seat and headed for the door at a dead run, no trace of a limp remaining.

Caught in shock for a brief moment, Duks closed his jaw on an exclamation and got up to run after her.

Chapter Thirteen

DAR TORE THROUGH the empty hallways, circling the fourteenth floor around the central elevator stack. She could hear scuffling ahead of her and she sped up, hurtling around the last corner into the corridor that held her office.

Ahead of her, in the semi darkness, she could see two figures wrestling, only one of which was familiar. "Kerry!" She let out a yell.

"Son of a bitch!" Kerry barked back. "Get this piece...ow!"

Dar reached the fight and didn't even slow down. She plowed right into both struggling figures, gently shoving Kerry back out of the way toward one wall as she took the person she was fighting with up against the other one.

"Let go of me!" The stranger yelped. "Hey!"

"Go to hell!" Dar said. "You're lucky I don't open the window and toss your ass out."

"Oh yeah, I'm scared."

The two were evenly matched in size, but Dar pinned Kerry's adversary against the paneling, resisting the urge to shake the woman like a terrier with a rat. "Hold still or I'll break your damn arm." She growled. "Ker, you okay?"

"Yeah." Kerry closed in behind her and put a hand on Dar's back. "I found this little creep in your office."

"My office?" Dar pressed harder. "Get the lights on."

"Dar, they're controlled by computer." Kerry reminded her.

"You're an IT professional." Dar gritted her teeth. "So go hack them."

"Yeesh. Okay." Kerry ducked into Dar's office, disappearing from view.

Her captive began to struggle, attempting to throw Dar off her. "Let me go, or you'll be sorry!"

Dar wasn't sure what was more painful, the cliché or the ache in her foot. The woman got an arm free and swatted at her. Dar blocked the blow with her forearm, then she grabbed hold of the other woman's shirt and swung around, slamming her opponent against the opposite wall.

"Bitch! You're so going to regret this!" The woman growled, grappling with Dar and trying to kick her.

"Not as much as you're going to regret this, or I'm going to enjoy it." Dar wrenched her arm free and took a step back, setting herself before she let loose with a right cross. It smacked into the woman's jaw, bouncing her head against the wall and knocking her out.

Dar simply released her and allowed her to slide down the wall to the ground. She shook her hand and flexed the fingers, silence once again settling over the darkened hall. "Ker?" She called out, wanting very badly to have the lights come on so she could see if she knew the woman.

"Hang on." Kerry's voice drifted in from her office. "I hacked into the wrong subroutine. Give me a minute."

"Hmm." Dar glanced around. "What'd you hit, the music system?"

"Plumbing."

Dar winced. "Oh boy." She leaned against the opposite wall as Duks appeared from the darkness to stand next to her. "It's gonna be a long night."

"Ah." Kerry rattled a few more keystrokes in, and was rewarded by a flood of light that made her wince. She straightened up from Maria's desk and stepped around it, heading for the door to the hallway. Rounding it, she hastened to Dar's side and they stood together looking down at the intruder.

It was a woman, tall with a lithe build and short cropped dark hair, dressed in a non-descript Dickeys shirt and trousers with well worn work shoes.

"Know her?" Dar asked.

"Um...no," she replied. "She's not the usual night gal on this floor."

"Considering the night gal is a night guy, no," Dar agreed. "I don't recognize her either."

"Hmm." Kerry rubbed her jaw. "That's a cleaning staff uniform."

"Uh huh," Dar agreed. "Please don't tell me she was cleaning my office."

Kerry snorted. "Maybe, if she was cleaning your desk drawers from the inside with a flashlight." She looked around. "Where did Duks go?"

"Calling the cleaning supervisor," Dar said. "They've got some explaining to do."

They certainly did. Kerry folded her arms over her chest. "What do we do with her? She's going to come around any minute Dar."

"Call security, I guess. I don't want to tie her up, but we don't know what she's going to do when she comes around, either." She leaned against the wall with one hand, pondering their options. "You okay?" she asked suddenly, looking at Kerry in some concern.

"More or less," Kerry murmured. "You want to duct tape her?"

Dar grimaced. "I'm probably bucking a lawsuit as it is for clocking the little bastard. I'd rather not have cruel and unusual punishment added to it."

"Huh?"

"You ever had to remove duct tape from any part of your body?"

"No." Kerry shook her head, then paused. "Have you?"

"Yes."

"Hmm. How about we lock her in the cleaning closet?" Kerry suggested. "Seems appropriate, and it's close by." She pointed to one in a series of identical doorways. "I don't really want to wrestle any more tonight. I think I pulled something in my back."

"Huh." Dar tried the door and found it open. She pushed it inward, and flipped the lights on, finding nothing more exotic than a mop bucket and a stack of cleaning cloths. There was room in the closet for a cleaning cart, but the cart was missing, presumably elsewhere in the building. "Good idea. Give me a hand."

They dragged the woman's limp body into the closet, laying her down on the tile floor and backing out, pulling the door shut behind them. Dar fished in her pocket and retrieved her keyset, trying the master key on the door and grunting when it turned to a locked position with a satisfying snick. "There."

"Ugh." Kerry leaned against the wall, wincing as she stretched out her lower back muscles.

"Is that the less part of the more?" Dar limped over to her. "You scared me half to death."

Kerry shifted and leaned against Dar instead. "My knight in shining armor," she said. "Boy was I glad to hear you calling my name. I grabbed her and she got away from me."

"Ah."

"I ran after her and got the back of her shirt, and next thing I knew, I felt like I was in a wrestling exhibition."

Duks emerged from a side hallway and walked toward them. "Ah." He looked around. "Did our little friend escape?"

"We put her in the closet." Kerry pointed. "Is the supervisor coming up?"

"He is, indeed," Duks reported. "Especially since he informed me that there should be no person on this floor at this time. I have been told they start cleaning on this floor and work downwards."

Dar nodded. "Makes sense, since I usually see them before I leave."

"Yeah," Kerry agreed.

A hammering from behind the closet door startled all of them. "Let me outta here!" A voice emerged, outraged. "You little bastards! You can't do this to me!"

"Shut up," Duks hammered back. "Or we shall leave you and go get ourselves a beer."

"Count me in," Kerry added. "I was in the copy room when I heard a noise coming from your office. I went in, and there she was, rooting through everything. Who in the hell is this, Dar?"

Dar exchanged glances with Duks. "Should we call the cops?"

Duks pondered this. "Let us wait to see what the cleaning supervisor has to say. He said he...ah." Duks nodded, and looked past them. "Here he is now."

They all turned as a tall, slim man with salt and pepper hair joined them. "Ma'ams, sir," the newcomer said. "I do not understand what is going on here. I signed off on this floor two hours ago."

The hammering started on the inside of the door again. "Bastards!"

The cleaning supervisor started, and took a step back away from the door. "What is this in my closet?"

"Someone in one of your uniforms," Dar informed him. "A woman."

"I have no women on staff this evening." The supervisor protested. "Certainly, I do not keep them on this late. It is not safe. I take care of my girls. They go home no later than eight p.m." He pointed down the hallway, where a cleaning cart, being pushed by an older man was approaching. "See? There is Carlos. He is my man here tonight."

Carlos spotted all of them outside the cleaning closet and stopped, looking puzzled. "Senor?" he asked hesitantly. "Hay un problemo?"

Duks stuck his hands in his pockets and rocked back and forth on the balls of his feet. "I think perhaps we need to call the police then," he admitted. "If this person is not part of your staff, then it is an intruder, and the authorities must be notified."

"You don't want to do that!" The woman's voice inside the closet was muffled. "I'm warning you!"

Kerry put a hand on Dar's arm. "Maybe we should talk to her," she suggested. "The way she's acting is very strange, Dar. I'd expect someone to either be scared poopless, or else be asking for a lawyer."

Dar considered the thought, and had to concede she had a point. The woman's actions had been strange, and maybe there was something to be learned from her. "Okay." She addressed the cleaning supervisor, "I'm going to assume this person just stole one of your uniforms, and maybe someone's ID. I'll find out, and let you know."

The man nodded. "It is good." He motioned Carlos to move the cart in the other direction. "Vamanos."

"Senor?" The older man was confused. "Como?"

The supervisor took him by the arm and led him off, leaving Duks, Dar and Kerry in the hallway facing the closet door. "Well?" Dar held her key up. "Do we?"

Duks shrugged his broad shoulders.

"Ker?"

Kerry also shrugged, lifting her hands slightly.

"Hey, you in there." Dar banged on the door. "If I open this, so we can talk, you cool it or you're gonna hit the dirt again, got me?"

"Ah." Duks exhaled gently. "That is the Dar I know."

"You better open this door! Don't worry, I'll talk. I'm not into physical abuse like you are."

Dar shook her head and stuck the key in the lock, turning it and shoving the door open. She spread her arms out and flexed her knees a little, wondering if their erstwhile captive was going to come out swinging.

As it happened, she didn't. The woman walked warily out, giving Dar a dour, suspicious look. "Hope you've got a good lawyer."

"You too," Kerry advised her. "Especially since you attacked me while trespassing."

"I didn't attack you." The woman scoffed.

"Yes, you did," Kerry responded evenly, "after I surprised you in the act of burgling Dar's office. So if I were you, unless you want to have this discussion with a police officer, I would start cooperating.?

The woman studied her, then flicked her eyes to the rest of them. "This isn't what you think," she remarked, reaching into her back pocket, halting when Dar reacted. "Take it easy," she cautioned, removing her wallet and opening it. "Here. See?"

She held out a card.

Dar took it, and glanced at it. "Military intelligence," she repeated slowly. "Interesting."

"My father always claimed that was an oxymoron," Kerry murmured.

It wasn't the reaction the woman had clearly been expecting. "I don't think you quite understand what's going on here," she said. "You're the subject of an investigation."

"Let's go inside." Dar indicated the outer door to her office. "Louis, maybe we have an answer to your issue as well."

"Perhaps we do," Duks agreed. "Perhaps we do."

The woman looked from one of them to the other. "Do you understand that this is a serious situation?"

"Do you understand that we quite probably issued your paycheck on this very past Friday?" Duks retorted. "Do not threaten us with the government. We know better. Now, please go inside, or else, as Dar says, we shall call the police."

"Yeah," Dar agreed. "Wait—let me ask you one thing." She addressed the woman, "Are you from the Army?"

The woman looked warily at her. "Yes."

Dar's eyes narrowed and she snorted softly, as she closed the door behind them.

DAR TOOK A seat behind her desk, and Kerry perched on the edge of it. Duks sat in one visitor chair, and their unwelcome guest elected to remain standing.

"Okay," Dar said, "Explain to me why I have a member of military intelligence breaking and entering in my office."

The woman smirked. "It's really simple," she said. "My boss assigned me to break in here and blow wide open your reputation for security." She spread her arms and turned. "And I did."

"Why?" Kerry asked.

"What?"

"Why did your boss ask you to do that?"

"Hey, I don't question my orders." The woman held a hand up. "I just do what I'm told. Now, if you'll excuse me, I've got a report to file, and believe me I'm going to enjoy it." She looked at Dar. "You made all kinds of claims, lady, and you run all kinds of things for the US Government. It really pisses me off that you're so full of shit."

"Now, wait a minute..." Kerry started to stand up.

"Oh, don't bother." The woman waved her off. "Please, let's not even get into this little conflict of interest perversion the two of you have going here."

Dar's eyes narrowed slightly. "I'd watch it if I were you."

The woman snorted. "If you cooperate, and you're very lucky, my boss might consider just getting all the government's contracts cut quietly, and not blast it all over the papers." She looked at Dar. "I wouldn't because I think you stink. But he might, because he thinks you could be useful to us."

"Does he?" Kerry said. She turned to her partner. "Dar?" Her voice trailed off as the pale blue eyes pinned hers, and she read Dar's expression. She quietly turned back around and folded her arms, watching the intruder in silence.

"I think he's nuts," The woman stated frankly. "But he's the boss." She held up a cell phone. "And now I can call him and tell him what I found." She started dialing, the smirk plastered seemingly permanently on her face. "And believe me, you're gonna pay for hitting me."

Dar had her fingertips steepled, and she regarded the woman with a surprisingly benign expression. "Kerry?"

"Hmm." Kerry glanced at her.

"Call the police," Dar said. "Tell them we've caught someone breaking and entering in the office. Tell security what's going on, and have them send a couple of officers up here."

The woman stopped dialing and stared at Dar. "What?"

Kerry picked up the phone and dialed.

"You didn't quite catch what I said, did you?" the woman asked Dar. "My boss wants to keep this quiet."

"I don't," Dar replied. "If you legitimately blew our security, then I want it out in the open."

Duks stared at her, his eyebrows lifting. "Ah, Dar..."

"We're a public company, Duks."

"Of course I know that," he said.

"She's here. She had a password into the system or else someone left the machine logged in. It's legit. I'm not hiding it," Dar stated flatly.

Duks subsided with a thoughtful look.

"Thanks." Kerry finished speaking into the phone. She depressed the hook then dialed again. "John?" Kerry Stuart. I need a few of your guys up in Dar's office right away, please."

"Matter of fact?" Dar went on. "When you're done with that Ker, put a call in to corporate communications. We'll need a press release."

The intruder slowly let her hand drop, with the cell phone in it.

"You're not serious."

"Sure." Dar half shrugged. "Don't worry. I'm sure your boss will be glad to explain to the press why you're here, and we'll be glad to explain how we found you, and how you were stopped from committing theft of proprietary technology that had nothing to do with security on any government account."

The woman's expression switched to wary. "I don't know what you're talking about."

"Don't you?" Dar inquired. "Well, then you've got no problem when the police take your fingerprints and match them against what's on the keyboard of the machine I confiscated from our Xerox room." She got up and circled her desk advancing on the woman. "You want to play in the big leagues? Fine, tell your boss, Captain Mousser, he can come down to Dade County jail and bail your ass out."

There was a soft knock on the door. Kerry crossed over and opened it standing aside to admit two of their night security guards. Unlike the day guards, the night men tended to be a little more serious, and these two, she knew, were off duty police officers. "Gentlemen, I found this person inside this office. The cleaning supervisor confirms she does not work for them. We've called Metro-Dade."

"All right, ma'am." The guards took up positions on either side of the intruder.

"Better call your boss now," Dar advised the woman. "I'm not sure what you'll be able to do once the police get here."

"How did you know his name?" the woman asked. "I didn't tell you that."

Kerry had been wondering the same thing herself.

Dar merely smiled. "Guess we all have our little secrets, don't we, Lieutenant?" She commented. "It's going to be interesting watching him — and you — explain why you were investigating government account security in a building that doesn't house any of it, of course."

The woman looked around the room. "This is..."

"The government systems are handled through our Houston office," Kerry told her quietly. "The Miami Ops center handles commercial accounts. Surely you knew that, right?"

Dar folded her arms as she watched their unwelcome intruder. The woman half turned and dialed a number, keeping her face averted and covering the mouthpiece of her phone with one hand. It was still a bad situation, she knew. There had been a breech, and there was no real way for her to whitewash it, save by the few details she'd already thrown forth.

Well, that, and the fact that the woman had not been successful in obtaining anything while she, Dar, had been watching. No telling how long she'd been at it and no telling what she'd sucked down when Dar hadn't been looking, since she wasn't apt to spend her evenings browsing the network.

Kerry sidled over to her side of the desk and eyed her, her back turned to the room and her expression open and very emotive.

Dar scrunched up her own face into a wry half grin in response, and both her shoulders moved slightly upward.

"We are so screwed." Kerry mouthed silently.

Dar nodded, keeping the same expression.

Surprisingly, Kerry now shrugged in return. "Oh well." She mimed.

Equally surprisingly, Dar understood the sentiment, and agreed with it. In the corner of her mind, a tiny bit of her ego was soothed by the knowledge that the breech, when it had come, hadn't come through her network. It had come, as security cracks often did, through the human end of the equation.

"Check the logs," she uttered softly. "Find out who logged into that workstation today."

Kerry nodded and slipped off the desk, crouching behind it and pulling Dar's keyboard over to her. After a moment, she knelt instead and rattled the keys, focusing her attention on the screen instead of the rest of the room.

The woman turned around and approached Dar, pausing when the security guards intercepted her with quiet, yet distinct intent. She held the cell phone out. "My boss wants to speak to you."

Dar let her wait while she considered the request. Then she got up and came around the desk, taking the phone and perching on the corner of the wooden surface to talk into it. "Yes, Captain?'

Kerry looked up from the monitor. "Dar?" she interrupted gently. "Marketing admin, four p.m., logoff twenty one hundred plus."

Dar's nostrils flared.

"That is an odd location for that resource." Duks commented. "Perhaps I should call Eleanor."

Dar blocked them out for a moment to listen to the phone. "What was that?"

"I said, Ms. Roberts, my intention was not to blow you out of the water," Captain Mousser stated.

"Not what your puppy dog said," Dar replied. "Get your story straight."

The man sighed audibly into the phone. "She's just a kid, and she doesn't understand complex politics. It was easier to just tell her that, anyway listen..."

"I'm not going to listen, Captain," Dar said. You decided to send some half assed kid in here to do god knows what, and she got caught. My bad for not running my own building services crew. Your bad for not doing your homework. So now we'll just let the press decide which one of us is the bigger asshole."

"Roberts, will you chill out?" the Captain hissed. "You're making this into a big deal, and it doesn't have to be!"

"You don't think trying to steal proprietary code is a big deal? I do!" Dar snapped back. "I don't give a rat's ass what your intent was, Captain! Figure out how you're going to defend that!"

There was a moment's silence. "Hey, that was just opportunistic," the Captain finally said. "She had a chance to go grab it so...you can't blame me! We've been trying to find a back door into that place for a week, and..."

"Mister, you are so screwed." Dar was merciless, though inwardly relieved she'd solved at least one mystery. "I'd get my ass down to Dade County jail if I were you, and bring cash. They don't take credit cards or government PO's." She got up and limped back around the desk, pausing to look out the windows at the moonlit sea.

Pressing a hand against the glass, she suddenly wished more than anything she was out there. A sigh fogged the window, and she looked up to catch the reflection of Kerry's sea green eyes gazing out at as well. Their glances met, and held.

"Roberts! Roberts! Jesus! You want this on page one? Really?" The Captain's voice rose. "C'mon! Get real!"

Dar turned and sat down. "I'd rather that, than have you holding some bullshit piece of nothing over my head. Get it out in the open, and we'll deal with it." Her mind was already busy with figuring out how to explain the whole damn thing.

To the press. To Alastair. God. To the board.

What a mess. She closed her eyes and welcomed the casual touch of Kerry's hand on her shoulder. Kerry didn't say a word, but the silent support was obvious. "So if you're done wasting my time, I've got a press release to arrange."

"Roberts." Mousser sighed. "Look, you have something to offer. Your skills are something I really, really want to add to the team I have supporting the country. Don't you care about your country? Don't you want to help it out?"

"I do my part providing civilian jobs, thanks," Dar said. "Are we done?"

"C'mon, Roberts, you're not a communist," he coaxed. "Uncle Sam's Army wants you."

"I'm gay," Dar stated the obvious.

"We can work around that."

Kerry's eyes nearly came out of her head as she listened.

Dar glared at the phone. "I'm a Navy brat." She added, "And my dad's a retired SEAL."

Silence. "Okay, that's a problem," he admitted. "But listen; can we chalk this one up to patriotism? Let my girl out of there, and we keep this between us."

Dar's phone rang. Kerry answered it. "Okay, thanks." She looked at Dar. "Police are downstairs."

Dar hesitated, considering their options. Duks chose that moment to come around the desk and lean close to her. He put a hand over the cell and caught her eye.

"This is not the explanation for our other problem, my friend. If you can avoid the publicity, do so." He murmured under his breath. "We have much bigger issues to deal with right now."

Dar hated swallowing her pride, but she hated making stupid mistakes even more. She gave Duks a brief nod, then lifted the phone back up. "All right," She snarled. "But you're gonna have to come up with some damn good assurances that your light bulb here isn't going to open her mouth to half the earth, since she's so proud of what she did."

The Captain chuckled. "Leave that to me." He sounded much surer of himself now. "Now...can we talk about that little program of yours?"

Dar looked up at the ceiling. "No," she said. "Right now, I have to get the cops out of my lobby."

"Then give my soldier her phone back. I'll be in touch with you tomorrow," the captain answered smugly. "Don't worry, Roberts. This is going to end up being good for both of us."

Dar shook her head and threw the phone back to its owner. Now she had the police to deal with. What the hell was she going to tell them?

"Let me go downstairs." Kerry patted her on the back. "I'll handle the cops, Dar. Don't worry about it." She circled the desk and headed for the door before Dar could stop her, not that she had any intention of trying.

"Okay." Dar turned to the two security guards. "Escort this person out of the building. Take her picture before you do, and I want to know how and where she got the cleaning department identification card."

"Ma'am." The nearer guard took hold of the intruder's arm. "Should we file an internal report on this?"

"Bet your ass you should," Dar replied instantly. "Get her out of here."

The lieutenant's smirk had returned, but it wasn't as brazen as it had been to begin with. She had closed her phone and put it away, and wasn't resisting the grip of the guard. She gave Dar a look of triumph as she was led off, but remained silent.

That left Duks and Dar alone in the office. Dar rested her chin on her fist and regarded her friend, who gazed back with an equally serious expression. "We're in trouble," Dar said.

"Yes," Duks agreed. "And the big problem is, if it turns out my people were compromised then that is something that will be very difficult to hide. If it comes out, then this will as well."

"I know." Dar felt very tired. "Let's schedule an executive meeting first thing in the morning. We all need to talk."

"Yes. We do," Duks agreed. "This is a time for teamwork."

The ultimate in non-team players let out a long, aggrieved sigh.

"It's time for something," she muttered. "Right now, I'm thinking maybe a beer."

"Perhaps two," Duks agreed solemnly. "After you, madam."

Dar logged Kerry out of her PC, and shut it off. She flipped the lights down as they left, shaking her head all the way to the elevator.

IT WAS AFTER midnight as they trudged back up the steps to the condo, Dar leaning against the wall as Kerry keyed in the lock and opened the door. Chino corkscrewed up to greet them, and Kerry distracted the dog long enough for Dar to slip inside and close the door behind her.

"Ugh." Dar limped across the living room and headed for the bedroom, holding a boot in one hand. "Ker, can you check in the mailbox to see if they dropped off those drugs?'

"Sure." Kerry gave Chino a kiss on the head, and then she ducked back outside to look for the bag. It was hanging neatly on the hook under their mailbox, so she grabbed it and scooted back inside. "It's here, hon."

"Yippee." Dar's voice floated in from the bedroom. "Y'know, I used to look back on all those long nights and stressful deadlines with some kind of half assed affection." She limped back in, now dressed in just a t-shirt and her underwear. "What drug was I on?"

Kerry handed her the bag. "Why don't you sit down, and I'll grab us some hot chocolate after I change," she suggested. "I need to decompress for a while. My head's spinning."

"Go change." Dar bumped her toward the bedroom. "I'll crank up the drinks." She continued on into the kitchen and set the bag down on the counter, leaving it there while she retrieved a glass from the cupboard and squirted herself some milk.

Her foot was killing her. The long evening encased in her boot had rubbed the injury raw, and her sock had been covered in blood when she'd taken the shoe off. She perched on a stool and added a handful of Advil to the antibiotics, swallowing them all with the help of a mouthful of her milk.

Chino trotted in and sniffed at her foot, giving it a sympathetic lick. Dar regarded the dog with a wry grin, then she got off the stool and retrieved the microwavable pitcher they used for their late night hot toddies.

She filled it with milk, and added the appropriate squirts of chocolate syrup, swirling the liquid around once or twice before she slapped the lid on and gave it a vigorous shake. She pulled open the lid and considered the contents, and satisfied with the consistency she put it in the microwave.

Seating herself back on the stool, she swung her legs back and forth a few times, idly tracing a long, thin white scar crossing her right kneecap. Free of her shoe, her injured foot was beginning to stop throbbing. She cautiously wiggled her toes.

Ick. They felt swollen. She brought the foot up to rest on her knee and examined it, scowling at the red, puffy skin and the tender area that covered the top and part of the bottom of her foot. It hurt. Her head hurt. Her shoulders hurt from the tension of the night, and she wished —

What did she wish?

Dar found herself too tired to focus on the big picture, and resorted to a short term goal instead. She wished she was tucked in bed with Kerry, and a cup of hot chocolate, and Advil. There, that was doable, wasn't it?

Kerry entered the kitchen wearing a knee length t-shirt. "For a day that started out really cool, it sure ended disgusting, didn't it?"

"Uh huh." Dar agreed mournfully. "I want to go back to yesterday."

Kerry came over and leaned against her, rubbing Dar's back with the tips of her fingers. "Did you take your drugs?"

"Uh huh."

"Tired?"

"Ugh." Dar closed her eyes and let her head rest against Kerry's. "I can just see tomorrow's gonna suck."

"Uh huh." Kerry glanced up as the microwave beeped. "I smell hot chocolate." She eased past Dar and removed two mugs from the cabinet, setting them down on the counter and leaning up to retrieve the pot. "Let's worry about tomorrow, tomorrow."

Oo, mental synergy. Dar snaked an arm around Kerry and held her gently, nuzzling her arm as she attempted to pour the hot chocolate out. "Thanks for taking care of the police, by the way."

"No problem." Kerry managed to get the beverage into the cups despite the distraction. "They were very understanding, once I explained about how big a company we are, and how many new hires we have, and how it was natural for someone to get lost on the wrong floor and wander into the wrong office and be discovered accidentally by me."

Dar sipped her chocolate. "You're kidding, right?"

"No." Kerry took her elbow. "C'mon, let's go curl up on the couch. I had all the time in the world, like the thirty seconds it takes the elevator to go from fourteen to one, to come up with that story. I thought I did pretty good."

"Hell of a lot better than I'd have done." Dar agreed, willingly allowing herself to be towed to the couch. She settled next to Kerry on the soft leather, and eased her foot up onto the table.

Kerry used the remote to start a quiet CD, and turn a seascape on the television screen. The lights were low in the room, and she exhaled as she allowed the peace of the moment to descend on her. The chocolate was sweet on her tongue and she could feel the warmth traveling down into her stomach, easing the slight uneasiness from a shared dozen ill-advised spicy chicken wings.

"Ker?"

"Mm?"

"Love you."

Thoughts of chicken wings flew out the window. "I never get tired of hearing that," Kerry admitted. "Love you too."

Dar draped her arm over Kerry's shoulders. "You know something?"

"Nope." Kerry leaned back and put her feet up next to Dar's. "My brain's a cheap plastic colander at the moment."

"Ah." Dar turned her head and nipped Kerry's earlobe. "I knew this yellow stuff reminded me of something." She puffed a bit of Kerry's hair up with a short breath.

"Spaghetti?" Kerry suggested.

"Corn silk."

"Hmm. I don't like corn silk."

Dar pulled back a little. "You don't?"

Kerry shook her head. "No. It makes me itch," She explained. "Every time I get us fresh corn I have to have someone in the store husk it for me. Otherwise I end up scratching my arms raw after I finish digging the suckers out of those honky wooden bins."

"Hmm." Dar took a sip of her chocolate. "Learn something new every day."

"Too bad, too, because I love corn, and I love the smell of it when it's fresh." Kerry went on, a touch mournfully. "Especially the white corn."

Dar considered. "You could wear gloves."

"Oh, Dar. Can you imagine me shopping in Publix in white gloves up to my armpits?"

"I saw someone shopping last year in a mink."

"Real?"

"Dead." Dar clarified, then paused. "Oh, I see what you mean...yeah, I think it was real."

"Ugh. That's so un-PC." Kerry shook her head. She reflected a moment more. "We're babbling like idiots, aren't we?"

"Not really." Dar exhaled, half closing her eyes. "Everything you've said so far makes sense." She put her cup down and put her arm around Kerry. "And you were right. That story you told the cops was a good one."

"Mm." Kerry got rid of her cup and half turned, snuggling into Dar?s embrace. "To hell with the cops. You tell me a story."

Both of Dar's eyebrows lifted, and her blue eyes widened. "What?"

"Tell me a story." Kerry repeated. "C'mon, I know you know some."

Dar searched through her memories, hoping her partner wasn't expecting a once upon a time kind of tale since she'd been reading things other than Jack and Jill since she'd been a pre-schooler, and Andrew had never subscribed to Mother Goose.

Did she know any stories suitable for Kerry's adorable ears? "Wanna hear about my tenth birthday?"

"Sure." Kerry pressed her ear against Dar's chest, listening to her heartbeat. It had that odd little echo beat, from the anomaly she had in her chest, a rhythm Kerry had become quite fond of.

"Okay," Dar said. "When I was ten years old, we moved from Florida to Virginia because that's where my dad was stationed for a while."

"Mm. I can't picture you in Virginia."

"Neither could I," Dar agreed. "I missed my friends on the base something awful, and I hated the new school I was in. They made us wear uniforms."

Kerry cocked an eyebrow.

"Yeah, I know. Military brat doesn't like uniforms," Dar acknowledged. "It was a skirt, Ker. What can I tell you?"

Kerry's nose wrinkled. "Pleated?"

"Yes."

"Uuuugh."

"Anyway, since I didn't know squat about skirts, I put the damn thing on backwards," Dar said, "And wore it to school that way." A faint, self deprecating smile appeared. "No one noticed until lunchtime, but then some pissass rich girls cornered me in the cafeteria and started teasing me."

"Kids are so cruel, sometimes," Kerry agreed softly. "Most of them steered clear of us, but there was always talk, and they were always careful to make sure I heard it."

"Mm...well, they were all mostly older girls, and I guess they figured I was safe to make fun of," Dar mused. "I'd promised my dad I wouldn't make trouble in school, that I'd give it a while until I got used to everything."

"Ah."

"First time I ever broke a promise to him."

"Mm." Kerry nodded gently against Dar's body.

"I took hold of the biggest of them..."

"Bigger than you?" Kerry interrupted.

"Yeah," Dar agreed. "I didn't hit my growth spurt until I was, I think, twelve or thirteen. Anyway, I grabbed the biggest one and just tossed her over onto the ground and ripped her skirt off."

"Oh gosh." Kerry covered her eyes.

"Then I asked her which one of us was more ridiculous looking." Dar half smiled at the memory. "She was crying, the other kids were laughing and then the principal showed up." She chuckled. "He told me I was going to get a spanking. I told him..."

Kerry giggled.

"...my dad was going to kick his ass," Dar finished. "So we all ended up in the principal's office, and they called in the girl's parents, and my parents, and it was quite the circus in there. It turns out the girl's mother was an old acquaintance of my mother's, but not a fondly remembered one."

"Oh, my god. Did you end up in jail?"

"No." Dar shook her head. "We ended up in Dairy Queen," she said "We'd both been suspended for two days, and I was just so pissed off. I told them I'd rather go to reform school than stay there with those stuck up pieces of –"

"Would you really have?" Kerry asked. "Rather been in reform school? Dar, you're not a criminal."

"I would have fit in better there," Dar replied honestly. "And my father said just to give him a little time, and he'd fix it so we could go back home."

"Did he?"

Dar nodded. "I found out later he gave up a big promotion and a job he really wanted for it," she said. "But when I asked him about that, he just said his family and us being happy was more important to him than what he did."

Kerry pondered that for a minute. "There's a moral to this story isn't there?"

Dar hugged her. "Maybe." She exhaled. "Or maybe I'm just being nostalgic. That jackass who broke into the office tonight reminded me of that girl."

Kerry shifted and raised her head, kissing her partner on the lips. "Your father's a smartie." She rubbed noses with Dar. "And I like stories with a moral." She gave Dar a hug back, burying her face into the side of her partner's neck, and biting her gently.

"Oo."

"Mm."

"What was that about morals?"

Kerry just chuckled.

DAR SPENT A good while after she woke before dawn just relaxing in the darkness, her eyes mostly closed as she listened to the soft cycling on and off of the air conditioner. It was comfortable in the bedroom, the conditioner putting enough chill into the air to make the warm waterbed surface under them feel good, and there was a sense of peace in the townhouse that was very appealing.

It certainly was appealing to Dar, who was perfectly content to lie there and enjoy it as she pondered the coming day.

"Meatballs," Kerry muttered, under her breath. "Banana compote."

Dar's eyebrow twitched and she turned her head slightly to get a better view of her still sleeping, yet surprisingly chatty, partner. "Ker?" she whispered.

"Pencils don't do it." Kerry insisted.

Instantly, Dar's mind was alive with possibilities and she tried to figure out what Kerry was dreaming of. Pencils? Meatballs? What was banana compote, anyway? "Keeeerrry?" she warbled softly. "I loooooovvveee you."

Very slowly, a green orb appeared, focusing on her and visible in the low light from the clock. "I thought I heard a gopher."

"Hi."

Kerry rolled over onto her left side and snuggled back up to her partner. "Honey, you can wake me up saying you love me any day of the week," she uttered. "But did you have to do it before sunrise?"

"What were you dreaming about?"

"I wasn't." Kerry shook her head, then paused. "Why? Was I babbling again?"

Dar chuckled.

"Y'know, Dar, I never used to talk in my sleep before I met you." Kerry complained. "I'm sure my brother and sister would have mentioned it."

"How do you know?" Dar asked, reasonably. "You guys didn't sleep in the same bed, did'ja?"

Kerry's face scrunched up. "No!" She poked the taller woman in the ribs. "But Angie and I went to camp together," she explained. "I never would have lived it down if I talked in my sleep. What was I saying?"

"Gettysburg Address."

Kerry chewed on her lip. "Can't believe I actually remember that. Must be subliminal." She shook her head and closed her eyes.

Dar put her arm around Kerry and exhaled. "You were actually talking about meatballs and bananas."

Kerry opened one eye again. "Together?" she asked a touch hesitantly. "Hmm. Maybe I was dreaming I was pregnant."

Dar considered the question. "Something you aspire to?" she queried cautiously, her mind flashing back to a certain dream she'd had near the beginning of their relationship.

"Not unless you're volunteering to make me that way."

Dar's eyes widened slightly. "I think we need to go back to sleep."

"Good idea." Kerry gave her a pat on the belly.

Dar pulled the covers up and tucked them around Kerry's shoulders. They had at least an hour before it was time to get up, and she intended on using every minute of the time productively. Peace settled back down over the room after a moment.

It didn't last that long. "Ker?"

"Mm?"

"You know I can't really make you pregnant, right"

"Sure you could." Kerry gave her another comforting pat. "You can do anything you put your mind to. I have total confidence in you."

Silence fell for another brief moment. Then Dar cleared her throat gently. "That old Christian school of yours was a little light on science, huh?"

Kerry chuckled throatily, her shoulder shaking. "You know, I do remember what I was dreaming about," she admitted. "I was organizing a potluck for our office."

"Ah. That's where the pencils came in," Dar mused.

"No one knew what to bring. No one had any idea of what the heck was going on. It was like a teacher's workday in Idiotville. She complained. "I'm glad you woke me up. I was just getting to the point where I was going to start..."

"Throwing food?" Dar suggested. "Seems to be a standard practice in our circle."

"Ahem."

They both chuckled. Then Kerry sighed. "Well, I'm up now." She lamented. "You?"

"Yeah."

"How about we have a biscuit on the porch and watch the sun rise then go over to the gym?" Kerry said. "I grabbed a new flavor coffee at the market the other day and I've been meaning to try it."

It sounded pretty appealing to Dar, who gave up on her snoozing plans with only a faint regret. She reached over and turned on the bedside lamp, which produced a soft glow calculated not to shock the eyeballs. Kerry had selected the appliance replacing a somewhat brighter one that had been a holdover from Aunt May's day. "Go go go."

Kerry waited for Dar to roll up out of the waterbed before she followed suit, rubbing her bare arms as the chill air hit them. She grabbed the shirt Dar tossed her and slipped into it, then briefly wished for a pair of slippers as she followed Dar out of the room.

Chino was already waiting at the back door, tail wagging gently as they entered the kitchen. Dar detoured to let the Labrador out, and paused on the steps to watch the pre-dawn stars twinkle in the sky.

The air was warm and full of moisture, and the scent of salt water and grass was thick. Dar sucked in a lungful, almost able to taste the richness on the back of her tongue as a breeze brushed over her body. She could remember air like this as part of her world from the time she was old enough to recognize anything. She spared a brief moment of nostalgia for a time when all it would have meant was another lazy summer day full of thunderstorms and dust, and maybe some coconuts to break open.

With a faint sigh, she turned and leaned on the door jamb, watching Kerry as she measured coffee from a lidded container into their coffee machine. Despite the faded shirt and sleep disheveled hair, or maybe because of it, she found herself smiling at the sight.

"So." Kerry leaned on the counter and watched the water start to percolate through the grinds. "We've got an executive meeting at nine. What's the angle you're going to put on that, Dar?"

"Shh." Dar circled her and kissed her on the back of the neck. "I don't want to talk about angles until we're in the car on the way there."

Kerry turned her head and peered up at her partner. "Just trying to mentally prepare," she protested mildly. "It's going to be a free for all, y'know."

"I know." Dar rested her chin on Kerry's shoulder. "Don't worry about it. We'll just take it as it comes. Now," she bumped her lightly, "what was that about sunrise and a cookie?"

"A biscuit." Kerry bumped her back with a tolerant grin. "I think I have some whole wheat crackers we could try."

Dar snorted.

"Yeah, okay. Grab the banana nut cakes from the fridge and I'll get the coffee." Kerry acknowledged. "And I'll figure out something safe to talk to you about."

Dar paused in the middle of removing a package of muffins, and looked at her. "That's not what I — "

Kerry raised her eyebrows.

"Ker, it's going to be an entire day of that crap. Any reason to start it early?" Dar asked plaintively.

"Yes." Kerry looked back at her seriously. "I want to be ready for it, and I want a comfort level with how you feel about all this stuff before we go in there. It would make me feel a lot better."

Dar blinked. "Oh."

"You asked." She shrugged slightly, a faint twitch starting at the corners of her mouth. "But I like being able to answer you honestly, and not have either of us freak out, you know that?"

On the verge of slightly freaking out, Dar relaxed instead. "Yeah," she agreed. "Sorry, I wasn't thinking." She put the muffins down and removed a package of whipped cream cheese, setting it down as well. "Story of my life lately."

"That's the second time you said that recently." Kerry poured the now finished coffee into a carafe and snagged two cups. "C'mon." She led the way to the sliding glass doors to their porch and paused, as Dar reached past her to unlock them and push them open.

They walked outside and settled down at the table, the sound of the surf now more audible as a fairly strong breeze fluttered their shirts against their bodies. "Oo." Kerry set her burden down and walked to the balcony, enjoying the fresh air.

Dar took a seat at the table and poured two cups of coffee, fixing Kerry's and setting it next to the other chair. She removed a muffin from the container and cut it in half, studiously covering both the flat surfaces with cream cheese.

Kerry came over and sat down, taking her cup and sipping at it. "Thank you."

Pale blue eyes flicked up and regarded her. "You're welcome." She handed Kerry half the muffin and took the other half for herself. "You know something?"

Kerry nibbled at her muffin. "You have no clue what you're going to do in that meeting," she stated, eyes twinkling very gently. "I figured that out while we were walking out here because if you did know what you were going to do, you'd have said it already instead of pushing me off since yesterday."

Dar took a bite of her muffin, more than a little disconcerted. "Um..."

"Am I wrong? It's okay if I am. I was just—" Kerry half shrugged. "You know." She slid one foot under the table and rubbed Dar's with it. "I don't want to rattle you, hon. I just feel rattled myself, and I hate that."

Dar, of course, hated it also. She wasn't really feeling rattled as much as she was feeling like she was not in control of whatever was going on and she hated that even more. Things were happening that surprised her, and knocked her off guard, and it was difficult to keep having to adjust her inner plans to account for totally bizarre?

Off balance. It struck a chord somewhere, and suddenly Dar remembered exactly why she hated feeling that way, and exactly when she'd been taunted about her reaction to it. "Huh."

"Dar?"

Everything had conspired lately against her, but was it just the vagaries of fate, or did she detect a subtle, long finger nailed hand behind it?

"Hello, Dar?" Kerry reached over and curled her fingers around Dar's wrist. "Earth calling?"

Dar cocked her head to one side. "I was just remembering something," she murmured. "Anyway, yeah, I think you're right, Ker. I mean...I know basically what we're gonna do." She leaned her elbows on the table and nibbled her way around the edge of her muffin. "We're gonna cancel that meeting."

"Uh?" Kerry got caught in mid-sip. "What?"

"You and I are just going to concentrate on the ship," Dar said firmly. "We've got a project to complete, and the rest of the stuff going on can wait. Duks can handle his security breach, and our security department can handle the cleaning staff."

Kerry rested her chin on her fist. "Um...okay."

"It's a distraction." Dar looked her right in the eye. "Someone's trying very hard to keep you, and I, off balance and not concentrating on this project." She bit her muffin in half, and watched crumbs litter the table. "We're not going to let them do that anymore."

Mental whiplash was no kinder than the physical kind Kerry

discovered. She studied her partner for a minute then merely shook her head. "Whatever you say, boss," she replied. "So, you want me to send a note to..."

"The battling burritos, yes." Dar sounded much more decisive now. "Tell them we'll be at the ship all day and nothing short of a hurricane better interrupt us." She sliced the other muffin in half and adorned it, then nudged Kerry's hand. "C'mon, we've got crunches to do, treadmills to pound...start chewing."

Obediently, Kerry did, glad at least that some sort of direction seemed to be coming back into her partner's attitude. Whether that direction was going to take them both off the road into the water, she didn't know, but heck.

Life was short. Enjoy the cream cheese while you could.

Chapter Fourteen

KERRY CROSSED THE baked, white concrete between the terminal and the ship, glad she'd put her sunglasses on as the sun reflected unmercifully off the pale surface. She was dressed in a pair of well broken in jeans, work boots, and a plain red pocketed t-shirt, and she blended in with the thick crowd of workers clustering around the ship entry in a state of controlled panic.

She had left Dar in the terminal, her partner intent on taking control of their office and everything that was processing through it. Unable to put on her own boots because of the swelling of her injured foot, Dar had reluctantly agreed to let Kerry take charge onboard and work with the install team.

Kerry knew, of course, that beach sandals or no, Dar would eventually break the rules and ramble after her, but for now she proceeded on the assumption that everything would be up to her to coordinate. They had a lot to do, and she felt relatively focused and ready for it. "Morning, guys."

Two of her IT techs turned, hearing her voice. "Morning, ma'am!" They both chorused. "Wow, what a mess, huh?"

"You got it." Kerry paused, seeing what appeared to be a logjam at the top of the gangway. "What's going on in there?"

"Oh." The taller of the two, a slim dark haired man named Carlos, grinned. "There's this guy up there who's yelling because we keep getting our stuff before he gets his. I think the man in charge inside likes us."

"The big guy?" Kerry hazarded a guess, holding a hand up over her own head.

"Si." Carlos nodded. "He sent up all the cabling patches to the main floor just now, and this other guy was waiting for some plugs and he had a fit."

"You know who that big guy is, don't you?" Green eyes twinkled.

"No." Carlos shook his head, and his companion did also. They were both fairly new hires, juniors in Mark's expansive department.

"C'mon." Kerry led the way up the gangway, nudging past a few construction workers. At the top she managed to squeeze past a man in a hard hat with a bristling red beard, ignoring his glare as she hopped onto the deck to see what was going on.

Carlos and his friend followed her, standing cautiously behind her as they got clear of the hatch.

"Ah do not care." Andy was standing, with his arms crossed over his broad chest, legs spread in front of a stack of boxes. "These here boxes go in whatever the hell order ah want them to."

Facing him was a lean man in an electrician's union t-shirt with a tool belt and a bad attitude. "Listen buddy, I'm gonna kick your ass if you don't cough up my stuff, unnerstand?"

Andy just looked at him and smiled. "We ain't got no time here for fun."

"You think it's funny?" The man advanced aggressively.

"Ah think you're an ass." Andy pointed at the narrow stairwell with one thumb. "So get your silly ass up them stairs fore I toss it overboard. Your damn stuff went up half an hour ago."

The man glared at him, but headed for the door. "You aint' seen the last of me. That's for sure."

The logjam broke and men started across the deck again, milling around and heading for various boxes and crates. Kerry scooted through them and headed for Andrew instead, cautiously followed by her techs. "Hey! Morning!"

Andy turned at the familiar voice. "Wall! Morning there, kumquat." He produced a grin for her. "You're an early bird."

Without hesitation, and despite all the commotion, Kerry walked up and gave him a big hug. "Boy, I'm glad you're here," she remarked. "Are you causing trouble taking care of us?"

Her father-in-law chuckled, a low, rumbling sound.

Kerry turned to the wide eyed techs. "Guys, this is Andrew Roberts," she explained. "Dar's daddy." she clarified, after a second. "Dad, this is Carlos and Jason, who work for us."

"Howdy." Andrew greeted them amiably.

"Hi," Carlos responded.

"Hello," Jason added, from his safe position behind Kerry. "Nice to meet you."

Kerry couldn't decide if the two were more intimidated by Andrew's size, or the fact that he was Dar's father. She gave them a tolerant grin, and pointed. "Go on upstairs. I'll meet you up there." She waited for them to retreat then turned back to Andy. "Having fun?"

Andy looked around, then back at her. "Little bit," he acknowledged. "My kid here?"

"Yep, in the building." Kerry pointed over her shoulder. "We've got a lot of work to do today."

"You get all that stuff settled up last night?" Andrew asked curiously. "Sounded like a rat in a teakettle all what was going on."

How would a rat get into a teakettle? Kerry wondered. "More or less," she said. "What's going on in here today? Seems like a lot of people are pissed off."

"Wall." Her father in law folded his arms again. "Folks don't like to naturally take turns, see, and in this here little box, ain't no way anything gets done unless folks do." He walked over and kicked a pallet. "Problem was, feller who was in here 'fore I was just let all this stuff show up any the hell way, and it was a big old mess."

Kerry looked around, realizing the cargo space was far more organized than it had been the last time she'd seen it. Pallets were lined up against the walls in orderly rows, each with a label on them, and men with pallet jacks were moving them out in a regular sequence. "Ah!"

"Folks don't like waiting." Andy shrugged.

"Especially when you put all our stuff first?" Kerry elbowed him gently in the side.

Blue eyes blinked innocently at her. "Ain't mah fault all them gizmos of yours come in labeled and regular when the rest of this here gunk we got to rip open to see what it is," he protested mildly. "I just get that there easy stuff out mah way first, that's all."

"Ahh!" Kerry put a hand over her chest. "My anally retentive labeling system. At last, someone appreciates it!" She smiled broadly. "I'm vindicated!"

Andrew chuckled. "Ah do like it," he agreed. "'Bout good enough for the Navy."

Kerry took that as the compliment it obviously was and grinned. "Thanks," she said. "Okay, I'm going to get working. If you need anything, I'll be upstairs and Dar's over there terrorizing everyone in case you hear yelling coming from the shore side area."

Andrew patted her on the back and sent her on her way. He waited for her to disappear up the stairs, before he returned his attention to the loading dock, observing the orderly movement with a judicious eye. "Hey, you all," he called over to two men standing near the far wall. "Watch this here thing. I'll be right back."

He walked across the gangway and down to the dock, ambling across the open space with a deceptive stride. Two forklifts dodged him, and he sped up a little as he made his way up the walk to the back of the terminal.

Ducking inside the door, he looked quickly around. It was almost as full of frenetic, yet purposeful motion as the ship hold, only here the bodies rushing around were covered in polo shirts and pressed chinos and the smell was of copper and new plastic rather than sump oil.

It was cool in here, too. Andrew appreciated that. He'd spent enough time in his life in places where air conditioning was unheard of to appreciate it now that he could pretty much have it at will. After a career spent in the military, he'd discovered that directing his own life and his own comfort was actually a pretty damn nice thing.

Ah. His eyes found what they were looking for. On the far side of the large room there was a large desk like area, raised up a foot or so, giving it a commanding view of the entire space.

Dar had taken it over, and was perched on a stool behind the counter, her laptop on one side of her and a pad of paper in front, her head bent over it as she wrote. Andrew found himself smiling at the sight, gazing at his daughter fondly as the head propped on one fist echoed a much earlier mental image he had of her.

He remembered watching her sit at the counter in their tiny kitchen down south in just such a pose, pouring over a comic book or a new magazine as she waited for them to have dinner. The look of absorption hadn't changed, or the rapid flicking as her eyes scanned across her subject with an intense focus he'd recognized as something he'd seen in himself on occasion.

It had always made him feel good...that echo. Andy knew he wasn't a stupid man, but he knew as well he wasn't no scientist and he'd taken a lot of pride in his daughter's accomplishments specially knowing he'd contributed to a bit of it in his own way.

Mah kid. He smiled, watching Dar shift restlessly as she wrote, recognizing the fidgets as well.

"All right." Dar finished writing and straightened, ripping the top sheet off the pad of paper and handing it to a waiting tech. "Get these units together, and get 'em on a flatbed. We'll start at the top of the ship and work down."

"Not from the bottom first, ma'am?" the tech queried. "Wouldn't it be easier?"

Dar leaned on her arms and pinned him with a cool, blue stare. "You think it's gonna be easier to carry those things up eleven flights of metal stairs now, or this afternoon?"

The tech looked at the list, then at Dar. "Oh." He scratched his jaw sheepishly. "Sorry, yeah. You're right. No elevators in there, huh?"

"No."

"Gotcha, on the way, ma'am." The tech trotted off with his list.

Dar shook her head and went back to her pad, then paused and turned her head, as though sensing her father's eyes on her. "Hey." She put her pencil down as she spotted him.

"Hey there, Dardar." Andrew came over and rested his forearms on the desk. "How are ya?"

Dar drummed her thumbs on the bad faux wood Formica. "Wanting this damn circus to be over. How's it going in there?"

"Not bad," her father said. "Saw Kerry go on up in there. She all right with them guys?" He expressed a little doubt. "Got some roughneck types up in them spaces up a ways."

Dar frowned. "My guys?" she asked incredulously. "Dad, most of them won't even cough hard in her presence."

"Naw, them contractors." Andrew shook his head. "'Lectricans and what all." He glanced around. "Not these here fellers. I figure they ain't most of 'em dangerous as bugs."

No, probably not. Dar glanced at the back door. "Well." She drummed the table again. "There's always a chance, I guess, but she's got some of the techs with her, and I'm not gonna be the one to tell her she can't be in there."

"Heh." Andrew chuckled shortly. "Well, I'll keep an earbug out."

He turned and looked around. "How's your laig?"

"Ick." Dar answered honestly. "Thanks for asking."

Andrew gave her arm a pat. "We'll get this thing done, Dardar. Don't you worry." He turned and headed for the back door, threading his way through the techs that all turned and looked after him.

Dar exhaled. She pulled her PDA out and tapped out a message, then unclipped her cell phone as it rang and checked the caller ID.

Duks.

With a sigh, she answered it.

"OKAY, LET'S START with the number one room." Kerry threaded her way through the hall, dodging rolls of carpet and stacks of steel supports. The two techs followed obediently after her, carrying the first of their heavy pieces of gear between them.

The hallways flickered with intermittent power, and they were full of workers all trying to get their part of the job done at the same time and mostly in the same space. Tempers were hot, the air was hotter, and Kerry already felt sweat making her t-shirt cling to her torso.

Not a nice feeling. Kerry had never enjoyed sweating though she didn't mind it in small doses, as when she was in the gym or if they were outside on the beach. But she liked the opportunity to limit it and have copious amounts of some kind of water at close hand.

At first, she'd thought she was being just too preppy about it, and for a while after they'd moved in together, she hadn't said anything about it one way or another to Dar, until she realized one morning that it was so muggy outside the windows in the town house were completely fogged over...

"Ugh." Kerry pressed her hands against the sliding glass doors, feeling the chill of them against her skin. "I'm sweating already."

Dar walked up behind her and looked over her shoulder at the misty scene. "Ah. Summer."

Well, Kerry told herself, buck up. It's only an hour, and you can't show your northern stripes yet. She straightened up a little and pushed off from the window. "Time's a wasting." She started for the door, only to be brought up short as Dar caught her around the waist with one long arm. "Urf?"

"You want to go running in that?" Dar queried.

Kerry peeked up at her. "Um...there's a choice?"

Dar leaned her arms on Kerry's shoulders and gazed into her eyes. "Sure," she said. "There's no rule that says we have to do anything we don't want to do, Ker."

"I thought you liked running."

"I like fitting into my clothes," Dar replied frankly. "Only idiots like spending the morning in air thick enough to make soup from, running in circles."

"Ah." Kerry felt better. "So you don't like sweating that much?"

"I don't like sweating at all." Dar grinned. "Or didn't the 65 degree constant AC in here tip you off to that?" She indicated the windows. "How about we go swimming instead?"

"Swimming?"

Dar nodded. "The big pool's great for laps."

Cool water and Dar in a bathing suit. Hmm. "You don't think I'm a wuss? Or a pathetic snowbird?"

Dar snickered. "We could start the morning off right and skinny dip."

"C'mon." Kerry turned her back on the fogged window feeling much friendlier to the humidity all of a sudden. "Race you to the pool."

"Ma'am?"

Kerry looked up and wiped the smile off her face, along with a healthy dose of perspiration from her forehead. "Sorry. What?"

"We have to take this upstairs, right?" the man asked. "Like, by walking?"

Kerry gave him a sympathetic look, as they edged past stacks of metal poles. "Unfortunately, yeah," she said. "I'll give you guys a hand going up with it," she offered. "I know it's heavy."

The closest tech released one hand off the switch and waved it at her. "Oh, no, no, that's okay, ma'am. We're fine! Honest."

"Yeah." The other tech grunted. "We can handle this."

Kerry gave them both a dubious look, and kept her comments to herself. She led the way to the wide center stair case and started up turning to keep an eye on the two techs as they trudged upward.

The steps had been stripped of carpet and were a treacherous combination of cracked wood and treading strips. Kerry could feel her boots sticking to them a little, and she kept her eyes on the ground trying to spot dangerous items like upward facing nails.

She was fairly sure her thick soled shoes would stand up to it, but given the accumulated grime in the stairwell, a puncture could possibly be life threatening.

A new frame had been welded in place for a handrail, but the top was still open metal studded with bolts. Kerry was very cautious in taking hold of it, and as she climbed upward, the light started dimming so she retrieved her flashlight from her back pocket and turned it on. "Careful," she warned. "I think they're welding up here."

"Great," one of the techs muttered.

Kerry paused on the landing as her PDA chirped. "Okay, let's break for a rest here a second." She stepped to one side of the landing and flipped the device open, as the techs let the switch rest on the steps. They were sweating, and breathing hard, and Kerry debated as to whether she should call them out on their macho.

Hey. Watch out for the tradesmen in there. Dad says they

look like a rough bunch.

Kerry regarded the note quietly. What exactly was Dar saying? That she was in danger, or were they in danger of getting knocked on the head and the switch swiped? She tapped out just that question and waited, keeping one eye on the techs.

He couldn't give a rat's ass about the guys or the switch.

Ah. Kerry looked around, but they were alone in the stairwell, and though she could hear workmen above them, so far everyone she'd seen had completely ignored her. I'll keep my eyes open. She assured her. You're gonna need to send me more little macho boys, though. Mine are giving out already.

She closed the device and put it away. "Ready?" she asked the techs. "Sure you don't want me to grab a corner of that?"

The techs hesitated, then moved over to allow her to join them on one side of the switch. Kerry took hold of a curved bit of metal and they lifted together, then started slowly up the stairs.

"SO, WHAT'S THE story?" Dar pressed the cell phone against one ear, as she reviewed a list of newly uncrated equipment. "John, did we get a case of fiber patch?" she called out. "If we did, find it!"

"Will do." John trotted off in search.

"I have just finished interviewing my four senior auditors," Duks said. "Three of them, I have no doubt about. They were as puzzled as I as to what was going on."

"Uh huh." Dar scanned the list again. "And the fourth?"

"The fourth one has admitted to being the person who started that activity last night," Duks answered calmly. "I have terminated them and begun legal proceedings."

Dar blinked. "You did...they did?" she blurted. "Just like that?"

"Just so," Duks agreed. "It was Adriene Blatklo, and she was unrepentant. Apparently there was some money involved in asking for the information," Duks said. "She has retained a lawyer already, and apparently believes we will not pursue the matter."

"Hell with that."

Duks snorted. "You may say that again, my friend. I got off the phone with Hamilton before I called you. At any rate, apparently that hole is closed. Have you heard anything more from our obnoxious friend from last night?"

"No."

"Excellent," Duks said. "I will say this; Adriene rather arrogantly informed me that I should not be surprised if she was the only one to be approached. Apparently our freeze on salaries is rather well known in the outside at the moment."

"Great." Dar sighed. "Well, I can't worry about that right now, Louis. I've got a project to bring in."

"I will let you get to it then," Duks said. "Have you spoken with Alastair?"

"No." Dar made a note on the page. "You want to call him? I'm busy." She glanced at her PDA, which had started to flash.

There was a significant pause, then Duks cleared his throat. "Of course. It is my department, after all."

"Great. Tell him I say hi," Dar said. "Talk to you later." She hung up, and set the cell phone down, then picked up her PDA and flipped it open. She read Kerry's note and answered it, then reviewed the response. "Uh huh."

Bodies she had plenty of. "Mark!"

Mark swerved and headed across the room to where she was sitting. "Yes, boss?" He leaned his arms on the counter. "Like your cubby here."

"Kerry needs help inside," Dar said. "Get half dozen guys and send them up to the deck eleven closet," she directed. "I don't want to hear she was lugging that damn gear around, got me?"

Mark grinned. "Do I get to tell her that?"

"NO." Dar glared at him.

"Ma'am." John trotted up with a box. "Here's the fiber patches...should I bring them to Ms. Stuart?"

"Yes." Dar pointed to the door, then turned her eyes back on Mark. "Have you sent those guys yet?"

"I'm going." Mark backed off. "Hey you want some coffee or something?"

Dar's eyes narrowed. "You insinuating I need some?"

Mark grinned. "I'm outta here, boss. You sound like the good old days." He turned and headed toward a group of technicians clustered around some boxes, grabbing some by the arm and calling others over.

Dar leaned back on her stool and pondered that, then returned her attention to the list of items. Kerry had done a very good job of ordering, and it looked like nothing had been left off the list. Most of their gear was in, and things were progressing fairly well.

She tapped a pencil on the counter and tried to figure out what to do next.

THE ELEVENTH DECK was mostly dark. As they walked up the last step, Kerry flashed her light around, peering down the hallway toward where their wiring closet was. On one end of the floor—the far end—electricians were working inside a panel, sparks flying as they welded something into place. "Hmm. This is going to be fun."

"It's creepy in here," the shorter tech commented.

"Yeah, it is," Kerry agreed. "Okay, let's get this thing mounted and plugged in." She led the way down the hall with her powerful light bobbing up and down with her steps and outlining the closed cabin doors. The scent had changed up here, from old mildew to new carpeting over old mildew, interspersed with fresh paint.

It was an improvement, but at the back of her tongue Kerry could still taste the age and decay. She suspected it would stay that way until some decent air conditioning could dry the air out a little. At least this high up, most of the diesel stench had dissipated.

As she walked, Kerry tried to imagine sailing on the ship to some place, her world bounded by the walls and the deep blue sea around them. It was hard; even though she'd spent time out on the Dixie, this was something else entirely.

This would be more like cruising in a slightly seedy, somewhat rundown hotel with a new coat of paint on it. Kerry had decided she would be interested in taking a cruise with Dar, but not on something like this. She'd found a sailboat cruise company in a magazine the other day and had already started planning. "Okay, watch it." She carefully stepped over a roll of carpet remnants left in the dark hallway.

"Urf." The tech in front grunted.

"Want to put it down a minute?" Kerry asked.

"No, we're good."

Men. Kerry sighed, though she suspected Dar would have given the same answer. She continued down the hall, becoming more and more aware of the darkness around them as they left the semi-lit stairwell behind. There were creaks all around as well, and a soft groaning somewhere as the ship shifted in its berth.

They reached the cross corridor that held their wiring closet, and she turned into it, the partially opened door moving inward as she pushed.

"Ayah!"

Kerry nearly hit her head on the roof as she jumped, the yell from inside the dark closet scaring her silly. "Yow!" She yelped, backing into the techs who dropped the switch on the deck with a solid thump. Since they and the hundred pound item were behind her, she was trapped near the door and she teetered for balance as she heard a clatter behind it. "Holy —"

The door yanked open and a large figure appeared. Faced with no retreat, Kerry flashed her light at it, her free hand lifting into an automatic defensive posture in front of her. Dar's warning rang in her mind and she felt a moment of panic, before her light illuminated the man's t-shirt and she recognized the name of their own cable vendor. "Oh."

"Jesus, lady!" the man exclaimed. "You scared the crap out of me!" He glared at Kerry. "I coulda been on a ladder in there, y'know!"

"Sorry." Kerry collected herself. "We're just trying to get this equipment in," she explained. "They told us the cabling was ready."

The man snorted. "Yeah, sure." He brushed by them. "Next time, watch it!"

Kerry peered after him, watching his back retreat into the darkness. "Hmm." She shook her head and tapped her flashlight against her palm. "Remind me to talk to his boss."

The techs wiped sweating palms on their jeans and took hold of the switch again. "Sounded like we woke him up," Carlos commented. "Not like we were sneaking down the hall, you know?"

"Exactly." Kerry turned and shoved the door open, entering the wiring closet and standing aside to let the men enter after her. If the hallway was stuffy, the closet was stifling, and held a hint of plastic and copper as well as old sweat and the faint scent of beer.

Not entirely pleasant. "Let's see what we've got here." Kerry motioned for them to block the door open with the switch as she studied the interior. Most of the small space was taken up by two tall racks bolted to the deck and reaching to the ceiling. In one, panels full of network jacks winked in her flashlight beam. The other was empty waiting for their equipment. "This is such fun to do in the dark." Kerry sighed. "Jesus. Okay, let me get over here." She went around the corner of the rack and tried to get into an angle that would allow her to put the light to good use. "Why don't you...ow!"

"Ma'am?" Carlos leaned toward her anxiously.

Kerry flexed her hand that she unwisely had put into the sharp angle of the rack. A sting alerted her, and she turned the flashlight on her palm that was now stained with blood. "Ugh." The slice was shallow, but long, like a two inch paper cut. "Figures. Watch out for this cross support guys, it's sharp."

"Ow." Carlos murmured sympathetically. "Bet that hurts."

It did. "Nah." Kerry stepped up to her macha. "Heck, if I could get a tattoo, what's this little old thing?"

The two techs stopped in the act of moving the switch into place. "You got a tattoo?" Carlos inquired. "Wow. I went with my cousin when he got his, and he screamed like a...um..." He gave Kerry a sheepish look. "Girl."'

"That's okay. So did I." Kerry smiled at them. "What do you think, here?" She indicated a spot in the rack.

"Yeah, that would be good." The techs picked up the switch and started to angle it into the rack. "Damn this thing weighs a ton."

Kerry watched them struggling. "Hang on." She wormed her way into the rack itself and knelt. "Here, set it on my knee, and then you can swivel it." She instructed patting the denim covered surface. "Otherwise you don't have enough space to really...yeah." She grunted a little as the weight of the device came down on her leg.

"Got it. Carlos, push it in further," the other tech urged. "Yeah...no, wait."

Kerry edged back against the back of the rack as the switch nearly pinned her in place. Her elbow knocked against something, and she heard the rattle of glass behind her, accompanied by the scent of stale beer. "Ah." She felt sweat running down her body, and her nose tickled from the dust. "How's it going guys?"

"Gotta get the rack nuts in," Carlos muttered. "One's in...wait...oh, shit. I dropped it."

"I got another one, here." His colleague handed it over. "Hurry up before we smush Ms. Stuart, and get our asses kicked into the bay."

Kerry smiled, as she took hold of the device with both hands and tried to keep it steady. It was a dead weight, and it was making her leg ache. She tried not to think about the ten others they had to install and leaned her head against the cool steel, blinking salty sweat from her eyes.

"Okay, got it...get that into place and I'll screw it in." Carlos said. "You okay, ma'am?"

"Just fine. Thanks," Kerry assured him. She felt the weight come off her knee as the switch was screwed into place. "Now I'm doing much better. You got it?"

"Got it." Carlos assured her. "You can come out of there now, ma'am."

Kerry eased up off her knees, then realized with the switch bolted into place, she was trapped inside the rack. "Oh, Jesus." She sighed. "Hang on...I need to climb up over the top of this thing." Her PDA beeped and she paused in the middle of getting a foothold on the side of the rack to open it.

I sent some help. They there yet?

Kerry looked around the cramped room. No, sweetie, and there's no room in here for them. I'm trapped inside a rack myself at the moment.

WHAT?

"Uh oh." Kerry put the PDA away and concentrated on escaping from her metal prison. She got a foot up on the support brace that had cut her and eased herself up and over the switch, catching sight of the two techs caught between wanting to help her and not wanting to be insubordinate. "I could use a hand, guys. If I fall on my head on the floor Dar's not gonna like it."

The techs jumped forward, unblocking the door and allowing it to swing shut as they reached for Kerry's hand. Her flashlight slipped from her sweaty fingers and dropped on the floor, turning itself off and putting them all in total darkness.

Everyone froze. "Um...."

Kerry sighed. "Find it." She eased back into the rack and pulled her PDA out, turning it on and using the meager light from the screen to give them as much help as possible. "This would be funny if it wasn't just so ridiculous."

More sweat rolled down her face as she waited for the flashlight to be found. "This is the glamorous part of our jobs, huh?"

Carlos laughed hesitantly. "Yes, ma'am...I think I got it," he said. "Oh, I think it broke."

Of course. Kerry rested her head against the rack. "Please try to fix it. If I have to call for help to get out of here, I'm never going to hear the end of it."

Her cell phone rang at that moment, and she opened it, not even having to glance at the caller ID. "Hi."

"You're stuck in a rack?"

"In the dark, in a closet, with a broken flashlight. But we're fixing it." Kerry informed her partner. "We'll be fine. Really."

"I'm sending my father to get you."

Kerry sighed. "Dar..." She protested. "We got the switch installed. We're fine. Honestly. Right guys?"

"Right." The two chorused obediently. "Hey." Carlos yelped suddenly. "Something just crawled on me!"

Kerry's eyes opened wide. "Uh..."

"Still okay?" Dar's voice sounded wry. "I heard that. Better hope it's only a roach."

"Urk." Kerry instinctively lifted her hand to the neck of her shirt, and twisted it a little, tightening the fabric around her throat in case something fell on her head and thought a journey inside her clothing would be a fun idea. "Don't suppose Dad has a nice big flashlight, huh?"

A loud bang sounded overhead, and the walls shook a little, producing a rattle of some things falling onto the floor.

"What was that?" Dar asked.

"I don't know." Kerry started looking for another way out, feeling around cautiously. "Hon, can I get back to you?"

"Okay. Hang tight," Dar said, briskly. "Bye."

Kerry clipped the phone to her belt. "Any luck?" she asked. "How about getting the door open?"

"Ma'am, I'm trying," the other tech said unhappily. "It's locked from the outside. There's no lock on this knob." He rattled the door, obviously yanking on it. "Do you hear that?"

"What?" Kerry asked.

"That noise."

They all listened, and Kerry now could hear a sound of water burbling. "Water." She concluded. "This is a ship. That can't be good in any sense." She put the thought of bugs aside and started climbing over the switch again, by feel alone. "Watch out!"

"Ma'am! What are you doing?" Carlos asked nervously. "Please be careful, you can...oh! Oh!"

Kerry felt her balance slipping and she made a grab for the railing, the sweat on her hands making her lose her grip. "Yeow!" She swung over the top of the switch and slammed against it, knocking herself sideways and tumbling over the support rail. "Look out!"

"Ma'am! Kerry!" Carlos made a grab for her, but he wasn't even close, and Kerry landed hard on her side knocking him back against the wall. "Oh!"

"Oof." Kerry felt the breath go out of her and she only barely kept her head from smacking the floor. The sound of water got louder, and she could suddenly smell something unpleasant over the scent of carpet and mildew and new electronics. "Uh oh."

"Uh." The sound of scrambling. "I think we better get off the floor."

Kerry sighed. "Can I go back to my ivory tower now?" She shoved herself up off the ground just as the stench of sewage flooded the closet and all they could do was hold their noses and hope for the best.

"Well, ma'am." Carlos sighed. "It can't get worse than this, can it?"

If Kerry could have found his mouth in the dark, she would have covered it. As it was, she just crossed her fingers, and hoped she had a spare pair of boots somewhere in the car.

DAR POPPED THE back door open and headed through it powering past the guard without so much as a glance in his direction. She pushed her sunglasses further up her nose as the glare hit her eyes, feeling the sharp blast of heat as the sun poured over her.

In the shimmering heat, the old ship looked scroungier than ever. Dar saw a crew of men gathering around the hull, armed with five gallon jugs of marine paint, and she suspected the old hull was about to take on new colors.

She strode past the forklifts, hopping onto the gangway and making her way up into the ship, trying not to limp too badly and hoping no one dropped anything significant on her mostly unprotected feet.

It wasn't smart to go into a construction area with beach sandals on, but Kerry needed something, and that made the risk irrelevant.

Looking right and left as she entered the storage hold she headed for the stairs slipping between two moving pallets just in time to keep herself from being smashed flat.

"Hey!" the man moving the pallet yelled. "Watch out, you crazy woman!"

Dar lifted a bare arm and waved at him, as she started up the steps. The heat already was oppressive, and she was glad she'd picked a tank top to wear with her jeans.

Two men coming down squeezed past her on the steps, muttering under their breaths, shaking their heads. "We ain't never gonna get this done. That guy down there fucked us up big time."

"I'm gonna kick his ass," the other man replied. "I don't care how big he is."

Dar paused as she turned the corner landing, and then shrugged and kept on going, figuring if the big guy he was talking about was the one she was related to, he could more than take care of himself. She rounded the turn and continued on up, taking the steps at a rhythmic trot.

Her foot hurt, but she put that in the back of her mind and concentrated on avoiding broken corners on the steps that might send her sprawling. It got darker as she went up until she arrived on the open deck, where the doors were thrown open to get some kind of breeze inside the stifling interior.

Abruptly, Dar felt slightly horrified that she'd sent Kerry in here with the team. What had she been thinking? It was a hell hole in here!

Aggravated, she increased her pace across the deck, moving inside and heading for the double wide stairwell that lead to the upper decks.

People were coming down the stairs, rubbing their eyes and complaining.

Dar became aware of a stench in the air that made her nose wrinkle in reaction. Sewage, but worse, old sewage that smelled like lots of dead things had reconstituted themselves and were now invading the inside of the ship. "Oh, gross."

Stifling the urge to hold her nose, Dar started up the steps, blinking a little as the fumes made her eyes water. She rounded the first landing and kept moving upward, the dimness and the smell getting worse every second.

"Gag," Dar muttered, getting a sympathetic look from two female crew members who were hurrying in the other direction. "What died?" she asked, pausing to call after them.

"Some stupid person put something down one of the toilets." The woman nearest to her stopped and explained. "It blew up the pipes. I tell you, these people who work on this ship are stupider than most of our passengers ever were."

Well acquainted with cranky marine heads, Dar winced. "Great." She turned and started up the steps again, hoping silently it hadn't been one of her people that had done it. None of them were stupid, but sometimes when you were under stress, you did things out of habit.

Dar took another flight and tugged her flashlight from its holder on her belt, turning it on.

Stop up an air pressure pipe, and what resulted was a blow out, usually in the middle of a wall somewhere, where the term 'shit hitting the fan' came to a new, pungent, and, occasionally, dangerous meaning.

"Ah, the romance of the sea." Dar heard voices up a level, and she redoubled her speed again, powering up onto the landing of the eleventh deck in time to hear someone blaspheme his mother in virulent Spanish.

She rounded the corner of the stairwell to find a dark hallway full of machinery, men, and a growing sludge advancing across the new carpet. Some of the men she recognized as hers. "All right folks. What's going on here?"

Half the crowd turned, obviously relieved to see her. "Ms. Roberts!" the closest one said. "They won't let us go any further."

Two of the ship personnel were blocking the passage, shoving the others back impatiently. "Go back," the taller one of the two said. "You cannot go here. Something is broken."

Dar edged through her staff, most of them backing up as much as they could in the crowded space to allow her through. "Some of our people are in that hallway," she told the crewman. "We need to go get them."

"There's a broken pipe." The crewman shook his head. "It is dangerous. They must purge the system first."

"Let's get outta here," one of the other tradesmen said, in a disgusted tone. "It stinks, and I don't give a crap if this stupid job gets finished or not." He turned and pushed his way out, followed by two others.

Dar heard a hammering down the hall. "Okay, look."

"You must leave, now," the crewman told her brusquely.

The hammering got louder. Dar stepped up to the crewman and tipped her head down slightly, glaring at him. "Mister, I am going down that hallway. You can move aside, or I can go through you. Your choice."

The man stared at her. "What?"

Dar took a step even closer. "Move," she barked. "Now!"

"You cannot—"

Dar shoved him without hesitation, keeping her motions short and hard. The man stumbled back and looked at her in shock, then exchanged looks with his companion and got out of the way.

"You are crazy! But if you want to go there and get hurt? Fine! Go! It will be your fault!"

Dar strode past him with the techs in tow. As they moved down the hall, the stench grew, and the sound of hissing, escaping air got louder and louder. "Kerry!"

"Over there, ma'am!" One of the techs pointed. "That's the door."

Two others approached it eagerly. "We'll knock it down, Ms. Roberts. Just give us a minute."

Dar paused. "Ker! Get back!" She pointed to the door with utter authority, and shone her flashlight on it. "You two get over there, and keep an eye on that pipe."

"Dar!" Kerry's voice came through the partition.

"Yeah!" Dar yelled back. "Hang on!"

Footsteps sounded coming toward them down the hall. "All right you people. Back off! This is a closed area," an authoritative voice said. They turned to see a uniformed officer heading their way. "Move it!"

"Kiss my ass." Dar challenged him. "I get my people out of here, we'll leave. Not before then. I don't care how much crap's going to come out of that pipe."

"You listen to me!" The man came up to them. "I'm the staff captain of this vessel!"

"And I'm the chief information officer of this company." Dar growled right back. "I could buy you and this whole piece of crap shrimp boat for petty cash, so take your stripes and your attitude and beat it, pinhead! "She looked at the two techs. "Do it!"

"You cannot—"

"Watch me!" Dar shot back.

"One...two..." The two techs turned their shoulders to the door.

The staff captain clenched his fists and glared.

Dar glared right back at him.

"You..." He started.

"Am in charge here." Dar completed the sentence.

"Paladar Katherine Roberts, you better not be out there in that damned sewage with your foot!" Kerry yelled at the top of her voice, nearly making the door metal rattle.

The techs all looked at Dar as a momentary silence fell.

Dar cleared her throat. "Do it," she instructed the techs. "Before I get my ass in real trouble."

The techs charged the door without any further hesitation slamming into the panel and crashing it inward. They stumbled inside as it opened easier than they expected, and there was a jumble of moving bodies in two flashlight streams.

A low rumble started up to their right, as the techs stumbled out of the closet and into the hallway, Kerry squished among them.

"You must get out of here. Now." The officer's voice was now more urgent than angry. "Please!"

Dar grabbed hold of Kerry's arm, and she ducked from behind a tall, sweating body. "Hey." She checked her over as best she could in the very dim light. "You alright?"

"Hey. Dar, are you crazy!" Kerry started tugging at her. "You gotta get out of here before you get sick!"

"Let's all get out of here." Dar pointed down the hall. "C'mon!"

The rumble grew abruptly into a roar, and out of pure instinct Dar grabbed Kerry and slammed her against the wall just as a blast of hot, fetid air and worse came down the passage, splatting full into the staff captain and knocking him back against the far bulkhead.

Then the hiss disappeared and silence descended.

"Oh, Jesu." One of the techs nearly threw up.

"Oh. Gross." Kerry muttered. "This is about the most disgusting..."

"Yeah." Dar inched toward the light, staying as far away from the sodden staff captain as she could. "It sure is."

"Ug, ug, ug." Kerry stifled a gag. "Dar, I'm gonna lose it."

Jaws clamped shut, Dar merely nodded, and nudged her faster. "Walk." She got out from between clenched teeth. Ahead of them, the hallway was blocked by a lot of bodies, men in jumpsuits yelling in a Nordic language.

A bell started to ring. The crowd of jump suited men shoved past them, ignoring everything in their haste to get down the corridor, carrying tool boxes and thick hoses.

"What happened to you?" One asked the staff captain. "Ah, you got shot, eh? Should be used to it."

"Oooohh," Kerry uttered under her breath. "Get me outta here." She squeezed past the men and got to the stairs, where the air was no cleaner. "Dar, I'm losing it."

"Hang on..." Dar got an arm around her, ignoring her own rebelling stomach. "Over here." She moved to the far end of the stairs, bypassing the men running up past them, all in ship jumpsuits. "How's your foot? Did you get it in that...um..."

"I have no idea." Dar steered her down another flight of steps. "Let's wait till we get outside...hey." The sharp scent of blood reached her nose. "Did you get hurt?"

Kerry held up a clenched fist. "Cut. Nothing major."

They reached the main deck landing and headed for the doors, getting outside just as all the power inside was cut, and the ship was plunged into darkness behind them.

"Ugh." Kerry went right to the railing and hung over it, willing a breeze to come up from the southwest and not from behind her. Her stomach was twisting in knots, the smell from inside the ship still in her lungs, and clinging to her clothing.

She closed her eyes.

"Let me see." Dar took her hand and gently opened it, studying the slice on her palm. "Ouch."

It wasn't working. "Dar," Kerry whispered. "I'm going to throw up."

"Aim down." Dar circled her wrist with gentle fingers and pressed against the inside of it.

Kerry opened one eye, to see the waters of Government Cut far below her. "Down?"

"Down."

Kerry watched the wavelets ripple past the ship, bumping into the hull. A bird flew lazily past, and then unexpectedly, plunged into the water after a fish.

She took a breath, then a second, filled with clean salty air, and felt the nausea subside. She released a breath, and looked over at Dar. "I think I'm okay." She took another few lungfuls of air, then glanced down at the deck, to study her partner's exposed feet.

The sandals were covered, almost up to the edge of the bottom, with an oily brown guck, but Dar's tanned skin was unmarked. Kerry's shoulders relaxed a little. "You escaped the crap monster."

Dar looked down. "Oh. Yeah," she murmured. "So I did." She turned Kerry around and examined her carefully. "So did you." She noted. "Except...er..." She glanced at a long, dark stain down the side of one leg.

"New rack crud." Kerry sighed. "I had to climb out of it."

Dar frowned.

"In the dark, in a room with roaches flying all around, and poop flowing on the floor. Dar that was not covered in my infrastructure classes." Kerry leaned against the railing, exhausted. "But at least we got the damn thing in."

Dar turned and leaned as well, looking back at the ship. Contractors were pouring out of it and heading for the upper gangway shaking their heads, while inside, bells were still ringing and alarms going off. "One down," she agreed with a sigh. "Seven to go."

It wasn't a very auspicious start.

KERRY LEFT HER boots outside the terminal, and in fact, crossed through it and out the front door heading for the Lexus. She remembered they had spare clothing in the back, and she fully intended on changing into it to get rid of the sewer scent she was convinced still clung to her shirt.

As she crossed to the parking lot, a small pickup swerved toward her and pulled up alongside. "Hi." Ceci waved, tipping her sunglasses down. "How's it going?"

Kerry walked over and leaned against the doorjamb. "You really want to know?"

Her mother in law grimaced. "Andy called me. Said they got thrown out of the boat while some repairs were on. I brought him some lunch," she said. "Tough day?"

"Ugh. Yes." Kerry agreed. "We're so behind schedule now, and we don't know when they're going to let us back on the ship."

Ceci leaned on the seat back. "Kerry, can I ask you a question?"

Hmm. "Sure."

"You and Dar, you're corporate officers."

"Yes." Kerry nodded.

"Maybe it's different here in Miami, but where I come from corporate officers don't do what you're doing." Ceci said bluntly. "They manage."

"I know."

"So?"

Kerry let her hands rest on the window frame, feeling the heat of the metal sting her cut hand. "Usually we do manage," she admitted. "Usually, someone else does this, but this job—Alastair asked Dar to handle it personally."

"Ah."

"There's a lot behind it," Kerry explained. "So here we are."

"We."

Kerry smiled.

Ceci reached over and patted her hand. "Good luck," she said. "How's Dar doing?"

How was Dar doing? Kerry thought back to the last sight she'd had of her partner, pacing back and forth in the terminal unable to do anything constructive. "She's a little freaked out because of the wait."

Ceci chuckled. "That's nothing new." She advised Kerry. "She absolutely positively hates waiting for anything."

Hmm. True and that reminded Kerry. "I know, in fact, maybe lunch is a good idea. I'll get her out of here for an hour or so until they reopen the ship." She tapped the window. "Thanks for the idea!"

Ceci pushed her sunglasses down and waved waiting for Kerry to step back before she continued driving out of the parking lot.

Lunch. Kerry continued over to the Lexus and keyed the lock open. She pulled the back door latch and peered inside, snagging her gym bag and tugging it over. "Let's see what we've got here." She unzipped it and rummaged through its contents.

"Okay, good." A pair of jeans landed on the seat, shortly followed by a shirt. She tended to keep changes of clothing for after work, as did Dar, since neither really wanted to get back into business clothing after working out.

Kerry reviewed her options, and fingered the shirt, which was a sleeveless muscle T. "Hmm. Not quite the image I was looking to project." She peered at the jeans. "And these are reeeally old ones, but at least it's clean." She pushed the jeans and shirt back in the bag, which already held her sneakers. Then she dug in the back of the car to see if she had anything for Dar stowed away anywhere.

"Hmm." She pulled out a few neatly folded bits of cotton. Workout shorts and a sports bra. "Much as I'd personally love her to change into this, I don't think it's going to work." Kerry regretfully put the items back, and shouldered her gym bag. Maybe, she considered, they could grab something at the mall when they went for lunch.

With that cheerful thought, she closed and locked the door and headed back for the terminal. Halfway back, she paused to let traffic go by, appreciating the intense light of the sun and the stiff ocean breeze. Being locked in the dark, with the bugs and the stench in that place had been hellacious, and for a moment she'd gained an understanding of Dar's aversion to closed in places.

It had gotten a little freaky in there, with her techs panicking a little, and the sound of those pipes so close. Hearing Dar's voice had been...

She ran her hands through her hair. She really wasn't the type of person who freaked out easily, Kerry knew. She'd handled some intense situations in the past few years, from being locked up in a damn psycho ward, to being trapped inside a burning hospital, to jumping in the raging ocean.

She was cool with it. But being in a dark room with roaches and crap? Kerry shuddered. That had freaked her out completely, and just when she'd been at the point where she'd started to tear at the door with her fingernails, there had been Dar's voice.

Instant no-freak.

Sweetest sound in the world. Kerry ran her fingers through her hair again, and shifted her shoulders, feeling the sun warm her skin. It had made her nuts to think of Dar standing out there in sewage, and that reminded her to get their shoes rinsed off.

Preferably by a firehose spouting industrial disinfectant.

Kerry proceeded across the road and trotted up the steps to the terminal. She entered the building and headed right to the restrooms, ducking inside the women's room. She was not surprised to find it empty. One thing about being in IT—you generally didn't have to wait on the bathroom if you were female.

Certainly, it was better than it was in the past, but still, she and Dar were in the vast minority in the building.

Kerry entered the handicapped stall and hung her workout bag on the hook, shedding her jeans and shirt and tossing them over the door. Briefly, she wished she could shower as well, but after a cautious sniff at the skin on her arm, decided a change would have to be good enough.

Rooting in the bag, she found fresh underclothes as well, and traded off, stuffing the others into a side pocket. "Okay." She removed the jeans from her bag and pulled them on, leaving the buttons unbuttoned. She then pulled the shirt over her head and tucked it in, fastening the jeans over it.

The waistband was a little loose, which surprised her. She dug in the bag, but she hadn't stuck a belt in there. "Hmm..." She turned and faced the mirror, checking the image with critical eyes. She touched her cheek, deciding her face also looked a little thinner than it had been. Was it the stress? Kerry knew they hadn't been exercising more than usual, so probably it was the tension she'd been under lately.

Oh well. She met her own eyes, seeing a wry twinkle there. "Guess I'll have to have an extra milkshake for lunch then." She stuffed her other clothes into the bag and grabbed her sneakers, unlocking the door to the stall and heading back out.

Emerging into the hall, she spotted Dar back at her podium, pecking at her laptop keyboard with one hand while leaning her head on the other. Dar's head lifted as she approached, and the blue eyes turned her way, looking her up and down as a rakish grin appeared.

Kerry set the bag down and leaned on the counter to put her sneakers on. "Something wrong?"

"With you? No," Dar said. "But we've got a big problem, Ker."

Leaving the laces of the first sneaker untied, Kerry straightened. "What's up?"

"They're not going to let anyone back on board for at least twenty four hours," Dar told her. "They've got the EPA in there now. Needs disinfecting before they'll clear us to go back in."

"But...wait." Kerry leaned on the counter. "I thought it was only that one deck?"

"Bacteria," Dar replied succinctly. "Got in the air system, or so they're afraid of."

Kerry closed her eyes. "Oh god." She stifled a reflex cough. "Can we get our lungs fumigated?"

Dar patted her hand. "I think we're okay," she said. "You feel better now?"

Kerry frowned. "Well, yeah, but what are we going to do, Dar? We didn't have enough time to install and test as it was...we lose a whole day. Jesus."

"I know," Dar acknowledged. "Pulling more people won't help."

"No." Kerry exhaled heavily.

The outer door slammed, and they both turned to see Peter Quest enter, spot them, and head in their direction with angry strides.

"Hmm." Kerry took the opportunity to put her other sneaker on, tying the laces as Quest arrived.

"Roberts, I just got out of a meeting with the inspectors," Quest said. "Can you explain to me why they informed me the blockage that caused this entire mess was some of your equipment?"

Dar and Kerry exchanged glances. "My equipment?" Dar pointed at her own chest. "Quest, look around you. My gear's bigger than a breadbox. How in the hell could it have caused a clog anywhere?"

Quest did, indeed, look around. Then he looked back at Dar. "I don't know, they just said it was IT stuff. There's a meeting outside in ten minutes with the ship's officers. I want you to be there, and explain what the hell's going on."

"Do you...um...have the IT stuff?" Kerry interjected. "Might be hard to explain otherwise."

"We have it," Quest said, grimly. "The EPA will be there to show what it was, and you'd better be too. If it turns out this is your fault, you're gonna pay." He turned and walked off, half turning as he did to point at Dar. "Big time."

Kerry stared at his back, and then turned her attention to Dar. "Now what?" She threw her hands up in exasperation. "Dar, I swear, this whole damn job is cursed."

Dar rubbed her temples, giving her head a tiny shake. "Guess you better call John." She sighed. "Since I know it's not our gear, the only thing left is his."

Kerry blew out a breath in a sputter. "So much for lunch." She pulled out her cell phone. "Damn it."

Dar got up. "Can I treat you to a Jamaican patty and a bottle of guava juice?" she asked. "Roach coach just pulled up outside."

Kerry paused. "Hang on, John." She covered the mic. "Dar, don't say roach and lunch in the same sentence to me for the next month, okay?"

Dar patted her on the shoulder, and limped off toward the door.

Damn it.

Chapter Fifteen

THEY MET ON the dockside shortly thereafter. Kerry sucked down the last droplets of her guava juice and dropped the empty container in the garbage outside the terminal door as she followed Dar across the sun bleached concrete.

A semi-circle of people were already out there. She spotted John's tall form and Quest, and several people she didn't know, along with the camera crew, which she did know. They all looked up as Dar and Kerry joined them, the strangers appearing a bit skeptical as they were introduced.

"Well, fine," a tall, thin man with an EPA badge said. "I was hoping...well, anyway. Here is what caused the accident." He held out a cardboard box and opened the flaps. A waft of sewer smell drifted out, and the group cautiously peered inside.

A grayish brown ball covered in gunk rested on the bottom of the box, a tangle of what Kerry identified as shielded cat 5 cable along with a snarl of the white cording that came in it to separate the strands. She looked up at their cable contractor. "John?"

The big man stepped forward and took the box, examining its contents. "Well, it's the stuff we're using, yeah," he admitted. "Looks like crap."

The camera man focused in on him, gaining himself a suspicious glare from the contractor.

"What does that mean?" Quest asked.

John looked at him. "It's ends left over after we finish a run. Got it all over the place the way we've been working," he explained.

"So one of your people did this? Dropped it in a toilet?" Quest asked, sharply.

John snorted. "I doubt it. Coulda been anyone, stuff's all over the place."

"That's true," Kerry agreed quietly, watching the EPA man from the corner of her eye. "That pipe was down the hall from one of our wiring closets, which was open."

"But," the EPA man objected, "It makes no sense for anyone to be carrying it around except for one of your workmen, does it?" He addressed John. "I mean, one of the other contractors would be carrying some of their supplies, tape, or electrical wire, or that sort of thing."

John shrugged. "Why would anyone be hauling a handful of that crap around?" he asked. "But I don't have anyone stupid enough to drop a ball of it in the toilet. Cigarettes, maybe, but not that."

Dar advanced and took the box. She looked at the ball of wire, noting its egg shape, and the tight wrapping around its middle that showed shredding from its travel through the pipes. With a grunt, she handed it back. "Could have been anyone," she said. "Or, who knows? Maybe one of John's guys left it on a sink somewhere and it got knocked into a bowl."

Quest snorted.

The inspector took the box back. He regarded the ball for a moment, then shrugged one shoulder. "That could be," he conceded. "We'd thought maybe someone did it on purpose, but you know, what you just said makes a lot of sense. I can see it."

Dar studiously did not look at the camera. "All those guys are working up there. I can't see someone doing this so they'd get covered in cr...sewage."

"Huh. Damn straight," John said.

Quest sniffed. "Maybe," he grudgingly conceded. "But now what? You're holding up my whole project in there!" He turned his aggressiveness on the EPA inspector. "So it was an accident, like Roberts said. When can we get back in there?"

"Twenty four hours, Mr. Quest. As I told you. Accident or not, you've got bio organisms in there, and they have to be fogged and sanitized. You don't want to get sued for getting people sick, do you?" The EPA man warned.

The camera swiveled to focus on Quest. From the look on his face, he was trapped and he knew it. "Of course not," he said. "But I want to get these guys back in there not a moment past twenty four hours. Can you guarantee me that?"

The camera moved back to the EPA man, who straightened a little. "Ah..."

"Or is it going to be one of those government things, were twenty four hours pass, and you all go out to play golf?" Quest pressed him. "I'm all for safety. I'll put this in your hands, but I need to know you're not going to screw me over for it."

Put on the defensive, the EPA man took a step back. "Well, in general, I suppose we can..."

"No general." Quest insisted. "I need to know. A lot of money's riding on this. You want to be responsible for that?"

"Of course not," the EPA man said. "Very well, we... I will guarantee you can be back inside that vessel after the twenty four hour decontamination process is complete."

"Okay." Quest seemed satisfied, holding his hand out for the man to shake. "We've got a deal then. I'll have these docks cleared."

The EPA men made a quick getaway, escaping the sun as they ducked through the gate and left the pier area.

John turned to Dar and put his hands on his hips. "Well, we lucked out. We'd just finished the last room when they rang the bell." He told her. "So..."

"Good work, John." Kerry congratulated him quietly.

"So what are you going to do, Roberts?" Quest interrupted. "I can't change the deadline." He turned and looked at the ship. "This thing'll never be ready."

Privately, Dar agreed completely. But she was aware of the focus on her, as the round camera eye swept across them. "Well, Peter I can't speak for your other contractors here, but my view is, we'll wait for the ban to be lifted, and do the best we can."

"Hmph." Quest made a grunting noise.

"We've gone to the wall on this project, and I'm not ready to drop it now," Dar continued. "If we run out of time, we run out of time, but we're going to be in there until the clock goes off."

Kerry folded her arms, content to let her partner shine in the artificial halogen spotlight.

"Bad luck," the cameraman commented quietly.

"Just another in a long series of challenges." Dar gave him a brisk nod. "Excuse us. We're going to see about securing the gear in there." She touched Kerry on the shoulder and turned to head back toward the terminal. John followed, and behind them they heard Quest and his entourage trooping back off down the pier.

Dar opened the door for them. "Jesus."

"That man figured to nail us with that thing, Dar!" John griped, as he passed in front of her, followed by Kerry. "All my guys in there busting their tails and I get that?"

Dar entered behind them. "John." She paused, waiting for him to turn. "Did you take a good look at that wire plug?" she asked. "That wasn't a bunch of scrap. That was tied up to be a bundle like that."

Kerry leaned on the wall with one hand. "What are you saying, Dar?"

Puzzled, John nodded his head. "Yeah. What are you saying? Someone did it on purpose after all?"

Dar glanced around, noting the techs still moving about the room. She waved them over toward the back corner, and waited for them to follow her. "After everything we've had to go through on this, I find it very hard to believe something like this happened naturally." She stated as they reached the back wall. "John, I'm not saying for a second it was one of your guys, but I don't think it dropped off a sink either. Can you ask all of them if they might have left a ball of the damn stuff anywhere?"

The contractor scrubbed his jaw, then nodded. "Sure, Dar. I'll ask 'em, but we were out of that area since eight a.m. Doubt any of 'em would remember. Some of the guys have gone home already, but I'll see what I can do."

Kerry blinked. "None of your guys were up there recently?"

"No." John shook his head positively. "My super keeps a close eye on 'em. Nice guys, good wire pullers, but they're lazier than hound dogs in summer most of the time."

"Huh." Kerry nibbled on the inside of her lip. "Someone wearing your company shirt was in that wiring closet when we got there."

Dar folded her arms and leaned against the wall, her head nodding slightly.

"Yeah?" John sounded honestly surprised.

"He was in there. We surprised him when we came in," Kerry said. "He was kinda rude," she added. "I made a mental note to talk to you about it. He was a tall guy, with brown hair, kind of curly, and he hadn't shaved recently."

John exhaled. "Could be half of 'em," he admitted. "Okay, let me gather 'em up and talk to 'em. See if any of 'em remember seeing you. I won't say why," he said. "Still doesn't mean he did anything."

"No, of course not," Kerry agreed. "But maybe he can confirm how the wire got near those pipes."

John grunted and nodded, then turned and walked across the room, heading for the front doors.

Kerry leaned against the wall next to Dar. "You really think it was on purpose?"

Dar nodded. "Yeah. Scraps are one thing, but that was wrapped so that it would fit down the pipe." She leaned against Kerry's shoulder. "It's just too coincidental, Ker."

Was it? Kerry pondered. "Or are we just getting paranoid?"

Dar studied the far wall briefly, then chuckled. "Just because I'm paranoid doesn't mean they're not out to get us." She pushed herself upright and laid an arm over Kerry's shoulders. "C'mon. Let's go sit down and figure out where we go from here now that we lost an entire day from our schedule."

Kerry circled Dar's waist with her arm as they walked, both of them slowing as they spotted their erstwhile friend reporter Cruicshank near the door, complete with a few of her camera people. "Oh, poot."

The reporter came forward. "Hello, ladies," she greeted them. "Now that the stakes have risen again, care to share a few words with me?"

Aware of the camera's red light turning on and focusing on them, Dar didn't so much as twitch, or remove her arm from Kerry's shoulders. "Sure," she replied amiably. "We've got plenty of time right now."

The television light turned on, framing them in silver. In the shadows beyond them, the techs paused, gathering to watch curiously as the reporter closed in, and opened her note pad. "Great. Tom, give me about sixty seconds, and then roll, all right?"

"Right."

Dar noticed the Herald reporter arriving too, taking a seat on one of the folding tables back out of the way and just watching.

One dark eyebrow curved up, and Dar's brow puckered in thought.

"All right, Ms. Roberts." Cruicshank began. "Now we have a

situation where all of a sudden, you're the underdogs. How does that make you feel?"

Dar exchanged looks with Kerry. Then she looked back at the camera. "I'm not sure we haven't always been the underdog in this," she commented with an easy smile. "Are you?"

Cruicshank looked up from her pad, pausing for a reflective moment. "Interesting question."

"Isn't it?" Kerry murmured.

"OKAY, SO NOW WHAT?" Kerry sat on a desk, swinging her feet a little. It was late afternoon, and the chaos had finally settled down. Cruicshank had left, the reporter had left, and she and Dar were alone in the small office.

Dar was lying on her back on the spare desk against the wall. "Let's take everyone out to dinner," she replied, her eyes closed. "Do some team building for the hell it's going to be from tomorrow on."

Kerry studied her denim covered knees. "Okay," she said." Someplace around here? Hard Rock, maybe? Or Bubba Gumps?"

"Hooters."

"Dar."

A blue eye opened. "Too politically incorrect, huh?"

"It's one thing for us to go to lunch there," Kerry said. "But taking the staff? Hon, there's two or three women in the team out there. How comfortable would that be for them?"

"Mmph." Dar grunted. "Yeah, I get you. Call Hard Rock. See if they have that side room available. What do we have, thirty?" Privately she doubted anyone on their staff would really mind, or kick up a fuss, but you never knew with people.

It didn't pay to take a chance, and she was a little abashed that Kerry had found it necessary to remind her of that. "Sorry. I was just in the mood for chicken wings," she added sheepishly.

"And a nice cold draft beer, yeah. But I'm sure we can get that somewhere else." Kerry got up and sat down in the desk chair instead, calling up a browser. She typed the restaurant's site in and got back a list of addresses, from which she selected the Bayside one.

Pulling out her cell phone, she dialed the number. "Did you say thirty?" She paused and held her hand over the mic. "With us?"

"Yeah." Dar nodded. "Twenty nine, something like that. Just say thirty."

"Gotcha." Kerry cleared her throat gently. "Hello, I'd like to speak to someone who can help me with a group reservation." She listened. "For thirty people." Listened again. "That's what I thought. I'll hold. Thanks."

Outside, their team was still getting gear ready for installation, soft clanks and thunks audible along with a low buzz of casual chatter.

Despite the problems with the ship, the atmosphere was one of efficient industry, and walking through the crowd Dar hadn't heard any griping at all.

Nice. Dar waited to hear Kerry say the words "You do? Okay. I'd like to reserve it." Sticking her head out, Dar observed the activity, then she sauntered out into the center of the large room and stood there, putting her hands on her hips.

She didn't need to say anything. One by one, the techs all stopped what they were doing and focused on her, the chatter in the room subsiding to nothing in about thirty seconds. Dar waited a few seconds more, then cleared her throat. "All right folks. You know what the story is. We're dead in the water until tomorrow, and then we're way behind the eight ball."

Thirty sets of eyes were pinned on her. "Better we bust our ass tomorrow than have to hang out in there today," Mark commented. "Man that stunk."

The two techs who'd been with Kerry nodded their heads vigorously. "Yeah, and working in the dark, that sucked too!"

Dar waited until silence fell again, then she resumed speaking. "It's going to be a tough couple of days. There'll be company support there while we're doing it, but before we start, I'd like you all to come over to the Hard Rock and be our guest for dinner tonight."

She could feel the shock in the room, as she flicked her eyes over the faces and caught the reactions. Surprise, certainly, and then muted delight. Dar smiled at them. "So get this stuff locked down, and we'll head on over. Okay?"

"Yes ma'am," Mark responded quickly. "You don't need to ask us twice...right guys?"

"Yeah."

"Heck yeah."

"For sure!"

Satisfied, Dar lifted her hand in acknowledgement and then walked back toward the office. She discovered Kerry inside, sprawled in the desk chair, spinning it idly. "We all set?"

"Uh huh." Kerry agreed. "We got the back room, and they're throwing in dessert free as long as everyone orders an entrée."

"No problem." Dar caught the back of the chair and stopped her partner's revolutions. "Not with this bunch. They're not the ice tea and carrot appetizer crowd."

Kerry gazed up at her with a wry expression. "Dar, I used to be one of the ice tea and carrot appetizer crowd."

"Nah." Dar looked fondly down at her. "You were a poser."

"A poser?"

"A poser." Dar leaned on the chair back. "I knew that the first time we had dinner together."

Kerry's face crinkled up into a grin. "Rats. Outed by a slab of cheesecake and a chicken wing."

Dar gently scratched the top of Kerry's head with her fingertips. "Did you check with the office? Everything calm there?"

Kerry gave the trackball on the desk a roll, exposing her email inbox when the screen saver cleared. "Couple of things. Three of those leads we got out of your hacker challenge turned into requests for pricing." She pointed. "Not really huge accounts but look...this one's in an area we haven't been involved in yet."

"Hmm." Dar studied the screen.

"I'm assigning someone to put together a design," Kerry said. "And I got a note from our friends in New York..." She clicked over. "They're opening another office in Hong Kong. They want pricing for infrastructure."

"Yeah?" Dar sounded quite surprised. "You got a note from Meyer?"

Kerry cocked her head. "Um...no, matter of fact. Hang on. "She rolled back a page. "Here...new name. Ellen Durst. Maybe he got an assistant?" She scrolled through the message until she reached the signature line. "Oh. No, I guess she's the VP now."

"Huh." Dar sniffed. "Hope Stewart didn't get booted. We're in deep kimchee if he did."

"Would she be asking us for pricing if Meyer took his place?"

Dar perched on the desk, getting her weight off her injured foot. "We're their current vendor." She mused. "So stands to reason... I don't know, let's find out." She pulled out her cell phone and dialed a number. "Hi. Stewart Godson, please."

Kerry leaned an elbow on the desk and watched Dar's face as she waited. She put her other hand on her partner's knee, rubbing gently in a circle with her thumb. It would be chilly in the restaurant, she suddenly remembered. They'd have to stop and get Dar something with more sleeves.

"Yes, thanks. It's Dar Roberts, from ILS." Dar supplied the secretary who intercepted the call. Now, either she'd be put off, or...

"One moment, ma'am, I'll put you right through." The secretary came back on the line, then bland hold music replaced her for a second, before a click sounded and a voice came through.

"Hello, there, Dar!"

Dar exhaled in relief. "Afternoon, Stewart." She glanced at Kerry, who gave her a thumbs up.

"What do I owe the pleasure of a call to?" Godson asked. "I was about to close up shop here and get on home. Don't tell me we've got problems!"

"No, no, not at all," Dar reassured him. "I just..." She hesitated. "Just was wondering how things were doing, with your program. It's been a week, now."

"Oh!" Godson cleared his throat, and apparently sat back in his chair based on the squeaks coming through the phone. "Everything's great! You have no idea how happy everyone is. It's been wonderful. First week in a month I've been able to get anything done without getting a phone call every ten minutes complaining," he said. "So rest assured, everything looks great from this end. How's it with you?"

Dar blinked. "Me? Oh, it's just been a typical week here, you know, Stewart," she replied. "Usual problems, usual weather...the odd pile of crap hitting the...um...fan." A smile appeared, as she watched Kerry first cover her eyes, then throw the back of her arm across them in a very theatrical gesture. "Glad things are going well. Listen, Kerry tells me you're putting in a new office in the Far East?"

"Yep." Godson sounded very, very smug. "Business has increased so much, partially due to my new system I might add, that we're branching out. Good stuff huh? Oh!" He ended the sentence with an exclamation. "Hey! You remember that guy of mine, Jason?"

Ah. "Sure." Dar drawled.

"You know that fella up and left last Friday? No notice at all, just picked up his papers and walked out. Said he had a better offer. What do you know? You were right! Shoulda listened to you right then, Dar!"

Kerry's eyes widened and she leaned forward a little as she listened. "Holy pooters!" She mouthed.

"Ahhh...yeah, he was a stinker," Dar remarked, her eyebrows hiked up to her hairline. "Any idea where he went? Not that I care."

"Nah." Godson said. "Didn't ask, he didn't tell, good riddance! I took a page from your book and decided maybe a gal would work better for me in there, and you know, it's been a week but Ellen's just been crackerjack. Good people! Matter of fact, can't wait for her to meet you. We were talking about you just yesterday."

Dar relaxed, one nagging problem taken off her conscience. "Well, that's good to hear, Stewart. Glad you got someone in there who we can work with. I wasn't looking forward to renegotiating our contract with Mr. Meyer. Hope whoever he went to work for fully appreciates...his...ah...style."

Godson chuckled. "Ellen's sharp, and would you know? She's a fan of yours. So you've got no worries, right? Anyhoo, time for me to head off to the little missus. Anything else you need to talk about, Dar?"

"Nope, just checking in. We'll get you those prices by end of the week, Stewart. Good luck on the new space, and congratulations."

"Thanks!" Godson replied. "Life's good! Take care, Dar! Give Ms. Stuart my hellos too, willya? Bye!"

Dar folded the phone up and tossed it, reversing her hand and grabbing it out of mid air as it fell. "Well, that's good news," she said. "I really thought we were going to get bit in the ass by my cantankerousness this time. Guess we got lucky."

Kerry patted her on the leg. "We have to sometimes." She got up, leaning over to log out of the computer. "Wonder where that little bugger went? Hope it's not to another of our customers."

Dar shrugged, getting up off the desk and waiting as Kerry turned the PC off. "I'll do a search later and see if he joined another public company." She put her hand on her partner's back as they walked out of the office, flipping the lights and closing the door behind them.

KERRY PUT HER MUG down and leaned back, chuckling a little at Mark's joke from across the table. She was on her second beer, and her plate held the scattered remnants of a relatively decent rack of spare ribs. Dar was sprawled in the chair next to her, long legs extended under the table as she nodded in agreement to what Mark was saying.

"I remember that," Dar said. "The entire building was overrun by red ants, and everyone ended up sitting on top of the network racks to get away from them." She reminisced. "Damned glad I missed that one."

Everyone chuckled.

"Yeah, you'd just gotten kicked upstairs," Mark said. "We sure missed you."

Kerry watched her partner from the corner of her eye, seeing the look of muted glee appear in her eyes, as her lips twitched into a grin. "I bet you did." She leaned on her chair arm. "There's nothing as comforting to have on a tough project as this thing." She indicated Dar with her thumb. "I can attest to that."

"Thing?" Dar leaned on her own chair arm and gave Kerry a raised eyebrow look.

"Ms. Roberts?" One of the techs spoke up shyly. "Is it true the fellow in charge on the boat is your father?"

Dar tore her attention from her partner, and picked up her glass of wine for a sip. "It's true," she said. "Some of you guys have met him before."

"Absolutely," Mark agreed. "He's a great guy, and he tells the funniest st—"

Dar looked at him.

"Stories about boats." Mark redirected his speech. "Really funny."

Nervous grins all around. "I think some of those contractors are scared of him," the first tech commented. "I heard them talking about him when they were out in back of the building using the pay phones."

Dar felt a little uncertain, unused to talking about her family in front of her staff. "Well, he doesn't take much crap."

"Gee." Mark took a swallow of his beer. "Wonder who that sounds like."

The tableful of techs chuckled again, this time a little less nervously when Dar joined in, lifting a hand in silent self deprecation. "Yeah, I come by it honestly," she assented. "But he's also retired Navy...he was a SEAL...that takes it to a different level sometimes."

"A SEAL?" One of the techs whistled. "Wow."

"That's pretty cool," another said. "I was in for six years. Those guys are tough."

"I was helping check off those switches that came in yesterday," one of the female techs spoke up shyly. "I was a little creeped out with those guys in there. They were making all kinds of comments, but then he came into the loading area and shut them all up." She looked over at Dar. "That was really cool."

Dar smiled.

"Dad's got a lot of old fashioned chivalry in him," Kerry spoke up. "One of those guys who's totally not embarrassed to open doors for women, or give them seats on a bus, you know?"

The men all looked a little embarrassed, themselves. "I, um..." The tech next to Mark cleared his throat. "Don't think girls like that stuff anymore. It's like, chauvinism, isn't it?"

Everyone looked at Kerry, to see what her answer would be. She took a sip of her beer, giving herself a moment to think about it. "Hmm." She pondered the complex ideas behind the question. "Opening a door for someone really isn't anything but a courtesy. I think—"

"I open doors for you," Dar commented.

"I think it depends how you were brought up," the woman tech spoke up suddenly. "It's like your parents teach you one way or the other. My mother was a big time radical feminist, and she always said it was condescending when men treated her like that."

"Yeah, my mom said the same thing," Mark agreed. "You open a door for her and she'd slam it in your face."

Everyone chuckled. "Well, I come from a very traditional family," Kerry said. "Though I think my father would have paid someone to be chivalrous for him if he could have gotten away with it. We were always treated like ladies, and let me tell you...it gave me a hive."

Everyone peeked at Dar next. "My mother's a pagan," She supplied agreeably.

Silence. Everyone looked at Dar in surprise, except Kerry. "Well, she is." Dar shrugged. "She's about as nontraditional as you can get, but she loves it when my dad does stuff like that for her."

"Really?" Mark asked.

"Yeah." Dar drained her wine glass and set it on the table. "But then, my dad doesn't do it for show. It's just how he is."

"And just how you are." Kerry gave her partner a fond look. "Daddy's girl."

Dar blushed slightly, almost invisibly in the reddish lamplight. Her eyebrows twitched, and she glanced at the rest of the table before looking back at Kerry.

"Well, my old man didn't give me anything but a hairy back." Mark broke the silence, drawing attention back to himself. "And probably a bum ticker," he added. "So it's a crap shoot, but like, you really can't win because if you do nice stuff like that, you got a fifty-fifty shot at best that the girl likes it, you know?"

Two of the guy techs nodded. "Yeah," one said. "My girlfriend is like this independent chick, yeah? She's pre-law, works in a woman lawyer's office, pro abortion, all that stuff, and I find out last week she really wants to get married, stop working, and have kids."

"Oh, god." The taller, blond female tech covered her eyes. "My husband hinted to me last night he'd like to have kids."

"So let him, Barb," Dar drawled. "He can stay home and take care of 'em."

Everyone laughed. Barb leaned forward, resting an elbow on the table. "That's really something women in our industry have to deal with that you guys don't," she said. "I've been turned down for jobs because I might start breeding. You know, that sucks. If you're a guy, that doesn't happen."

"Hey, we breed." Mark protested. "I've had to give plenty of guys' time off to go take care of their kids."

"Three months?" Barb asked him.

"Well..."

"It's hard enough to keep even in this business as it is, being female," Barb said. "Nobody thinks women belong in technical fields, even today." Her eyes tracked briefly to Dar and Kerry. "I have to tell you, you guys were the reason I even applied here."

"We take flack," Kerry responded quietly. "There are a lot of people out there that don't think Dar and I should be doing what we're doing, and it takes a lot more effort than you think to get past that."

Mark looked between them. "You guys are making me feel like a jerk, just because I got a Y in the big ol' chromo-dice throw." He protested. "Hey, it's not our fault! I hire most of the women who apply. They are just really, really few and far between!"

Barb leaned back, and nodded. "Mark, I know that. You should see the looks I get from other women when I tell them what I do. You'd think I was telling them I was a car mechanic."

Dar chuckled wryly. "Well, given what my other choice of profession was, my family is very glad I picked this one," she said. "But I'd have made a lousy sailor anyway."

Mark leaned back. "No offense, DR, but that would have been a big waste of brain cells."

"Yeah," Barb agreed. "That's for sure."

Dar shrugged modestly.

Someone approached, and cleared their throat gently. Dar looked up to see their reporter friend Elecia standing there, hands behind her back and a diffident expression on her face. "Ah. Evening."

"Hi," the woman said. "I know you probably think I'm stalking you all, but I happened to be having dinner over there." She pointed to a corner of the restaurant. "Mind if I ask your group here a few questions?"

Dar studied her briefly, then shrugged and turned back to the table. "You guys mind talking to a reporter?"

Various reactions, ranging from wariness to outright alarm faced her.

"Hey, relax." The reporter chuckled. "I'm from the Herald, not Panic Seven," she said. "I'm doing a story on the work you all are doing at the pier, and I just had a few questions about some of the things you were talking about."

Kerry still had her doubts. She knew Dar respected the woman, but after their experiences of the past few weeks, no reporter seemed trustworthy to her, if any ever had. "You know, Ms Rodriguez, these folks have worked really hard the past few days, and they're going to have to work even harder in the next few. Is it really fair to disturb them during a moment of peace, here?"

Rodriguez studied her. "You know what being a reporter is like, Ms. Stuart," she responded conversationally. "It's like being addicted to everything. You never have enough. You always want more, more, more...every question brings up another question."

Kerry merely waited, giving the woman her best incomprehensible stare.

The reporter looked at Dar, who folded her hands over her stomach and refrained from comment. Then Rodriguez shrugged. "No, it's not fair, and my husband's going to kick my ass since it's the first time I've seen him all week." She turned to the table. "Some other time, ladies and gents. Good luck, by the way."

With that, she turned and left, walking down the small flight of steps and sliding into a half hidden banquette table near the window.

Everyone was silent for a few moments, then Carlos, who'd been in the closet with her that day, cleared his throat a little. "Thanks, Kerry," he murmured. "This whole news and filming stuff is kinda getting old."

"Tell me about it." Kerry sympathized. "We've had these people in our faces for weeks." She glanced after the reporter, then looked at Dar. "You want to go talk to her?"

"Nope." Dar seemed content to stay right where she was. "I hear a hot brownie sundae calling my name." She tapped her thumbs against each other, and looked around the table. "Anyone else interested?"

The atmosphere relaxed, and everyone leaned back, sharing dessert menus as the serving staff cleared the table of their dinner plates. Kerry waited for the buzz of conversation to rise, and then she leaned closer to Dar. "Was that a mistake?"

Pale blue eyes turned her way, warmed from within as they met hers. "For them? No," Dar answered.

"For us?" Kerry persisted.

Dar shrugged. "Nah."

Kerry frowned. Dar reached over and smoothed the furrow in her brow with her thumb, then she ruffled Kerry's hair.

Oh well. Kerry silently exhaled. Just another pass of the dice.

To be continued...

OTHER MELISSA GOOD TITLES

Tropical Storm

From bestselling author Melissa Good comes a tale of heartache, longing, family strife, lust for love, and redemption. *Tropical Storm* took the lesbian reading world by storm when it was first written...now read this exciting revised "author's cut" edition.

Dar Roberts, corporate raider for a multi-national tech company is cold, practical, and merciless. She does her job with a razor-sharp accuracy. Friends are a luxury she cannot allow herself, and love is something she knows she'll never attain.

Kerry Stuart left Michigan for Florida in an attempt to get away from her domineering politician father and the constraints of the overly conservative life her family forced upon her. After college she worked her way into supervision at a small tech company, only to have it taken over by Dar Roberts' organization. Her association with Dar begins in disbelief, hatred, and disappointment, but when Dar unexpectedly hires Kerry as her work assistant, the dynamics of their relationship change. Over time, a bond begins to form.

But can Dar overcome years of habit and conditioning to open herself up to the uncertainty of love? And will Kerry escape from the clutches of her powerful father in order to live a better life?

ISBN 978-1-932300-60-4

Hurricane Watch

In this sequel to "Tropical Storm," Dar and Kerry are back and making their relationship permanent. But an ambitious new colleague threatens to divide them --- and out them. He wants Dar's head and her job, and he's willing to use Kerry to do it. Can their home life survive the office power play?

Dar and Kerry are redefining themselves and their priorities to build a life and a family together. But with the scheming colleagues and old flames trying to drive them apart and bring them down, the two women must overcome fear, prejudice, and their own pasts to protect the company and each other. Does their relationship have enough trust to survive the storm?

Enter the lives of two captivating characters and their world that Melissa Good's thousands of fans already know and love. Your heart will be touched by the poignant realism of the story. Your senses and emotions will be electrified by the intensity of their problems. You will care about these characters before you get very far into the story.

ISBN 978-1-935053-00

Eye of the Storm

Eye of the Storm picks up the story of Dar Roberts and Kerry Stuart a few months after Hurricane Watch ends. At first it looks like they are settling into their lives together but, as readers of this series have learned, life is never simple around Dar and Kerry. Surrounded by endless corporate intrigue, Dar experiences personal discoveries that force her to deal with issues that she had buried long ago and Kerry finally faces the consequences of her own actions. As always, they help each other through these personal challenges that, in the end, strengthen them as individuals and as a couple.

ISBN 978-1-932300-13-0

Red Sky At Morning

A connection others don't understand...

A love that won't be denied...

Danger they can sense but cannot see...

Dar Roberts was always ruthless and single-minded...until she met Kerry Stuart.

Kerry was oppressed by her family's wealth and politics. But Dar saved her from that.

Now new dangers confront them from all sides. While traveling to Chicago, Kerry's plane is struck by lightning. Dar, in New York for a stockholders' meeting, senses Kerry is in trouble. They simultaneously experience feelings that are new, sensations that both are reluctant to admit when they are finally back together. Back in Miami, a cover-up of the worst kind, problems with the military, and unexpected betrayals will cause more danger. Can Kerry help as Dar has to examine her life and loyalties and call into question all she's believed in since childhood? Will their relationship deepen through it all? Or will it be destroyed?

ISBN 978-1-932300-80-2

Thicker Than Water

This fifth entry in the continuing saga of Dar Roberts and Kerry Stuart starts off with Kerry involved in mentoring a church group of girls. Kerry is forced to acknowledge her own feelings toward and experiences with her own parents as she and Dar assist a teenager from the group who gets jailed because her parents tossed her out onto the streets when they found out she is gay. While trying to help the teenagers adjust to real world situations, Kerry gets a call concerning her father's health. Kerry flies to her family's side as her father dies, putting the family in crisis. Caught up in an international problem, Dar abandons the issue to go to Michigan, determined to support Kerry in the face of grief and hatred. Dar and Kerry face down Kerry's extended family with a little help from their own, and return home, where they decide to leave work and the world behind for a while for some time to themselves.

ISBN 978-1-932300-24-6

Terrors of the High Seas

After the stress of a long Navy project and Kerry's father's death, Dar and Kerry decide to take their first long vacation together. A cruise in the eastern Caribbean is just the nice, peaceful time they need — until they get involved in a family feud, an old murder, and come face to face with pirates as their vacation turns into a race to find the key to a decades old puzzle.

ISBN 978-1-932300-45-1

Tropical Convergence

There's trouble on the horizon for ILS when a rival challenges them head on, and their best weapons, Dar and Kerry, are distracted by life instead of focusing on the business. Add to that an old flame, and an aggressive entreprenaur throwing down the gauntlet and Dar at least is ready to throw in the towel. Is Kerry ready to follow suit, or will she decide to step out from behind Dar's shadow and step up to the challenges they both face?

ISBN 978-1-935053-18-7

Storm Surge

It's fall. Dar and Kerry are traveling — Dar overseas to clinch a deal with their new ship owner partners in England, and Kerry on a reluctant visit home for her high school reunion. In the midst of corporate deals and personal conflict, their world goes unexpectedly out of control when an early morning spurt of unusual alarms turns out to be the beginning of a shocking nightmare neither expected. Can they win the race against time to save their company and themselves?

Book One: ISBN 978-1-935053-28-6
Book Two: ISBN 978-1-935053-39-2

Coming Next from Melissa Good

Partners

After a massive volcanic eruption puts earth into nuclear winter, the planet is cloaked in clouds and no sun penetrates. Seas cover most of the land areas except high elevations which exist as islands where the remaining humans have learned to make do with much less. People survive on what they can take from the sea and with foodstuffs supplemented from an orbiting set of space stations.

Jess Drake is an agent for Interforce, a small and exclusive special forces organization that still possesses access to technology. Her job is to protect and serve the citizens of the American continent who are in conflict with those left on the European continent. The struggle for resources is brutal, and when a rogue agent nearly destroys everything, Interforce decides to trust no one. They send Jess a biologically-created agent who has been artificially devised and given knowledge using specialized brain programming techniques.

Instead of the mindless automaton one might expect, Biological Alternative NM-Dev-1 proves to be human and attractive. Against all odds, Jess and the new agent are swept into a relationship neither expected. Can they survive in these strange circumstances? And will they even be able to stay alive in this bleak new world?

OTHER YELLOW ROSE PUBLICATIONS

About the Author

Melissa Good is a full time network engineer and part time writer who lives in Pembroke Pines, Florida with a handful of lizards and a dog. When not traveling for work, or participating in the usual chores she ejects several sets of clamoring voices onto a variety of keyboards and tries to entertain others with them to the best of her ability. You can find other info at www.merwolf.com.

CPSIA information can be obtained at www.ICGtesting.com
Printed in the USA
LVOW041250200113

316441LV00003B/351/P